The Man Who Painted Roses

The Man Who Painted Roses

The Story of Pierre-Joseph Redouté

by
ANTONIA RIDGE

FABER AND FABER
3 Queen Square
London

First published in 1974
by Faber and Faber Limited
3 Queen Square London WC1
Printed in Great Britain by
Western Printing Services Ltd, Bristol
All rights reserved

ISBN 0 571 10554 8

© Antonia Ridge, 1974

Contents

⊞ ⊞ ⊞

Contents

Foreword

⌘ ⌘ ⌘

The charming roses painted well over a century and a half ago by
Pierre-Joseph Redouté still enchant countless people the world
over.

But what manner of man was this painter of roses? I set out to
learn all I could about him. Before I put pen to paper, however, I
decided to follow the advice of the sixteenth-century philosopher,
Montaigne:

> In studying this kind of history one must be prepared to read
> and keep an open mind on all manner of writers, past and present,
> those who write abominably, and those who write admirably.
> They deal with the same subject in many a way, and it is only by
> studying them all, without prejudice, that one can learn and form
> one's own opinion.

I was fortunate. I was permitted to study at leisure the archives
and other relevant documents stored in the ancient Abbey of Saint
Hubert in the Belgian Ardennes, and then to spend long, rewarding
days in the Royal Library of Brussels and also in the National
Museum of Natural History in Paris.

As I read on and on, I found I not only had to 'keep an open mind',
I also had to sift and assess a mass of evidence that was sometimes
disturbingly contradictory. But Montaigne was right. I began to
form my 'own opinion' of Pierre-Joseph Redouté, his family and
friends, and the turbulent days in which he lived.

Here is no orthodox biography but the story of Pierre-Joseph

Redouté as I myself now so clearly see it, a story that is firmly based on a close study of all manner of contemporary evidence.

It will be reward indeed if you now come to share my regard and warm affection for Pierre-Joseph Redouté.

Acknowledgements

❈ ❈ ❈

I am grateful to Monsieur Jean Gyory, Head of the Public Relations and Press Department of the Belgian National Tourist Office in Brussels and Monsieur Claus, Director of the Belgian National Tourist Office in London who gave me invaluable help which enabled me to work among the archives stored in the ancient Abbey of Saint Hubert, and to study, with the kind assistance of Mademoiselle Tassoul, in the Royal Library of Brussels.

I must thank Madame Lilianne Kells of the Belgian Embassy in London, and Madame Gabrielle Duprat, Professor Yves Laissus and Professor Jean-F. Leroy of the National Museum of Natural History of Paris who all most courteously helped me in my search for data. I was also permitted to see the superb 'Miniatures du Roi', the 'Vellums', and study those painted by Pierre-Joseph Redouté and his brother, Henri-Joseph Redouté.

I am grateful to Mademoiselle Françoise Bibolet, Keeper of the Archives of Troyes, and Frau Karin Schreyer, Editor, of Munich, who both helped me with the historical data on the turbulent days in which Redouté lived.

I was most kindly received when I visited Fleury-Meudon. Monsieur Henri Albert gave me a copy of his fascinating history of Meudon. Monsieur Roux-Devillas gave me photographs of Redouté's house before it had to be demolished. On the site he has built a charming villa, and in his garden the magnificent cedar given to Redouté by the Empress Josephine still flourishes. I was delighted to study Monsieur Roux-Devillas' unique collection of letters and documents relating to the life and times of Redouté.

Acknowledgements

I shall also remember with warm pleasure the visit I paid to the Chelsea Physic Garden where the Curator, Mr. W. G. MacKenzie, gave me a list of the plants which were growing there in the days when Redouté was in London.

Above all, I can never hope to thank adequately Doctor André Lawalrée of the National Botanical Garden of Belgium, the eminent authority on Redouté, who was at all times so generously ready to help me.

I

Charles-Joseph Redouté

This is the story of Pierre-Joseph Redouté who was born on 10 July 1759, and who asked nothing better of life than to earn his bread by painting flowers.

He loved them all, every flower that grew, but he is best known for the roses he painted, the charming roses that then grew in many a royal and cottage garden, as well as the wild ones that you can still see – if you are fortunate – blooming in hedgerows just as they did when Pierre-Joseph was a boy.

You will certainly have seen copies of the roses he painted. They hang on countless walls, they decorate lamp-shades, tea-trays, waste-paper-baskets, calendars, finger-plates, tea-towels, ladies' scarves – the list is endless.

Pierre-Joseph, a perfectionist if ever there was one, would certainly have winced to see the quality of many of these reproductions but he would also have been moved and proud to know that the roses he loved to paint still captivate so many hearts the wide world over.

Time and again I have heard people declare that Pierre-Joseph Redouté was French. He most certainly was not. He was Belgian to the backbone and proud of it. He was born in the quiet village of Saint Hubert lost in the lovely forests of the Belgian Ardennes, and he did not come into this world with a fine silver spoon in his mouth. Far from it. In fact, one day in 1772 a conscientious monk, the Keeper of Accounts of the ancient Abbey of Saint Hubert, sighed as he compassionately considered the tax liability of Pierre-Joseph's father, Charles-Joseph Redouté. Presently that fair-minded monk dipped his feather-pen in his massive inkwell and recorded that Charles-Joseph Redouté, a painter and decorator employed since 1744 on the decoration of the Abbey, could in all justice be taxed only on:

> One small house, classified as Third Class.
> One small garden thereto attached.
> Three goats.

This was just as well, for that small Third-Class house, the small garden thereto attached and those three goats accurately summed up all Pierre-Joseph's father owned in this world.

Moreover he had a wife and five children to support, two girls: Jeanne Marie and Anne-Marie, and three boys: Antoine-Ferdinand, Pierre-Joseph and Henri-Joseph, all five blessed with excellent health and appetites.

Fortunately he was also blessed with an excellent wife – quiet, sensible and the soul of thrift, who daily worked miracles with the vegetables from that small garden, the cheese made from the milk of the three goats, and – most important of all – the modest wage paid to Charles-Joseph by My Lord Abbot of Saint Hubert.

It was also fortunate that their Third-Class house was No. 8 Rue du Four – the Street of the Oven, the village baker's oven. In fact No. 8 was right next door to the oven, so, as Charles-Joseph often declared, it was the very house for the busy mother of five ravenous children who made short work of three great loaves of bread a day. She had only to mix her dough, set it to rise, then briskly shape it into loaves and send one or other of the children galloping next door with them to Monsieur their Baker to bake in his vast oven – for a modest charge, of course.

There was never any need for Monsieur their Baker to stand at his open door and blow a trumpet to announce that yet another batch of bread, hot, crisp and golden brown, was safely out of his oven as bakers had to do in the great city of Brussels, or so Charles-Joseph maintained. Ah no! In the village of Saint Hubert the wondrous smell of new-baked bread sang for itself loud and triumphant, all along the Rue du Four and far beyond.

Then being next door to the baker made No. 8 a doubly warm and interesting house. There were always women and children bringing loaves to be baked, or waiting to collect them. And one never waited in unprofitable silence. One naturally caught up with all the news, not only of Saint Hubert but also from villages and farms from miles around – thanks to 'les marchands du Bon Dieu'.

It sounded very saintly to be sure – 'les marchands du Bon Dieu', the merchants of the good God. But they were really pedlars, who, with pack on back, trudged from one village to another, calling at many a lonely farm as they went, selling prayer-books, rosaries, holy pictures, medals and other easily carried 'objects of piety'. They also sensibly carried bobbins of thread, packets of needles, and a small but well-tried selection of ointments and elixirs, all guaranteed to work wonders – if applied or swallowed with the right dose of faith.

Everyone, even the ungodly, was always glad to welcome 'les marchands du Bon Dieu' for they were the most gifted of talkers who knew just how to serve up the latest news and gossip, and so they could always count on a good meal and a warm bed for the night, not to mention a profitable sale or two.

All in all then, that small Third-Class house, No. 8 Rue du Four, could not have been in a more convenient, warmer and livelier spot. However, as all the neighbours knew, it was nevertheless providential for the backs and stomachs of Pierre-Joseph and his four brothers and sisters that their papa was commissioned now and then to paint a flattering portrait, or a fine dramatic scene from the Holy Scriptures, to hang on a wall of the home of some local dignitary. Not that these occasional commissions ever brought in much money. Charles-Joseph's tight-fisted patrons had no hesitation whatever in reminding him, as they haggled over the price, that he wasn't precisely another Rubens or Rembrandt.

This was undoubtedly true. Charles-Joseph was talented and hard-working but he was no genius. When he was young he had been taught to paint by his father who had been taught by *his* father, who had also been taught by *his* father. This was how it went in the family, one talented Redouté after another teaching his sons who generation after generation took to paint as ducks to water. And were therefore agreeably ready to listen to paternal advice and criticism – just as Charles-Joseph's three sons now listened to him.

In fact from the cradle on, Pierre-Joseph and his two brothers knew precisely what they were going to do in life – paint like papa, of course. And all three could deftly handle brushes and paint long before they had to sit on the hard benches of the Abbey School, and reluctantly learn to use dull ink and pens. At the age of five, for instance, young Pierre-Joseph was only too happy to oblige some admiring neighbour with a brightly coloured, and highly imaginative, picture of any one of his favourite saints. But, as the long-suffering monks of the Abbey School groaned, he showed a deplorable lack of enthusiasm in learning to write and spell, and his grammar was even more deplorable. Yet, give him paint and brushes, and he would eagerly turn out picture after picture of all the saints in the calendar.

No-one, by the way, ever seems to have wondered if Pierre-Joseph's two sisters might also have inherited the Redouté talent and love of painting. But this was not in the least astonishing. In that day and age, in so modest and hard-up a family, it was taken for granted that it was their duty to devote any talents they had to helping their mother with the cooking and cleaning, the darning and sewing, tending the garden, and driving the three goats out to feed on the sweet herbs growing on the fringe of the nearby forests. And industriously knitting too, of course, as they kept a vigilant eye on the goats.

Later they could hope to marry and become excellent, thrifty wives and mothers, just like their own mother, and lead just as quiet and unremarkable lives. And one must be honest, those good daughters asked for nothing better.

In many ways then, Pierre-Joseph and his brothers and sisters were fortunate. They had a small, crowded but very real home, the best of mothers, and the most lively and interesting of fathers.

Their papa, you must understand, had not only travelled but he had an excellent memory and he was a born 'raconteur'. He could tell a story, relate some incident so eloquently that they never grew tired of hearing it. Indeed it had a way of becoming more dramatic, more fascinating, at every retelling.

Often of an evening, when it grew too dark to paint, Charles-Joseph would hold forth, for instance, on the long-dead and mysterious Crusader in the family, who, clad in shining armour, had galloped off one day from his home in Dinant to lend a Christian hand in slaughtering the Turks and the Saracens; and thus make sure of eternal bliss by helping to deliver the Holy Land from these infidels.

Charles-Joseph regretfully had to admit that not a soul in the family had ever been able to discover just what glory that long ago Chevalier Redouté had acquired. No doubt he was one of those infuriatingly silent and modest knights. But he must have galloped gloriously back to Dinant for he was not only buried there, in the Church of the Crusaders, but thanks to him, every male Redouté since then had the solemn right to be buried there as well.

However, the descendants of their family Crusader had been hard-working, ill-paid painters earning their bread all over Belgium. And no Redouté, as he lay on his death bed, had ever demanded a financial miracle of his sorrowing family, commanding them to transport his lifeless body all the way to Dinant and bury him, regardless of cost, by the side of their long-dead Crusader. And very sensible of them, said Charles-Joseph, since one cannot enjoy one's own funeral, no matter how grandiose and costly whereas one can enjoy life even if one's pockets do not bulge with silver florins.

Then off would go Charles-Joseph reliving his 'beaux vingt ans', the beautiful days when he was in his shining twenties without a sou or a care in the world. And though Pierre-Joseph and his brothers and sisters must have heard it all a hundred times and more, they dearly loved to hear their papa tell how once *his* papa had taught him all he knew, he had kissed his family good-bye and merrily set out for Paris.

Paris! Now that was the golden city! Every young artist dreamed of studying one day in Paris. But Charles-Joseph could not fly there straight as a crow, he had to tramp there on foot, stopping every now and then to earn his supper and a bed for the night by painting the portrait of a prosperous tradesman, or a pious picture to hang on the wall of some village church.

Not only this, but as he went, Charles-Joseph always made a conscientious détour to knock at the door of any well-known and successful master-painter. One could be sure that the studio of such a man would be packed with eager students, watching, listening, as the master painted and lectured. And if one hadn't the cash to pay for these lessons, one paid by doing any job around the studio from cleaning the brushes to stoking the stove or sweeping the floor.

And this was splendid. As soon as a student showed real promise, he would be accorded the privilege and honour of painting some minor detail in the background of the masterpiece then in hand – a distant tree, for instance, or a dog or a cloud in the sky.

The master would then stand back, study this detail, ruthlessly criticise it, analyse why it made him grind his teeth; and set to work to transform it, talking hard, giving illuminative advice with every stroke of his brush. And the students, rapt and listening, would behold that tree, dog or cloud become harmonious part and parcel of the masterpiece, one to which the master could then sign his name with a magnificent flourish.

In short these lessons were splendidly entertaining as well as instructive. Moreover no hard-up student with any real talent need ever starve, for successful master-painters with more orders than any one pair of hands could hope to accomplish, would often employ a whole troop of lesser painters working full-time painting the time-consuming but necessary background details. Charles-Joseph could easily have found such employment but he didn't relish forever painting distant trees, clouds and dogs, no matter how good the pay or how famous the master-painter.

No, he longed to get to Paris, wonderful, exciting Paris. And admit it, he also had dreams of becoming a master-painter himself one day with a studio of his own and admiring students hanging on *his* every word.

But ah, where were they now, the snows, the dreams, of yester-year?

Then to the young Redoutés' relief, their volatile papa would cheer up and tell how there he was at last – in Paris. And how he had at once grandly enrolled in the famous Academy of Saint-Luc. But now he not only had to find the money for his fees, he also had to find a place to sleep, and even more necessary, he had to eat. So again, in all his free time, he cheerfully painted to order, at an agreed price, portraits, or scenes from the Holy Scriptures, or some heroic feat of Hercules or any other classical subject a client happened to fancy.

Heavens, the lofty pictures, the flattering portraits Charles-Joseph had painted! And at the gallop too, hunger being so excellent a spur. Indeed he had lost count of his artistic output, but he trusted that his pictures still added a note of pious dignity or classical erudition to the walls of tight-fisted patrons of the arts all over Paris.

Sometimes the market for all this would dry up, and then Charles-Joseph would walk the streets of Paris from one theatre to another and find work painting the scenery for some romantic play, or decorate the walls of a theatre with garlands of roses, for instance, with laughing cupids or nymphs swinging upon them.

In short, Charles-Joseph had preferred to turn his hand to any branch of painting rather than starve artistically and most uncomfortably in some chilly garret. And a fine rollicking time Charles-Joseph had managed to enjoy too! Paris, it seemed, did something to a student. It went to his head, it loosened his tongue so that he would sit up half the night with other hard-up students making one cup of coffee or a glass of wine last as long as possible, avoiding the eye of the waiter, as they eloquently set the world to rights, or better still, aired their views on what was so wrong with 'Art Today'. And illustrated their theories with many a tale.

There was the story, for instance, of the pompous student boasting away at the top of his voice that he'd invented a unique method for 'purifying colours', an incomparable method that he intended to keep a close secret of course.

Now listening to all this bombastic nonsense was that great but most unpretentious painter – Jean-Baptiste Chardin. And presently he could stand no more.

'And pray, who informed you, Monsieur,' demanded Chardin, 'that one should paint with colours?'

'But . . . but, Monsieur,' stammered the purifier of colours, very taken aback to recognise the great Chardin, 'with what else can one paint?'

'One makes use of colours,' said Chardin, as if speaking to some village idiot, 'but one paints, Monsieur, with feeling.'

And to paint like Chardin, would sigh Charles-Joseph, one certainly had to paint with something that sprang from one's very soul. And Charles-Joseph would look at his three sons and sternly advise them never to forget this.

But these solemn moments of exhortation never lasted long, and off would go Charles-Joseph again, telling how he'd revelled in wandering around Versailles, admiring the marvellous palace there, the gardens, the fountains, the graceful statues of Greek or Roman gods and goddesses with the quiet waters of lovely lakes rippling around them.

And he too had jostled and pushed his way into the palace through the scented and magnificently attired ladies and gentlemen and all the crowd of lesser sightseers who day in, day out, and far into the night were permitted to wander round, free and easy as you please.

One could even watch, at a discreet distance, the Royal Family of France, most regally dressed, eating their supper, but Charles-Joseph had no opinion whatever of this strange royal French custom. Every family ought to be able to eat without a crowd of spectators watching their every mouthful.

So Charles-Joseph preferred to squeeze into some corner of one of the palatial apartments where he could stand at his ease and gaze up at some wondrously painted ceiling depicting gods and goddesses disporting themselves on High Olympus and where Apollo, the sun god, bore a striking resemblance, if you please, to His Majesty King Louis XIV of France. Or Charles-Joseph would turn and behold the stately lilies of France glowing in the moonlight along the border of the velvet green of a lawn.

Ah yes, when in Versailles, one felt that the Kings of France had no doubt whatever that they were heaven's royal representatives on earth, and that all this regal splendour was therefore only due and proper.

But never believe, would say Charles-Joseph, that Versailles was a glorious triumph for France, and France alone! Ah, no! One had only to turn one's head and listen, and one heard the unmistakable accents of other Belgians. A whole army of Belgian artists had taken part, and were still taking part in creating and maintaining all this splendour. Never forget that, would say Charles-Joseph.

All this talk of Versailles always came round to that princely Benedictine monk, Dom Celestin de Jong. Now he had spent some years in Versailles as the honoured guest of His Majesty, King Louis XV; and no royal guest had ever graced Versailles with more impeccable dignity – an aristocratic prelate after the King's own heart.

But then came the day when Dom Celestin was appointed My Lord Abbot of Saint Hubert in the Belgian Ardennes, yes, their very village. So imagine now, would say Charles-Joseph, Dom Celestin arriving in Saint Hubert and descending from his richly decorated coach and gazing about him.

Their tranquil village, the fields, the forests all about it, were his domain; and there in the heart of the village towered their vast and ancient Basilica and the Abbey beyond. For a thousand years it was here that Benedictine monks had prayed, taught the young, and cared for the sick. But it was the ancient Basilica that down the years had stirred the souls of men for it was here that great Saint Hubert lay at rest, Saint Hubert, the patron saint of hunters everywhere.

It was to their ancient Basilica that century after century pilgrims made their way from all over Christendom to implore protection from the mortal bites and savage onslaught of the wild beasts of the forest. It was here that they brought the tormented souls already bitten or savaged to be cured, or to die absolved of all their sins.

At least one must charitably believe, said Charles-Joseph, that Dom Celestin, late of Versailles, reflected on all this as he stood there that day. But the cold truth must be told. That princely prelate surveyed their gaunt ancient Basilica, the austere Abbey beyond, with considerable distaste. A far cry, this, from the splendour of Versailles!

And Dom Celestin forthwith decided that it was his high mission on earth to make both Basilica and Abbey shine to the glory of God, great Saint Hubert, and Dom Celestin de Jong. In that pious order, of course, but definitely to the glory of all three.

For this, however, Dom Celestin would have to recruit a whole army of architects, painters, decorators, gardeners and a host of other skilled craftsmen. He let no grass grow under his feet and presently among all those who received an invitation to travel to Saint Hubert and begin work forthwith on this pious project was that all-round, hard-working, and not expensive, Belgian painter and decorator – Charles-Joseph Redouté. Yes, their papa.

Now this certainly explained why Pierre-Joseph's lively father gave up his happy-go-lucky life in Paris. But he may well have suddenly realised with a shock that the years were whisking by, that he was now in his elderly thirties, and that his dream of becoming a famous master-painter was as far away as ever. It was high time he found some settled and regular employment, and where better than in the lovely Ardennes of his own native land, and with the high-sounding title of 'Decorator and Painter' of so famous and ancient a Basilica and Abbey.

And a fine stir he had caused too among the girls of Saint Hubert. Tall and handsome, and with all the swagger and panache of an artist straight from Paris, and still unmarried! But he'd had the good sense to fall in love and marry, not the village beauty, but quiet, sensible Marguerite-Josèphe Chalon.

Presently Charles-Joseph had 'une corde à la patte' as his merry and unattached friends in Paris would have put it, and there was indeed a rope tied about his wandering feet. He had a wife and children to support and his only steady source of income was the wage he received for painting and decorating the Abbey.

This painting and decorating was however very much to Charles-Joseph's taste. There was nothing at all monotonous about it. It covered a surprisingly wide field of artistic jobs from painting flattering portraits of Dom Celestin's distinguished visitors to hang on the Abbey walls, to painting pictures of the saints to hang in the side chapels of the Basilica, or, by way of a change, decorating the panels of the stately coaches of Dom Celestin with his coat of arms encircled with intricate scrolls and garlands of flowers, all in vivid colours and no sparing of the gold leaf.

Charles-Joseph was still decorating and painting the Abbey and Basilica when Dom Celestin died, leaving behind a resplendent Basilica, and a most regal Abbey worthy of Versailles itself, with fountains playing in the courtyards, marble colonnades, spacious and richly furnished apartments with magnificent parquet floors – works of art in themselves – and tall windows opening on balconies from which one could survey the admirably kept gardens, the orchards of fine fruit trees and the green forest beyond.

Dom Celestin had even gone one better than Versailles. He had walled in one stretch of lovely woodland where the wild creatures of the forest could safely shelter and where the animal or bird-lovers among his aristocratic visitors could watch them at play.

But soon all Saint Hubert was buzzing with the news that Dom Celestin had also left behind a right regal and most alarming mountain of debts, so alarming that his outraged successor, Dom Nicolas Spirlet, promptly buried him with the utmost economy and secrecy, somewhere in the Basilica one said, but with never a memorial, a flagstone with his name and coat of arms carved upon it, not even a righteous 'sic transit gloria . . .'. So search where you may, you can discover no trace, no record of that magnificent prelate's last resting place. Dom Spirlet had seen to that.

Then burning with indignant zeal, Dom Spirlet set to work to place the tottering finances of the Abbey on a firm and profitable footing, and so pay off in exemplary time that mountain of debts.

Unfortunately for all concerned, Dom Spirlet was convinced that he had a heaven-sent gift for making quick and easy money, and he plunged head-first into a series of wildly ambitious and ill-planned business ventures: tanneries, sawmills, breweries, chemical works turning out potash and nitric acid, even the scientific breeding of sheep and horses. And as fast as one get-rich-quick venture failed, he would borrow more money and, nothing daunted, set up another.

Yet even with all these losing concerns on his hands, Dom Spirlet was also fiercely determined to maintain, even to improve, the newly-restored splendour and dignity of the ancient Basilica and the Abbey.

This, of course, was providential for the Redouté family in that crowded Third-Class house, No. 8 Rue du Four, for Charles-Joseph remained on the pay-roll of the Abbey. And day in, day out, he went on with the painting, the decorating, and took any opportunity to earn a little extra by painting a portrait or a pious picture for anyone who agreed to pay him cash down. And in any free time he went on teaching Pierre-Joseph and his brothers to paint.

Charles-Joseph also went on telling his neighbours that he was never the one to boast, as everyone knew, but he had not studied in the famous Academy of Saint Luc in Paris for nothing. Ah, no! So mark his words. The village of Saint Hubert would one day be proud of his three sons.

Then Charles-Joseph would crash down to earth again and say ah, well, if the village of Saint Hubert and the rest of this hard ungrateful world proved unappreciative, no son of his need ever starve as long as he had his two hands, and paints and brushes.

He, Charles-Joseph Redouté, their papa, had seen to that.

2

Dom Hickman

❈ ❈ ❈

As you may well imagine, Pierre-Joseph was to remember his native village of Saint Hubert with warm affection all his life long. He never forgot that warm, crowded Third-Class house, his lively father, and his quiet devoted mother; not to mention the dramatic flinging up of hands as the neighbours gossiped about the cost of the splendours achieved by princely Dom Celestin de Jong. And hard on this, the equally spectacular whirlwind of business ventures of Dom Spirlet. No boy could wish to grow up in a more interesting village.

There were, however, two days in the village calendar that Pierre-Joseph was to recall with special emotion: the Monday of Pentecost, and the third day of November. On those two days, as soon as it was dawn, from far away would come the sound of chanting, and along the rough track through the forest and down the hillside to the village would come a long procession of pilgrims, carrying banners and singing litanies to great Saint Hubert. They had come on foot from all over Luxembourg, the Ruhr, the Saar, the Moselle and many other distant parts.

Behind them rumbled a couple of farm-carts drawn by great strong horses, and in these sat or lay those too old or sick to trudge the long rough road to Saint Hubert, and sometimes among them would be a poor demented soul, tugging at the chains that bound him safely to the side of the cart.

Last of all would rumble a most desolate cart with a load of coffins. Yes, coffins. One had to be realistic. There were always some pilgrims who died on the way to Saint Hubert, or on the way back.

Still chanting and praying, the pilgrims would begin to climb the flight of stone steps of the ancient Basilica, and through the wide open doors would stream a soft and lovely light. Even in November the pale autumn sun always seemed to come shining through the tall windows and set alight the high vaulted roof, the pillars of softly coloured stone so that a gentle rainbow of gold, green, blue and rose would welcome them there.

And up and up would soar the solemn music of the organ, the chanting of the monks, and one had only to look at their faces to know that the pilgrims had forgotten their weariness, the long rough road, even that last desolate cart.

And up and up would rise the age-old plaintive petition:

> *Oh, Saint Hubert, Saint of love,*
> *Saint of honour, dark fears beset me!*
> *Guard me, protect me from Satan's rage*
> *His fearsome, demoniac madness!*
> *Grant that I may be given the grace*
> *To serve God in peace*
> *To the end of my days!*

The demoniac rage – the rabies – they feared so much was terrible indeed. Yet Pierre-Joseph secretly found it strange and most difficult to understand why Saint Hubert had become the patron saint of hunters since he himself had been rebuked for his passion for hunting in so miraculous a way – by the vision of a stag with a cross of gold shining between its antlers. Surely then, Saint Hubert ought to be the patron saint of the hunted stag and all the other wild beasts of the forest, not the protector of those who hunted them.

One day Pierre-Joseph had spoken about this to Dom Hickman, and that understanding monk had been silent for a while, and then said that Saint Hubert had been rebuked, not for hunting, but for his overwhelming passion for hunting for hunting's sake, forgetting to think of his duty to God. He had actually been out hunting in the forest on Good Friday when he had seen that stag with the golden cross shining between its antlers.

But the older one grew, said Dom Hickman, the more one realised that men had the most convenient of memories. As the centuries went by it was they who had decided that Saint Hubert was the patron saint of hunters. The good Saint might well have been astonished at this, but being a Saint now and therefore infinitely compassionate, how could he turn a deaf ear to poor souls who were terrified of being cornered, savaged one day by some mad dog or a wild boar in the forest. Having been a hunter himself, he could be counted upon to understand this.

One also had to realise that since time began the wild game of the forests and the fishes that swam in rivers and streams had been a god-send to many a needy and hungry family. And a delicious one as Pierre-Joseph well knew.

Pierre-Joseph enthusiastically agreed. In the years to come it would give one an appetite just to listen to him singing the praises of the delicacies of his native Ardennes – the hams and sausages smoked over fires of wild broom gathered on the hillside, the fresh fish caught in the sparkling little forest streams, not to mention the pâtés made from the succulent meat of some young wild boar or other game when the hunting season was in full swing.

Not that these unsurpassed delicacies were everyday fare in that Third-Class house! His papa would bring some home from time to time, in lieu of hard cash for a portrait or a painting. But now as he stood there that day, listening to Dom Hickman, it seemed to him that the comforting logic of all he was saying summed up that good monk – his head high in heaven but both his sandalled feet firmly on the earth below.

Dom Hickman. . . . Now there was a monk, a friend, Pierre-Joseph was never to forget, though he little realised then how much he would owe him in the years to come.

Dom Hickman was not one of these righteous pedantic monks who daily lamented that they were in danger of losing their immortal souls in the battle to teach blockheads like Pierre-Joseph to spell and write grammatically.

No, Dom Hickman was the most friendly, and to Pierre-Joseph's mind, the wisest and most knowledgeable of monks. He was medical practitioner, scientist, herbalist, apothecary and philosopher all rolled into one. But being a monk he was not permitted to visit and examine the sick who from far and near sent to him for help and advice. So he did the next best thing. He carefully recorded all their symptoms as related by some anxious relative or sympathetic neighbour, and then just as carefully recorded all the remedies he recommended and prepared for them.

And this filled Pierre-Joseph with admiration. Dom Hickman conscientiously set down the details of his failures as well as his successes. Indeed he would say that his failures often taught him far more than his successes.

Pierre-Joseph knew all this for once he escaped from the hard benches of the Abbey School, he loved nothing better than to help Dom Hickman in the secluded garden of the Abbey where all manner of herbs grew in straight neat rows. Many of these, when gathered, were spread out to dry in the sun for future use in the making of savoury stews and sauces in the Abbey kitchen, of course. But there were also many others needed by Dom Hickman for his medicines, lotions, pills, salves and plasters. So there were sweet-smelling borders of lavender, rosemary, thyme, camomile, marjoram, tansy, as well as bright beds of marigolds, columbines, monkshoods, snapdragons, wallflowers and many other gay and homely flowers. And in every spare corner Dom Hickman loved to plant a rose-bush or two, saying great Saint Benedict would certainly have approved of this. He himself had planted rose-bushes with his own saintly hands outside the cave in which he had taken refuge to pray and meditate.

Then Dom Hickman was also not one of those austere monks who demanded the young to be eternally silent. On the contrary, once he saw how interested Pierre-Joseph was in his healing flowers and herbs, they would both talk away as they worked; and presently he began to open Pierre-Joseph's young eyes to matters far beyond the tranquil herb-gardens of Saint Hubert.

He would lament, for instance, that the medical men of the day knew precious little more than the ancient Greeks and Romans about the causes and treatment of plagues and fevers, or even the most commonplace of everyday ailments. It seemed they now arrogantly dismissed the excellent advice of a certain Hippocrates, a great Greek thinker and the Father of Medicine, who more than two thousand years ago had done his learned best to knock a little common sense into the hard heads of men.

Hippocrates had advocated fresh air and sunlight and keeping the body clean. But what did doctors do now, heaven forgive them? When called to a sick-bed, they at once ordered the windows and shutters to be tightly closed, shutting out God's good air and the blessed light of day. And no matter what the malady – bronchitis, griping pains in the belly, rheumatism, apoplexy, sore throats – they immediately set to work to purge and bleed the sweating and terrified sick.

Then Pierre-Joseph should always remember, said Dom Hickman, that some maladies were caused by distress of the mind and not of the body. So Dom Hickman was interested in reports of the experiments of a learned Herr-Professor-Doctor in Vienna, Franz Anton Mesmer. Now this Herr-Professor-Doctor Mesmer it seemed, used magnets and soothing and reassuring words to restore the inner harmony of his patients.

But what an unholy scandal it would cause if Dom Hickman dared to try experiments of this kind here in Saint Hubert!

However, Dom Hickman would quietly experiment in his pharmacy with something else, something he called 'Fluid Electricity'. He had a French translation of a book about this written by a famous scientist who lived in the far-away English Colony of America. Dom Hickman had shown this precious book to Pierre-Joseph. It was called *Experiments and Observations on Electricity made at Philadelphia in America by Monsieur Benjamin Franklin*.

Pierre-Joseph listened attentively and did his best to understand when Dom Hickman explained that lightning was nothing but this 'Fluid Electricity'. But all this scientific explaining was of no comfort whatever when dark menacing clouds gathered over Saint Hubert and the thunder roared and the lightning flashed, and Pierre-Joseph's mother, her face as white as a sheet, would run here and there, dousing the whole house, and everyone in it, with holy water.

And Pierre-Joseph, his heart beating like a drum in spite of all the holy water, would wish heaven could arrange matters so that Monsieur Benjamin Franklin could keep all this Fluid Electricity over there in Philadelphia, America. Saint Hubert could do without it.

Presently Dom Hickman began to tell Pierre-Joseph tales of his own childhood, and Pierre-Joseph would listen, wide-eyed, absolutely spellbound.

Dom Hickman's father had been a rip-roaring professional soldier, in plain words, a mercenary, always ready and eager to fight in any war – on the side that offered the better pay, of course. In fact there was a verse in the Book of Job that always set Dom Hickman praying most urgently for the repose of his father's warlike soul!

> *He saith among the trumpets, Ha, ha;*
> *and he smelleth the battle afar off,*
> *the thunder of the captains,*
> *and the shouting.*

Behind this ha-ha-ing professional warrior, all over torn and quarrelling Europe, had trailed his unhappy wife and his twelve ragged, barefooted children. Dom Hickman had been one of those children, and even as a small boy he shrank from the thought of ever becoming a fire-eating warrior like his father. All the jubilant ha-ha-ing, the sounding of trumpets, had never drowned the cries of the dying left abandoned on the battlefields after every glorious victory. The very thought of war had always made Dom Hickman's young soul sick with horror.

Yet he had to do something in life; and one could bluntly say that bleak necessity had decided him to become a monk. Not the highest of motives, heaven forgive him, but he had never regretted it. And he daily prayed that kind and tolerant heaven would also never regret it.

Honest Dom Hickman had been swift to realise that he had no gifts whatever for scholarship, or contemplation, or anything else spiritually uplifting. So he had earnestly prayed for a chance, an opportunity, to show his love of God, his gratitude for quiet security by being useful in some humbler, workaday way. And heaven had heard his prayer.

One day a learned old doctor arrived at the Abbey to end his days in pious tranquillity. He had been a most eminent man, the personal physician of His Royal Highness, the Prince of Liège. And this kindly old man had been most distressed to discover that the Abbey Pharmacy was in a lamentable state, thick with dust, festooned with spiders' webs, and not a remedy left on any of the shelves, for the simple reason that for many years there had been no apothecary among the monks of Saint Hubert.

So that courageous old man had summoned up his failing strength to put matters right, and was most grateful when Dom Hickman had begged to be allowed to lend a willing, if untrained, hand.

In return, the old doctor had not only taught Dom Hickman the rudiments of pharmacology but he began to lend him books on anatomy, medicine and chemistry, and had helped and encouraged him to master them. And when this saintly old man died, there was Dom Hickman the only apothecary and medical adviser in Saint Hubert.

But being a monk, nobody had to pay Dom Hickman for advice and medicines. So the physicians for miles around, enthusiastic purgers and blood-letters to a man, had no brotherly love whatever for Dom Hickman. However, Dom Hickman did his Christian best to love these unenlightened neighbours as himself – even if he did most heartily disagree with them.

At times Dom Hickman would need certain wild plants, or the flowers or bark of some forest tree for his remedies, and Pierre-Joseph loved to go with him to search for them. For hours on end they would roam the countryside around Saint Hubert, the meadows, the forests, and soon Pierre-Joseph became quick to spot and recognise many an unremarkable but health-restoring flower or herb.

To Pierre-Joseph there was something most lovely about the vast, lonely forests of Saint Hubert. They would sometimes come across a joyous little stream, for instance, where silver fishes flashed between the mossy stones; and when spring came, Pierre-Joseph would catch his breath and stand caught up in enchantment to behold a whole carpet of wild lilies of the valley, or a patch of sweet-smelling violets.

And Dom Hickman would stand looking about him and say Solomon in all his wisdom must have stood, just like this, beholding the eternal miracle of spring, when he burst into song:

> *For lo, the winter is past. The rain*
> *is over and done.*
> *The flowers appear on the earth,*
> *the time of the singing of birds is come,*
> *and the voice of the turtle is heard in our land.*

In the forests about Saint Hubert, said Dom Hickman, they had even more cause to rejoice. Their winters were always bitterly cold but now the icy snow was 'over and done', and the air was full of the singing of joyous birds.

One spring day, however, Dom Hickman, striding ahead suddenly froze in his tracks, and when Pierre-Joseph scrambled up to join him, there below them, in the very heart of the forest, they saw a most unlovely sight, My Lord Abbot Spirlet's latest business venture – a blast-furnace!

Dom Spirlet had discovered this charming spot where two little rivers met, and he'd at once decided that this was the ideal place to establish a blast-furnace. Here was water in plenty to harness and drive the machinery, there was iron ore to be had close by, and all around grew the trees of the forest to provide the charcoal for the furnace.

There it now stood, belching smoke, that monastic ironworks, and nearby towered the most dismal of sights – a slag heap. All this in the heart of the lovely forest of Saint Hubert!

Presently Dom Hickman abruptly turned and strode away, and Pierre-Joseph followed him; but not a word did Dom Hickman say all the way back to the Abbey. So Pierre-Joseph was silent too.

Pierre-Joseph knew, however, what all the gossips of Saint Hubert were saying. The iron ore turned out by that forest blast-furnace was proving so costly to produce that nobody could afford to buy it! And the wit of the village was going round saying that the alchemists of old had far more sense than My Lord Abbot Spirlet. They squandered fortunes trying to transmute base metal into gold. Their Lord Abbot was reversing the process. He was successfully transmuting gold into base metal – iron that nobody had gold enough to buy.

Soon Dom Hickman was doing far more than teach Pierre-Joseph to recognise flowers and herbs; he began to pay him the compliment of explaining their virtues. He would say, for instance, that all down the ages, both pagan and Christian apothecaries had made sovereign remedies from the flowers and the hips of the rose. Indeed it seemed there was one rose called 'The Apothecary's Rose', and Dom Hickman would say that if ever he were made Lord Abbot – from which unlikely and most uncomfortable miracle heaven preserve him! – he would surround his pharmacy with a whole plantation of these and other roses, not only to provide these tried and proved remedies, but also for the delight of the sick. And admit it, for his own delight as well. Just as great Saint Benedict had done.

Indeed, said Dom Hickman, to his mind great Saint Benedict had shown far more wisdom than another monk who had preached that it was permissible to smell a rose in order to cure a headache, but one had to limit this rose-smelling to one or two deep sniffs, and these only to relieve pain. Otherwise, one would be in mortal danger of becoming sinfully addicted to pleasure.

To Dom Hickman, the scent, the very sight, of a rose in bloom was a glimpse of heaven itself. And young Pierre-Joseph solemnly said that he agreed with great Saint Benedict and Dom Hickman. He too thought that roses were the most beautiful of all flowers.

And a boon to all apothecaries, added Dom Hickman. One should never forget that.

Then Dom Hickman went on to talk of another boon to all apothecaries – the tall purple foxgloves that grew in the forest. Infusions of the dried leaves of these stately flowers gave God-sent relief to those afflicted with dropsy or spasms of the heart.

Even the humble arnica that grew so wild and free around Saint Hubert was a boon. It had the kindest way of soothing painful sprains and bruises. And Dom Hickman seeing the bees buzzing and fussing around his beds of scented flowers in the herb garden would sing the praises of the honey of young bees for which the Abbey of Saint Hubert was deservedly famous. Honey, too, was a blessing from heaven; moreover it was one of the Abbey's few money-making concerns, for rich merchants from Brussels and other great cities would send for supplies and cheerfully pay good prices for it.

One day as they were making their way back to Saint Hubert, Dom Hickman began to speak again of that saintly old physician from Liège, and how one evening just before he died, he had taken out a rare and precious manuscript, a beautiful Latin version of a poem written, said the old physician, all of nine hundred years ago by a humble monk in that greenest of all islands – Ireland. And he had translated this poem to Dom Hickman, and as he listened, Dom Hickman had the strangest feeling that this long-ago monk was capturing in words all Dom Hickman had always felt but could never hope to express.

Dom Hickman considered that this monk must have been meditating on life after death, and that this poem was a cry from the heart, and though Dom Hickman wasn't word-perfect, far from it, this was how he recalled that Irish monk's appeal to heaven:

> *I wish, oh Son of the Living God,*
> *Oh ancient and eternal King,*
> *For a little hut hidden in some wild-land.*
> *And that this may be my dwelling-place.*
>
> *Close by, and all about it on every side,*
> *A lovely wood to shelter the wild birds,*
> *The many-voiced birds, nesting,*
> *Hiding there within its quiet shelter.*

All looking south for warmth,
And good earth with many gracious gifts
Such are kind to all the plants that grow
Whilst across the floor a little stream would flow.

This is the husbandry I would choose
And I will not hide it,
Fragrant leeks, hens, salmon, trout, bees . . .
And I to be sitting there, resting a while.

Resting a while and praying,
Praising God in every place.

Dom Hickman said he always found himself picturing all this when he chanted the words of the Psalmist:

This will be my rest for ever,
Here will I dwell.

If the good God in his mercy gave Dom Hickman his wish, then he too would ask for just such a rustic corner of heaven. That would be bliss indeed, whereas a celestial mansion, now, that would positively dismay him.

Fascinating and delightful as all these talks were, it was the flowers they gathered that now began to captivate Pierre-Joseph's young heart. He would stand and gently hold one in his hands and be lost in wonder at the delicacy, the unexpected loveliness of even the most everyday flower. And Dom Hickman, quick to observe his delight in flowers, began to permit him to slip off his wooden clogs, and tiptoe behind him in his stockinged feet into the splendid library of the Abbey where learned monks sat or stood at magnificently carved desks, meticulously copying rare and beautiful old books and documents.

Dom Hickman would silently lead Pierre-Joseph to a far corner of the library where the ancient 'Herbals' were stored, and he would allow him to take them from the shelves and sit at a desk and pore over them. Not that the cramped notes and observations set down by those herbalists of old interested Pierre-Joseph – he was never fond of closely printed words – it was the illustrations that strangely fascinated and yet repelled him. They were so lifeless, so wooden.

Now if one could only paint those flowers as they really were, growing and blooming out there under the sky, paint them 'with feeling' as great Chardin had painted, what a 'herbal' that would make!

Then Pierre-Joseph would ruefully look down at his hands. All the Redoutés had big, strong, capable hands, but his were enormous! And with such stumpy clumsy-looking fingers! They were ugly, the ugliest hands in all Saint Hubert.

But they were the very hands, his papa declared, to paint great powerful scenes from history such as Julius Caesar being stabbed to death, or the mighty battles waged by the Greeks and Romans of old. Pierre-Joseph could earn good money, make a name for himself, painting the famous heroes of antiquity – Alexander, for instance, slaying the foe to left and right.

Rich aristocrats liked to hang these blood-curdling masterpieces on the walls of their châteaux; important burgomasters would commission them to adorn the walls of their town halls. They were a visible and stirring proof of classical erudition.

As he listened to his papa's hopeful plans for his artistic future, Pierre-Joseph's heart would sink like lead into his wooden clogs. How could he paint scenes like this when he wasn't in the least interested in history, not even in Julius Caesar or Alexander or any other conquering hero. And the very thought of painting bloody battle-scenes made his own blood run cold.

So Pierre-Joseph listened in silence to his papa's enthusiastic exhortations.

On the night of 9 July 1772, Pierre-Joseph lay in his bed and gravely considered tomorrow.

Tomorrow, 10 July, he would be thirteen years old, a responsible age, when every self-respecting lad in Saint Hubert was expected to be earning the bread he devoured, and everything else he needed as well.

Moreover, money was tighter than ever in that small Third-Class house, No. 8 Rue du Four, even though Pierre-Joseph's older brother, Antoine-Ferdinand, was now on the Abbey pay-roll and helping their father in every possible way. But my Lord Abbot Spirlet's disastrous money-making enterprises had reduced the Abbey to such dire financial straits that the painters and decorators – the dwindling few who still remained – were being paid less and less, and more and more irregularly. And as his father mournfully declared, all he had to show for all his years of decorating and painting was that one small house, one small garden and three goats. Nothing more.

So tomorrow Pierre-Joseph would pack his palette, brushes, a supply of paints and paper and a change of clothes, and set out to look for work. From tomorrow on, he must make his own way in life. And there was nothing dramatic or heroic about this. Nobody in Saint Hubert would be in the least surprised. His mother might be quieter than usual as she packed some bread and a chunk of cheese for him to take, and kissed him good-bye. But she too realised that now his father had taught him all he knew, Pierre-Joseph, at the manly age of thirteen, must stand on his own two feet. There was no work for him in Saint Hubert.

And Pierre-Joseph saw himself trudging along the roads from one village to another, from one great city to the next, offering to paint portraits or pictures, or decorate walls or ceilings with gay painted garlands and scrolls, just as his father and many other painters had done before him. He too would be hard-headed and business-like, offer to paint a picture or portrait at a reduced price if a meal and a bed for the night were thrown in as well.

And he would do as his father urged him to do. Whenever the opportunity came his way, he would find the time to visit some lovely old church or cathedral or some majestic town hall, and respectfully study the masterpieces hanging there, painted by the master-painters of old.

Then whenever possible he would make his way to the studios of successful master-painters, and offer to hew wood, draw water, fetch and carry, tackle any job in lieu of the fees he could never hope to pay in hard cash.

Yes, all this he would do, just as his father had once done.

Tomorrow then, when dawn broke and the cocks began to crow, he would become a man and forever put away all childish things. It was as simple and inevitable as that.

Then a sudden desolation shook Pierre-Joseph and he tried to find comfort in thinking that, if he worked hard, he might become a master-painter one day, with a studio crammed with respectful students. And he would send handsome sums of money home to his proud and aged parents, and he would sit of an evening in a great armchair upholstered in rich flowered silk or maybe scarlet Utrecht velvet, and there would be wax candles in silver candlesticks burning on the polished table. And he would hold forth mightily in the soft candlelight to his own sons and daughters, telling them stories of Saint Hubert, and the Crusader in the family, and good Dom Hickman.

And thinking of all this, Pierre-Joseph at last fell asleep.

3

Letter from Antoine-Ferdinand

※ ※ ※

At dawn next day, 10 July 1772, Pierre-Joseph, aged thirteen, set out from Saint Hubert.

As they watched him go, his father suddenly very eloquently indeed began to assure his silent wife that there went a lad who would come to no harm. And heavens above, what a golden chance he had! He could wander where he pleased as he worked his way, behold with his own two eyes the rich, artistic treasures of his native land – on all of which, he, his papa, had given him his considered professional opinion of course.

Take, for instance, the masterpieces of their Pieter Breugel. Now he could paint a village wedding or some other rustic feast-day with such gusto, such relish, that one could positively see old Pieter there, enjoying himself right heartily as he painted away.

With his talents, their Pierre-Joseph might well become another Pieter Breugel.

On the other hand, if Pierre-Joseph decided to dedicate his life to painting loftier subjects, such as altar-pieces, well, there was no finer example in all Christendom than the one in their Cathedral of Saint Bavo in Ghent. Painters came from all over the world to study it, and every one of them would stand before it, speechless with awe and wonder.

If, however, their Pierre-Joseph decided to concentrate on portrait-painting, then again he would be working in the best of all possible worlds. Rich merchants, noblemen, princes from other lands thought nothing of travelling to Belgium, or inviting Belgian painters to cross the sea and paint, at a princely price, portraits of themselves and their families.

Charles-Joseph could rattle off a whole catalogue of world-famous Belgian portrait-painters; and as he had so often told his sons, there had never been any need for their Jan van Eyck to inscribe a portrait with the Latin affidavit:

> Johannes van Eyck fuit hic.
> (Jan van Eyck was here.)

One had only to have two eyes in one's head to know Jan van Eyck had indeed been there. One could almost believe that the people he painted were still breathing, as alive and alert as on the day he painted them.

In short, their Pierre-Joseph need never want for inspiration wherever he wandered or whatever he chose to do.

And, went on Charles-Joseph, reputable master-painters all over Belgium would certainly have heard of the Redouté family, painters every one for many a generation. In all modesty, these eminent master-painters might well have heard of how much he, Charles-Joseph Redouté, had contributed to the regal splendour of the Basilica and Abbey of Saint Hubert. Ah yes, they could be counted upon to take a friendly interest in Pierre-Joseph – once they saw for themselves how talented he was. And how well taught.

Then, carried away on the wings of imagination and paternal pride, Charles-Joseph declared he could see the trail of fine pictures or portraits or altar-pieces their Pierre-Joseph would leave behind him as he wandered along. Mark his words, people would say in the years to come: 'Ah, now that was painted by Pierre-Joseph Redouté, one of the three gifted sons and pupils of Charles-Joseph Redouté, himself no mean painter!'

Then crashing down to earth, Charles-Joseph said that he knew, none better, that no Redouté had made a fortune or acquired the wide renown his talents richly deserved, but neither had any Redouté starved to death in a garret.

And their Pierre-Joseph was not in the least likely to blot the family record by ignominiously dying of starvation. He was as strong as an ox, his head was set firm and square on his broad shoulders, and he could briskly paint any subject a client had in mind.

Moreover he had so pleasant a way with him. Everyone liked their Pierre-Joseph. Everyone.

'Yes,' said his quiet mother, 'yes.' And turned away and left it at that.

Maybe she was seeing again one July day just three years ago when My Lord Bishop had travelled from Liège to confirm the young Christians of Saint Hubert and the countryside around. As My Lord Bishop could hardly be expected to travel frequently all the way from Liège, he had economically confirmed a whole batch of children, regardless of age.

There before the high altar, very solemn and awed, had stood her three sons: Antoine-Ferdinand, aged thirteen on that very day, Pierre-Joseph, aged ten, and little Henri-Joseph aged three, only three, and holding tight to Pierre-Joseph's hand.

All three sons confirmed at one and the same time.

Moved as any mother would be on so solemn an occasion, there was something most poignant for their quiet mother to see her three sons standing there, side by side. Please God, this was how it would be all their lives long. They would always be true brothers, one to the other. But Antoine-Ferdinand was now sixteen, and growing more and more restive, saying he ought to make his way to Paris and find better-paid work.

And there went Pierre-Joseph, aged thirteen.

And here, tugging at her apron, was little Henri-Joseph, aged six, crying and begging to go with Pierre-Joseph and seek his fortune too in the wide world far from home and Saint Hubert.

The years that followed were not precisely as Charles-Joseph had so rosily predicted on that sunny July day. True, Pierre-Joseph did not starve in any garret, but he often went footsore and hungry. And as he worked his way from one village to another, and then on to this city or that, he certainly left behind many a cut-price portrait of some worthy tradesman or local dignitary. He would also often paint, at an agreed price, a scene from Holy Scriptures to hang on the wall of a village church. Sometimes in these pious scenes he would be requested to paint his patron, together with his wife and children, all suitably sanctified and attired, singing away in some celestial choir, or standing reverently, but conspicuously, behind the three Kings of Orient. No-one in those days considered this presumptuous. On the contrary, it was an act of faith, intelligent anticipation of divine approval of one's upright behaviour on this earth.

But no satisfied patrons were ever to declare in the years to come that they had at once recognised a budding genius in young Pierre-Joseph Redouté, an up-and-coming Rubens or Van Eyck. On the contrary, to them he was a pleasant sturdy lad with the most homely of country accents, and such enormous hands, that they were staggered to learn he wanted work, not as a labourer or mason, but as a painter. And they were even more staggered to discover that he could indeed paint a presentable portrait and at a very reasonable price too, if one threw in a square meal and a bed for the night – though many a time the square meal turned out to be black bread spread with bacon fat or a bowl of vegetable soup, and the bed a bale of straw in a barn.

Then, as Charles-Joseph had claimed, the master-painter of this and that city had indeed heard of the Redouté family, and willingly gave Pierre-Joseph a free place among his fee-paying students, on the understanding that he made himself useful. But not one of these master-painters was ever to declare that he had immediately seen that young Pierre-Joseph had such outstanding talent that one day he might well make a name for himself.

On the other hand, they were not astonished when Pierre-Joseph began to acquire a modest but sound reputation as a good 'all-round' painter and decorator. He was competent, reliable, industrious and cheerful. Prosaic, maybe, but it meant that Pierre-Joseph could now count on finding work of one kind or another.

At times, for example, he would be engaged by a master-painter in charge of decorating a rich nobleman's château, or the grand town residence of a wealthy merchant. And Pierre-Joseph would nimbly climb up ladders and scaffolding and paint, as directed, all manner of artistic details, as up on the lofty, ornate ceilings went the bluest of skies peopled by many a Greek or Roman god and goddess. Very much the vogue, these Greek and Roman divinities, and Pierre-Joseph would wonder why, since no-one now believed in them. However, his job was to do as he was bid. So over the massive doors, between the richly gilded panelling would go scenes from Greek or Roman mythology, Venus, for instance, rising from the waves, chastely draped in her golden hair, or Orpheus playing his lute on high Olympus.

In short, Pierre-Joseph was fast becoming a competent painter and decorator, just like his father, Charles-Joseph, and his older brother, Antoine-Ferdinand.

As Pierre-Joseph wandered from one job to another, he always listened eagerly to tales of great painters, both living and dead. And he began to wish that he'd had the good luck to be born thirty years earlier. Then he might possibly have had the chance to work in the studio of a certain Dutch master-painter, Jan van Huysum who died in 1740, nineteen years before Pierre-Joseph came into this world.

Everything he heard about Jan van Huysum fascinated Pierre-Joseph. To begin with, Jan had also been one of three brothers: Jan, Justus and Jacob; and like the three young Redoutés, they too had been taught by their father, Justus van Huysum.

But their father had been a shrewd level-headed Dutchman who made a comfortable living painting peaceful pastoral landscapes. So he must have been staggered when young Justus belligerently took to painting the most ferocious, the bloodiest of battles. Pierre-Joseph was not in the least surprised to learn that Justus had died at the early age of twenty-two. Those battles had obviously proved too much for him.

The story of his brother, Jan, was altogether different. All his life long he had painted fruit and flowers – above all, flowers, the most handsome arrangements of all manner of delightful flowers. And it seemed that the flowers he painted were so lovely that one would swear they were still alive, blooming on the canvas.

As for the third brother, Jacob, he'd had the sound Dutch common sense to realise he was no genius like Jan. But he was a competent painter and a born copyist. So he sensibly spent his life profitably copying his brother Jan's masterpieces.

Fortunately for both Jan and Jacob, the Dutch have a passion for flowers, and rich merchants willingly paid astonishingly high prices for Jan's pictures or one of Jacob's copies to hang on the walls of their stately houses.

Then sometimes the burgomaster of a prosperous Dutch city would pay Jan excellent money for a painting to adorn their imposing Stadhuis, or if the City Fathers jibbed at Jan's prices, they did the next best thing, they would buy one of Jacob's excellent copies of his brother's paintings.

So there had never been one small Third-Class house, one small garden and three goats for the van Huysums. Papa van Huysum had always earned a comfortable living, so had Jacob. But it was Jan who had done far better. He had become wealthy and famous, revered by all Holland and discerning painters everywhere.

And all by painting flowers!

Now Pierre-Joseph had no love whatever for writing letters, but he was a loving and dutiful son, so from time to time he would laboriously compose and send a letter to his family in Saint Hubert. And though Charles-Joseph always groaned at Pierre-Joseph's atrocious spelling and glaring grammatical mistakes, he and his quiet wife were naturally delighted to learn of his steady if not dramatic progress. But when a letter came to say that Pierre-Joseph was now planning to work his way to Amsterdam, Charles-Joseph was outraged.

Why Amsterdam, he demanded. Heavens above, one would imagine that he had already exhausted the wonders of his own native land.

Presently, cooling down a little, Charles-Joseph conceded that one should always strive to be fair-minded. An ambitious young painter *could* learn from the works of some of these Dutch painters – Frans Hals, for instance, Vermeer or Pieter de Hooch. And above all, of course, from that giant of art – Rembrandt. Now his work positively took one's breath away, a sobering, indeed shattering experience for any painter, young or old.

So maybe, all in all, their Pierre-Joseph might well profit by a stay in Amsterdam.

Once in Amsterdam, Pierre-Joseph stood respectfully before the great masterpieces of Frans Hals, Vermeer, Pieter de Hooch and great Rembrandt. But his father would certainly have been outraged at the way he paid his respects at a most irreverent gallop, and then hurried away as if he hadn't a moment to lose, and then stand for hours on end, lost in wonder, before the flower-paintings of Jan van Huysum.

There they bloomed, those flowers, masses of flowers, every one so exquisitely painted that they caught at his very heart. Yet, as he stood there, Pierre-Joseph felt a secret longing to take those great bouquets from those handsome vases, those massive jardinières, and study each flower, one by one, and try to discover by what miracle they seemed to be still alive, still scenting the air about them.

And how explain that in one great bouquet there were some flowers that bloomed only in spring, others that one only saw in summer, and some that bloomed late in autumn?

Pierre-Joseph began to ask questions and learned that Jan van Huysum would first see in his mind each of his magnificent flower arrangements; and as he was never hard up, he could afford to wait until he had a choice, hand-picked specimen of each one of the flowers he had decided to include. Once he had painted it in its appointed place he would get on with something else – paint a dish of fruit, for instance, until the next flower he wanted came into bloom. In this way he would paint his bouquet over the seasons till at last, there they bloomed – a whole calendar of lovely flowers.

Presently, as he stood there, Pierre-Joseph began to have the youthful audacity to ask himself why cram so many perfect flowers into one vase, one jardinière? How wonderful it would be if he could earn his bread painting just two or three flowers in a slender vase, or even one single flower.

But who would give good money for a painting like that? If people ordered a flower-painting, they expected value for money, a handsome arrangement of flowers packed into a grand vase standing on an imposing marble slab. And as Pierre-Joseph had to eat, he too tried his hand at massive bouquets but his heart bled for every flower he jammed into some blue Delft jug or vase.

He also earned so little that he began to work his way back to Belgium again where he could at least count on steady work. But as he trudged along the country lanes and roads he began to stop here and there, open and search in the battered, cheap portfolio he now carried everywhere with him, and find pencils and odd ends of paper and swiftly sketch any flower that seemed to call good-day to him as he came near. And if he hadn't paper to spare, he would stand and look and look at a flower, and then file it lovingly away in his memory.

One day Pierre-Joseph asked himself why keep all those lightning sketches, these vivid memories locked away so unprofitably? Why not give himself the delight of using them?

So now when he managed to get a commission to paint a portrait, he began to slip in a flower or two, and tell any dubious client that this was just what great Jan van Eyck had done. Why, he'd once painted the portrait of some wealthy and most important-looking gentleman wearing a magnificent fur hat on his head. But what was that rich burgher holding in his beringed right hand?

One pink, just one homely scented pink.

Then if Pierre-Joseph managed to get a commission for an altar-piece or some pious picture for a village church, he would strew the green grass beneath the feet of angels, saints and martyrs with the everyday flowers of this world, daisies, buttercups and cornflowers, all painted from memory or with the help of those lightning sketches.

And again he would pleasantly win over any critic by saying that in the world's finest altar-piece, the one in Ghent, the famous brothers, Hubert and Jan van Eyck, had painted a whole hedge of roses and vines, and they had positively bejewelled the grass beneath the feet of the Heavenly Host with just such flowers.

All of which would have made his father's hair stand on end.

Charles-Joseph had so eloquently exhorted him to study the *composition* of this great altar-piece, observe with what mastery the brothers Hubert and Jan van Eyck had grouped and painted the angels, the white-robed virgins, the martyrs, holy hermits, the pilgrims and lesser worshippers, not stand there concentrating on the flowers growing beneath their celestial feet.

Once back in Belgium, Pierre-Joseph soberly reminded himself that he was now sixteen and as they would have said in the homely patois of Saint Hubert: 'i n'aveu nin en fayée mastoke' – he hadn't a sou in his pocket.

So he was grateful when he was at once offered work by a master-painter called André, who had been engaged to decorate the Château of Carlsbourg, the regal mansion of the Duke of Bouillon.

To his delight, Maître André raised no objection whatever when Pierre-Joseph ingeniously introduced flowers wherever space permitted. When ordered, for instance, to add an artistic detail or two to a painting of some holy saint, he would contrive to make him hold a branch of a sweet wild rose or one of the loveliest of all the flowers of spring – the one so rightly called 'narcisse des poètes'.

Then if Maître André was ordered to decorate one of the spacious rooms in the classic Greek or Roman style, Pierre-Joseph could be counted upon to paint the most jovial of plump Cupids perched high in a tree, but at the foot of that tree, Pierre-Joseph would paint, from memory, a splendid tangle of the flowers, the tall graceful grass, the sprays of honeysuckle that had so often enchanted him as he trudged along some lane or forest track.

But Pierre-Joseph was an honest lad. He was well aware that Maître André paid him good money to paint as briskly as possible, not enjoy himself for hours on end painting flowers for which no Greek or Roman would have said thank you. So Pierre-Joseph took good care to paint all these flowery embellishments at the gallop, and never once did Maître André complain. Maybe he didn't even notice them.

It was now when Pierre-Joseph, carefree and happy, was working for Maître André that he received news that sent him hurrying home to Saint Hubert, his young heart heavy as lead within him.

His father was ill, so ill that one feared for his life.

Pierre-Joseph arrived just in time. His father lay dying, and there was nothing Dom Hickman or any physician in the world could do for him. And early on the grey cold morning of 23 December 1776, his sorrowing family 'closed his eyes', as one so gently put it in those days.

Christmas that year was bleak indeed in that Third-Class house, No. 8 Rue du Four. It was small, crowded, cluttered, but it had always been so lively, warm and cheerful a home. Money had always been tight but Charles-Joseph had always been so merrily sure that good fortune and fame were waiting for him just around the corner. For thirty-two long years, day in, day out, he had laughed and sung as he added to the splendours of the ancient Abbey and Basilica. Now he lay silent in death, as unknown to fame as the day he arrived in Saint Hubert.

And all his quiet widow owned in this world was that Third-Class house, the small garden, the three goats and a pathetically small sum of money she had managed to save, sou by sou, over the years.

But that gentle unselfish woman had no need to fear the future. Antoine-Ferdinand was now earning good money in Paris; Pierre-Joseph could also count on steady work there in Belgium; and those two good daughters, still unmarried, were with her in Saint Hubert. Between them they would take care of their mother and their ten-year-old brother, Henri Joseph; they would see they were never in want.

Then ten-year-old Henri-Joseph had set his heart on becoming a painter too, of course, but now his papa was no longer there to go on teaching him, they would have to manage to send him to some master-painter to finish his apprenticeship, someone with a studio not too far from Saint Hubert where Pierre-Joseph, whenever possible, could keep a brotherly eye on him.

Henri-Joseph had always loved and admired Pierre-Joseph, and his sensitive young face lit up when Pierre-Joseph, seeking to console him, said who knew, maybe one day they would both become master-painters. Think of it, the Brothers Pierre-Joseph and Henri-Joseph Redouté, master-painters with a splendid studio of their own.

Once everything was settled, Pierre-Joseph had to return post-haste to Carlsbourg; he could not linger long in Saint Hubert not earning a sou. But before he left, he went to see Dom Hickman and found him plunged in most unusual gloom.

It seemed that the finances of the Abbey could now be summed up in four words:

> Debts? Enormous
> Credit? Nil

But all undismayed, my Lord Abbot Spirlet was now enthusiastically engaged in yet another money-making enterprise, one that would wipe out all those enormous debts and leave abundant reserves as well. And this time it was in the sacred name of Freedom as well as High Finance.

Ah yes, Freedom, sighed Dom Hickman. And said he supposed Pierre-Joseph had heard that the English were also up to their necks in debt, and having trouble with their American Colonies as well.

The English, said Dom Hickman, had been waging war for years all over Europe, and in Asia and Africa as well – not to mention fighting rip-roaring sea battles on all the Seven Seas. But one always had to pay for wars, no matter how glorious.

And he had heard that the English now had to find millions of their English pounds – pounds, not francs – to pay for all this far-flung warfare. And they had decided, without consulting them, that their American Colonies were to have the patriotic privilege of helping to settle this stupendous National Debt. And without as much as a by-your-leave, they'd clapped the heaviest taxes upon them.

However, these American colonists, all lovers of freedom and justice, had blazed with anger at this high-handed treatment and were now up in arms, openly resisting the armed forces sent out to subdue them and collect those taxes.

And what had all this to do with their quiet Abbey in the village of Saint Hubert in the peaceful forests of the Ardennes?

Well, these rebellious Americans, explained Dom Hickman, had chosen one George Washington to be their leader, a godly upright man, so they said, and a highly astute one for he'd had the good sense to send their celebrated Benjamin Franklin to Paris to ask for French help in their fight against the English.

Yes, brilliant Benjamin Franklin, who had written that admirable book, *Experiments and Observations on Electricity*.

The French, always enchanted to embarrass the English, had warmly welcomed Benjamin Franklin and were sending agents all over Belgium to buy cannons, guns, ammunition of all kinds, to send to the American freedom-fighters. And My Lord Abbot Spirlet was now, if you please, busily turning out cannons, yes, cannons, in that blast-furnace in the heart of the forest. All of which he confidently expected to sell at a very good price to the King of France who would then dispatch them to America.

To think, mourned Dom Hickman, that here he was, doing his humble best to heal the sick, to patch up the maimed, and My Lord Abbot was bent on turning out cannons to blow up whole regiments of Englishmen on whom he'd never set eyes. And all in the sacred name of Freedom!

Providentially for those Englishmen, My Lord Abbot was excellent at theory but lamentably unpractical. He was not in the least interested when the great iron foundries in Liège began to use cheap coke instead of expensive charcoal in their furnaces. Neither could he be convinced that theory was not enough, that one needed a lifetime of practical experience to turn out cannons. Under his detailed instructions his blast-furnace was turning out a vast quantity of costly iron that ought, theoretically, to be perfect for the casting of cannons. But either that costly iron or the casting was faulty, for so far, it was always the cannon that blew up whenever one tried to fire off a cannon-ball.

Then abruptly changing the subject, Dom Hickman said he had learned that Herr-Professor-Doctor Franz Mesmer was planning to go to Paris where reports of his methods of healing were arousing the greatest interest. If Pierre-Joseph ever went to Paris – as he might well do one day – Dom Hickman knew he could count on him to send him any details he could gather about this most un-orthodox of doctors.

Then Dom Hickman began to speak most earnestly to Pierre-Joseph saying that his father's death was a grievous loss to all who loved their ancient Basilica and Abbey. God knew he had been given the most meagre of worldly rewards for his labour, but in his work he had left behind the best of memorials. Pilgrims and poor souls in distress would see all about them the work of Charles-Joseph Redouté shining to the glory of God and Saint Hubert, and would surely be comforted.

Dom Hickman then spoke of the years that lay ahead for Pierre-Joseph, saying it was foolish, indeed dangerous, for any man – be he monk, artist, scientist, doctor – to become self-satisfied. The longer one lived, the more one should realise how pathetically little one had learnt. So Pierre-Joseph should do as his good father, God rest his soul, had wished. As he worked his way, he should go on studying the wondrous art treasures of his native land, and whenever possible seek the sound advice and tuition of the best possible master-painters, working for them for next to nothing if necessary. A full belly was not an indispensable vade-mecum to any achievement.

If he remembered this, Pierre-Joseph could hope to become a credit to his family, just as his father, may he rest in peace, had always so confidently predicted. Above all he would learn to make the best possible use of the gifts which the good God had un-doubtedly bestowed on him.

Then Dom Hickman quietly blessed Pierre-Joseph and sent him on his way, reassured and comforted.

When the decoration of the Château of Carlsbourg was com-pleted, Pierre-Joseph, still very sobered by the death of his father, began to work his way to Liège. It was in this city that the distin-guished family of master-painters, the Cocklers, had established their famous studio.

The Cocklers, like the Redoutés, had always been painters, but unlike the Redoutés they had an astute flair for making money. For generation after generation they had worked only for the most generous and appreciative of patrons, among them, Monseigneur, the Prince-Bishop of Liège; they had also painted portraits of many a foreign royal family and noblemen. So there had never been any lack of money in the family; and generation after generation of young Cocklers had enjoyed the advantage of studying for some years in Italy, a veritable Paradise for any young artist.

All of which added a splendid lustre to their family reputation, of course, so it was not astonishing that young painters flocked from far and near to learn from the famous Cocklers of Liège.

Fortunately for Pierre-Joseph the Cocklers had heard of the modest Redouté family, but they were obviously taken aback when a seventeen-year-old lad with the most homely of country accents and enormous and clumsy-looking hands, turned up one day and announced that he was Pierre-Joseph Redouté who had recently been helping Maître André with the decoration of the Château of Carlsbourg. And who would now be grateful to have the privilege of studying in their studio and making himself useful in lieu of fees.

However, there was something so pleasant and disarming about this unlikely-looking young painter that the Cocklers took him on as a non-fee-paying student. But Pierre-Joseph had to eat, and when driven to it, buy shoes and clothes; he also religiously sent every sou he could spare to his mother in Saint Hubert. To earn all this, in every moment of his free time he again painted cut-price portraits, scenes from the Holy Scriptures or the Lives of the Saints, and in this precarious way managed to spend a whole year in Liège.

The Cocklers must certainly have appreciated his skill, and the speed at which he worked, for when the year was up, he set out to work his way to Luxembourg with two profitable commissions in his pocket. He had been invited, thanks to the Cocklers, to paint two portraits, one of a distinguished military gentleman, Monsieur the General Bender, and one of an enthusiastic patron of the arts, Her Highness the Princesse-Baronne de Tornaco.

It was when he was busily engaged putting the finishing touches to these two portraits that Pierre-Joseph had interesting news from Saint Hubert. My Lord Abbot Spirlet had publicly announced he was no longer prepared to oblige the King of France with cannons to send to America.

The truth was that although those cannons, theoretically, ought at last to be deadly efficient, they still had the most deplorable way of exploding whenever one attempted to demonstrate their efficiency by firing off a cannon-ball. Not that My Lord Abbot was prepared to admit this. On the contrary, he announced with considerable hauteur that though the French had placed definite orders for his cannons 'no money had followed'. It was this perfidious refusal to pay up that had obliged My Lord Abbot, to quote his own words, 'decisively to abandon the manufacture of cannons destined for America'.

Pierre-Joseph laughed aloud at this masterpiece of whitewashing, but his heart grew warm as he pictured Dom Hickman trudging through the forest of Saint Hubert, searching for his medicinal herbs and quietly chanting a grateful 'Te Deum'. Knowing Dom Hickman as he did, Pierre-Joseph could well imagine that as he chanted, Dom Hickman was quite prepared to believe that some peace-loving angel had lent an avenging hand in blowing sky-high those abominable cannons.

The portrait of Monsieur the General Bender, blazing with gold braid and magnificent military decorations, was much admired. Especially by the General himself.

Her Highness the Princesse-Baronne de Tornaco was equally delighted with her portrait, so delighted that she told Pierre-Joseph he simply must go to Paris where his talents as a portrait-painter would be well rewarded. And she sat down at her elegant writing-desk and wrote him letters of introduction to present to certain noble patrons of the arts in Versailles. Pierre-Joseph thanked the gracious lady, and stowed these valuable letters away in one of his pockets.

Then as nothing succeeds like success, Pierre-Joseph immediately received more invitations to paint the portraits of other notabilities in Luxembourg. But this didn't fill him with elation. Far from it. He was no fool. He knew his portraits were good, adequate, and that he could now easily make a comfortable living painting nothing but portraits. But something within him cried aloud that this was not for him. He recalled the quiet farewell words of Dom Hickman, and, once he had sent home most of the money he had earned, he set off again.

This time, as he worked his way, he would study far more earnestly, far more diligently, the great masterpieces of his native land. And so discover, please God, what was so lacking in his own depressingly adequate work.

So Pierre-Joseph, in search of inspiration, once more took to the roads and wandered from one lovely old city to another, conscientiously visiting cathedrals, churches, museums and town halls. He stood, awestruck, before many a magnificent altar-piece; he shuddered and turned away from harrowing pictures of the torments of the damned, and cheered up again to behold some joyous and naïve Nativity with angels and shepherds and the Three Wise Men all singing and rejoicing so merrily that one could not gaze at them and not rejoice too.

He also saw many a small, unpretentious picture of some homely and familiar scene, a ragged but jovial beggar, or a child playing with a doll, an old man with his grandchildren, all painted with such meticulous and loving details that one knew that those masters of old had been spellbound, deeply moved by all they saw about them in everyday life.

Then there were the excellent, lifelike portraits they had left behind. But it was the background to these portraits that always captivated Pierre-Joseph. There would often be a small, open window, and through this one caught a glimpse of some distant and enchanting landscape, or more delightful still, a garden with every plant, every bush and tree in full bloom.

So many, so varied, so inspiring these masterpieces of old! Yet, once out again on the country roads and under the open sky, Pierre-Joseph would find himself thinking only of those enchanted gardens, or the beauty of a painted lily in the hands of a Madonna.

And as he trudged on, he was forever stopping to wonder at the loveliness of the wild flowers growing in the meadows, hedgerows and forests. And out again from his bulging portfolio would come pencils and paper and he would try to capture their grace and charm, and presently it seemed to him that his heart as well as his battered portfolio overflowed with flowers, nothing but flowers.

At times he would sternly tell himself that this was no way to become a successful painter, and a wave of guilt would sweep over him to think how disappointed his father would have been to see him so indecisive, still earning so little money, wasting his time, thinking only of flowers.

Moreover the years were whisking by; no painter could afford to wander forever earning his bread as he went. He must be sensible, hard-headed, decide what to do in life.

Paint portraits, as the Cocklers had so strongly advised him to do . . .

But the thought of churning out portraits, year after year, for the rest of his life, made his heart grow heavy with dismay. Ah, no, heaven deliver him from so safe, well-paid and joyless a future.

At this moment out of the blue came a letter from Antoine-Ferdinand. He was still in Paris but he was now engaged on the most interesting of jobs. He was helping to decorate a new theatre where companies of Italian singers would come to sing their amusing operettas. French operas, wrote Antoine-Ferdinand, were immensely lofty and dignified, but these Italians sang the gayest, the most diverting of operettas.

Antoine-Ferdinand was not only helping to decorate the walls and ceiling of this new theatre, he was also designing and painting the scenery; everything to be as gay and full of colour as possible. Nothing muted or sober for these Italian nightingales!

Would Pierre-Joseph care to travel to Paris as speedily as possible and work on all this with Antoine-Ferdinand? The pay was not princely but it would give Pierre-Joseph an excellent start in Paris.

Moreover Pierre-Joseph would not be taking a risk for Antoine-Ferdinand was beginning to make a name for himself as a reliable decorator. In fact the future now looked so assured that he'd decided to marry. His wife was the most agreeable of girls, modest, quiet, pious, very like their mother. They couldn't afford to rent more than a couple of rooms but Pierre-Joseph would be very welcome there at any time. However, as they had no spare room to offer him, Antoine-Ferdinand would begin hunting for one at a reasonable rent for Pierre-Joseph as soon as he had a reply. So would Pierre-Joseph promptly let him know if he was interested in this offer of work.

Interested! Pierre-Joseph was enchanted. It would be a splendid tonic to try his hand at something so gay and novel. And he scrawled a note to Antoine-Ferdinand, bundled together his few possessions, and hurried home to Saint Hubert to kiss his mother and assure her he would write whenever possible. He also asked her to be sure and let Dom Hickman know how sorry he was he hadn't had the time to see him – Dom Hickman was somewhere in the forests that day. And Pierre-Joseph picked up his battered portfolio and his bundle of clothes, and set out to make his way, this time to Paris.

Now behind him Pierre-Joseph certainly left a long, long trail of all manner of paintings, just as his father had predicted.

But where are they now, all those paintings, those portraits?

Maybe some still hang, unsigned, on the walls of old farms lost in the countryside, or on the walls of village churches. There were two pictures, both signed: P. J. Redouté, so they say, one of the Blessed Virgin and one of the Child Jesus; the colours of both pictures had faded over the years and the Blessed Virgin and the Child Jesus were obviously painted by a very young artist. The flowers and fruit, however, with which he encircled them were beautifully, indeed astonishingly well painted.

They also say there were once three pictures in the Château of Carlsbourg which were considered to be the work of young Pierre-Joseph Redouté, one large and two smaller ones. The large one, they say, was meant to hang over a fire-place, with a smaller one on the wall on either side. And whoever ordered this trio must have had a predilection for Cupids, for each picture showed a plump and merry Cupid perched on a leafy branch of a forest tree, all three revelling in some rollicking, classical joke.

If Pierre-Joseph did indeed paint this trio of pictures, then he must have had the time of his young life painting from memory, or with the help of the sketches stuffed in his portfolio, the flowers, grasses, tangles of briar and ivy that grew, so they say, about all three of those forest trees.

But no-one can now show you these pictures. There have been several fires over the years in the Château, so they may well have gone up in flames. Or maybe they were removed, banished from sight, by some straitlaced authority who decided that plump and ribald Cupids were altogether out of place when the Château became a school for boys.

As for the many portraits Pierre-Joseph painted, younger generations of Belgians may well have decided that these portraits of their great grandmamas or portly great grandpapas were quaint but no works of art and simply not worth keeping, though maybe, of course, they dutifully stacked them with other unwanted bric-a-brac in a corner of an attic, and they are still there, forgotten, gathering the dust to this very day.

All that is certain is that Pierre-Joseph was only too happy to leave them all forever behind him as he set out that day for Paris.

4

The King's Garden

In all the ten years Pierre-Joseph had been working his way along
the roads of his native land, he had been only too happy to obey the
Scriptures and 'consider the lilies of the field, how they grow' and
'to take no thought for the morrow'. Above all 'to consider the lilies
of the field'. Pierre-Joseph was always ready to snatch at any opportunity to obey that agreeable exhortation.

As for taking 'no thought for the morrow', well, when he earned
good money he always sent a generous part home to his mother; the
rest had a way of slipping like sand through his fingers. He never
could coldly think of the morrow and turn a blind eye, a deaf ear, to
others who also knew what it is to wonder just when, and how, they
would again earn the price of a meal. In short, Pierre-Joseph had
precious little in hard cash to show for his ten years of happy-go-
lucky wandering.

It was not surprising then that he set off for Paris in the cheapest
possible way – on the roof of the stage-coach that rumbled once a
week from Brussels to Paris. The moneyed passengers sat on
cushioned seats inside the coach with curtains at the windows to
keep out the draughts; but up on the roof sat Pierre-Joseph with a
few other hard-up passengers, making themselves as comfortable as
possible among the luggage.

The journey took three days and the stage-coach stopped at night
at a roadside inn where the passengers had to pay for supper and a
bed. So it was fortunate that Antoine-Ferdinand was waiting to welcome Pierre-Joseph to Paris, for once again, as they would have said

in Saint Hubert, 'i n'aveu nin en fayée mastoke', he hadn't a sou in his pocket.

Pierre-Joseph was also relieved to learn that there were still weeks of decorating to be done before the new Italian Theatre could announce its grand opening night with a 'Magnificent Season of Gaiety, Splendour and Song' for all of which Antoine-Ferdinand had agreed to paint the scenery.

There was to be no monotony about these gay operettas. As fast as one troupe of singers exhausted their repertoire, another troupe would arrive and demand, pronto! new romantic scenery for *their* operettas. Indeed Antoine-Ferdinand had been warned that he might well have only a day's notice for the scenery needed for that very night. So they'd often have to work at breakneck speed.

Then there was still decorating to be done on the walls of the theatre. So all in all, Antoine-Ferdinand could confidently predict they had at least two years of steady employment before them. And he was counting on Pierre-Joseph to roll up his sleeves and begin work the very next day.

Antoine-Ferdinand took Pierre-Joseph straight home to meet his young wife, and she was just as Pierre-Joseph had hoped she would be, very pleasant and homely. Over the good soup she had ready for them, Antoine-Ferdinand said he knew that Pierre-Joseph didn't enjoy letter writing, but he could count the letters Pierre-Joseph had sent him on the fingers of one hand. So now he'd like to hear something of all Pierre-Joseph had been doing in the last ten years.

Pierre-Joseph laughed and said well, he'd try; and he began to list the master-painters for whom he'd worked at one time or another, and the grand houses he'd helped to decorate. But he prudently thought it advisable not to mention how much time he'd spent painting flowers. Antoine-Ferdinand would certainly not have approved of that.

Presently Pierre-Joseph came to the time when he'd made his way to Luxembourg to paint the portraits of Monsieur the General Bender and Her Highness the Princesse-Baronne de Tornaco. And Antoine-Ferdinand was most impressed to learn that the Princesse-Baronne had been so pleased with her portrait that she'd given

Pierre-Joseph letters of introduction to influential patrons of the arts in Versailles who might well be interested in having their portraits painted.

'But this is excellent!' cried Antoine-Ferdinand. 'Letters like this do not grow on every bush! Once we've finished with the Italian Theatre we must look for other work. And it seems to me that you would indeed be well advised to go on painting portraits. These letters of introduction will then be of immense service to you! You must put them somewhere safe. Maybe you'd better leave them here with me until you need them.'

'Good idea!' said Pierre-Joseph, and still talking away as carefree as you please, he began to fumble and turn out his pockets, and then his bulging portfolio, and out tumbled stubs of pencils, brushes, sketches of flowers, paints and a hundred other oddments.

But no letters.

Search where he might, there were no letters. That reluctant portrait-painter had lost them, and heaven only knew where. He couldn't even remember when he had last set eyes on them.

Now Pierre-Joseph was always to remember, with gratitude, that gracious lady, the Princesse-Baronne de Tornaco, but never once did he feel a pang of regret at the loss of those potentially useful letters. Indeed, in the years to come, it seemed to him that fate *meant* him to lose them for now began a new life altogether different from anything he had ever imagined.

To begin with, the room Antoine-Ferdinand had found for him was just what he would have chosen himself. There was space enough for all his needs, a bed, a table, a chair and a couple of hooks on the door to hang up his few clothes. And as Antoine-Ferdinand had said, with Paris so crowded, and rooms so hard to find, Pierre-Joseph was fortunate to find any place at all at a rent which wouldn't swallow up most of what he earned.

True, it was up three steep flights of stone stairs, but what does that matter when one is twenty and can fly up stairs two at a time, fling open one's door, rush to the window, fling that open, and gaze out all over Paris.

Ah yes, that small room was idyllic, all a young artist could ask.

Then the very next day, Pierre-Joseph began to work with Antoine-Ferdinand, helping to finish decorating the walls of the new theatre with garlands of flowers ten times larger and gaudier than any that bloom in our everyday world. He also lent a hand in painting the romantic scenery, with Antoine-Ferdinand forever imploring him to keep in mind that when one went to an Italian operetta, one expected to feast one's eyes as well as one's ears. So if Pierre-Joseph *had* to make flowers sprout about every green cardboard tree, or riot all over romantic cardboard ruins, then for heaven's sake would he kindly make those flowers so dramatic, so blazing with colour, that even the hard-up, but vociferous, critics packed high under the roof or at the very back of the theatre could see and admire them too.

Pierre-Joseph therefore obliged with highly imaginative and spectacular flowers, most passionately coloured, telling himself that flowers like these might well bloom in the make-believe land of Italian operettas.

Once back in his room, however, he would sling his coat on the bed – or occasionally on a hook on the door – and gaze for a moment over Paris. Then he would sit down at his table and set to work to paint a real flower, any flower at all he had been able to beg from the friends he was beginning to make who were lucky enough to have a patch of garden. And they began to tell others about this young Belgian who painted flowers in all his free time – just for the love of it! And one would never credit how beautifully he painted them. Yet one would never imagine this to behold him. He was the homeliest of young men with enormous, clumsy-looking hands, the strong hands of a blacksmith, one would say. One could easily imagine him shoeing a cart-horse, but painting flowers? Never!

This good-natured gossip began to pay dividends and soon Pierre-Joseph was never short of flowers to paint.

But what became of all those flower-paintings? No-one knows. Pierre-Joseph probably gave them away as fast as he painted them.

Then Pierre-Joseph quickly discovered that his father had been right – Paris certainly did something to a young man; and when it grew too dark to paint, Pierre-Joseph began to enjoy many an evening in one of the coffee-houses that seemed to be springing up like mushrooms all over Paris. And as he listened to other young men eloquently airing their views on a thousand and one topics, he realised he had come to Paris at the best, the most exciting of times.

Splendid gardens, it seemed, were all the rage. Wealthy men thought nothing of paying dedicated botanists to go on voyages of discovery to far distant lands, risk their lives in steaming jungles or high untrodden mountainsides to bring back – if they were fortunate enough to survive – living plants or seeds or cuttings of shrubs, trees or flowers completely unknown in Europe. It added an extra lustre to any princely garden to have the one and only specimen of a flower or plant from some far-away land growing there, the envy of all other wealthy garden enthusiasts.

But best of all, there in Paris, only a brisk walk from Pierre-Joseph's room was one of the most magnificent of these gardens – le Jardin du Roi – the King's Garden. And this royal garden soon became a Paradise on Earth for Pierre-Joseph.

It was, as everyone said, 'a botanical wonder', most artistically and lavishly planted with rare and beautiful trees and shrubs and the loveliest of flowers. But it was far more than 'a botanical wonder', it was a veritable university, for in the spacious grounds there was a Museum of Natural History where learned professors gave lectures on botany, zoology and mineralogy. And as Natural History, as well as wonderful gardens, was all the rage, these lectures, above all those on botany, were very well attended, especially by young ladies, beautifully dressed and chaperoned by their fashionable mamas or the most watchful of governesses.

Pierre-Joseph, however, was not in the least interested in these lectures, not even those on botany with all those charming young ladies so raptly listening. His own free time was far too short to listen to any professor no matter how learned. All he asked was to wander, lost in delight, among the beds of flowers, and then come to a sudden halt when he saw a flower newly open, the bloom still on every petal. And he would swiftly bring out paper, pencils, brushes, paint and seek to capture its joyous loveliness; and as he painted, the whole world, time itself, seemed to stand still and silent.

Now the gardeners employed in the Jardin du Roi were highly qualified professionals, but gardeners the world over are a kindly race, quick to sense, to respond to a genuine love of flowers, and presently the gardeners in that royal garden grew interested in the homely young man who spent so much time there painting flowers. They began to exchange a civil word or two with him, and they liked his friendly unpretentious ways, his warm Belgian accent. They were also interested to learn that he earned his bread and the rent of his room helping to decorate the new Italian Theatre, and that this was why he always came hurrying into the Jardin du Roi as if he hadn't a moment of daylight to squander. And to crown all, he painted flowers for the sheer delight of it, nothing more! And when they looked at his paintings, they too marvelled how he could paint so delicately, so beautifully with those enormous and ugly hands of his.

Soon they began to watch out for him and tell him to hurry over to this or that corner of the garden where some flower was about to come into bloom. And Pierre-Joseph's homely face would shine with gratitude as he thanked them, and he would hurry away to behold what surely must be one of the most gentle, most innocent sights on earth – a flower slowly unfolding its petals.

So there was Pierre-Joseph now, working industriously all day with Antoine-Ferdinand in the new Italian Theatre, and then racing off to the Jardin du Roi to spend every possible moment left of daylight blissfully painting the flowers blooming there. And when night fell, he would join the friends he had made in their favourite café and listen to them arguing away on the infallible, the only way to put the whole world right. But Pierre-Joseph began to notice that sooner or later the talk would always come round to the latest folly of Her Majesty Queen Marie-Antoinette.

It seemed that Her Majesty also dearly loved a garden, and as she was always in the van of fashion, she was determined, regardless as always of cost, to outshine all other royal garden-lovers. And she had ruthlessly set to work to transform the grounds around Le Petit Trianon – her own private palace in Versailles.

Admittedly it had once been surrounded by a monstrous array of greenhouses full of a vast variety of pampered and exotic plants, but Marie-Antoinette promptly had all these cleared away, except those in which strawberries grew in delicious profusion. Her Majesty was very fond of strawberries.

She had also ruthlessly ordered every tree and shrub growing about the greenhouses to be uprooted. All this to make room for the building of a fairytale hamlet set in the most idyllic of rural scenes, with rippling streams, delightful little cascades and a lovely lake. Every drop of the water for this had to be brought all the way from Marly but one paid skilled engineers, of course, to see to the tedious technical difficulties involved.

And, by the way, said one of Pierre-Joseph's friends, some of the trees and shrubs that Marie-Antoinette had ordered to be uprooted, had been replanted in the Jardin du Roi. Pierre-Joseph ought to inquire about their health, ask if they had recovered from this royal affront, the next time he chatted to those friendly gardeners.

But to come back to Her Majesty's rustic hamlet. Her Head Gardener, Monsieur Richard, had a dedicated love of trees so Her Majesty encouraged him to buy and plant the loveliest, the most graceful of trees to cast a green, and costly, shade on her fairytale hamlet.

Only Her Majesty's intimate friends were ever invited to her hamlet but everyone said it was delightful, especially in the spring when a host of scented hyacinths – Her Majesty adored hyacinths – and gay tulips and irises bloomed there, outdoing Solomon in all his glory. And all acquired in Holland at enormous expense from those bulb-loving but hard-headed business men, the Dutch.

It was also delightful, so they said, to catch a glimpse of Her Majesty and her intimate friends whiling away the hours playing at being shepherds and shepherdesses or milkmaids and their rustic swains, in that fairytale hamlet.

And in the warm summertime, the Queen and her ladies, rustically attired in white muslin gowns with broad sashes of coloured satin about their waists, ethereal gauze fichus floating about their necks, and wide straw hats on their heads, would trip around gathering posies of roses and honeysuckle, and then sit down in the cool shade of the costly trees on the banks of one of the rippling streams, and enjoy delicious strawberries, with cream straight from the fairy-tale dairy.

After this they would be restfully rowed about on the lovely artificial lake in charming gondolas, flying the Queen's own colours of blue and white.

Ah yes, Her Majesty, Queen Marie-Antoinette adored to live the simple rustic life – regardless of expense.

As for His Majesty, King Louis XVI, what was he doing whilst the Queen and her ladies so idyllically whiled away the sunny hours? It seemed he was never happier than when out hunting in the forests around Versailles, a brother in spirit to Saint Hubert himself – before that huntsman saint had been confronted with that reproving vision, of course.

When His Majesty was not out hunting, he still loved to escape whenever possible from the suffocating, tedious etiquette, the stiff, inflexible ceremony of the Court of Versailles.

Pierre-Joseph's friends magnanimously admitted they sympathised with His Majesty's longing to escape from all this, but what did His Majesty do? He would shut himself up, alone, in a workshop, and concentrate on making, or mending, locks – locks of any kind! Or else he would spend hours drawing elaborate maps of the world.

'Chacun à son goût!' would say Pierre-Joseph's friends. This might be His Majesty's idea of bliss and contentment but they, ah, now they could think of far more exhilarating ways to spend their free time if they wore the crown and no impertinent questions ever asked, no matter what the cost.

As Pierre-Joseph listened to all this, he began to feel a secret sympathy for both the French King and the Queen. From all he heard, they were forever spied upon by a thousand malicious eyes. Maybe it was a wondrous relief to the King to be alone and try to *master* locks. Maybe, as he drew those elaborate maps, he was dreaming of some Utopia on earth where he would be King by divine right – he could never escape the heavy burden of kingship laid on him by heaven – but in this new Utopia, all his ministers, courtiers and subjects, would be upright, contented and loyal.

As for the Queen, well, Heaven knew that she'd never had the chance to learn first-hand how unromantic was the lot of a real-life shepherdess or milkmaid, above all on a bitter winter day.

Pierre-Joseph said nothing of this to his critical friends. After all, he wasn't even French; and as they were not slow to remind him, he was the most unpractical Belgian they'd ever set eyes on. The proof? The way he squandered all his free hours of daylight painting pretty flowers! A fine lucrative pastime that was for a hard-up artist! It had never yet brought him the price of a cup of coffee. Then they'd slap him on the back and magnanimously cry again: 'Chacun à son goût!'

Presently the talk would come around to the war in America where the French were still generously helping the American freedom-fighters to drive out the tyrannical English. An alarming drain on the Exchequer, of course – all wars devour money – but this was surely the best of all wars with so lofty a cause, and plenty of glorious victories. And so conveniently far away!

It was also gratifying to think that the English might boast, with some truth, that Britannia ruled the waves, but it was France who was showing the world that she led the way in 'navigating the skies' as the King himself had so unexpectedly, and aptly, put it.

The first glorious ascent into space was made soon after Pierre-Joseph arrived in Paris. A brightly painted balloon had sailed high over Versailles and drifted for all of eight minutes before it made a successful landing a whole mile and a half away. Admittedly men had been experimenting for centuries with balloons, but this was the first to carry passengers: a cock, a lamb and a duck. And not in the least flustered by this momentous flight, those three level-headed creatures seemed to wonder what all the fuss was about when they were escorted, amid wild excitement, to the Royal Zoo in Marly to spend the rest of their lives in honourable monotony and comfort.

Two months later, all the coffee-houses were again buzzing with excitement. Two noblemen had paid for the construction of a far more magnificent balloon, and they were bent on becoming the first two men to soar into space. But to their dismay His Majesty the King was refusing his royal permission – the skies over France were also his by divine right. And presently exasperated by their insistent entreaties, His Majesty barked that if two men had to risk their lives in this way, then they had his permission to fetter two criminals together and send *them* up in their magnificent balloon.

'What, Sire!' exclaimed one of the noblemen. 'You would allow two base criminals to be the first men to soar into God's great sky!'

'And in this manner, demonstrate to the world the glory of France!' astutely added the second nobleman.

That did it! His Majesty at last gave his royal permission, and early one fine November morning, in the Bois de Boulogne, the two noblemen, elegantly clad in blue velvet, white silk stockings, and tricorne hats adorned with feathers, climbed solemnly into their magnificent balloon. As the ropes were cast off and the balloon slowly rose, the two noblemen politely doffed their feathered hats and bowed to Pierre-Joseph and all the other excited spectators down there on earth.

That balloon sailed all of six miles before those two first aeronauts in history landed, safe, sound and triumphant, twenty-five minutes later.

Soon after this, everyone was talking of the trip a certain Madame Thible was planning to make in yet another balloon. Pierre-Joseph gathered that all Paris, all Versailles, knew Madame Thible. She was an operatic singer with the most powerful voice, and Madame had decided to be the very first woman to soar into space. And as up and away soared Madame in her balloon, she absolutely surpassed herself, singing at the top of her powerful voice a song specially composed for the occasion:

'Oh, to travel in the clouds!'

Ah yes, the Paris into which Pierre-Joseph had stepped was the liveliest, the most fascinating, the most dramatic of cities. But his best, his happiest hours were always those he spent in the Jardin du Roi where he too lived in a dream world all his own, a tranquil world of flowers.

Then came a red-letter day in Pierre-Joseph's life, and it could not have come at a better time. The work on the new Italian Theatre was almost finished, and everyone, including the Italian singers, was delighted with both the decorations and the scenery. Already Antoine-Ferdinand had excellent offers of more work, and not only from other theatre-managers but from the wealthy owners of fine houses in other French cities. A safe lifetime of decorating now lay before them, said Antoine-Ferdinand, very gratified and confident. And then sharply demanded to know why Pierre-Joseph was sitting there, listening to him, silent as the grave, showing no eagerness, no enthusiasm whatever.

Just in the nick of time to save Pierre-Joseph from this safe life-time of decorating theatres and fine houses, came this red-letter day. He was in the Jardin du Roi engrossed in painting a delicate little flower – he didn't know its name, names meant nothing to Pierre-Joseph – when he became aware that a gentleman was standing by his side, watching him.

'Monsieur, I like your work,' said this gentleman. 'How would you like to paint some flowers especially for me? I would pay you, of course.'

Pay him! Pierre-Joseph couldn't believe his ears but before he could stammer a word, the gentleman was explaining that he was an art-dealer. He would entrust Pierre-Joseph's paintings to the eminent engraver, Monsieur Demarteau, who would reproduce copies of them in colour. These would be put on sale, at a modest price, by the art-dealer. They would serve as models to students and others interested in flower-painting.

That day Pierre-Joseph walked home on air, all the more so as he had learnt that the eminent engraver, Monsieur Demarteau, was also a Belgian. Pierre-Joseph allowed no grass to grow under his feet and presently, paintings completed, there he was eagerly learning a new skill – the first principles of engraving and colour-printing in the workshop of Monsieur Demarteau. And again he was living from hand to mouth, for naturally Monsieur Demarteau could not be expected to pay much to an apprentice no matter how eager and gifted.

Antoine-Ferdinand, throwing up both arms in exasperated dis-may, exclaimed that first, Pierre-Joseph had carelessly lost those valuable letters of introduction from Her Highness the Princesse-Baronne de Tornaco, and now he was just as carelessly losing the chance of a good safe future in decorating.

Ah well, if one black day, Pierre-Joseph found himself evicted from his room for failing to pay the rent, without a coat to his back, not even the price of a meal in his pocket, Antoine-Ferdinand would always come to the rescue.

Pierre-Joseph, touched by this brotherly solicitude, warmly thanked Antoine-Ferdinand, and not in the least discouraged, went on with his apprenticeship under the expert guidance of Monsieur Demarteau. And living from hand to mouth, of course.

Now the art of engraving and colour-printing in those days fell far short of the high standards we have grown to expect today. But everyone then thought Monsieur Demarteau's work was admirable, everyone that is, except that novice, Pierre-Joseph Redouté.

He looked at those admirable copies of his flower-paintings and secretly longed to take each one in turn and with a loving stroke of the brush here and there, transform them; make them look, not like copies, but as if each one of them had just been painted by him, as fresh and alive as on the day it came into bloom in the Jardin du Roi.

But Pierre-Joseph sternly reminded himself that he had been paid, in hard cash, for the originals of these engravings. Moreover he was truly grateful to kindly Monsieur Demarteau who took such pride in the excellence of his work. And who was he, Pierre-Joseph Redouté, a hard-up unknown painter, to offer improving suggestions to such an eminent engraver! So Pierre-Joseph stifled this artistic arrogance.

But if ever he was given the chance, this subtle touching up of every copy of his paintings was just what he would do, so help him God!

Then Pierre-Joseph laughed aloud. It was almost as if he, Pierre-Joseph Redouté, was making a solemn vow to seize with both hands a chance, a golden chance, that was not in the least likely to come his way.

.   .   .

As the days, the months, went by, Pierre-Joseph grew more and more friendly with the gardeners of the Jardin du Roi and he became very interested in all they could tell him of the history of the many beautiful trees, shrubs and flowers that grew there. He was moved to look at a flower, or a graceful tree, and think that it was a native of China or Japan, the Cape of Good Hope or some other far-distant land. And that there it grew now, quite happily, under the sky of France.

In the days to come it was strange and poignant to recall how interested he became in all the gardeners could tell him about a gay and courageous young botanist, Monsieur Joseph Dombey, who at that very time was far away in Chile, or maybe it was in Peru, risking his life again to bring back still more unknown plants and flowers to add to the glory of France.

True, both Chile and Peru belonged to Spain, but those Spaniards were no fools. They had given permission to Monsieur Dombey to travel where he pleased on condition that he took with him two Spanish botanists, and that they brought back with them two specimens of every discovery, together with two copies of all their observations and notes, one set of all this for Spain, one set for France.

Pierre-Joseph would often think of intrepid young Monsieur Dombey, and wonder if he would ever have the good luck to meet him when he returned triumphantly to France. A botanist like this would certainly have a thousand hair-raising tales to tell of his adventures in Chile and Peru. And it would be fascinating to see the new flowers he would certainly bring back with him.

Then came another red-letter day in Pierre-Joseph's life, and this one too could not have come at a better, a more providential time. Pierre-Joseph had learned all he could from friendly Monsieur Demarteau but the last thing he wished to do was to earn his bread as an engraver. He had simply wanted to learn, first-hand, just how one made copies of original paintings.

He also had no wish whatever to work again with Antoine-Ferdinand, especially now. Antoine-Ferdinand was seriously thinking of accepting a profitable invitation to decorate a large country house some miles from Bordeaux.

Bordeaux? Ah no! All Pierre-Joseph asked was to stay on in Paris, take on any job no matter how ill-paid or uninteresting as long as it covered the rent of his room, provided a frugal meal, and left him a few hours of daylight to call his own, and spend, as happy as a king, in the Jardin du Roi.

His outspoken friends in their favourite café would look at him with exasperated affection, sitting there, making one cup of coffee or a glass of wine last as long as possible, and declare he must be weak in the head. He had such talent, he could paint so easily, so quickly, why then this mania for painting flowers? Apart from one modest sum paid him by that art-dealer, it hadn't brought him in a sou, not one solitary sou. And never would!

They were wrong. On that second red-letter day Pierre-Joseph was peacefully giving 'no thought for the morrow', considering 'the lilies of the field' growing in the Jardin du Roi, when a quiet, authoritative voice made him start.

By his side stood a soberly but well-dressed gentleman. Pierre-Joseph had sometimes noticed him closely examining some tree, bush or flower newly planted in the garden. At times he stopped for a brief moment as if curious to see what Pierre-Joseph was painting. Then he would turn, without a word, and go on his way.

But now he was standing there, obviously waiting to have a word with Pierre-Joseph.

'Monsieur Redouté,' he said in a quiet, precise voice. 'I will come straight to the point. I have made a few inquiries about you and I have seen some of your work. I think it shows great promise.'

The gentleman certainly had a gift for coming straight to the point for before Pierre-Joseph could utter a polite word or two in return, he was explaining that he was a botanist and that he was now engaged on an important botanical publication which he planned to bring out, at his own expense; and that he was interested in finding skilled artists to illustrate his work, artists who truly loved painting flowers.

'Painting flowers!' cried Pierre-Joseph. 'Why, Monsieur . . .'

'Wait,' said the gentleman, very abrupt and authoritative.

And he warned Pierre-Joseph that he would have to be prepared to study botany very seriously indeed under his guidance. The illustrations for his work would have to be absolutely accurate, every minute detail most faithfully observed and portrayed. All this, as well as beautifully painted. No easy achievement, warned the gentleman.

Then he curtly said that if Pierre-Joseph was interested, he could offer him steady and well-paid work.

'Monsieur . . .' stammered Pierre-Joseph, and hesitated, embarrassed not to know this gentleman's name.

'L'Héritier,' said the gentleman. 'I am Charles Louis L'Héritier de Brutelle if one must be precise. And if one had the time. So "L'Héritier" will do.'

Then still in the same dry voice he said, 'Well?'

'Monsieur,' said Pierre-Joseph, 'I ask for nothing better.'

'Nevertheless, you must think it over. I do not expect an instant decision. If you are of the same mind in a month's time, then come to see me at this address.'

He handed Pierre-Joseph a card, shook hands, and left him standing there, his head in a whirl, asking himself if all this was a dream.

But no, there he stood in the Jardin du Roi, with this card in his hand. And presently he reverently stowed it in one of his pockets, one with no torn lining, no hole.

Pierre-Joseph was taking no risks – not with this card.

5

Flight to Soho Square, London

Antoine-Ferdinand was worried, but not about his own future. He was steadily making a name for himself as a first-class and reliable decorator. He felt that his father would have been pleased, indeed proud, of his eldest son.

But what would their papa have made of his second son, Pierre-Joseph! Torn his hair, no doubt, with bewildered exasperation to see him still living so cheerfully from hand to mouth, turning down all offers of work no matter how well-paid, if they meant leaving Paris, or left him with no free hours of daylight to paint the flowers of the Jardin du Roi.

It was incomprehensible to sensible Antoine-Ferdinand, the way Pierre-Joseph seemed to have decided that the only world that mattered was the flowery world of the Jardin du Roi. Everything in the real world outside was obviously unimportant to him. And no amount of brotherly advice, exhortations or even sharp criticism had the slightest effect on him. He would not even try to justify squandering his talents, his time, in this unprofitable way, regardless of the future.

So Antoine-Ferdinand was worried. Like all the Redoutés he had a strong sense of duty to his family, and it was he, Antoine-Ferdinand who had been responsible for bringing Pierre-Joseph to Paris. He had meant well but now he felt he had made a mistake, a grave mistake. It would have been far wiser to have encouraged Pierre-Joseph to remain in Belgium where he had been earning good money painting portraits of eminent people.

Antoine-Ferdinand was therefore more than interested when Pierre-Joseph came in one evening, positively radiating happiness, and poured out his story of meeting Monsieur L'Héritier in the Jardin du Roi.

'Oh, I assure you', cried Pierre-Joseph, 'I have thought it over. In fact I've done nothing but think it over. I wondered if it could really be possible to make a living painting flowers. But now I know it is the one thing I have always longed to do. And I've decided I've been most fortunate to meet Monsieur L'Héritier.'

Antoine-Ferdinand, level-headed and practical as always, soberly agreed that Pierre-Joseph had indeed been fortunate. Monsieur L'Héritier would never have made such an offer without giving it the most careful consideration. He was recognised everywhere as the most upright, the most conscientious of men – even by his critics.

'Critics!' cried Pierre-Joseph. 'But how could one criticise such a man!'

Antoine-Ferdinand, throwing up both arms, said it was high time that Pierre-Joseph began to take an intelligent interest in the important people of Paris. Now he, Antoine-Ferdinand, kept his ears open so he could tell Pierre-Joseph that Monsieur L'Héritier had the reputation of being cold, sarcastic, very abrupt in his manner and with no charitable inclination to 'suffer fools gladly', or indeed to suffer them at all. All of which made his offer to Pierre-Joseph the more gratifying of course.

And well-informed Antoine-Ferdinand could also tell Pierre-Joseph that Monsieur L'Héritier not only came of a wealthy family, he already had considerable means of his own; and it was well known that he took the greatest pride in his two large well-kept gardens, one there in Paris, the other in his country estate in Picardy. In both gardens he delighted to grow flowers, plants, shrubs or trees not yet known, much less grown, by any other French botanist. It was also common knowledge – except it seemed to Pierre-Joseph – that Monsieur L'Héritier always generously rewarded any botanist, or traveller from distant parts, who brought a new plant of any kind to his notice.

Moreover Monsieur L'Héritier could easily have devoted all his time to this one passion of his, but no, he was a man with the highest sense of duty and justice and was recognised by everyone to be one of the most conscientious of magistrates. . . .

'Magistrates!' echoed Pierre-Joseph, unable to believe his ears.

'Monsieur L'Héritier is also a magistrate,' insisted Antoine-Ferdinand and added, very significantly, 'and at the Cours des Aides.'

Then correctly reading from Pierre-Joseph's face that he hadn't heard of the Cours des Aides either, Antoine-Ferdinand again threw up both arms and said one would imagine Pierre-Joseph had been living on the moon and not in the very heart of Paris.

It seemed that the Cours des Aides was one of the most ancient of French Tribunals, established to protect honest Frenchmen against all unjust or illegal taxation. No easy task, this! Year in, year out, it waged courageous war against even the most powerful of corrupt Ministers of the Crown, not to mention high and mighty noblemen who deemed it right and proper that the heavy burden of taxation should be the patriotic duty of the poor and lowly with no cash to pay wily lawyers to protect them.

Ah yes, said Antoine-Ferdinand, heaven only knew what would happen to ordinary hardworking French taxpayers if there were no Cours des Aides to come to their aid. All Paris, all France, knew that no magistrate of that ancient tribunal ever truckled to the powerful, or turned a deaf ear to the obscure and unimportant.

Antoine-Ferdinand, now thoroughly enjoying instructing his ill-informed brother suddenly broke off, and very worried indeed, demanded to know what Pierre-Joseph had done with the card Monsieur L'Héritier had given him. For heaven's sake don't tell him that he had lost that too! Monsieur L'Héritier was the most precise, the most punctilious of men, not at all the man to tolerate such inexcusable carelessness.

Without a word, Pierre-Joseph reverently pulled out the card, showed it to Antoine-Ferdinand, and then carefully stowed it away again in that one safe pocket.

'Thank heaven,' sighed Antoine-Ferdinand, and meant it most

devoutly. No need now to worry about Pierre-Joseph. Monsieur L'Héritier was going to take him in hand, train him to become a botanical artist. Hardly a brilliant or lucrative career of course. Their father would turn in his grave to see Pierre-Joseph wasting his talents on painting flowers to illustrate botany books.

But one had to be realistic. This work for Monsieur L'Héritier would not be work at all for Pierre-Joseph. It would be something he loved to do, already insisted on doing, deaf to all appeals to use his common sense and think instead of a safe, secure future working with Antoine-Ferdinand.

So Antoine-Ferdinand's heavy load of responsibility fell from him; and he gratefully thanked God for Monsieur L'Héritier.

Now began the most rewarding and certainly the most instructive years of Pierre-Joseph's life.

To begin with, Monsieur L'Héritier was a first-class botanist and the very fact that he was self-taught made him all the more compelling and authoritative. Pierre-Joseph would listen, enthralled, as Monsieur L'Héritier taught him to examine a flower in such minute and exact detail that presently he could list the reasons why it must belong to this or that of the many families of plants.

And this moved Pierre-Joseph most strangely. At first he had secretly dreaded such coldly scientific examination. What if all this meticulous analysis numbed his sudden dear delight at the sight of a wild rose in a hedge or a gay scarlet poppy dancing in a cornfield?

But now it startled him to realise how much, how very much he had been missing. The closer he examined a flower, the more clearly he saw how charming and delicate were the tiny details he had never noticed before. Truly a flower was more than a joy, it was a miracle fashioned by the hand of God.

Then it was delightful and most comfortable to work in Monsieur L'Héritier's spacious library, the walls lined with valuable and handsomely bound books, the works of world-famous botanists and scientists. Sometimes Monsieur L'Héritier would take down one of these books and the hours would fly as together they pored over it.

Presently Monsieur L'Héritier did more than give his opinion on the value of a book, he began to talk to Pierre-Joseph of the men who had written them, and it was clear that he had met, talked, argued, and carried on a learned correspondence with many a remarkable man.

As always, Monsieur L'Héritier's comments were so pungent that Pierre-Joseph listened with respectful interest, and to his own surprise he began to be extremely well informed about famous men whose names had never before roused a spark of interest in him. One day, for instance, Monsieur L'Héritier took down an unpretentious book from a shelf and remarked that in his opinion this was the world's most readable and unusual botany book. He opened it and showed Pierre-Joseph the title-page:

LETTERS ON BOTANY
by
Jean-Jacques Rousseau

Monsieur L'Héritier said he was well aware by now that Pierre-Joseph had no interest whatever in politics, but he must have noticed how the very name Jean-Jacques Rousseau, sparked off the most violent of arguments in the most peaceful of cafés.

Pierre-Joseph apologetically said that he had a way of becoming deaf as a post when political arguments began to rage about him, but even so he had heard enough to know that to some Rousseau was a menace to society, while to others he was a genius who had pointed out the way to the solution of all the world's problems.

Monsieur L'Héritier said Pierre-Joseph had hit on the very epitaph for Jean-Jacques Rousseau; and that to his mind, heaven had been deplorably short-sighted in bestowing so many gifts on one man.

Jean-Jacques Rousseau was, for instance, an excellent musician; he had written a gay and very successful light opera; he had even composed a ballet.

Then he had written a most romantic and highly successful novel, *La Nouvelle Heloise.* This had set all the ladies weeping like fountains and made romantic young men positively yearn for some sad unrequited love so that they might droop, lost in melancholy, preferably against a weeping willow tree from which their touching despair could be observed, of course. And, added unsentimental Monsieur L'Héritier, this had set the fashion for a flood of equally romantic novels, not only in France but all over Europe.

Then having roused so much tender emotion, Rousseau dipped his pen in acid and began to set the world right. He declared that progress in the arts and sciences did not make men happier. On the contrary, all this progress corrupted men, made them increasingly unhappy.

Men, wrote Rousseau, were born good and noble. It was society that corrupted them, and the only way to escape this sinister corruption was 'to return to Nature'. This set the fashion, often in the most unlikely circles, for flying back, when convenient, to rustic simplicity. Queen Marie-Antoinette and her ladies were enchanted, for instance, to play at being shepherdesses or milkmaids in her fairytale rustic hamlet in Versailles.

Then 'Property is Theft!' thundered Jean-Jacques Rousseau, but he nevertheless often lived in comfort at the expense of some liberal-minded rich landowner who recognised his genius and wished to help him. But sooner or later he quarrelled with every one of his benefactors, and for that matter with everyone else as well. Indeed he was so touchy and suspicious that, as someone rightly observed, Rousseau always seemed to think that those who made people laugh, were always making them laugh at him.

Presently Rousseau set to work on a second and again most successful novel, an educational one this time; in fact the title was *Emile or Education*. And one had to admit that the hero, young Emile, had enjoyed the most idyllic of educations, for the book was packed with new and high-minded theories on how to bring up and teach a child.

Other people's children, caustically added Monsieur L'Héritier. Rousseau himself had scandalised everyone by living with a dim-witted woman called Thérèse Levasseur. Thérèse, one gathered, might be dim-witted but she could cook and darn, and she looked pleasant enough. However, she had inconsiderately presented Jean-Jacques Rousseau with no fewer than five children, all endowed with

powerful lungs and protesting non-stop at the top of their voices –
at the prospect of having Jean-Jacques Rousseau as their papa, no
doubt.

As night fell on the day when each protesting infant was born,
Jean-Jacques would wrap it in a blanket and deposit it on the steps
of the Foundling Hospital. And bolt, before one had time to open
the door.

He openly admitted this, querulously demanding how he could be
expected to write, earn a living, with five squalling children to dis-
tract him. Moreover, he would loftily declare he had rendered his
five children the finest of service. Later on they would be sent to
work on farms, and so spend their lives in noble simplicity uncorrupted by society.

'For God's sake!' cried Pierre-Joseph, appalled to think of those
five unwanted children, forever branded as 'foundlings', condemned
to a life of drudgery. Not that all farmers had hearts of cold
stone, but more often than not the farmers who took in these
foundlings had to work all the hours God gave, break their own
backs to earn their black bread, their bowl of soup, and pay their
taxes.

No-one ever asked, went on Monsieur L'Héritier, what Thérèse
felt, and she certainly did not have the solace of reading that great
educational novel, for the simple reason that she could not read,
write or even count. Jean-Jacques had never thought it necessary to
teach her.

Fair-minded Monsieur L'Héritier then added that Jean-Jacques
Rousseau was not the first, and he certainly would not be the last
philosopher who knew precisely how other men should live, but
never deemed it necessary to prove their theories by the way they
themselves lived. One had to admit, however, that many of his
theories, his ideals, were excellent, if one also believed, that is, that
all men were born good and noble.

Then Rousseau had undoubtedly had his share of bigoted persecution, above all for his outspoken views on the sanctity of
money and marriage. Stones had been hurled at his windows, he had
been greeted with savage abuse, he had been expelled from Paris and

from the self-righteous Republic of Geneva. Small wonder then that he began to suffer from a persecution mania, always convinced that he was going to be the victim of some sinister plot.

Rousseau was all of fifty-two, said Monsieur L'Héritier, when he began to take an interest in botany. 'My dialogue with plants', he wrote, 'came only after humanity had refused me its companionship.' And certainly the only happy peaceful hours this cantankerous genius had ever known were those he spent wandering in the countryside, studying the flowers of the fields and hedgerows. In fact, in one outburst of poetic enthusiasm he had pictured himself 'botanising for all eternity in the Elysian Fields'.

Monsieur L'Héritier added that he wondered how long the shade of Jean-Jacques Rousseau would wander before meeting the astonished shade of Aristotle and immediately shattering the celestial peace of those Elysian Fields by picking a quarrel over some species of asphodel. Asphodels, it seemed, bloomed eternally in the shining spaces of that classical Abode of the Blessed.

However, to come back to the *Letters on Botany* by Jean-Jacques Rousseau, Pierre-Joseph might like to borrow it, perhaps consider illustrating it one day.

Pierre-Joseph hastily said that reading any botany book was a penance for him. He did not add that he would rather starve than illustrate the work of the genius who had so callously abandoned his five children. And his heart grew warm to remember his own parents. They'd had no fine theories on how to bring up *their* five children; it had always been a struggle to feed and clothe them, but they had loved them, cared for them as best they could, and all five had grown up happily in that crowded Third-Class house in Saint Hubert.

And Pierre-Joseph decided that gifted Jean-Jacques Rousseau must have been a detestable character and that it was small wonder that humanity had refused him companionship.

No, Pierre-Joseph had no wish whatever to borrow that man's botany book and Monsieur L'Héritier would never convince him that he ought one day to consider illustrating it.

In the years to come, Pierre-Joseph was to remember this, and be ashamed to think he had been so self-righteous, so ready to hurl his own small stone at a most unhappy man.

Some time later, Monsieur L'Héritier began to talk to Pierre-Joseph of a very different man. This one lived in England, in the great city of London, and his name was Sir Joseph Banks. He was, it seemed, a very rich and enthusiastic botanist and scientist, who thought nothing of fitting up ships at his own expense and undertaking expeditions to distant shores to collect plants on which no botanist had ever set eyes.

Sir Joseph himself had once sailed with an intrepid sea-dog, a certain Captain Cook, on a voyage that took them far across the oceans to the continent of Australia, or New Holland as the Dutch still insisted on calling it. Nobody knew much about that vast new continent, and Sir Joseph had been in the seventh heaven of delight when they sailed one day into a magnificent bay and discovered that a thousand strange and lovely plants, flowers and trees grew all about it. Sir Joseph had at once given that wondrous bay the best of all names: Botany Bay.

It was however the story of how Sir Joseph had first become interested in botany that most fascinated Pierre-Joseph. When young, Sir Joseph had been sent to a famous English school, Eton College, where only wealthy families could afford to send their sons. This college was on the banks of the River Thames in which the young gentlemen of Eton often enjoyed a swim.

One warm summer evening, young Sir Joseph had dawdled so long in the cool waters of the Thames that by the time he scrambled out and dressed again, all his companions had gone, scurried off no doubt to wrestle with their Latin verse or some other task set for that evening by their masters.

But young Sir Joseph, like young Pierre-Joseph, was no model pupil. He was already late and due for punishment so he saw no reason to hurry now. As he went sauntering along the lanes he began to look for the very first time at the wild flowers growing in the hedgerows. The more he looked, the more they fascinated him, and it was a salutary shock to this wealthy, well-educated boy to realise how blind he had been to all this loveliness, and above all, to realise how crassly ignorant he was. He did not know the name of any one of these flowers! And there was no Dom Hickman in that famous school to whom young Sir Joseph could turn for help.

So Sir Joseph did the next best thing. In all his free time he would lie in wait for the country women who earned a few pence by gathering 'simples' – the wild flowers and plants needed by pharmacists for their remedies. These women were delighted, and secretly astounded, when this well-spoken young gentleman offered to pay them sixpence a time – a princely sum in those days – just to tell him the names and all they knew of the 'simples' they were gathering.

That year when Sir Joseph went home for the summer holiday, to his delight he found a battered old book in his mother's dressing-room. One of its covers was missing but inside were illustrations and descriptions of many of the 'simples' collected by those women of Eton. This book was called *Gerard's Herball* and it was held in reverent esteem by English botanists and pharmacists. To them it was as indisputable as the Bible; they believed it, every word.

When that holiday came to an end, young Sir Joseph carried *Gerard's Herball* back to Eton with him as if it were the most valuable book in the world. However he would still lie in wait for the gatherers of 'simples', but now to their astonishment he began to turn the tables on them. It was he, this strange young gentleman, who began to tell *them* the names and healing properties of plants and flowers they had never gathered before. But as he still handed out those welcome sixpences, everyone was well satisfied.

So it began, the brilliant botanical career of Sir Joseph Banks. Just like the beginning of a fairytale, thought Pierre-Joseph, for Sir Joseph was now one of the world's most eminent botanists. It seemed he had a spacious house in a fine London Square – Soho Square. Here he had a magnificent library with every known botanical and scientific book on its shelves. Here too he had a superb herbarium – a vast and carefully indexed collection of dried flowers and plants from all parts of the world. And Sir Joseph was the most generous and hospitable of men. He always welcomed all botanists, all scientists, no matter what their nationality, and permitted them to study at their leisure his unique collection of books and his priceless herbarium.

Now Pierre-Joseph knew that Monsieur L'Héritier also had a fine and meticulously indexed herbarium. As he had explained to Pierre-Joseph, it was often not possible for botanists to bring back a flower in bloom, one they wished to study. They therefore had a scientific way of drying and pressing it between specially prepared sheets of paper. In this way they could study in midwinter an interesting flower they had discovered months ago, indeed sometimes years ago. In short, a comprehensive herbarium was an indispensable part of a botanist's equipment.

And, added Monsieur L'Héritier, very dry and sarcastic, a botanist's herbarium was very different from the latest vogue in charming pastimes for fashionable young ladies. They too had a passion for collecting and pressing flowers, the ones with romantic names, forget-me-not, honeysuckle, love-in-a-mist, and so on. As often as not their collections were bound in covers of azure-blue or rose-pink velvet or satin. Very ladylike and appealing and most appropriate to show admiring young gentlemen after dinner in the candlelight, declared unromantic Monsieur L'Héritier.

Now Pierre-Joseph was no fool; he realised the scientific value of Monsieur L'Héritier's herbarium. Nevertheless at times his heart would grow cold and heavy at the thought of that herbarium. What if Monsieur L'Héritier presently required him to paint nothing but those pathetic flowers, plucked in their full beauty and scientifically dried and pressed flat in the interests of botany?

One day, however, it seemed as if Monsieur L'Héritier knew what was in Pierre-Joseph's mind for he abruptly said he had not mentioned it before, but he had decided from the start that all the illustrations for his new work were to be drawn and painted from life. Every flower, every plant would be depicted just as it grew under the sky of France. And hearing this, Pierre-Joseph's spirits rose like boiling milk.

Then came the memorable day when Monsieur L'Héritier was able to show Pierre-Joseph the first instalment of his grand project –

Pierre-Joseph had no part in this one of course, the illustrations for it had been commissioned long before Monsieur L'Héritier had engaged him.

There was only one word for that first instalment – magnificent. It was beautifully bound and printed, with excellent illustrations, and the Latin title stood out bold and clear:

STIRPES NOVAE

Pierre-Joseph had a smattering of Latin, enough to know that this meant NEW PLANTS. But when he saw that opposite each full-page illustration there was a detailed, scientific description written in Latin by Monsieur L'Héritier, he wished he had been more attentive and appreciative when the good monks of the Abbey School of Saint Hubert had striven to hammer a little Latin into his unscholarly head. Latin was the universal language of all scholars, botanists and scientists. And very sensible too, thought repentant Pierre-Joseph; '*Stirpes Novae*', for instance, could be read by botanists the world over.

Pierre-Joseph, examining and wondering at the technical excellence of Instalment One felt a surge of pride to think that he was to be entrusted with the illustrations for Instalment Two. Suddenly he remembered his father's story of the great painter, Chardin, how he had said: 'One makes use of colours but one paints with feeling.' He too would 'paint with feeling', put all his heart as well as his new botanical knowledge into his illustrations for *Stirpes Novae*, and so demonstrate his gratitude to upright dedicated Monsieur L'Héritier.

Thus garlanded with good resolutions, and a list of 'New Plants' drawn up by Monsieur L'Héritier in his pocket, into the Jardin du Roi one day strode Pierre-Joseph. This was the most wonderful day of his life. Today he was to begin his new career. Today he was Pierre-Joseph Redouté, botanical artist, entrusted by Monsieur Charles-Louis L'Héritier de Brutelle to illustrate Instalment Two of *Stirpes Novae*.

Moreover there was to be instalment after instalment of *Stirpes Novae*. From this day on, a flowery future shone before him. All his

morrows he could 'consider the lilies of the field', and be paid to do
so!

And Pierre-Joseph, not for the first time, most gratefully thanked
heaven for Monsieur L'Héritier.

To Pierre-Joseph's delight, many of the new plants and flowers
on Monsieur L'Héritier's list were growing there in his Paradise on
Earth, the Jardin du Roi. And as chance would have it, the first on
the list was a flower successfully grown from a seed sent over from
Peru by that gay, intrepid young explorer, Joseph Dombey.

Monsieur L'Héritier had given a Latin name to this Peruvian
flower: 'Dombey Lappacea', an acknowledgement, and a compliment too of course, to Joseph Dombey. But such a heavy, wooden
name, thought Pierre-Joseph, for so delicate and graceful a flower.
And Pierre-Joseph thought how apt and poetical were the names
countrymen gave to flowers. He remembered how he had been
wandering one day through the forests with Dom Hickman, when
something had made him run ahead. He had seen a patch of beautiful
little white flowers, ones he had never seen before, and he had gone
down so suddenly on his knees to look at them that poor Dom
Hickman almost went sprawling over his clogs.

But then Dom Hickman had stood there as if he too was lost in
delight at the purity, the delicacy of those charming flowers. However, Dom Hickman had not known their name. These flowers were
so shy and rare that as far as Dom Hickman knew they were not
mentioned in any botany book or herbal. But he believed that in
Germany they were called 'star flowers'.

Pierre-Joseph, recalling this, made a mental note to describe this
starlike flower to Monsieur L'Héritier. Maybe it was one he had not
yet come across.

But to work now! Here he was studying that Peruvian flower,
and as he looked at it, he wondered how gay young Joseph Dombey
was faring in far-away Chile or Peru. Then he pulled out paper and
pencil, and forgot Joseph Dombey, Chile and Peru and all the rest
of the world as he began to sketch 'Dombey Lappacea'.

.   .   .

To his immense satisfaction, Pierre-Joseph now had the means to pay a visit from time to time to Saint Hubert. But presently a grey shadow began to darken those joyous reunions. His quiet mother was growing old and tired, and Pierre-Joseph was always grateful to remember that before she died, she had one last God-given comfort. She knew that her two good daughters would soon settle in homes of their own, and that quiet Henri-Joseph was to join his two brothers in Paris.

Henri-Joseph was sensitive, retiring, diffident, and he had always been very fond of Pierre-Joseph. Happy-go-lucky Pierre-Joseph would be good for him in every way. Antoine-Ferdinand and his wife would be kind to him too. Between them they would care for Henri-Joseph and see he found work, for he too had great talents.

And knowing all this, that gentle selfless woman died as quietly and undramatically as she had lived.

Their mother had been right. Henri-Joseph was happy to be with his brothers in Paris, and Monsieur L'Héritier, outwardly so brusque and bleak, was kindness itself to this shy but talented young artist. Soon Henri-Joseph was painting flowers and plants so accurately, so meticulously, that Monsieur L'Héritier began to entrust him with some of the illustrations he needed for future instalments of *Stirpes Novae*.

But this staggered both Pierre-Joseph and Antoine-Ferdinand. Their quiet brother found a room for himself and began to spend all his free time painting, not flowers, but a sea shell or a tortoise, and stranger still, lizards and snakes, even the deadly 'crotale horrible' – the rattlesnake. He would tramp all the way to Marly just to have the pleasure of drawing and painting from life some reptile in the Royal Menagerie there.

Henri-Joseph soon silenced all criticism however, for he showed such aptitude, such delicate accuracy in all this, that he began to be employed by zoologists who needed just such a specialised artist to illustrate their work.

But Antoine-Ferdinand would still wonder at times what their father would have made of his two younger sons. He had foreseen so different, so brilliant a future for them. At least he, Antoine-Ferdinand, had been faithful to family tradition. Behind him he would leave, please God, many a stately mansion decorated, made beautiful by a Redouté. But where were the fine portraits, the majestic paintings of lofty subjects their poor papa had so confidently expected of Pierre-Joseph and Henri-Joseph? Dreams, all empty dreams.

Pierre-Joseph was besotted with flowers, and Henri-Joseph, for God's sake, with reptiles! There was no understanding either of them.

Ah well, their poor papa had at least been right in the most modest of his rosy predictions. Neither Pierre-Joseph nor Henri-Joseph would starve to death in a garret, not while there were wealthy botanists and zoologists ready to employ them to illustrate their work.

Then as so often happens when one is counting one's worries, Antoine-Ferdinand added yet another to his list. Now Pierre-Joseph had steady employment, why on earth did he not get married? He showed no interest whatever in any of the suitable girls they would invite when he was expected to spend an hour or so with them. Oh, he was polite, friendly enough. But interested? Not in the least.

Again Antoine-Ferdinand need not have worried for one day Pierre-Joseph realised with a shock that he was galloping on to the ripe age of twenty-seven. He was still more astonished to realise he was beginning to think how pleasant it would be to fling open the door of an evening and find not a cold empty room but a loving wife, a warm home, and hot soup waiting for him.

Yes, Antoine-Ferdinand was right. It was high time that Pierre-Joseph, now a botanical artist with a steady income, thought of marriage.

To be honest, Pierre-Joseph was also thinking of his brother, Henri-Joseph. From the start, Henri-Joseph had insisted on renting a room of his own, but he was a lonely, solitary young man, very slow to make friends. True, Antoine-Ferdinand and his wife always made him welcome but he was always more at ease with Pierre-Joseph. It would be a comfort to know that he could also count on a welcome in Pierre-Joseph's warm home, once Pierre-Joseph had found that suitable and loving wife of course.

Now this may seem singular, indeed wellnigh unbelievable to the cynical, but it was nevertheless true that for generation after generation the Redoutés had not only been talented painters, they also had a most enviable flair for finding themselves the most suitable of wives. And Pierre-Joseph was to prove no exception to this excellent family tradition.

On 27 February 1786, he married Marie-Marthe Gobert, a sensible little Parisienne who asked for nothing better than to love and cherish Pierre-Joseph. She loved everything about him, his amusing Belgian accent, his easy-going, friendly ways, his warm-hearted generosity and his wonderful gift for painting flowers. Indeed all their lives long, Marie-Marthe thought Pierre-Joseph was wonderful; and to Pierre-Joseph Marie-Marthe was truly 'far above rubies'. Not that Pierre-Joseph ever put this into words of his own. He couldn't better wise old Solomon who certainly knew all there is to know about women, as well as a host of other eternal truths.

That same year, 1786, Pierre-Joseph at last met Joseph Dombey. But all the gaiety had fallen from that intrepid young explorer. This was not astonishing for he had a sorry story to tell. Oh, not about the perils he had faced in Chile and Peru! Joseph Dombey thrived on a life of excitement and danger. No, the expedition had been a great success, and Joseph Dombey had come sailing back to Cadiz with the collection of his life. Most precious of all was a fine unique number of living plants which he had lovingly tended all the long stormy way back from Peru. He could hardly wait to bring all this to Paris.

Then the blow fell. It had of course been agreed from the start that France and Spain were to have equal shares in everything collected in Chile and Peru. And before he set sail, Joseph Dombey had most faithfully kept his side of the contract. Nobody denied this.

But, as Monsieur L'Héritier acidly commented, it would have

been far wiser if Joseph Dombey had insisted on bringing the whole collection back to Spain and splitting it there, under the eagle eyes of the Spanish authorities.

Instead of which, the Spanish half had been dispatched on a Spanish ship. Nobody denied this either. Indeed it was fortunate that the two Spanish botanists decided to prolong their stay in Peru, for the ship carrying their half of the collection sailed away, and since then, all was silence. That ship was missing, at the bottom of the ocean one feared.

Joseph Dombey had sailed on another Spanish ship bound for Cadiz but to his dismay, when this ship safely docked, the Spanish authorities had promptly impounded the whole of his half of the collection, and a long, legal wrangle began. But the wrangling was not the worst. The unique living plants he had risked his life to collect, had tended so tenderly all the long sea-journey back to Cadiz, were locked up in the Spanish customs-house, and to his anguish, they drooped and died, all for want of proper attention.

Month after month dragged by but at last Joseph Dombey was graciously permitted to leave Cadiz but with only half of his share of what remained of the collection. The other half was confiscated by the Spanish authorities.

Now Joseph Dombey had no means of his own. It was the French Government who had granted him the money to travel to Chile and Peru, rightly considering that all the new botanical knowledge he would collect would add to the lustre of civilised France. True, Joseph Dombey, through no fault of his own had not brought back any unique living plants but he had returned with a remarkable herbarium and careful and copious notes and observations. So he confidently expected to be congratulated and given the necessary funds to publish all this new botanical knowledge.

To his bitter disappointment nobody was in the least interested. No-one in authority seemed to realise the value of his herbarium, and all appeals were blandly ignored. And to add to this distress, not only had he run out of money, he was also now in debt.

At this black moment of misery and despair, Monsieur L'Héritier stepped in. It was he who persuaded the Director of the Jardin du

Roi that France ought in all honour to settle the debts incurred by Joseph Dombey and also to grant him a modest pension for life.

In this way Joseph Dombey at least had the consoling dignity of feeling that he was not accepting charity. This was a belated official recognition, an acknowledgement of all he had sweated and toiled to achieve to add to the botanical wonders of France.

But far, far more rewarding to Joseph Dombey, Monsieur L'Héritier persuaded the indifferent French authorities, who had, legally, taken possession of that unique herbarium, to hand everything over to him. In return Monsieur L'Héritier would publish, at his own expense, and to the glory of France, a comprehensive study, with illustrations, of the new flowers and plants discovered by Joseph Dombey in Chile and Peru and now scientifically dried and pressed in that herbarium.

In short, Joseph Dombey would not have risked his life in vain in Chile and Peru. And Joseph Dombey too thanked heaven for Monsieur L'Héritier, and at once began to make plans for yet another voyage of discovery.

But no sooner was all this settled than menacing clouds again began to gather. That herbarium certainly seemed to be 'yoked to inauspicious clouds', and it was fortunate that Monsieur L'Héritier happened to be in Versailles very early on the morning of 9 September 1786. Quite by chance he heard that the Spanish Government had suddenly lodged the strongest objection to a French botanist being allowed the glory of publishing the first account of the flowers and plants gathered in Chile and Peru by the two Spanish botanists, and Joseph Dombey.

Peru and Chile, and everything that grew there were, by divine right, the property of Spain, and Spain alone. And Spain was now demanding the immediate return of Joseph Dombey's herbarium, together with all notes and observations. When those two Spanish botanists returned to Spain, they must have the honour and glory of publishing the first account of that expedition.

All of which seemed reasonable enough to the indifferent authorities in Versailles, especially as the French Government had no wish, just then, to offend Spain.

Monsieur L'Héritier listened to all this in outraged silence, and set off post-haste for home. And at once sent an urgent message to Pierre-Joseph and another trustworthy friend, Doctor Broussonet – who was also an enthusiastic botanist.

All that day, Monsieur L'Héritier, with the help of his wife and his two friends, worked long and hard, carefully packing Joseph Dombey's herbarium. When night fell, a carriage drew up before Monsieur L'Héritier's residence, the driver politely handed in Monsieur L'Héritier and his luggage; Monsieur L'Héritier leaned out to kiss his wife and shake hands with his two friends. Then he said a quiet 'Au revoir', and drove away into the night.

Only Madame L'Héritier, Doctor Broussonet and Pierre-Joseph knew where he was going. He was going to seek the hospitality and the help of that famous and sympathetic botanist – Sir Joseph Banks of Soho Square, London.

6

The Royal Gardens of Kew

At first the disappearance of Monsieur L'Héritier caused no surprise, aroused no suspicions whatever in Versailles. Monsieur L'Héritier never thought it necessary to explain his movements to anyone outside his family and a few chosen friends; and knowledgeable busybodies decided he must have gone off again to 'botanise' on his estate in Picardy.

As the days wore on, however, the Spanish envoys, waiting for him to hand over Joseph Dombey's herbarium, began to grow suspicious and impatient, and were presently outraged to discover that Monsieur L'Héritier was definitely not on his estate in Picardy. They were, understandably, even more outraged when they learned that this French botanist had had the audacity to travel post-haste to London under the pretext of paying a visit to the world-famous Sir Joseph Banks, and that with him had gone Joseph Dombey's herbarium.

The English were not in the least likely to listen, much less to yield to any demand for the extradition of a friend of Sir Joseph Banks, or force him to hand over that herbarium. And all the glory lay in being the first to make known these new botanical discoveries, the first, the very first. No doubt Monsieur L'Héritier, safe and snug in London, was already hard at work on that herbarium, the devil take him. And gradually the sound and fury died away, precisely as Monsieur L'Héritier had predicted.

There had, however, been one awkward and anxious moment when Monsieur L'Héritier first set foot in England and was confronted by suspicious English customs officials. They demanded to know just why this Frenchman had taken the trouble to bring this collection of dried flowers and plants with him to England. Why England?

Monsieur L'Héritier, strained and exhausted, could not even begin to explain; he simply did not know enough English. But he managed to make them understand that he and these dried flowers were on their way to Sir Joseph Banks of Soho Square, London.

Sir Joseph Banks! That did it. Every Englishman was proud of Sir Joseph, even if they did guffaw at the lampoons of would-be wits who in every age, in every land, relish ridiculing any outstanding man. There was this one for instance:

> *I'm honoured, stared at, wheresoe-er I go.*
> *Soon as I enter a room, lo! all ranks*
> *Get up to compliment Sir Joseph Banks.*
> *'Lord, that's Sir Joseph Banks! How grand his look,*
> *Who sailed all round the world with Captain Cook!'*

But everyone, including those customs officials, did indeed honour Sir Joseph Banks, and now the very mention of his name proved a veritable 'Open Sesame!' This French gentleman must be a botanist friend of Sir Joseph, all those dried plants and flowers were intended for him. No more questions were asked and out through the customs shed and on to the stage-coach for London went Monsieur L'Héritier and the Dombey herbarium.

Now as they packed the herbarium on that anxious day, Monsieur L'Héritier, no doubt to reassure and comfort his wife, told them that from all he had heard, Sir Joseph was also very fortunate in his family life. His wife and spinster sister, Mademoiselle Sarah Sophia Banks, were both devoted to him and bitterly disappointed the gossips by their real affection one for the other. 'My ladies', Sir Joseph called them, and wherever he went, they both went too.

So Lady Banks and Mademoiselle Sarah Sophia, as well as Sir Joseph, could be counted upon to welcome Monsieur L'Héritier. All botanists, all scientists of repute, were always made welcome in that hospitable house in Soho Square.

Unfortunately Sir Joseph and his ladies were away in their country house in Lincolnshire when Monsieur L'Héritier arrived at Soho Square, and he was received by Sir Joseph's devoted librarian, Mr. Dryander – 'Old Dry' as he was affectionately called, and not without reason – by the Banks family.

'Old Dry', though punctiliously polite, certainly did not welcome Monsieur L'Héritier with open arms. In fact he was secretly shocked at the way this French botanist, giving no courteous advance notice whatever, had descended so unceremoniously on the august doorstep of Sir Joseph.

Presently, 'Old Dry' was even more shocked to learn that this Frenchman, without as much as a by-your-leave, had used the name of Sir Joseph Banks to slip through the English Customs with an important herbarium that might cause a lot of legal trouble with both the French and the Spanish Governments. Most disturbing, decided 'Old Dry'.

Moreover, Monsieur L'Héritier's abrupt manner of making a request also upset him. This uninvited Frenchman would ask in the most peremptory way to consult this and that in Sir Joseph's library or herbarium. And presently 'Old Dry' wrote to Sir Joseph saying that although he was well aware that Monsieur L'Héritier was a French botanist of considerable importance, he was a 'strange fellow', and he felt he ought to keep an eye on him.

The truth, was, of course, that Monsieur L'Héritier hadn't the least idea he was upsetting 'Old Dry'. He would also have been appalled to learn that at first, thanks to 'Old Dry's' complaining letter, Sir Joseph had also been furious with him, until he received Monsieur L'Héritier's letter giving the full and poignant story of poor Dombey's herbarium.

When honest 'Old Dry' learned of this, he began to understand the interest of this taciturn 'strange fellow' in the Peruvian and Chilean flowers and plants listed and classified in Sir Joseph's herbarium. No need now to be so on guard, so suspicious. Monsieur L'Héritier only wished to study and compare them with the ones collected by the unfortunate Joseph Dombey. Indeed, as the days, the weeks sped by, conscientious 'Old Dry' began to respect, if not like, this dedicated French botanist.

Then something very strange amazed 'Old Dry'. Monsieur L'Héritier suddenly shelved the Dombey herbarium, put it completely on one side. So this, thought 'Old Dry', was how he was keeping his solemn promise to unfortunate Joseph Dombey! A fine way for a gentleman and a botanist to behave! Sir Joseph was equally dumbfounded. What was this 'strange fellow' up to now? And Sir Joseph wrote to a friend:

> Monsieur L'Héritier is still here to the amazement of everyone and has given no sign of returning. He has left off working at Dombey's herbarium and now runs most diligently from garden to garden, buying plants in profusion and books without end.

Monsieur L'Héritier, as usual, saw no necessity to explain why he had suddenly decided to run so diligently from one London garden to another.

A pity, for if they had known, both Sir Joseph and 'Old Dry' would have been exceedingly touched.

Meanwhile as Monsieur L'Héritier ran diligently from garden to garden in London, over in Paris, Pierre-Joseph and Marie-Marthe had become the proud parents of a little daughter.

She had been christened Marie-Joseph but soon Marie-Marthe began to say there were already thousands and thousands of little girls called Marie-Joseph, and a very good pious name it was too for any child. But wouldn't it be delightful if their Marie-Joseph had a more musical, a more unusual name – just for everyday use, of course. And what about Josephine? Josephine sounded just right for their little Marie-Joseph.

Easy-going Pierre-Joseph of course agreed. Hadn't great Shakespeare once declared that a rose by any other name would smell as sweet? And seeing Marie-Marthe's astonishment to hear him quote Shakespeare, Pierre-Joseph grandly said this was one of the worthwhile literary quotations he had bothered to memorise.

So little Marie-Joseph Redouté became Josephine Redouté, and she was known by that name, with her full approval, all her life long.

. . .

Now before Monsieur L'Héritier set off so hurriedly for London, he had left a long list of the flowers he wished Pierre-Joseph to paint or sketch whilst he was away, enough work to keep him busy for many a long day. To Marie-Marthe's relief he had also instructed his wife to go on paying Pierre-Joseph.

The days, the weeks, slipped peacefully by and from time to time a letter from London would arrive for Pierre-Joseph. It would be from Monsieur L'Héritier, asking for details of this or that plant, and if the engravers he had engaged were turning out the high standard of work he expected from them. Pierre-Joseph must keep an eye on them. He also wrote that he had found comfortable rooms not far from Soho Square and that he still wished all news of him to be kept secret.

In April 1787, Pierre-Joseph received another letter from Monsieur L'Héritier, and at first he stared at this one as if he couldn't believe his eyes. Then he read it aloud to Marie-Marthe.

'Mon Dieu!' gasped Marie-Marthe. 'Read it again! Slowly this time.'

Monsieur L'Héritier wrote that he was engaged, not on the Dombey herbarium, but on work to which he attached great importance, work which he wished Pierre-Joseph to illustrate. He would therefore be grateful if Pierre-Joseph, without a word to anyone, would join him immediately as the illustrations he required would be ones of flowers and plants growing in a certain garden near London. All expenses would be paid of course by Monsieur L'Héritier, and he would rent a comfortable room for Pierre-Joseph in the house in which he himself was living. Then came a few helpful hints on the clothes Pierre-Joseph would do well to bring with him.

Silk stockings were horribly dear in London, so were shoes. But everyday stockings of wool or cotton were cheaper and better than in Paris.

'Silk stockings indeed!' snorted Marie-Marthe. 'One would think you were going to England to drink tea with royalty.' And haughtily added that the stockings she knitted for Pierre-Joseph were as good, and probably better than any he'd find in London. And that he already had a good supply of them. However, he had better find the time to buy himself a stout pair of good leather shoes.

But it was the next paragraph of Monsieur L'Héritier's letter that made Marie-Marthe indignantly throw up both arms. These English must be crazy! When thrifty people began to tell their tailors to use wooden buttons and cover them with scraps of the same material as the coat or waistcoat they had ordered, the English button-makers had kicked up such a fuss that a law had been passed making this illegal. All buttons had to be bought from button-makers and anyone defying this could be fined a fixed sum for every illegally cloth-covered button.

It had been enough, said Marie-Marthe, to wear out any woman, to get Pierre-Joseph to see he simply had to order a new coat or waistcoat, and now she'd have to go out and buy bone or metal buttons and snip off all his sensible cloth-covered buttons or he'd risk being fined over there in London. A fine state of affairs, fumed Marie-Marthe, when button-makers could lay the law down like this. Then seeing the look on Pierre-Joseph's face, she briskly said, 'But you'll go of course! It will be a wonderful chance to see London, and all those English gardens.'

At the end of that same week, Pierre-Joseph set off for London, England, with a good supply of sensible hand-knitted stockings, a new pair of stout leather shoes, and bone and metal buttons on his two coats and waistcoats.

Marie-Marthe hugged and kissed him, made him swear he would write from time to time and waved him merrily off without a tear. It was only when he had gone that Marie-Marthe began to weep and then told herself to stop behaving as if she'd never set eyes on Pierre-Joseph again. At this opportune moment, little Josephine began to make herself heard. The poor child was hungry.

Pierre-Joseph was never to forget Sir Joseph's wonderful house in Soho Square. Every morning, the fine library, the spacious reception rooms and the museum were open to visitors. Coal fires burned bright in every room, and discreet servants silently offered everyone freshly made coffee or tea and delicious buttered rolls, and tended the warm, glowing fires.

Monsieur L'Héritier explained that this fine hospitable house had become a rendezvous for all those 'who cultivated the sciences'. There, on the handsome polished tables, they could always find the latest books and pamphlets on every branch of science from botany to mineralogy. In the library, shelf upon shelf of scientific books lined every wall, and upstairs in a vast room one could study, at leisure, Sir Joseph's superb herbarium.

Pierre-Joseph, gazing in wonder at all this, thought of Dom Hickman. How he would have loved to behold, to study all these books in this welcoming, warm English house! Sir Joseph Banks must be the most generous of men to use his great wealth in this admirable way. A man after Dom Hickman's heart.

Pierre-Joseph said nothing of this to Monsieur L'Héritier. He knew Monsieur L'Héritier liked to come straight to the point, and keep to the point, not go wandering off down any conversational byway.

So there they sat one morning, in one of the fine reception rooms of Sir Joseph's house in Soho Square before a bright English coal fire, with delicious coffee and rolls to refresh them, and with Monsieur L'Héritier coming straight to the point about this new project of his.

He was certainly not abandoning the Dombey herbarium. He intended to go on with it once he could safely return with it to France. But as he now found himself so unexpectedly in London, he had decided that this was the chance of a lifetime to study the magnificent variety of new plants and flowers growing in English gardens, above all in the Kew Gardens on the banks of the Thames, the property of His Majesty, King George III – Farmer George as his people affectionately called him. It seemed that Farmer George and Sir Joseph were the best of friends, they both loved gardens, but at the moment they were even more interested in the breeding of sheep.

Monsieur L'Héritier was not in the least interested in sheep but he was grateful that His Majesty, Farmer George, had had the good sense to make Sir Joseph his royal adviser in all matters that concerned Kew Gardens. As Pierre-Joseph would discover, there were numerous rare new flowers and plants from many a distant part of the world growing in that royal garden, some of them still unnamed.

Then Monsieur L'Héritier pulled a paper from his pocket and told Pierre-Joseph that this was only a rough draft, but it would give him an idea of the title-page and the foreword he intended to write for the book he had in mind.

It was, of course, in Latin, but with a curt word of help here and there from Monsieur L'Héritier, Pierre-Joseph understood the title was to be:

AN ENGLISH GARLAND

or

RARE PLANTS

which are cultivated in the
Gardens around London
especially
In the Royal Gardens of Kew
observed
From the year 1786 to the year 1787

It was the carefully composed Foreword however that surprised and moved Pierre-Joseph. Monsieur L'Héritier, outwardly so bleak, intended this English Garland to demonstrate his gratitude for the hospitality and the help he had received in England.

'I dedicate and offer', began the Foreword, 'this work to the English Nation,' and it went on to say that Monsieur L'Héritier would always gratefully remember how courteously everyone had received him, how scholars showed themselves so ready to reveal their treasures and how men learned in botany had generously assisted him.

Then Monsieur L'Héritier abruptly said he was showing this to Pierre-Joseph so that he would understand the great importance he attached to this English Garland. And he refolded the paper, re-placed it in one pocket, and from another he drew out a list of the flowers he wished Pierre-Joseph to paint. He then gave him concise directions on how best to travel to Kew on one of the hundreds of small boats plying for hire on the River Thames. And the very next morning, Pierre-Joseph found his way to Kew Gardens and strolled around, delighted to discover that the English also had a Paradise on Earth so close to their crowded smoky city of London.

Day after day, Pierre-Joseph returned to Kew and nobody showed the least interest in the homely-looking foreigner with the enormous clumsy hands who couldn't speak a word of the King's English. He had Sir Joseph's permission to come there to draw and paint flowers, so they let him get on with it and never once glanced or commented on anything he was doing. A pity, for today one can find no mention, no record, of the long days Pierre-Joseph Redouté once spent among the flowers of Kew.

It was perhaps the wonderful variety of a stately flower known as amaryllis that grew in one of the greenhouses there that most fascinated Pierre-Joseph. A thousand years and more ago, the great Roman poet, Virgil, had sung the praises of an enchanting young shepherdess called Amaryllis, or so Monsieur L'Héritier had once told Pierre-Joseph.

Well, thought Pierre-Joseph, that long-ago shepherdess would have been flattered by the poem, and even more so to behold the variety of lovely flowers that now bore her name. All first cousins, these flowers, but now meeting for the first time in Kew Gardens on the bank of the English River Thames, after long and perilous journeys from their native homes in far-away Japan or China, the Cape of Good Hope, Brazil, the East Indies or Mexico.

And yet these stately flowers were also first cousins to the gentle scented jonquils, the 'narcisses des poètes' that Pierre-Joseph had loved to paint as he wandered, young, and often hungry and footsore, along the roads of his native land.

Even in those days the sight of any lovely flower had made him forget he was hungry. But now he had learned so much from Monsieur L'Héritier, it filled him with wonder to think how the wide world over, heaven had scattered so vast a multitude of flowers to give joy and delight to all who paused to consider them.

Pierre-Joseph took another long look at the amaryllis he was about to paint that day. This one had come from China, and Pierre-Joseph could well imagine some Chinese poet composing verses as he beheld it. Such lovely tawny-yellow petals, the very colour for a Chinese flower!

Then he rapidly began to sketch and paint that amaryllis, and forgot China and Chinese poets and everything else until a great bell clanged a loud warning that he must pack up and hurry away unless he wished to be locked in for the night in Kew Gardens.

Now Monsieur L'Héritier with his customary efficiency had not only rented a comfortable room for Pierre-Joseph in the house where he himself lodged, he also recommended a couple of eating-houses and coffee-houses where Pierre-Joseph would certainly meet other artists from France and Belgium.

One evening in one of these coffee-houses, Pierre-Joseph met the Belgian artist, Pierre-Philippe Tassaert. He too came from a family of painters, and one friendly word led to another and so did the cups of coffee followed by a convivial bottle of wine. Presently Monsieur Tassaert was telling Pierre-Joseph how one of the stern grandpapas in his family had always shown his sons the door the day they reached the ripe age of twelve. Yes, out they had to go and earn their own bread, and as they went he would thunder that if any one of them dared to bring discredit on the honourable name of Tassaert, he would take the skin off his back, no matter where he was, so help him God.

His daughters had the luxury of staying at home, making themselves useful of course, until they reached the age of sixteen, then out through the door they too had to go, with the same dire parental warning.

And this Tassaert, sitting there, had wandered even further afield than Pierre-Joseph. He had worked, as a lad, in the London studio of the famous English portrait painter, Thomas Hudson. From there he had crossed the rough sea to Ireland. Yes, Ireland. And an accomplished lot of eloquent talkers these Irish were! Never a dull moment in that green island. In fact Monsieur Tassaert had so enjoyed his stay in Ireland that he had married an Irish girl.

And here he sat in this most English of coffee-houses, and though Pierre-Joseph would never believe it to look at him, he was now

Monsieur the President of the Society of the Artists of London. That grandpapa in the family would have been proud of him, a Tassaert, born in Antwerp, lording it over the Artists of London. And earning excellent money too, painting portraits, landscapes, not to mention soul-stirring scenes from the Scriptures, or of English, Greek, Roman, any period of history a client fancied from the Queen of Sheba setting forth to meet Solomon to English Oliver Cromwell singing Psalms at the top of his voice as he slaughtered the Irish.

This slaughter of the Irish had taken place a hundred years and more ago now, but one heard tales over there that made one's hair stand on end. In fact the most fearsome of Irish maledictions was still 'the curse of Cromwell on ye!' As for Monsieur Tassaert's Irish wife, she fairly spat at the very mention of Psalm-singing Oliver Cromwell.

The versatile President of the Society of Artists of London then said he was often well paid to copy some masterpiece, and though he would scorn to boast, it took an expert to decide which was a genuine Van Dyck and which was a copy painted by Pierre-Philippe Tassaert.

Over yet another bottle of wine, Monsieur the President of the Society of Artists of London sadly shook his head at Pierre-Joseph's lack of ambition. From all he heard, Pierre-Joseph could paint a good portrait at the drop of a hat. He could make a fortune here in London. Everyone of importance in England simply had to have his portrait painted – preferably by a foreigner. This added tone to any portrait. Why then waste his talents, his time, on illustrating books which would only interest botanists? True, botany was all the rage just now. But would it be the rage in the future? Who could foresee this? Whereas portraits, now they would never go out of fashion,

Ah well, if illustrating botany books was all Pierre-Joseph asked of life, 'chacun à son goût' cried the tolerant President of the Society of Artists of London, just as Pierre-Joseph's friends in Paris had done. And they drank to this liberal sentiment, and parted the best of friends.

. . .

The Royal Gardens of Kew were not the only ones that delighted Pierre-Joseph. He also found his way to Chelsea where there were some fine houses and well-kept gardens. But it was not to see these that Pierre-Joseph returned again and again to Chelsea. It was to visit the famous Apothecaries' Garden there, the Physic Garden as it is now known. It was here that apothecaries, botanists, physicians and medical students came to study the many medicinal flowers and plants that grew there, every one with some healing quality all its own.

Once, it seemed, four magnificent Cedars of Lebanon had grown there, two each side of the gate. Two had been cut down to make more room for plants but two still remained, very stately to behold.

However it wasn't these stately Cedars of Lebanon that so impressed Pierre-Joseph, it was the orderly beauty of the beds of flowers and plants that grew there, family upon family of medicinal plants, herbs and flowers, some known from ancient times, others far newer discoveries. There was one modest, but very sweet smelling flowering plant for instance that had first been found in North Africa, and it was labelled Reseda Odorata. But someone in France had given it a far more poetical name: Mignonette. One needed half a dozen English words to translate this – sweet, charming, dainty, and other endearing adjectives – so the English had also decided to call it mignonette.

As Pierre-Joseph wandered along the trim paths between the flower-beds, he thought how Dom Hickman would have rejoiced in this scented garden planted with many of the flowers he himself had grown in the Abbey herb garden of Saint Hubert, or trudged so patiently in field and forest to gather. And how he would have loved to learn of the healing qualities of the many new plants which he never had the privilege to see.

Pierre-Joseph repentantly told himself he must write a long letter to Dom Hickman, explain why he was now in London, tell him about the Royal Gardens at Kew, and the Apothecaries' Garden in Chelsea. He would also mention that the Herr-Professor-Doctor Mesmer was now in Paris and astounding everyone, even Her Majesty Queen Marie-Antoinette, or so one said.

Yes, Pierre-Joseph would sit down and write a long letter to good Dom Hickman.

Dom Hickman was never to read that letter. At the very time Pierre-Joseph was thinking of him with so much affection in the Apothecaries' Garden of Chelsea, Dom Hickman lay silent, still in death before the high altar of the ancient Abbey of Saint Hubert, and all about him echoed the solemn chanting of the Mass for the Dead.

'Dies Irae', chanted the monks, 'Day of wrath, day of mourning!'

So desolate, so terrible a hymn to chant about the lifeless body of kind, homely Dom Hickman who had dearly loved to gather the healing herbs of garden, field and forest. Dom Hickman who had thirsted after knowledge and never harmed any man, woman or child.

'Spare, O God, in mercy spare him,' implored the monks.

Even the most charitable of those chanting monks was convinced that Dom Hickman had dire need of all their supplication for the manner of his death had been most reprehensible, most unmonastic.

With no authority whatever, with no word of approval from My Lord Abbot, Dom Hickman had decided it would be profitable to ascertain how long a man could live without eating or drinking. This would be of immense comfort to a traveller lost in some barren, waterless wilderness. He would know he need not give up hope of survival for a specified number of days.

So Dom Hickman, without a word to anyone, began to fast, for naturally he was conducting this experiment on himself. Day by day he grew gaunter and weaker until he realised he had arrived at the dangerous, tenuous line between life and death. It was time to eat and drink otherwise he would be guilty of the mortal sin of deliberately bringing about his own death.

Once recovered from Experiment One, Dom Hickman began his equally important, to him, Experiment Two. He would now discover how much food and water the human stomach could accommodate. This again would be of immense value to a traveller, a missionary for instance, setting out to cross some sandy desert. He could carry an adequate store of food and water in his own stomach to sustain him for a specified number of days.

But alas for Dom Hickman, his long-suffering stomach rebelled; and he had died, of all things, of over-eating and over-drinking. Now he faced his Maker; and all the poor and sick of Saint Hubert and for miles around were sorely distressed. This was no way for a monk to die, and they crossed themselves and prayed that God would have mercy on his soul.

The monks, mournfully chanting stanza after stanza of 'Dies Irae', thought it would surely need a miracle of intercession if Dom Hickman was to 'escape the avenging judgement', since it was his baleful love of experimenting that had sent him hurtling so ignominiously into eternity. And up to the vaulted roof echoed and rang that terrible cry:

> '*O that day, that day of wrath, of sore distress and*
> *of all wretchedness, that great and exceeding bitter day!*
> *Spare O God, in mercy spare him!*'

Pierre-Joseph was stunned when the news of Dom Hickman's death reached him late that July.

He bitterly reproached himself. Why had he not overcome his reluctance, his dislike of writing even the simplest of letters? Why had he comfortably assumed that Dom Hickman would always be there in Saint Hubert, just as he loved to remember him?

And there was no comfort in thinking that he had always meant to go back to Saint Hubert and tell Dom Hickman how he had now found the happiest of all ways to earn his bread, and tell him how much he owed to him.

All the way to Kew that day, Pierre-Joseph thought only of Dom Hickman, how wisely he had talked to him, how he had opened his young eyes to the flowers of fields, forest and hedgerow.

Presently Pierre-Joseph found himself standing before one of the flowers he had planned to sketch that day, a foxglove that had newly arrived from the shady woodlands of the sunny island of Madeira. But as he stood there, Pierre-Joseph seemed to see again those other purple foxgloves that grew in the forests of Saint Hubert, and to hear the homely voice of Dom Hickman telling him what a blessing an infusion of the dried leaves of these handsome flowers was to poor souls afflicted with spasms of the heart.

Then out of the blue came the memory of another day when Dom Hickman had told him of the poem written by a humble Irish monk who had lived all of six centuries ago, and how this poem had captured in words all Dom Hickman felt, but could never put into words.

For the first time that day, Pierre-Joseph smiled, picturing Dom Hickman being warmly welcomed at the Gates of Eternity by that Irish monk who would take him by the hand and lead him to his 'hidden little hut' with the beautiful woods all about it and the 'many-voiced birds' singing among the green branches of the celestial trees, and the little brook rippling joyously 'across the floor'.

How could there be a Day of Wrath for good Dom Hickman! With this gentle Irish monk, he too must surely be 'sitting for a while, praising God in every place' of that rustic corner of heaven. Together they would sing, 'This is my rest for ever. Here will I dwell.'

Very naïve, very unorthodox, to be sure, but having settled Dom Hickman so suitably in eternal bliss, Pierre-Joseph at last began to sketch Digitalis Sceptrum, the foxglove from Madeira.

7

By Appointment to Her Majesty
Queen Marie-Antoinette

Early in December 1787, Pierre-Joseph came back again to Paris, much to the joy of Marie-Marthe and little Josephine.

But was that traveller able to answer his wife's eager questions about the sights of the great city of London? No, he was not. Indeed one would imagine he hadn't had a moment to spare to look at any one of them, not even the Tower of London or the Castle of Windsor. But the flowers, the plants, the trees of the Royal Gardens of Kew and the Apothecaries' Garden in Chelsea, now he could, and did, talk for hours on end about them, grow positively poetical in fact.

It was days later, for instance, that Pierre-Joseph casually remarked that there was a full-size replica of a pagoda in Kew Gardens, precisely as in the romantic Far East, and with no fewer than eighty dragons decorating the angles of its gilt roof, every dragon covered in glittering coloured glass.

No, Pierre-Joseph hadn't actually spared a moment to count those dragons. One of the gardeners had pointed to them one day and then held up his ten fingers eight times, so Pierre-Joseph had concluded there must be eighty of them. And yes, that pagoda did look very striking standing there under the cool English sky; and then off would go Pierre-Joseph and grow rapturous about some flowers that grew in a heated greenhouse of Kew, such brilliantly coloured flowers that they were called 'Birds of Paradise Flowers', though it seemed that the unpoetical English had also dubbed them 'Bird's Tongue Flowers'.

Oh yes, Pierre-Joseph could talk most eloquently of the gardens, the flowers he had seen in England, but ask him about the English people he had met and one would suppose he had only set eyes on Sir Joseph Banks, Madame his wife, Mademoiselle his sister, a gentleman known to the Banks' family as 'Old Dry' and a young English artist by the name of James Sowerby.

And all Pierre-Joseph knew about them was that Sir Joseph was a very busy man with a thousand scientific interests, and that Madame his wife was very gracious and kind but not in the least interested in anything scientific, only in collecting antique china. And Mademoiselle Sarah Sophia? Well, to tell the truth she was a most intimidating English lady, very tall, very blunt, with a deep commanding voice, who obviously didn't give a rap about her appearance.

When pressed to describe just how this formidable English lady was dressed, Pierre-Joseph was infuriatingly vague about that too, except that he had noticed, in fact one couldn't help noticing, that she always had two enormous pockets, one on each side of her skirt, into which she stuffed books, pamphlets, letters and all manner of documents. But a very clever lady for all that, and a most devoted sister to Sir Joseph. It was she who had made careful copies of the interesting diaries kept by Sir Joseph on his voyages of discovery.

'Old Dry'? Well, he was a very formal Swedish gentleman who as far as Pierre-Joseph could judge spoke fluent and excellent English. He kept Sir Joseph's library and herbarium in impeccable order and positively radiated icy silent disapproval of any absent-minded visitor who all unwittingly upset the exact order of Sir Joseph's army of books. Understandable, of course, but a little in-human, this Swedish mania for order.

James Sowerby? Now he was a very likeable young painter who before Monsieur L'Héritier arrived in London had made a meagre living painting portraits and giving lessons, and not enjoying either. But this was all the work he could find to do. In his free time, however, he delighted in painting flowers and this had led him to study botany, with all his well-meaning friends exclaiming heaven help poor James Sowerby for none of his flower-paintings and 'botanising' would ever earn him the price of a pair of boots. Just as Pierre-Joseph's friends had once done.

As if by some miracle, out of the blue Monsieur L'Héritier had appeared and discovered James Sowerby just as he had discovered Pierre-Joseph and he had at once engaged him to help with the illustrations for his *English Garland*. In short, Monsieur L'Héritier was the very first botanist to give James Sowerby the chance for which he had been praying. And now eminent English botanists were also fast discovering James Sowerby and offering him work illustrating *their* botanical books and journals. So James Sowerby could also look forward to a lifetime of the work he loved; and he too must be thanking heaven – in English of course – for Monsieur L'Héritier.

This about summed up all Pierre-Joseph's impressions of his months in England, and as Marie-Marthe exclaimed, he wasn't in the least ashamed to admit he hadn't learned more than two or three useful words of English, flowers being flowers in any language. He hadn't even gone out of his way to take a look at the English King and Queen or any of their large family of royal children. Maybe this was just as well since he couldn't have shouted 'God bless Your Majesties!' with the rest of the crowd, and more suspicious still he wouldn't have been able to join in a single verse of 'God Save the King', much less 'Rule Britannia'.

Pierre-Joseph merrily agreed; but oh, if Marie-Marthe could only have seen the flowers of Kew Gardens or strolled between the beds of sweet-smelling herbs in the Apothecaries' Garden of Chelsea, she would understand that these were the best of all memories.

What country could ask a foreign visitor to cherish better ones?

Monsieur L'Héritier was also cherishing excellent memories of his stay in England. He had quietly returned to Paris, and not a question had been asked about the Dombey herbarium, though with his customary prudence he had arranged for this to be forwarded to him later on, when he judged it safe to do so.

With him, however, he had brought all the illustrations for his *English Garland* together with his carefully composed Latin text. To Pierre-Joseph's secret amusement, Monsieur L'Héritier now began exchanging argumentative letters with 'Old Dry'. It seemed that 'Old Dry' did not always approve of the Latin names given by Monsieur L'Héritier to the English flowers of his Garland.

But this was moving, a real tribute to 'Old Dry'. It was to him Monsieur L'Héritier turned when he decided he needed a few lines from a truly English poem that would voice his esteem for England.

'Old Dry' found the very lines. They came, so Monsieur L'Héritier told Pierre-Joseph, from a long poem entitled *The Seasons*, composed by a poet called James Thomson, a great lover of nature and of freedom for all mankind.

When Part One of the *English Garland* was published in 1788, at Monsieur L'Héritier's own expense, of course, there on Page Two were those truly English lines of poetry:

> *O vale of bliss! O softly-swelling hills!*
> *On which the* Power of Cultivation *lies,*
> *And joys to see the wonders of his toil.*
>
> . . . .
> . . . .
> . . . .
> . . . .
>
> *Happy* BRITANNIA! *where the* QUEEN OF ARTS,
> *Inspiring vigour,* LIBERTY *abroad*
> *Walks, unconfin'd, even to thy farthest cotes,*
> *And scatters plenty with unsparing hand.*

Pierre-Joseph, looking at this, decided that one had need of that large space, all dots, to recover one's breath before one tackled the resounding last four lines.

One felt, as Monsieur L'Héritier translated them, as if one wasn't listening to a poem but to trumpets sounding triumphantly in some wondrous land where LIBERTY did indeed walk abroad from coast to coast, scattering plentiful harvests and a wealth of flowers with unsparing hand as she went.

One of the English naturalists who, in Monsieur L'Héritier's own words, 'had showed themselves so ready to reveal their treasures' was a gentleman named Mr. J. E. Smith. Now he had been fortunate indeed. The great Swedish naturalist, Linnaeus, had died in 1778, leaving behind him a vast and valuable collection of books and manuscripts and an unrivalled herbarium. Pierre-Joseph gathered that Mr. Smith had managed to acquire all this treasure for the sum of one thousand and eighty-eight pounds and five shillings.

Pierre-Joseph had not attempted to work out how much this was in French francs but Monsieur L'Héritier obviously thought it was worth every shilling. He had always been a disciple of Linnaeus and he had been most grateful, in his own sober, taciturn way, when Mr. Smith invited him to come when he pleased and study this unique collection. Pierre-Joseph felt that these occasions were as solemn as a pilgrimage to Monsieur L'Héritier. He would have given much to spend days consulting this treasure trove, but he had so much else to do whilst he was in London. And he had to think of returning to his family in Paris.

Monsieur L'Héritier had also been interested to learn that Mr. Smith and two of his naturalist friends had met one day in a London coffee-house, and as they drank their coffee they had discussed the excellent idea of forming a 'Linnean Society' there in London. Before he returned to Paris, Monsieur L'Héritier knew that Mr. Smith and his friends had been successful. There was now a 'Linnean Society of London'.

Once back in Paris Monsieur L'Héritier must have spoken of all this to his naturalist friend, Doctor Broussonet, and before long, there sat Pierre-Joseph at the very first meeting of the 'Linnean Society of Paris', very flattered to have the honour of being listed as a Founder Member of so learned a society.

Then long before his dramatic flight to Soho Square, London, Monsieur L'Héritier had been justly proud of his own fine collection of books, and like Sir Joseph Banks he had always been ready to allow other botanists to consult them, though they certainly could not count on hot tea or coffee and delicious buttered rolls as well.

But Monsieur L'Héritier now seemed bent on having a library equal to that of Sir Joseph. This, of course, explained why he had 'run so diligently' about London, 'buying books without end'. And why even now, with all these on his shelves, he was forever buying still more books there in Paris.

All these erudite books were expensive, of course, but Monsieur L'Héritier was a wealthy man so it wasn't this passion for books that puzzled his friends. No, it was the way he lived.

'The books he brings out are superb,' wrote one of these friends, 'but his table is frugal and his clothes simplicity itself. He spends twenty thousand francs a year on botany, but he goes everywhere on foot.'

Pierre-Joseph knew all this but now it began to fill him with a strange feeling of compassion for this dedicated, austere man. It was almost as if his conscience was forever nagging him, reproaching him for spending so much on his one absorbing passion in life. Those frugal meals, his simple clothes, going everywhere on foot, maybe they all made him feel better.

Fortunately, Madame L'Héritier was a devoted wife; whatever her husband did was right and proper in her eyes, and she was proud that her husband was such an eminent botanist. But their eldest son, Jacques, shared none of his father's interest in botany, or in his fine collection of books, or anything else his father did.

A sad pity, thought Pierre-Joseph, for in his own bleak, unde-monstrative way Monsieur L'Héritier loved his children. It would have been wonderful for him if Jacques had shared his interests instead of being so indifferent, indeed almost hostile.

Pierre-Joseph decided yet once again that he himself was the most fortunate of men. True, he and Marie-Marthe had the most modest of homes but when he opened the door of an evening, there was Marie-Marthe, with her warm welcoming smile, and there was little Josephine running to meet him shouting 'Papa! Papa!', and proudly holding out a paper on which she had painted, all by herself, the bluest of forget-me-nots or a bright yellow buttercup.

Then came another momentous day in Pierre-Joseph's life, or as he chose to express it to Marie-Marthe, he had the honour of making the acquaintance of a nobleman, a duke no less – one dead and buried a century or so ago.

When asked to talk sense, Pierre-Joseph said that to make the acquaintance of this high-born nobleman, one had to whisk back through the last hundred years of French history and come to a halt at the time when King Louis XIII sat uneasily on the throne of France.

Nothing in the least heroic about Louis XIII; he was king only in name. It was the all-powerful Cardinal Richelieu who dominated both the young King and the Kingdom of France, and who had, so Pierre-Joseph had now learnt, made sharp, short work of all who conspired against him.

It was a bitter blow to the sad young King when it was discovered that the most dangerous, the most merciless of all these conspirators was his own brother, Gaston, Duke of Orleans. But even His Eminence, Cardinal Richelieu, could hardly order the royal head of the King's brother to be hacked from his neck. So he packed the perfidious Gaston off to his ducal castle of Blois on the banks of the River Loire and icily 'requested' him to remain there for the rest of his life. To make sure Gaston obeyed this 'request', His Eminence, the Cardinal, posted a whole army of secret police about him.

Now Gaston was undoubtedly the most undesirable of brothers, but he was no fool. He was polished, cultivated and very rich, and he sized up the strength of the secret police watching his every move, and decided to make the best of his enforced exile from Paris.

He determined to make Blois the most renowned of all French castles. This in itself would give him immense pleasure and he would have the added delight of knowing it would cause His Eminence, the Cardinal, to gnash his teeth.

So Gaston employed expert gardeners and set them to work to create superb gardens all about his castle, and pleased them mightily by spending princely sums of money on rare and beautiful trees and flowers so that the gardens of Blois became a delight to behold: 'A fair jewel set in the heart of sweet France, second only to the Garden of Eden before Adam took the bite of that apple', sang the strolling minstrels, and thus adroitly made sure of an excellent supper, and wine without limit, in the kitchen of Blois.

Then to add to the glory of Blois, Gaston added a menagerie of exotic animals never before seen in France. All this too with a regal disregard of the cost. But it was in his aviaries that Gaston took the greatest pleasure. In them flew and sang the loveliest of birds, all the colours of the rainbow, that had come from many a far-distant land.

And what, just what, had all this slice of royal history to do with Pierre-Joseph, botanical artist, demanded Marie-Marthe. Indeed, why this sudden interest in French history at all? Hadn't Pierre-Joseph declared a thousand times that it had always been a penance for him to learn even the first two pages of the history of his own native land?

Pierre-Joseph said, ah yes, but a momentous event had fired him to ask a whole catechism of searching questions. So if Marie-Marthe would now permit, they would return to Gaston, Duke of Orleans, in his wondrous Castle of Blois.

Gaston was, of course, well versed in Latin, so he would certainly have been aware of the mournful old adage: 'Sic transit gloria mundi.' Gaston, however, was not prepared to allow the glory he had created on earth to pass away in centuries to come.

He therefore engaged the most gifted of artists and paid them handsomely to paint the loveliest, the rarest flowers in his garden and the most beautiful birds in his aviaries. These were all to be painted 'd'après le naturel', from life, on the finest vellum and 'en miniature'.

'En miniature' in those days had nothing at all to do with small-scale paintings. It meant they had to be painted in 'gouache', colours blended with a precise mixture of water, honey and gum. Gouache, said Pierre-Joseph, had certain advantages. One could leave off painting and return when one pleased to add yet another layer, superimpose one colour on another with the most charming results.

Indeed, one writer had declared that 'one needed to be a sorcerer to divine the order and manner of these exquisitely superimposed colours'. And Gaston's collection of 'miniatures' was truly exquisite.

When Gaston died, he dutifully left this collection to his nephew, King Louis XIV, who had brought it to Versailles and at once recognised that it was unique, absolutely priceless. And announced forthwith that it would be the royal duty of every King of France to go on adding to Gaston's collection.

His Majesty had therefore created a new, well-paid and permanent appointment: 'Painter to the King for "La Miniature"'. The fortunate artist given this appointment had to see to it that at least twenty-four 'miniatures' were added every year to the collection. The birds to be painted were to be the newest arrivals in the Royal Aviaries of Versailles; the flowers were to be the ones blooming for the first time under the sky of France – in the Jardin du Roi.

The very flowers that Pierre-Joseph was now painting for Monsieur L'Héritier's *Stirpes Novae*!

Now came the grand finale to Pierre-Joseph's historical discourse. The present 'Painter to the King for "La Miniature"' was a friend of Monsieur L'Héritier, a genial Dutchman by the name of Gerard van Spaendonck. And it seemed that he had been quietly observing Pierre-Joseph at work, and now he had approached him.

He, Pierre-Joseph Redouté, was going to have the honour of adding from time to time a flower-painting to the rich collection of Gaston, Duke of Orleans.

When Marie-Marthe recovered her breath and wiped her eyes, she said well, what would Pierre-Joseph's well-meaning but Doubting Thomas of a brother, Antoine-Ferdinand, think of this! Not to mention all those other well-meaning friends who plainly thought Pierre-Joseph was wasting his time, his talents on painting flowers.

Then she demanded to know more about this discerning Monsieur van Spaendonck. He was, it seemed, a man after Pierre-Joseph's own heart, very friendly and unpretentious. He had studied first in his native land and Pierre-Joseph had been pleased to learn he had then had the good sense to wander on and study for some time in Antwerp.

At first, just like Pierre-Joseph, he had lived from hand to mouth, tackling any artistic job that came his way. But unlike Pierre-Joseph, he was thrifty. He had saved every possible guilder until he had enough to travel on to Paris.

Once safely in Paris this level-headed Dutchman decided to specialise first in something artistically safe, something that would do more than keep the wolf from his door. He began to decorate the lids of small porcelain boxes, delightful boxes to hold comfits or tobacco, every box a joy to handle and set down on a table, a real 'objet de luxe'.

Soon a porcelain box decorated with a graceful spray or vase of flowers, with the initials V.S. became all the rage. Indeed to this very day it is a collector's dream to come across a porcelain box with the lid decorated and signed with the initials: V.S.

But Monsieur van Spaendonck was a serious artist; he had no intention of spending his life decorating the lids of porcelain boxes, no matter how profitable. When he again had saved enough money, he turned his back on porcelain boxes, and began to paint flower-pieces in the grand manner of the old Dutch artists, and these brought him even wider fame. Then as if to prove the old French saying, 'Rien réussit mieux que le succès,' 'nothing succeeds better than success,' in 1774 Monsieur van Spaendonck had been appointed 'Painter to the King for "La Miniature" '.

This did not mean that he himself was expected to paint every one of the new additions to the collection. No, he was responsible for them, but he had every right to employ occasional expert help.

This was very convenient for Monsieur van Spaendonck, for he had also become a most successful master-painter giving regular classes in the Jardin du Roi attended mostly by fashionable young ladies, closely chaperoned by Mesdames their vigilant mothers or their governesses. In short, Monsieur van Spaendonck was as busy as he was successful. Over the years he had contributed no fewer than fifty-six paintings to the 'Miniatures du Roi', and now he felt he could at times employ other artists whom he considered worthy of the honour.

Then Pierre-Joseph had been delighted to hear that Monsieur van Spaendonck had decided that all future paintings for the collection were to be painted, not in the time-honoured gouache of Gaston's day, but in water-colours.

Paintings in gouache, no matter how reverently handled, had a heart-breaking way of scaling over the years. The lovely super-imposed colours became so much rainbow dust at the intake of a breath.

But this was not the only reason that had made Monsieur van Spaendonck decide on water-colours. He, too, had come to the conclusion that one could not better clear, pure water-colours, to capture the subtle, elusive charm of a flower.

Ah yes, Pierre-Joseph was enchanted to know he would be required to paint in water-colours.

By the way, said Pierre-Joseph, it was not now academically correct to refer to Gaston's collection as 'Miniatures' since all the new additions were no longer painted in gouache. So sticklers for correct nomenclature – and heaven knew one met them by the dozen in the world of botany – these sticklers now insisted on call-ing the collection: 'The Vellums of the King'. But old names have a way of refusing to die, and Pierre-Joseph had a feeling that Gaston's rich collection would always be best known as the 'Miniatures du Roi'.

The collection was still in Versailles, in handsome volumes, eighty paintings in each volume, all magnificently bound in red morocco with the arms of the Kings of France tooled in gold on the covers.

Marie-Marthe's face shone with pride. Think of it! Flower-paintings by Pierre-Joseph were now going to be preserved for all time in that royal collection in the Palace of Versailles!

Wait, wait a moment, implored Pierre-Joseph. He wasn't precisely galloping straight into one of those handsome red morocco volumes at crack of dawn tomorrow. Heavens, no! At first he would have to work under the close supervision of Monsieur van Spaendonck but this would be a privilege. He had shown Pierre-Joseph some of his own 'miniatures' and they had taken Pierre-Joseph's breath away, they were so delicately, so perfectly beautiful. Gaston, Duke of Orleans, would certainly have approved of this Dutchman's additions to his rich collection.

And one more word of warning! Marie-Marthe was not to have rosy dreams of Pierre-Joseph immediately earning vast sums of money. One was paid so much, not a franc more or less, for every new painting added to the collection. Furthermore, it was only when Monsieur van Spaendonck decided that there was a rare new flower worthy of a place in the collection that he would invite Pierre-Joseph, or another artist he could trust, to have the honour of painting it.

Monsieur L'Héritier showed no surprise when Pierre-Joseph turned up next morning and told him the good news. He simply shook hands with Pierre-Joseph and said 'Monsieur van Spaendonck is showing his customary good sense.' Then he abruptly changed the subject and said he wished Pierre-Joseph to go immediately to the residence of one of his wealthy friends, Monsieur Cels, who had sent him a line to say that a certain new plant was about to flower in a sheltered corner of his garden.

Pierre-Joseph, hurrying away, was not in the least chilled by the way Monsieur L'Héritier had received his good news. The longer he knew Monsieur L'Héritier, the better he understood him. And he had made it clear from the start that though Pierre-Joseph could count on being regularly employed on the illustrations for *Stirpes Novae* this did not mean that he expected Pierre-Joseph, in all gratitude, to turn down all other offers of work. Monsieur L'Héritier did not believe in clapping handcuffs of any sort on any artist, on any honest man.

In fact it might well have been Monsieur L'Héritier who, without a word to Pierre-Joseph, had spoken to Monsieur van Spaendonck, asked him to take a look at the work Pierre-Joseph was doing. It would be so very like him.

From time to time Pierre-Joseph would still spend a convivial evening with the friends he had made when he first came to Paris, and they would sit in their favourite café and talk and laugh as merrily as before.

But now, sooner or later the talk would be of a brave New France, a France where men would be brothers, all equal, all free, as in the new independent America.

It stirred the blood to think how many freedom-loving Frenchmen lay buried in American graves, heroes every one in the fight to free the new Americans from the tyranny of Britain.

No wonder freedom was now in the very air over France, they said. Any fool could see that France was fast sliding into bankruptcy though prices and taxes were forever soaring. The time was ripe for reform. And reform they talked until they were hoarse.

The Court of Versailles always came first under attack. For years, they said, the Queen had been showering princely pensions on her friends and their families. The King had been equally munificent regardless of the fact that the mountain of national debt was piling up higher and higher. As for the vast army of royal servants, they hadn't been paid for months, sometimes years. Not that this need wring one's heart, they all had ingenious ways of feathering their nests in the extravagant splendour of that glittering Court.

Take the head chamber-maids for instance. They could earn a comfortable and easy 600,000 francs a year just by selling candle-ends, for the Palace glowed from dusk to dawn in the light of thousands of wax candles, each candle replaced every day of course.

As for the multitude of noblemen who daily danced attendance on their Majesties and jostled for royal favour, many of them had great estates in the country which they never deigned to visit, exile from Versailles being considered worse than death itself. They left everything to their astute stewards who also feathered *their* nests as they squeezed every possible sou from the sullen and half-starved peasants.

Noblemen had great need of money for it vanished like snow in high summer at the Court of Versailles. Magnificently attired in velvet and brocade, they hunted by day and danced the gavotte, the minuet and the pavane all night, or gambled fortunes away. So head over heels, deeper and deeper in debt they went, and then, gay as you please, borrowed still more money.

Presently somebody would quote the story of how the King had turned one day to His Grace, the high-born Archbishop Dillon and said, 'My Lord Archbishop, I am informed that you are in debt, heavily in debt.'

His Grace, the Lord Archbishop, raised amused eyebrows.

'Sire, I shall have to ask my steward. I will then have the honour of giving your Majesty a report on my financial position.'

This noble detachment was typical of the Court of Versailles. One would imagine they expected gold to rain down from a sympathetic heaven one day, and obligingly solve this tiresome lack of money. Meanwhile, on with the dance, the gambling, whilst France went galloping faster and faster down the slippery slope to bankruptcy.

And off would go Pierre-Joseph's friends hurling quotations at one another from the writings of Voltaire, Diderot, Montesquieu and Jean-Jacques Rousseau as they hotly argued on the best, the infallible way to take France by the neck, and the rest of Europe too, transform them and the whole Universe as well into Utopia, a free and idyllic brotherhood of men.

One evening someone startled them by solemnly saying he was praying that a second Saint Martin would soon appear. A popular and most successful saint, that one. The proof? No fewer than 3,600 churches in France bore his name, and well over 400 villages. And how had that saint, once a fire-eating warrior, so successfully converted their pagan ancestors? Backed by a force of brawny disciples he had marched from one village to another in ancient Gaul and promptly destroyed their pagan idols before he set to work to convert the villagers, laying about him with his stout wooden staff on any truculent heathen who was reluctant to see the light.

This was met with a gale of merriment. Then suddenly sober again, they would begin to denounce many a ridiculous and outdated by-law. Take, for instance, travel in a stage-coach along the roads of France. As Voltaire had put it:

'From post-house to post-house one changed the law as one changed horses.'

Everywhere a fine legal tangle conceived in the distant past and still flourishing now in 1788! Everyone had his own panacea of course and louder and louder, and more and more heated would grow the arguments till somebody would point an accusing finger at Pierre-Joseph and yell, take a look at that Belgian, he hadn't been listening to a word anyone said for the last hour or so. Pierre-Joseph would agree and say that French politics, indeed any brand of politics, were beyond him. He had been born politically deficient. At this they would fling up their arms and laugh again for they liked easy-going, friendly Pierre-Joseph, and someone would say even Saint Martin would have scratched his head over a Belgian like this.

Just think of it! He had been four years in Paris and he could have earned a packet by painting portraits. But no, there he sat, tranquilly drinking his coffee and admitting he was still painting nothing but pretty flowers.

One night someone asked if it was true that Pierre-Joseph had recently been painting the flowers growing in Her Majesty Queen Marie-Antoinette's costly garden of the Petit Trianon.

Well yes, said Pierre-Joseph. He'd been given permission to do this, thanks to Monsieur Desfontaines, an eminent botanist and a friend of Monsieur L'Héritier. But heavens, no! He hadn't set eyes on the Queen or been inside any of the cottages of Her Majesty's rustic hamlet. Neither did he know if the rumour now sweeping Paris was true – that the walls of Her Majesty's little theatre in Versailles were covered with sparkling diamonds.

Highly unlikely, said Pierre-Joseph. Those theatre walls were probably covered with a mosaic of cheap bits of ordinary glass. And why on earth was everyone so ready to believe that Marie-Antoinette had squandered yet another fortune on diamond-covered theatre walls?

And yes, he would admit that he wasn't a reliable witness since he had eyes for nothing except the gardens, and the flowers growing there.

•　　　•　　　•

Making his way home, Pierre-Joseph would soberly reflect that his friends were right. He was content to live in his own quiet small world. The work he was doing had its own rewards. Monsieur L'Héritier had become far more than an exemplary employer; it was plain that he now regarded Pierre-Joseph as a friend. He never lost a chance to introduce him to his influential friends in the world of botany, many of them wealthy gentlemen with well-loved gardens of their own, where Pierre-Joseph often went to paint some new flower which Monsieur L'Héritier had decided to include in a future instalment of *Stirpes Novae*.

To add to the spice of life, Monsieur van Spaendonck would sometimes summon him to the Jardin du Roi to paint a flower on costly vellum to add to the 'Miniatures du Roi'. It did not occur to Pierre-Joseph to resent the fact that it was tacitly understood that he left his work unsigned. Monsieur van Spaendonck was responsible for all the new additions, he had every right to sign his name on his own paintings, but all the rest were anonymous.

But what did it matter? Pierre-Joseph had the honour and glory of contributing to the rich collection of Gaston, Duke of Orleans.

The influential friends of Monsieur L'Héritier were at first vastly amused by this homely Belgian artist, with the hands of a blacksmith and a rustic accent straight from his native Ardennes. He was positively refreshing, he was always at his ease, never in the least awed by rank and riches. They loved flowers, so did he, and it was crystal clear that to this likeable man, this was all that mattered.

When they watched him paint, however, or saw some of his work, they forgot the rustic accent, the homely language. They were no longer amused. This man was far more than a painstaking, well-trained botanical artist. Every flower he painted seemed to bloom on the paper, fresh, enchanting, and yet absolutely accurate.

Now maybe one of these influential gentlemen remembered that Her Majesty Queen Marie-Antoinette liked to hang paintings of her favourite flowers on the walls of her rustic cottages in her fairytale hamlet.

Maybe this gentleman spoke to one of the Queen's ladies about the Belgian artist who was astounding them all with the accuracy and beauty of his flower-paintings. But no-one knows for sure.

All that is certain is that Pierre-Joseph raced home one day, flung open the door, and cried:

'Marie-Marthe, take a look at me. Take a good look at me.'

Marie-Marthe obediently took a good look at him.

'Well,' she said, 'you remind me of my husband, Pierre-Joseph Redouté.'

'Marie-Marthe,' said Pierre-Joseph, 'here stands Pierre-Joseph Redouté, Painter to Her Majesty Queen Marie-Antoinette of France!'

8

The Midnight Cactus

Painter to Her Majesty Queen Marie-Antoinette!

It sounded magnificent to be sure. No wonder Marie-Marthe immediately saw Pierre-Joseph in brand-new and most gentlemanly attire, strolling around the gardens of the Petit Trianon, pausing now and then to select a few of the loveliest flowers, and then being bowed into one of the romantic cottages of Her Majesty's fairytale hamlet, where he would arrange these flowers in a charming Sèvres vase or maybe in one from Japan.

Presently in would float the Queen in one of her ravishingly simple muslin gowns, wide satin sash around her waist, and Pierre-Joseph would teach his royal pupil to paint that charming vase of flowers.

This idyllic picture of Pierre-Joseph teaching Queen Marie-Antoinette to paint is still told, and moreover believed, to this very day. So you can easily imagine Marie-Marthe's disappointment when the newly appointed Painter to the Queen roared with laughter and said the Queen wasn't in the least interested in learning to paint.

Her Majesty, however, loved her gardens, and it pleased her to decorate the walls of the cottages of her hamlet with lifelike paintings of her favourite or rarest flowers. Pierre-Joseph had been awarded the honour of being at the Queen's command whenever she decided to have another flower painted.

Well yes, agreed Pierre-Joseph, he had indeed come a long, long way since he arrived in Paris six years ago, among the luggage on the top of a stage-coach, hungry, penniless and completely unknown.

However, one had to be hard-headed, realistic. This royal appointment was all honour and no pay, or so Pierre-Joseph had gathered. Even if there were some financial reward attached to the title, the royal finances were in such chaos that Pierre-Joseph would be fortunate indeed if someone thought it necessary to pay him for painting a flower for the Queen.

But why look on this blank side of the medal? Pierre-Joseph, Painter to Her Majesty the Queen, was going to celebrate his royal appointment. He and Marie-Marthe and little Josephine were going to get up at crack of dawn on Sunday next, take one of the passenger boats down the Seine and spend the whole day in Meudon, wander in the forest there, and eat a festive meal in a small inn warmly recommended by one of Pierre-Joseph's friends.

Now Parisians had long enjoyed a day's outing to Meudon, but it was a discerning Roman, Julian, nephew of the Emperor Constantine, who centuries ago had first sung its praises.

'I have discovered a charming spot,' he wrote, 'only five hundred "stades" from the city, where you will not be pestered by importunate merchants. You will leave the city behind you as you ride along the bank of the river till presently you will see some cultivated fields. Crossing these you will enter the forest. It will be best to follow the little stream there, and don't hesitate to let your horse enter the water. He will not sink, the stream is not deep.

'If you presently decide to proceed on foot you will tread on a carpet of sweet-smelling grass and thyme, and you will find the most profound peace and quiet if you then desire to lie on your back for a while and peruse a book.

'Then, to rejoice your eyes still further, you should climb a little higher in the forest and below you will see the river. Nothing more pleasant than to watch the ships tranquilly sailing to and fro.

'You will meet no-one as you go on your way, and soon you will be wandering through vineyards. The vines there are small but the wine they make from them is delectable, scented and a little sharp. Why are there not more of these vines elsewhere in Gaul?

'Still higher in the forest you will come across a few huts built of wood and clay, but the inhabitants are friendly. They will offer you honey fit for the gods on High Olympus.'

Julian, the Roman, had certainly spent a most enjoyable day in Meudon, and so had many others ever since. Young ladies on a day's outing there with their papas and mamans were still enthusing about 'charming Meudon' and 'amiable Meudon'; and Pierre-Joseph and Marie-Marthe soon decided that Julian the Roman, and these modern young ladies were not exaggerating. Indeed when it was dusk and they had to board a boat back to Paris they too had lost their hearts to 'charming, amiable' Meudon. Pierre-Joseph had also lost his heart to that 'delectable wine' – Julian had not exaggerated that either.

As for little Josephine, that Sunday was an enchanted day, sunlit and rose-scented. She was to remember all her life long how her papa had gently bent down a branch of a briar-rose and told her to look how beautifully the good God had made those delicate flowers. And look, how generous He was! Here was a whole hedge of them filling the air with a heavenly scent.

Then, just as Julian the Roman had done long centuries ago, they had climbed high in the forest and looked down on the Seine peacefully flowing far below. The air here was wonderful, full of the scent of pine-trees rejoicing in the sun; and the moss, the grass and thyme beneath their feet, were warm and scented too. And as they wandered on, little Josephine exclaimed and capered with delight to catch a glimpse of a deer, or a rabbit scuttling away, busy on some important business of its own.

The 'huts built of wood and clay' had long disappeared of course, but here and there were fine mansions set in spacious gardens. There was one of these mansions, however, that made the tears come to Marie-Marthe's eyes. It was the royal château with a splendid, ornate orangery where orange trees grew in wooden tubs on wheels, ready to be wheeled out into the open when the weather was kind.

The gardens of all these fine mansions, even those around the royal château, were sadly neglected. It was not this, however, that distressed Marie-Marthe. It was the thought that within the royal château lay the little Dauphin, heir to the throne, only eight years old, and surely the most piteous child in all France. He had been brought to the château so that he could breathe the pure, sweet air of Meudon. The innkeeper of the inn where they had eaten their meal, had readily accepted Pierre-Joseph's invitation to sit down and take a glass of wine with them, and he had been moved as he spoke of that pale, tortured little boy. He had, one said, a malady of the bones, and slowly and most cruelly he was growing more and more deformed and suffered more and more agonising pain.

The people of Meudon dearly loved the little Dauphin and only a few months ago they had been delighted to catch an occasional glimpse of him riding on the back of his favourite donkey, or dressed in a sailor-suit, taking a few painful steps leaning on the arm of one of his tutors.

But not now, said the innkeeper, not now. The little Dauphin now lay very still in his great bedroom; and Her Majesty, his mother had sent down sumptuous furniture from Versailles and rich tapestries, porcelain vases, and a hundred other costly ornaments so that her little son could feel royally at home as he lay in his room.

He had, so one said, been presented with his first gun, sword and two pistols, all beautifully engraved by the famous Auguste, goldsmith to the King. But those gold-encrusted weapons lay neglected, unloved by that pale deformed little boy. Instead he would ask for pots of sweet-smelling flowers to be brought up to his room and placed where he could see and smell them, hyacinths, jonquils, roses and jasmine.

One sunny day he had asked if the orange trees could be wheeled out and placed where he could see them through his tall windows. But there had been no money spent on the upkeep of the orangery for many a year, and when old Rossignol, the head – and now the only gardener – and the official keeper of the orangery, had struggled to wheel them out, the wheels were so rusty and the wooden tubs so rotten that he had not dared to bring them out for fear they fell apart.

Poor old Rossignol! Like so many royal servants he hadn't been paid for God knew how long. Everyone knew he hadn't tasted meat for the last two years, that he lived on black bread and vegetables, that he had no shoes to his feet, no hat to wear on his head. Yet, barefooted, bareheaded, he still wore his tattered old livery, decked with tarnished gold braid, as he faithfully and lovingly watered and tended the King's orange trees, and the pots of flowering plants he kept alive in the shelter of the orangery, and sent up to the room of the Dauphin. He had been desolated when he found he could not wheel out those rotten tubs, and so give a little pleasure to that uncomplaining gentle child, maybe even make him forget his pain for a moment at the sight, the scent of orange trees in bloom.

Now, said the innkeeper, the little Dauphin lay, not in his magnificent bed, but on a billiard table; yes, as true as God was in heaven, on a billiard table. He could no longer endure his soft yielding feather bed and all his pleasure now lay in the sweet-smelling flowers growing in pots about that hard, flat table.

Poor child! said the innkeeper. Heir to the throne, but surely one of the most afflicted of children. He could not romp and play in those royal gardens, grow rosy and strong in the good air of Meudon. No, they kept his windows shut tight to keep out the draught; and his one and only pleasure was a little nature about him in the airless grandeur of that stately room in the château.

Presently they paid the innkeeper, thanked him for an excellent meal, and went back to wander again in the forest.

'If only all the world were as peaceful and kind as this!' sighed Marie-Marthe.

'Yes,' said Pierre-Joseph, 'If only. . . .'

Then a smile lit up his homely face. 'Listen,' he said, 'one day we'll buy a house in Meudon.'

'Make it one with an orangery too, while you're at it,' said Marie-Marthe.

'Of course,' said Pierre-Joseph, 'I promise you an orangery too, and I will see to it that the tubs never become rotten or the wheels rusty. And the garden will be full of flowers, hundreds of flowers.'

'Wonderful!' said Marie-Marthe, and took his hand as they wandered on with little Josephine dancing ahead.

All too soon they had to hurry down the track that led to the river bank, and take a boat back to Paris.

A house in Meudon! A delightful dream to be sure. But for the life of her Marie-Marthe could not see them ever buying even the smallest house anywhere. Pierre-Joseph was still the generous, warm-hearted man she had married. He was eternally lending money to one or the other of his hard-up friends, bringing them home to meals, offering them a bed for the night, 'taking no thought for the morrow', no thought at all.

But that was Pierre-Joseph, the man she loved, and in Marie-Marthe's eyes everything he did was good and right. And they were fortunate, far more fortunate than so many families in France. They had their home, and many good friends, above all Monsieur L'Héritier who never forgot to pay Pierre-Joseph which was more than one could say those days of many a high-born gentleman. So they were never hungry, never cold, they had clothes on their backs and shoes on their feet, and above all they had love and quiet happiness in plenty in their modest home. What more could a woman want?

So Marie-Marthe sensibly waved a fond farewell to that dream-house, complete with garden and orangery, in 'charming, amiable' Meudon as they sailed along the river that lovely evening, back home again to Paris.

That day in Meudon was to be the last completely carefree and happy day Pierre-Joseph and Marie-Marthe were to know for many a dark year. Pierre-Joseph was soon to realise that he had been appointed 'Painter to Queen Marie-Antoinette' on the very eve of the French Revolution, surely the most tragic years in the history of France.

They were there, in Paris, all through the Revolution, and yet it would often seem to Pierre-Joseph that he lived in another world, a quiet safe world, not there in the very heart of Paris.

He was not alone in this. Far from it. One student, for instance, at the very height of the troubles in Paris, wrote to his anxious father in Bordeaux: 'All is quiet here.'

That student was writing the sober truth. All was quiet in the small scholastic world in which he lived and worked – just as it was in the tranquil world in which both Pierre-Joseph and Henri-Joseph worked. Indeed it was amazing to look back and recall that never once did they lack employment, and how in spite of enormous difficulties, botanists and scientists still found ways and means to publish their books and pamphlets for all of which they needed illustrations.

So all through the Revolution, Pierre-Joseph still drew and painted the flowers growing in his Paradise on Earth, though that lovely garden had been stripped of its royal name and had become the Jardin des Plantes – and this is what it is called to this very day. Day in, day out, Pierre-Joseph would be caught up in the unfailing peace and delight of that world of flowers, and the cruel quarrelling world outside would seem infinitely remote and strangely unreal.

This did not mean, however, that Pierre-Joseph callously wore blinkers, that he was not in the least concerned even when the hideous guillotine was set up on what is now called the Place de la Concorde.

True, he was not French, he had no love for, no interest in, politics, but for some time now it had become a pleasant habit to spend some hours every Sunday afternoon with Monsieur L'Héritier and a few of his chosen friends in his house on the Place Vendôme. But now the agreeable talk of plants and flowers and new botanical publications invariably came round to the latest, and always more ominous, news from Versailles.

And this was moving – Monsieur L'Héritier seemed to be glad to 'unpack his heart with words' to these friends whom he knew he could trust. So Sunday after Sunday, Pierre-Joseph, sitting there in that quiet house on the Place Vendôme, saw the Revolution through the eyes of honest, upright Monsieur L'Héritier.

It was heart-rending to recall how warmly Monsieur L'Héritier and his friends had welcomed those first revolutionary days. To them, and to many other liberal and cultivated men and women, this was to be no bloody, violent upheaval but the peaceful dawn of a new era for France. At long last, so they thought, France would have a democratic government, a parliament chosen by the people, *all* the people, and Louis XVI would go down in history as the first constitutional monarch of France, a king very like Farmer George of England. No longer would any French monarch be able to plunge his kingdom into disastrous unwanted wars, and pile up mountains of debts. No longer would any French king be able to dismiss all legal opposition to his every wish with an imperious 'C'est légal, parce que je le veux' – 'It is legal because I wish it.'

In 1789 the King announced he had decided to summon the 'States General', the ancient name for the assembly of the chosen representatives of the Church, the Nobility, and the People – in that order of diminishing importance, decidedly in that order. But Monsieur L'Héritier, obviously very satisfied to learn this, quoted the comment of a witty marquise who, on being assured that decapitated Saint Denis had walked all of six miles carrying his head in his hands, had said 'It's not the distance that matters, it's the first step that counts!'

No King of France, it seemed, had deigned to summon, much less consult, the States General since 1614. Even now, Louis XVI would certainly not have taken this step if he hadn't been faced with financial ruin. However, said Monsieur L'Héritier, this was the all-important 'first step', the one that counted.

Later on Pierre-Joseph would throw up both arms to recall how regally, with what ceremony that 'first step' was organised. As the States General had not met for so long, out from Versailles poured a flood of detailed instructions on the correct attire for the occasion.

The Cardinals, chosen to represent the Church, were to be clad from head to foot in scarlet silk and wear a surplice of fine lace. The chosen representatives of the Nobility were to be attired in black satin with waistcoats of cloth of gold, gold buttons, lace cravats, and white plumed hats. But the Third Estate, the representatives of the People, were to be soberly and befittingly dressed in plain black cloth, simple muslin cravats, no feathers in their hats, and no pretentious gold buttons, no gold trimmings of any sort.

In short, as Monsieur L'Héritier tartly commented, there was to be no democratic sartorial nonsense. The status of every representative was to be plainly evident, recognisable at a glance.

Moreover the States General, thus attired, were to meet, not in Paris, but in Versailles where the King could get on with his hunting whilst the States General between them got on with finding ways and means of raising the vast sums of money needed to save France from bankruptcy.

To all of which the King would listen, but reserve his divine right to sanction or veto.

Then, as everything had to be done with impressive ceremony, there was to be a solemn inaugural procession – in Versailles of course. Behind the Blessed Sacrament would walk the King, the Queen, every member of the Royal Family and the States General, each carrying a tall lighted candle. The Third Estate in their plain black attire would walk in the rear of that solemn procession, of course.

Then 'noblesse oblige', the little Dauphin had to be present. A truckle bed, covered with cushions, was therefore placed on a convenient flat roof, and the Dauphin was brought all the way from Meudon to lie on that truckle bed and watch this edifying procession of the nation's representatives who, with his father's royal approval, were to have the honour of saving France from bankruptcy.

When he had dutifully watched this solemn candle-lit procession, the little Dauphin was taken back to Meudon. Every movement, every jolt, must have been agony for that pain-racked child, and a month later he died in quiet Meudon, surrounded by his only delight on this earth, those pots of sweet-smelling flowers.

Marie-Marthe listening to the bells of Paris tolling for the death of the little Dauphin, crossed herself and ordered heaven to bless old Rossignol, and said for once she devoutly approved of the last words addressed to all the royal descendants of Saint Louis:

> *Fils de Saint Louis, monte, au ciel!*
> *Son of Saint Louis, ascend to heaven!*

This little son of Saint Louis would surely mount straight to heaven which was more than one could believe of many of his royal ancestors.

But life must go on, and the dead child's little brother was at once proclaimed Dauphin, heir to a most precarious throne for already the representatives of the Church, the Nobility and the People were fiercely quarrelling, and the King would be seen to fall asleep in the thick of a most passionate debate – His Majesty would be tired after a day's hunting.

On 12 July it seemed to Pierre-Joseph that all Paris was seething with angry indignation, with rumours flying fast and furious. The King, one said, was already regretting taking that 'first step' for the Third Estate was refusing to be treated as Third-Class Frenchmen. They'd had the courage to insist on one body of representatives, the National Assembly, to speak for the nation.

The King, one said, urged on by the Queen of course, was determined to crush this newly formed and dangerously democratic National Assembly – by force, if necessary. He had already ordered crack cavalry troops to encircle Versailles and Paris – most of them detestable Austrian or Prussian mercenaries.

All that Pierre-Joseph knew for certain was that Monsieur L'Héritier was one of the men entrusted to elect the deputies to this new National Assembly and that he was beginning to look haggard and grey with worry at the way things were going. As Monsieur L'Héritier saw it, one had to tackle that formidable mountain of national problems coldly, impartially, objectively, not be swept along on torrents of frenzied speeches that might well lead to senseless, unproductive violence. If ever there was a time when one needed to listen to the quiet Voice of Reason, it was now, said Monsieur L'Héritier. And in Versailles as well as Paris, and by the King and Queen as well as the National Assembly.

On a warm day that July, a fiery young writer, Camille Desmoulins, stood on a table in the garden of the Palais Royal in Paris and spoke most passionately to a great crowd of Parisians, urging them to resist all 'Turkish despotism'. Suddenly a detachment of hated mercenaries, the 'Royal German', came galloping into the garden and sent the crowd flying for their lives.

All that night and the next, the bells of Paris boomed the tocsin and no-one slept as angry crowds roamed the streets. And the following day, the fourteenth of July, the grim walls of the Bastille, the most hated prison in France, went crashing to the ground.

And sadly ironical it was to remember how all the orators and poets then burst into triumphant song, saluting the 'Fall of the Bastille' as the 'Defeat of Despotism' and the 'Dawn of Liberty'.

'Tremble ye tyrants!' sang one poet, Jacques Delille.

Monsieur L'Héritier reported that the King, if not visibly trembling, was certainly shaken by the Fall of the Bastille, and was now sanctioning every reform demanded by the National Assembly. But on every possible occasion he still slipped away and went on hunting in one or the other of the forests near Versailles.

Then this was to seem poignant later on: no-one spoke openly of Revolution. No, the National Assembly to a man always spoke of National Regeneration and sought to achieve this miracle by floods of words, thousands upon thousands of high-sounding words.

Meanwhile up and up soared the unemployment, the price of food, above all the price of bread. But wine! Now that year wine was dirt-cheap and most plentiful, and it would seem to Pierre-Joseph that there were tipsy orators ranting away in every café, on every street corner, drowning the 'Voice of Reason' in which Monsieur L'Héritier so passionately believed.

But what poor devil, thought Pierre-Joseph, felt inclined to listen to the 'Voice of Reason' with his belly full of cheap, strong wine and no bread to sober him down, and no bread to give his hungry children. And with the orators with the loudest voices bellowing that there was bread to be had in plenty in Versailles, fine white bread, and enough flour stored away to feed all Paris.

All hoarded deliberately by the Queen of course – 'the Austrian' they called her, and 'Madame Deficit', and blamed her for all the nation's woes, spitting at the very mention of her name.

The King? Oh, he was well meaning enough, but how could he know anything of their misery? Nobody told him, 'the Austrian' saw to that. And as always happens at times like this, the riff-raff, the violent extremists, began to roam the streets only too eager to demonstrate how democratic they were by looting and senseless destruction.

To combat this, to restore and maintain order, a force called the National Guard was formed, and Monsieur L'Héritier was appointed commander of the battalion for his district of Paris. Pierre-Joseph could tell that he did not relish this appointment but he accepted it as a duty.

On Tuesday 6 October that year – Pierre Joseph never forgot that date – Monsieur L'Héritier returned home very late from Versailles. Pierre-Joseph was waiting there to show him the work he had done that day, but for the very first time, Monsieur L'Héritier wearily waved it aside and sank down on a chair.

His face was grey with fatigue, and something else, something infinitely sad. It was the face of a man who sees all his high hopes for the future, all his ideals, about to be betrayed.

'Today,' he said, his voice hoarse and spent, 'today has been a nightmare . . . a nightmare.'

It seemed that the King had again slipped away from Versailles to go hunting, this time in the forest of Meudon where Pierre-Joseph, Marie-Marthe and little Josephine had spent so happy a day.

Presently a sweating dispatch-rider had come galloping through the forest in search of him. An angry mob of Parisians, thousands of them, many of them women, were marching on Versailles, every one of them armed with a weapon of some sort, pitchforks, sabres, lances, bludgeons, pokers, they were even pulling along cannons lashed on rough carts with rope, and as they went they were shouting:

'The King to Paris! The King to Paris! We want bread! Bread! We demand bread!'

The King listened in silence to this, and then turned to the gentlemen with him, and said 'Messieurs, la chasse est finie' – 'Gentlemen, the hunt is over.'

And without another word he had turned and galloped away through the autumn splendour of the forest, back to Versailles.

It was fortunate, said Monsieur L'Héritier, that he and his battalion were there in Versailles when the mob stormed in, for a group of them immediately began to attack and kill the King's Bodyguard. God only knew how, but he had managed to halt what would certainly have been a mass-murder.

Pierre-Joseph did not say so but he knew that it was not only Monsieur L'Héritier's brusque, authoritative voice, it was surely also his reputation as a just and upright magistrate that had averted that wholesale massacre.

Monsieur L'Héritier, head in his hands, said it was a nightmare procession that then set out for Paris. The King, the Queen and the terrified little Dauphin rode in a carriage that slowly crawled along with the mob yelling and singing all about it, shouting that they were bringing back 'The Baker, the Baker's wife and the Baker's boy'.

Riding ahead on horseback were two hideous women holding aloft on long pikes the heads of two of the King's Bodyguard they had murdered, God forgive them; and behind this macabre procession rumbled carts laden with sacks of flour looted in Versailles, and decked with branches torn from the lovely trees of the Petit Trianon.

In this ignominious way King Louis XVI, Queen Marie-Antoinette and the terrified little Dauphin were brought to Paris, and ordered to take up residence in the Palace of the Tuileries.

And many a time in the dark days that followed, was Pierre-Joseph to think that the hunt was indeed well and truly over. Never again was that well-meaning but weak and irresolute King to go hunting in any forest. Never again was the Queen to see her gardens of the Petit Trianon, sail in her gondola, or play at being a fairytale shepherdess or milkmaid in her costly rustic hamlet. As for that pitiful child, the four-year-old Dauphin, he was to go down in history as the 'Dauphin of the Imprisonment'. Already this was literally true for the Palace of the Tuileries was now nothing more than a prison for the Royal Family of France.

From that day on, it seemed to Pierre-Joseph that every time he sat down to a cup of coffee in a café, the very air was charged with angry rumours: 'on dit . . . on dit . . . on dit . . . ', one says . . . one say . . . one says. . . .

One said that the King's two brothers and other noble cowards who had fled abroad were inciting every monarch in Europe to send armies to subdue France.

One said that the Queen was secretly urging, imploring, her nephew, the Emperor of Austria, to invade France.

One said ... one said ... one said ..., and with every rumour the anger mounted.

Then, as if to demonstrate there was truth behind all the rumours, the Royal Family made an incredibly foolish and inept attempt to escape and seek the protection of the Austrian army already massing on the frontier. But they were recognised and arrested at midnight in the village inn of Varennes.

Nothing more humiliating than the way in which the King, the Queen, the little Dauphin and his sister, and the King's sister, were brought back to Paris. They sat huddled together in a heavy coach, exhausted, covered with dust, and this time there were no triumphant yells, no ribald singing, only silence every step of the way to the Tuileries, most ominous, sinister silence.

In April 1792, Pierre-Joseph devoutly thanked heaven for his own tranquil home for it was then that he and Marie-Marthe became the parents of another little daughter.

She was christened Marie-Louise, a good sober name, said Marie-Marthe, one she could sign with dignity when she grew old, grey and wrinkled. And having decided this, Marie-Marthe at once began to consider some more poetical, more musical name for everyday use for their second little daughter, and finally selected Adélaïde, all in rippling syllables: A-dé-la-ïde, a caress of a name for little Marie-Louise, didn't Pierre-Joseph agree?

Pierre-Joseph of course agreed, and so little Marie-Louise became Adélaïde, just as her sister, Marie-Joseph, had become Josephine.

April that year had never seemed more lovely to Pierre-Joseph, with all the trees in the Jardin des Plantes bursting into leaf and the birds singing most joyously.

But alas for France and all the high hopes of Monsieur L'Héritier, the extremists were fast gaining the upper hand, shouting down sweet spring itself, bellowing treason at all who opposed them. And finally they intimidated the weak irresolute King into declaring war against the Emperor of Austria, Francis II, Marie-Antoinette's nephew.

It was then that Pierre-Joseph saw Monsieur L'Héritier grow old overnight, and something in his face made Pierre-Joseph remember Dom Hickman. This was how he had looked, that good old monk, the day he had told Pierre-Joseph that the blast-furnace set up in the peaceful forest of Saint Hubert was to turn out cannons to blow sky-high men in far-away America.

But what could Pierre-Joseph say then? Or now? Nothing, nothing at all.

Then it came, the invasion of France, to the north by the Austrians, to the east by the Prussians; and the arrogant Prussian, General Brunswick, issued an ultimatum to the French nation: the King was to be reinstated forthwith, with full honour and power as before, or Paris would be destroyed, razed to the very ground.

It only needed this to set fire to the fury of the mob in Paris. They made straight for the Tuileries, murdered the Swiss Guards on duty there, and the Royal Family were hustled away and put under lock and key in the grim ancient prison of the Temple to await trial for treason and other crimes against the nation. And an angry wave of patriotism swept France, from town to town, from village to village. So there was no outcry, only fervent approval when it was decided to conscript every able-bodied Frenchman, and off they went by the thousand marching to fight the invaders, and as they went they sang the new revolutionary song, the battle-song composed by a young officer from Marseilles – the song that was to become the national anthem of France: 'La Marseillaise'.

By September that motley ragged army of conscripts, dressed in anything military on which they could lay hands, had sent the proud disciplined armies of Prussia and Austria reeling back again across the frontier, and then gone marching triumphantly on into Belgium.

Both victors and vanquished were soaked to the skin as day after day the rain poured down, and the cold windswept roads were strewn with thousands of French, Austrians and Prussians, dying most miserably of dysentery and tormented by vermin.

But war is war and there in Paris, Pierre-Joseph's jubilant friends were clapping him on the back, expecting him to look the picture of gratitude as they assured him that the glorious Revolutionary Army of France would soon rid his native land of the Austrians who had ruled there for many a century.

'All Belgium will soon be ours,' they said, as if this change of occupying forces would be Paradise indeed for the freedom-loving Belgians.

And very premature was all the rejoicing, the dancing, the singing in the streets of Paris. Every monarch in Europe, badly shaken by the victory of that raggle-taggle Revolutionary Army, immediately began to raise armies to invade and crush France. Far, far worse, civil war broke out in France itself and Frenchmen slaughtered Frenchmen all in the name of 'la douce France', sweet and gentle France.

It was now that Pierre-Joseph had the strangest, the most desolate experience of his life.

He was ordered to come to the Temple to paint a certain cactus about to come into flower, a cactus belonging to the Queen. Heaven only knew why the Queen had been permitted the luxury of keeping this cactus, or why she was now allowed to call in Pierre-Joseph to paint it. Stranger still, he was commanded to be there, at the Temple, paints and brushes at the ready, at half past ten that night. The cactus would begin to unfold its petals at a quarter to eleven, and it would be in full bloom at midnight, precisely at midnight.

Pierre-Joseph, very puzzled and troubled, at once went to see Monsieur L'Héritier who assured him that it was a well-established fact that many cacti had an extraordinary reputation for punctuality, though no-one had been able to explain this. So there was no known reason why this royal cactus always chose the dead of night to come into bloom. But it could confidently be expected to be in full bloom that midnight – even in a prison.

Marie-Marthe could never persuade Pierre-Joseph to talk of what he saw or heard that night. All he would say was that the Royal Family were in one airless, closely guarded room in the Temple, with no privacy whatever. And it was heart-rending to see the little Dauphin, a pale ghost of a child, starting, crying out at every sound, with his mother haggard and worn, trying to soothe and comfort him.

The cactus, thank God, lived up to its reputation for punctuality. At a quarter to eleven, it slowly began to unfold its petals, and Pierre-Joseph prepared to paint it; and the little Dauphin watching that flower slowly, gently opening, at last fell asleep.

At midnight, precisely at midnight, it was in full bloom, and Pierre-Joseph immediately began to paint it. No-one spoke until he had finished, then the Queen looked at it, and said, 'Thank you, Monsieur,' as if she was regally dismissing him. And a grinning guard marched him out saying, 'A cactus! Of all the God-forsaken flowers!'

That was all. Not another word would Pierre-Joseph say. And Marie-Marthe was often to wonder what became of that painting, the very last Queen Marie-Antoinette was to commission.

No-one knows. Maybe it was carried away by one of the guards who sold it for the price of a bottle of wine or a loaf of bread. Maybe it still hangs on some wall in Paris, its tragic history all forgotten. This, however, is certain – that cactus was the only flower that made Pierre-Joseph's heart ache just to remember it.

9

Napoleon Bonaparte

In the days when Pierre-Joseph had wandered, looking for work, along the roads of his native land, he had at times turned and hurried away, sickened to see a 'Danse Macabre' painted centuries ago along the wall of some village church. In every one a grinning skeleton, Death itself, went capering, dancing along, claiming one terrified victim after another.

It now seemed to Pierre-Joseph that cruel malicious Death went capering and dancing along the streets of Paris, and that terror and hatred danced with him. Life outside the Jardin des Plantes had become a never-ending nightmare. Nothing, no-one, was safe any more. Terror stalked everywhere.

Royalty in France had been abolished for ever, and the year 1792 declared Year One of the Republic of France; and the fanatical politician, Robespierre, was rasping 'Terror? Terror is simply prompt justice, severe and inflexible.'

'Prompt justice' with a thunderous roll of the drums drowned the King's last words as he stood on the scaffold. 'Prompt justice' sent the Queen to the guillotine, seated on a rough plank slung across a dung-cart, hands tied behind her back. 'Prompt justice' permitted that dung-cart to come to a halt at one point so that the famous portrait-painter, David, could sketch her on her way to the scaffold.

So savage, so cruel a sketch! This straight-backed woman, hands tied behind her, hair chopped off, face sunken and haggard, could this be the elegant, pleasure-loving Queen Marie-Antoinette?

Pierre-Joseph seeing a copy of this sketch in pride of place in a shop window, had turned away. Surely in the years to come, men would no longer guffaw at the sight of a woman going to her death in a dung-cart? Surely it would silence them, for with every stroke of his vindictive pencil, David had all unwittingly invested Marie-Antoinette with a moving courage and infinite dignity.

Monsieur L'Héritier and his few closest friends still spoke freely and openly before Pierre-Joseph when they met to spend an hour or two together every Sunday. It was now clear that they saw nothing but black trouble ahead. The ignominious execution of the French King and Queen would certainly outrage every monarch in Europe.

They were right. In 1793, France was again invaded by the Austrians and the Prussians. But again the raggle-taggle, the ill-equipped French army rose magnificently to the occasion. They might despise their bungling politicians quarrelling away in Paris, but they were not going to permit arrogant foreign tyrants to lay France in the dust, destroy their high hopes, their burning belief in liberty and equality for all men. And again they defeated and drove back the invading armies.

Now the Austrians had long occupied North Italy and they had again taken possession of Belgium. Authority, sitting on its backside in Paris then decreed that their victorious army should now have the honour and glory of driving the Austrians from both these territories.

But munitions, weapons of all kinds were desperately needed, so all over France, in towns and villages, arsenals were hastily set up and munition-workers toiled day and night. Even in 'charming, amiable' Meudon, they began turning out cannon-balls, fire-balls, and bullets in great ramshackle wooden sheds in the grounds, and in the ground-floor apartments of the royal château where the little Dauphin had suffered so cruelly and died.

Pierre-Joseph was moved to learn that old Rossignol, regardless of the din, the inferno all about him, was frantically bent on saving the orange trees in their rotten wooden tubs in the ornate orangery there. Now, however, he had to toil harder than ever fetching and carrying his great cans of water, for there was none in any of the artificial little streams or lake. The lead pipes that fed them had been torn up, one needed all the lead one could lay hands on for cannon-balls.

Monsieur L'Héritier said he doubted if old Rossignol had ever read the works of the great thinker and satirist, Voltaire, yet he must be the only man in 'charming, amiable' Meudon who woke every morning and doggedly quoted Voltaire to himself:

'We must work in the garden.'

It was poignant to recall later on that as old Rossignol so doggedly tended his orange trees, the English who were besieging the port of Toulon were staggered and mortified to find themselves outwitted and defeated by the brilliant tactics of an obscure and fiery little officer from Corsica with the resounding name of Napoleon Buona-parte.

'Mountains of brilliant flames!' boasted Napoleon. 'Like immense waves of the sea, turn by turn, soaring high to skies of fire and then sinking into the oceans of flames below. Oh, it was the grandest, the most sublime, the most terrifying sight the world ever beheld!'

Hastily leaving this sublime sight behind them, the English ships went sailing fast away and the Republican Army came marching into the smoking gutted port. The fiery little Corsican officer, however, was given no immediate chance to demonstrate still further his military genius. He was mortified to be rewarded with a post in the topographical department of the Republican Army in Paris, the dullest of jobs, surrounded on all sides by maps, maps, and still more maps, and no military action whatever.

And there sat the fiery little officer, hating every moment of this peaceful employment, and whiled away the leaden hours by writing the history of his native Corisca.

It was now that Robespierre and his supporters decided that 'prompt justice' demanded the head of any citizen who held danger-ously liberal or tolerant views, any one who had had cause to feel grateful to any hated aristocrat, any one who 'had not constantly manifested their attachment to the Republic'.

This gave vindictive wretches with a grudge to settle, a splendid opportunity to denounce many an innocent man or woman; and those few hours spent every Sunday with Monsieur L'Héritier and his friends became sombre indeed. No-one was safe from these infamous denunciations. André Chenier, who had proclaimed so joyously, poor poet, that Tyranny was dead; Camille Desmoulins, the young writer who had harangued the crowd that day in the gardens of the Palais Royal, both had been denounced and their heads had fallen into the bloody basket of the guillotine. The famous scientist, Lavoisier, had also been denounced and lost his head. And one Sunday, Pierre-Joseph was appalled to learn that Antoine-Auguste Parmentier too had been beheaded.

Pierre-Joseph had never met Parmentier, but he admired all he had heard of him. He had given his whole life to bettering agriculture in France. He reminded Pierre-Joseph of Sir Joseph Banks of Soho Square, London; Louis XVI had been no Farmer George, but Parmentier had succeeded in persuading him to order a field of potatoes to be planted, and to wear a potato-flower one day in his royal buttonhole and so help to silence the ignorant scoffers who swore that potatoes would poison anyone gullible enough to dig them up and cook and eat them.

Parmentier had done far more. He had planted field upon field of potatoes and left them unfenced, unguarded, so that the poor and hungry could safely pilfer them and prove for themselves that potatoes when cooked were a real food, a godsend now that bread was so wickedly dear.

But Antoine-Auguste Parmentier had hobnobbed with royalty, so the guillotine sliced off his head.

Then came shattering news. Monsieur L'Héritier had been thrown into prison and was awaiting trial!

He had been denounced by some anonymous citizen who had probably been offended by his caustic and abrupt plain-speaking. And well may the Scriptures say 'Cast thy bread upon the waters for thou shalt find it after many days,' for it was Joseph Dombey who indirectly saved Monsieur L'Héritier from the guillotine. Yes, Joseph Dombey, the gay and courageous young explorer and botanist whom Monsieur L'Héritier had saved from despair and destitution when he returned from that expedition to Chile and Peru.

But it was not official recognition of this kindly act that saved Monsieur L'Héritier. Ah no! As Monsieur L'Héritier said with quiet bitterness, gratitude was now a suspect emotion – it cluttered up the execution of 'prompt justice'. It was thought essential however that the first years of the revolution should go down to posterity with a shining reputation for encouraging all the sciences as well as 'prompt justice'. Citizen L'Héritier had therefore been reprieved so that he might finish his work on the rich herbarium Joseph Dombey had brought back from Peru – the herbarium Pierre-Joseph had helped him pack before Monsieur L'Héritier had so hurriedly left Paris with the herbarium, and sought refuge in the hospitable house of Sir Joseph Banks of Soho Square, London.

And now Monsieur L'Héritier owed his life to that very herbarium!

Joseph Dombey was never to know this. Some months previously he had managed to obtain a permit and the necessary funds to set off for the new Republic of America in search of still more plants and flowers unknown in France. But again ill fortune dogged him. A sudden tempest forced the ship in which he sailed to alter course and take shelter in a small harbour of the island of Guadeloupe. When he managed to board another ship bound for America, that ship had been captured by pirates. And they had carried off Joseph Dombey and flung him into a dark prison cell on the island of Montserrat in the West Indies. They expected to wring a handsome ransom from his anxious relatives, or failing them, from the French Government.

But no help came, no kindly ray of hope, and Joseph Dombey had died of grief, misery, heat and near starvation in that dark stifling prison cell. He had not even had the consolation of knowing that the herbarium he had brought back with so much difficulty from Peru and Chile, had saved the life of his benefactor, Monsieur L'Héritier.

It was heart-rending to think of that intrepid young botanist dying forsaken, forgotten, in that oven of a prison cell. Then

Pierre-Joseph remembered the many flowers and plants from distant lands now blooming in gardens all over Europe, thanks to Joseph Dombey.

Men, as Dom Hickman had warned Pierre-Joseph, had the most convenient of short memories, but even if they forgot the name of Joseph Dombey, those plants and flowers would surely be the best of memorials to that gay and courageous young French explorer and botanist.

Among the many women denounced by 'patriotic' citizens, and now in prison awaiting 'prompt justice', was an attractive young widow with the dangerously aristocratic name: Marie-Joseph-Rose de la Pagerie de Beauharnais. She had been born on the sunny island of Martinique and her high-born but hard-up papa had brought her to France to marry the son of an old friend, the Marquis de Beauharnais.

And a most unlovable husband he had proved to be! He was forever lecturing her, criticising her accent, her spelling, insisting she must improve her mind, leaving her at home with dry-as-dust books to study while he was out and about enjoying sparkling talk with more cultivated ladies, dancing with them at glittering balls in Versailles.

He too had been denounced, and had lost his head, and his young widow was frantic with shock and worry. Even if she was spared, she had no money and two fatherless children to support. What would become of them? Dear God, what would she do?

Sleeping on the straw of that same crowded cell was another young woman, a plain homely little woman, who did her best to comfort that young widow.

She was the niece of a Doctor Curtius who ran a popular museum of lifelike wax figures in Paris. The Doctor had discovered that his plain little niece also had a gift for wax modelling, indeed some said she outshone the good Doctor, and soon she was helping her uncle to model wax figures for that popular museum. She also had a real flair for displaying them, with rich draperies in the background, and lights playing on them in the most dramatic way whilst soft music added to the enchantment.

Pierre-Joseph had once taken Marie-Marthe to this museum, and she had declared that it was better than going to the theatre.

Doctor Curtius had always 'constantly manifested' his 'attachment to the Republic' and his niece had always dutifully obeyed her good uncle. If she had opinions of her own, she had prudently never voiced them. So what crime had she committed?

She had taught the King's sister, a most virtuous and pious spinster, Madame Elisabeth, to model in wax. Madame Elisabeth had undoubtedly been kind and generous to her, she therefore had cause to be grateful to a hated aristocrat.

She had been denounced by a jealous 'patriot' who danced and pulled comic faces to divert the audience of a small theatre near the museum of Doctor Curtius.

Fortunately the Doctor had some influence in government circles and after three months of misery in that crowded cell, she was released. But behind her, she left that attractive young widow, Marie-Joseph-Rose de la Pagerie de Beauharnais, still dreading the fatal day of 'prompt justice'.

When she and Pierre-Joseph were alone of an evening, Marie-Marthe would sometimes look at their second little daughter, Adélaïde, sleeping in her cradle and sigh that this was a fine time for the poor child to come into the world and no mistake. Everything one was used to, was being abolished. The seasons, the months, the days of the week, they had all been given fanciful new names, and there was no longer the time-honoured seven-day week. No, they now had 'decades', every 'decade' being ten of these new fancifully named days. Ironical, if you please, for one now had to labour nine days to have one day's rest.

And how could one expect the young to grow up well-mannered when one was forbidden to teach them to address their elders with a polite Monsieur, Madame, or Mademoiselle. Now a child had to be drilled into calling everyone Citizen or Citizeness, and to address them all with a familiar 'tu' and never a respectful courteous 'vous', even to the most venerable of citizens.

Citizen Pierre-Joseph Redouté said well, he always endeavoured to remember in public, or when making out a bill, that everyone in France was now a citizen or a citizeness but here, at home, one could mercifully forget all this enthusiastic abolishing.

Marie-Marthe was not to be silenced. And what about the feast-days, she demanded, the dear old feast-days they had loved to celebrate? They too had been abolished, even the most joyous of them all, especially to a child, the lovely feast-day of Christmas.

Why in heaven's name abolish all this? But heaven, of course, was no longer to be invoked. Religion had been declared 'burnt out'; it too had been abolished.

Ah well, said Marie-Marthe, Citizen Robespierre could rant and rave and abolish away, but Christianity had survived for nearly 2,000 years; it would certainly survive Citizen Maximilien Robespierre!

Marie-Marthe took good care however to voice all this only to Pierre-Joseph. A woman could have her head sliced off for treasonable talk like this.

Pierre-Joseph, listening sympathetically, said one need not let this crop of obligatory new names poison one's life. Take his Paradise on Earth for instance. When it lost its royal name, and became the Jardin des Plantes, as far as he knew not a plant, tree or flower had thereupon resentfully withered and died.

Pierre-Joseph said he was also relieved that the genial Dutchman, Citizen van Spaendonck had been spared, and that he had been officially declared to be responsible for 'The Art of Drawing and Painting all the Productions of Nature'. Unfortunately the money at the disposal of Citizen van Spaendonck was not as bountiful as the 'Productions of Nature'. So Citizens Pierre-Joseph and Henri-Joseph could no longer count as often as before on earning a useful fee for the pleasure of adding a new painting now and then to the 'Miniatures du Roi' – the 'Vellums' as one was now expected to call this royal collection.

The 'Vellums' were still stored in Versailles but one heard countless tales of the wanton destruction there of beautiful furniture, priceless pictures and books. It would be a crime if the 'Vellums' were reduced to ashes on some fanatical patriot's bonfire.

However, Pierre-Joseph came home one evening and announced that for once he had some excellent news to report. The 'Vellums' were not only safe but they had been transferred under the vigilant eyes of his good friends, Citizens van Spaendonck and Desfontaines to the best and safest place for them, the Jardin des Plantes. They were now, every volume of them, in place of honour on the shelves of the National Museum of Natural History there.

Marie-Marthe said she supposed this was a ray of sunshine, a revolutionary bouquet, one might even call it, to the memory of Gaston, Duke of Orleans, though she could well imagine how that royal gentleman would have relished it. Here Pierre-Joseph silenced her by dramatically pulling a paper from his pocket. 'That is not all', he said. 'Listen!'

It has been decreed that the Collection of plants and animals, painted from life, now in the National Museum of Natural History, must not be interrupted, and that it is essential to maintain emulation between the artists. . . .

When implored to put the rest of his news in plain French, Pierre-Joseph said he must confess that he would hardly have thought it essential for artists to be officially stimulated to vie with one another, but now emulation was going to be made financially as well as artistically worthwhile.

A guaranteed yearly sum of 6,000 francs was to be paid to the artists, judged in open competition, to be worthy of adding paintings to the 'Vellums'. And, of course, Pierre-Joseph and Henri-Joseph would be among the competitors.

Three months later Marie-Marthe was proudly proclaiming that she had always known what the result of that competition would be. Both Pierre-Joseph and Henri-Joseph had come through with flying colours. Both had been appointed 'Painters attached to the National Museum of Natural History', Pierre-Joseph for botany, Henri-Joseph for zoology.

The genial Dutchman, van Spaendonck, was still to be in over-all charge of the 'Vellums', it would still be he who decided just what new painting to add to the collection. But now Pierre-Joseph was to sign his name to his paintings of flowers, and Henri-Joseph sign his paintings of reptiles, shells, fishes, snails, worms and all the strange rest that fascinated him.

To Marie-Marthe, it wasn't only Gaston's magnificent collection that had been saved for all time, it was also the signed work of the gifted brothers, Pierre-Joseph and Henri-Joseph Redouté. This too was now safe for ever.

Three months later Pierre-Joseph received a letter from Saint Hubert that was to sadden him for many a day.

· It said that the French army had come marching in to liberate Saint Hubert from the Austrians though no-one had set eyes on an Austrian for many a long day, and Dom Spirlet, who had always been anti-French and pro-Austrian, had prudently fled.

Nevertheless the village of Saint Hubert had to be officially liberated, and liberation had to be officially paid for. So a horde of rapacious officials had moved in behind the army of liberation and a crippling contribution towards expenses had been clapped on the village. That done, the liberators set to work to requisition cattle, pigs, sheep and horses, and stores of fodder and sacks of grain.

Then as religion had been officially abolished for ever, all visible signs of it had to be removed. The liberators began by tearing down the iron crosses that had stood for centuries along the quiet country roads, the lanes, the forest tracks leading to Saint Hubert.

They then turned their attention to the ancient Basilica and the Abbey. They stripped them of pious pictures, portraits, statues, furniture, chandeliers, the tiles on the roof, the lead piping, anything and everything movable, and put the lot up for sale.

The ancient Basilica and the Abbey, so splendidly restored and decorated, regardless of cost, by the princely Dom Celestin, and then by Dom Spirlet, now stood ravaged, desolate, despoiled.

For the very first time, Pierre-Joseph was glad that his father was dead. He had worked for thirty-two years helping to decorate the ancient Basilica and the Abbey. He had died in poverty, his only worldly possessions that one small Third-Class house, the garden and three goats. But in his own merry way he had been deeply religious, he had confidently believed that he was helping to make the Basilica and the Abbey shine to the glory of God and great Saint Hubert for many a century to come.

It had all been laid waste. Thirty-two years of work, and not a picture, a portrait, an altar-piece, now remained of the work of Charles-Joseph Redouté.

And Pierre-Joseph buried his face in his hands and wept, not only for his father, but for the ancient Basilica and Abbey he had loved as a child. After a thousand years of work and prayer, the very heart of his village was dead, desolate.

At long last came the day when the citizens and citizenesses of Paris tore into the streets, laughing, singing and dancing.

The Reign of Terror was over! Robespierre, accused of plotting to become Dictator, had been given a savage dose of his 'prompt justice, severe and inflexible'. His own head had been sliced off by the guillotine.

And among the prisoners who came stumbling out into the blessed light of day was that attractive young widow with the high-sounding name, Marie-Joseph-Rose de la Pagerie de Beauharnais, weeping for joy to hug and kiss her two fatherless children.

She forgot she had no money. She had her two children, and she was free. Free! She had escaped Robespierre's 'prompt justice' in the very nick of time.

Presently a new government was elected – the strangest, the most unwieldy collection, groaned Citizen L'Héritier. It consisted of two houses of deputies. One was composed of 250 men, aged at least forty, every man of them married or a widower. These were known as the 'Ancients' as if, commented Citizen L'Héritier, matrimony and increasing age infallibly made a man a wiser politician.

The second house had 500 members so they were known as the 'Five Hundred', and every one of them was at least thirty. In short, the government of the Republic of France would no longer suffer from the disadvantages of hot-headed youth.

Then to lend them an air of wisdom and dignity, all the deputies were to wear togas as if they were so many Roman citizens.

Clad in their togas, the 'Ancients' and the 'Five Hundred' then solemnly elected 'five Directors', and as Citizen L'Héritier caustically remarked one would think to behold their five 'Directors' that they were the five principal characters in some lofty opera with a classical theme, all about to burst into heroic song.

The artist, David, of all people, had been commissioned to design the ceremonial dress of the five 'Directors'. Clad in scarlet velvet, they glittered with lavish gold embroidery, they wore wide silk sashes about their waists, silver buckles shone on their fine leather shoes and their scarlet hats were adorned with feathers.

The five 'Directors' were not the only citizens who began to delight again in fine clothes. Dandies, buttoned tightly into fantastic coats, chins buried in enormous silk cravats, began to strut around in long, pointed shoes, and more sober citizens gaping at them gave them the very name: 'Incroyables!' – 'Unbelievables!'

As for the latest feminine fashion, Marie-Marthe declared that one would imagine that modesty had now been abolished. Elegant women wore the most transparent of low-cut gowns, gauze was all the rage, and as they tripped along, they waved long-handled lorgnettes. They too had ironically been given the very name: 'Merveilleuses!' – 'Marvellous!'

And as the five velvet-clad 'Directors' and the 'Ancients' and the 'Five Hundred' delivered fine long patriotic speeches, and the 'Incroyables' and the 'Merveilleuses' strolled in the fashionable garden of the Palais Royal, the army of the Republic was still fighting the Austrians in Italy and angry rumours began to sweep Paris. Their soldiers were in rags, their boots were falling off their feet, they hadn't been paid or sent supplies for God knew how long. And there in Paris, speculators with the conscience of vultures, were making fat fortunes, and the price of food was soaring higher and higher.

.　　　.　　　.

On the evening of 16 March 1795, as Pierre-Joseph came out of the Jardin des Plantes, he was startled to see crowds of people staring at great flames from a distant fire leaping high into the sky. When night fell, that fire was still fiercely blazing, lighting up the dark sky with a vivid flood of crimson light.

Soon everyone was saying that it was Meudon that was on fire, 'charming, amiable' Meudon! All those great ramshackle wooden sheds full of bombs and kegs of gunpowder were an inferno of flame.

The next morning, the newspapers came out with the headlines: 'Full and Exact Details of the Great Fire of Meudon!' One had only to read between the lines to learn that it had been a fatal mistake to tear up the lead pipes that fed the artificial lake and little streams there. Even the most valiant of firemen cannot achieve miracles without an abundance of water, and the lake and the little streams were now as dry as the Sahara Desert. However, when morning came, the fire at last smouldered and died, but not a wooden shed remained, and the ground floor of the lovely château was gutted and black with smoke.

There was one unimportant item of news that delighted Pierre-Joseph and Marie-Marthe. Old Rossignol had assumed a splendidly convincing military authority. He had commandeered a squad of the Austrian prisoners of war who had been brought in to help fight the fire and marched them off to tug and heave his orange trees in their rotten wooden tubs to a place of safety.

And this, decided Pierre-Joseph, must have been a real pleasure to that squad of Austrians who had right willingly obeyed old Rossignol with many a deferential 'Jawohl, Herr Hauptmann!' 'Zu Befehl, Hauptmann!' Saving orange trees must have been a picnic compared with heaving out kegs of gunpowder or loads of bombs from blazing wooden sheds.

Once his orange trees were safe, old Rossignol had marched his Austrians back to help him keep the flames from reaching the orangery. And again this was a pleasure; they took axes and demolished and carried away everything inflammable about it.

And Pierre-Joseph hoped with all his heart that in the confusion old Rossignol had also managed to commandeer bread, sausage and a few bottles of wine to offer his willing, sweating Austrians.

All this while, come rain, come shine, every Sunday Pierre-Joseph still spent some hours with Monsieur L'Héritier and his few close friends. They had all rejoiced when Monsieur L'Héritier had been saved from the guillotine, but almost immediately he was again 'engulfed in a sea of troubles'. Madame L'Héritier had always understood her husband's passion for botany, she had been the most devoted, the most capable of wives and mothers. So Monsieur L'Héritier had happily left home, children, everything to her. He was therefore stricken with shock, grief and a devastating sense of loss when Madame L'Héritier, after a short illness, suddenly died. And he was left with the full responsibility of bringing up and educating his five children.

He was a conscientious man, he did his best, but he found it hard to show his children that he truly loved them. It was a bitter blow to him when his eldest son, Jacques, always a difficult young man, had packed a bag one night and left home, without a word to his father, not even an affectionate line to his brothers and sisters.

To Pierre-Joseph's mind, it was providential that Monsieur L'Héritier had so great a love for botany for now it became his only consolation. He had lost a great deal of money during the Revolution, and his great work, *Stirpes Novae*, had to be drastically cut, yet this did not prevent him from planning for the future.

He had been glad to take a minor post in the Ministry of Justice, and now as he walked from his house to the Ministry across the Place Vendôme, he began to notice the tiny plants, mosses and lichens growing in the cracks between the stones under his feet. And he began to bring specimens home with him as carefully as if they had been rare orchids, and the closer he examined them, the more they fascinated him.

All he could afford to do now was make meticulous notes but one day he would publish his findings, with illustrations by Pierre-Joseph, of course. Between them, said Monsieur L'Héritier, they would startle all other botanists with a most original book: *Flore de la Place Vendôme*.

Who knew, it might even startle and attract the attention of the heedless hundreds who daily trudged across the Place Vendôme, blind as bats to the fascinating world of tiny plants and mosses growing in the cracks in the stones beneath their feet.

Then there was still Joseph Dombey's rich herbarium. Now that was a sacred trust and Monsieur L'Héritier planned to set to work seriously on it once he had the necessary time and also the money needed to make its publication a truly handsome tribute to Joseph Dombey.

Pierre-Joseph, knowing all this, realised more and more that Monsieur L'Héritier was surely the best of friends for even now with so heavy a load of responsibility at home, so little time to devote to his own botanical work, he still took the warmest interest in all Pierre-Joseph was doing.

One day he began to talk to him about the family of plants known to botanists as Succulent Plants, ones with thick fleshy leaves but often with flowers of surprisingly delicate beauty. Monsieur L'Héritier dryly said he was well aware that Pierre-Joseph was not interested in any herbarium, no matter how valuable a comprehensive collection of dried flowers was to a botanist. So Pierre-Joseph would have a certain sympathy for these succulent plants. No botanist had ever yet succeeded in making a reliable herbarium of *them*. No matter how scientifically, how respectfully, one attempted to dry and press them for future reference, they invariably took their revenge by becoming completely unrecognisable.

It would be an excellent idea, said Monsieur L'Héritier, if Pierre-Joseph began to paint any succulent plant in bloom that he chanced to see in some greenhouse, commence a whole collection of these paintings. With the necessary Latin botanical notes, they would make a first-class, indeed unique publication, one that would be welcomed by all professional botanists and students, as well as enthusiastic garden-lovers who delighted in growing these interesting plants in the shelter of a greenhouse.

But one would have to wait to publish this, said Monsieur

L'Héritier, suddenly gloomy again, until times were better – they could hardly grow worse. Nevertheless Pierre-Joseph would be well advised to consider the idea.

Pierre-Joseph did not wait to consider the idea. He at once began to look out for succulent plants in any greenhouse in which he worked. And as always, Monsieur L'Héritier was right. They certainly were fascinating. It staggered Pierre-Joseph to discover how many of them had the same mysterious sense of time as the royal cactus that had bloomed at midnight in that dark and tragic room in the Temple. Not that they all opened at midnight. Far from it. Every one of them seemed to decide for itself just when, and for how long, it would bloom. Pierre-Joseph would come home and amaze Marie-Marthe with stories of their incredible punctuality. There was one, for instance, called the 'Candle of the Big Flower' growing in the greenhouse of a friendly gardener Pierre-Joseph knew. Year after year, this 'Big Flower' began to unfold its petals at precisely six-forty of the evening of the fifteenth of March. Always that date, always at that time. By seven o'clock it would be in full bloom, and filling the greenhouse with a lovely scent. Then slowly it would begin to fade, and by eight o'clock its short, scented life would be over and done.

Then there was another that opened its petals at eight in the morning and closed them at midday, and never mind about the sun shining bright in the sky and all the other flowers wide-open about it.

There was, it seemed, another more obliging one that chose to open at three of an afternoon and remained in full bloom until nightfall.

There was no end, said Pierre-Joseph, to the variety of time-tables for blooming determined by those independent plants. Pierre-Joseph himself hadn't the least idea of their correct Latin names; he would have to leave all that to the botanist who wrote the Latin text, if and when the chance came to publish the book.

But now he was delighted to drop everything the moment he saw a succulent plant about to bloom; and he would stand there caught up in the same eternal wonder, watching it slowly open, and suddenly he would know the moment had come. And he would sketch and paint it, his great clumsy hands moving with amazing speed and delicacy as he captured the fleeting perfection of that flower in full bloom.

It never occurred to Pierre-Joseph to think that he could not count on a franc of reward for all these paintings. He knew that Monsieur L'Héritier might never again be able to afford to bring out costly publications at his own expense. He also knew that it would be well-nigh impossible to find a publisher willing in those uncertain days to risk money on bringing out a book on succulent plants no matter how unusual and how well illustrated.

Then there would be the question of the necessary Latin text to accompany his paintings. Not only was Pierre-Joseph's Latin as elementary as a schoolboy's, but he realised, none better, that it would take a highly qualified botanist to write that text. And that botanist would expect to be paid.

Yet none of this worried Pierre-Joseph. These paintings might never bring in an extra franc but Pierre-Joseph knew they were the best work he had yet achieved. And that was all that mattered.

It was therefore just as well that Marie-Marthe could count on Pierre-Joseph's regular income as 'Painter attached to the National Museum of Natural History', and so far, thank heaven, both Pierre-Joseph and Henri-Joseph were still kept busy with other work for botanists and zoologists who even now had the money to pay them for illustrating their pamphlets and books. Otherwise a woman would have gone crazy struggling to feed and clothe her family with the cost of living forever rising.

Who could wonder that the five velvet-clad 'Directors', the 250 'Ancients' and the 'Five Hundred' were fast becoming more and more unpopular. As Monsieur L'Héritier acidly commented, they were neither loved, respected nor trusted.

How could they be, demanded Marie-Marthe. As they argued and made fine patriotic speeches, the war against Austria and England dragged on and on, and now there were no splendid consoling victories and the speculators were making even fatter fortunes as up and up rose the prices.

'God help us all!' groaned Marie-Marthe. 'A family-sized loaf of bread now costs sixty francs, and the price of a pair of shoes takes one's breath away – 1,000 francs!'

All a woman could do was pray for a miracle to save France, and whilst awaiting the miracle, pray that nobody in the family would wear holes in the soles of their shoes.

Monsieur L'Héritier gloomily shared Marie-Marthe's conviction that it would take a miracle to save France. Bankruptcy, starvation, ignominious defeat now stared the Republic in the face, and no-one had any confidence in their quarrelling, mutton-headed politicians. Presently fierce rioting broke out in the streets of Paris, and daily became more violent, more dangerous.

'Now heaven have mercy on us!' said Marie-Marthe, 'and save us from yet another glorious Revolution!'

It is dubious if heaven lent a hand in quelling the rioting in Paris, but the fiery little Corsican officer, Napoleon Buonaparte, most certainly did. He had been fuming away behind his peaceful desk in the topographical department of the army in Paris, aching for the chance to demonstrate his military genius again. This insurrection, for instance, he had worked out a foolproof strategy to crush that! If only he could get these half-wits in authority to listen to him.... !

This explains why one day very few Parisians had ever heard the name of Napoleon Buonaparte, and the next, it was on everyone's lips. Young General Buonaparte had been given his chance, and he had crushed the rioting with ruthless and lightning efficiency. And he was promptly rewarded, he was given the command of the army fighting the Austrians in Italy. All at the gallop.

Before he went he decided to marry – also at the gallop. And the story went round that late one chilly night there was an almighty banging and thundering on the door of a Parisian mayor, and a Corsican voice – no mistaking that accent – barking at him to leap out of his warm bed, light candles, get out his Marriage Register, and marry two citizens.

Only when the candles were lit did Monsieur the Mayor observe that this impatient bridegroom was a General, and the bride a most elegant and charming lady. He did not take much notice of their names at the time, but he did remark how the Corsican General stood tapping an impatient foot when the bride was required to write her names in full as the law required. As time went by Monsieur the Mayor was to re-live that whirlwind marriage a thousand times, every time adding more fanciful trimmings. But there were those two names in his Marriage Register for all the world to see:

GENERAL NAPOLEON BONAPARTE
MARIE-JOSEPH-ROSE DE LA PAGERIE
DE BEAUHARNAIS BONAPARTE

And as Monsieur the Mayor later pointed out, the bridegroom had gallantly added two years to *his* age, and the charming bride had subtracted five from hers. They were both twenty-eight.

Notice too how the impatient Corsican General had cut the Italian 'u' from his name. Bonaparte looked better than Buonaparte for a General with a brilliant career before him in the Army of France.

That night the General also cut short his bride's resounding litany of names. From that night on, she was to have a name of *his* choosing. She was to be Josephine, wife of General Napoleon Bonaparte.

Thirty-six hours later General Napoleon Bonaparte was on his way to Italy; and Pierre-Joseph was on his way to the Jardin des Plantes.

Pierre-Joseph had, of course, heard talk of all this – one would have to be deaf as a post *not* to have heard it – and on Sundays Monsieur L'Héritier and his friends would also discuss this latest slice of French history, and Pierre-Joseph would sit there and listen.

There were times as he listened when Pierre-Joseph would remember how as a boy in Saint Hubert, he had cultivated a most reprehensible gift for sitting bolt upright on his allocated space on a long wooden bench, looking the picture of earnest attention, but all the while, he would be miles away seeing the primroses, the wild lilies of the valley, the violets that forever bloomed in a secret enchanted world of his own.

Ah yes, that youthful blockhead, Pierre-Joseph Redouté, had

successfully eluded all but the most elementary of education, above all when it came to history. How ironical then that for years now, once outside his quiet home and the peaceful gardens in which he worked, there had been no escape from history, most violent history in the making. One would have to have a heart of cold stone to sit there every Sunday and not listen and share his friends' terrible anxiety for the fate of France.

Ah well, today he was on his way to the Jardin des Plantes to paint one of the humbler succulent plants, the common, everyday house-leek; and presently as he studied its fleshy leaves, its red star-like flowers, he remembered how Dom Hickman had sung its praises, saying an infusion of its leaves made an excellent gargle for people afflicted with sore throats and that one could make a soothing plaster with it to clap on a painful ulcerated leg. Last and just as beneficial, when given in judiciously small doses, it helped children suffering, poor lambs, from diarrhoea.

Pierre-Joseph, remembering all this, lovingly painted that house-leek and wished with all his heart that the ills of the quarrelling world outside the Jardin des Plantes could be healed in so homely and simple a way.

10

The Artistic and Scientific Commission

Marie-Marthe had good reason to remember the year 1796. It was then that Pierre-Joseph was officially awarded free accommodation in the ancient royal Palace of the Louvre.

Even in the old days artists under royal patronage had been given free accommodation there, and the new rulers of France had decided to continue this practical way of encouraging the Fine Arts.

Not that those thus rewarded were given any of the fine palatial rooms. They were lodged in obscure quarters where the narrow dirty corridors stank to high heaven on a hot summer's day.

But, said Marie-Marthe, one did not have to linger in those ancient dusty corridors, but just hold one's nose and hurry to one's rooms as fast as one's legs could carry one, remembering all the while that one need no longer worry about finding the money to pay the rent.

This wasn't the only break in the clouds that year. Pierre-Joseph began to return from his Sunday visits to Monsieur L'Héritier feeling far more cheerful. Even Monsieur L'Héritier was cautiously admitting that France might yet be saved – and by the fiery little Corsican, General Napoleon Bonaparte.

Already the cafés of Paris were singing his praises. One said he was positively electrifying the army in Italy. All those ugly rumours had been right. When he stormed on the scene, the men were indeed in rags, with no boots on their feet, half-starved, forced to pillage the food of the people they had come to liberate. In short they had been so abominably treated that they were smouldering with resentment.

But their new Commander had known just how to put fresh heart, fierce courage into those demoralised men. 'The Little Corporal' they called him, and soon worshipped the ground on which he trod.

'You have no weapons, no boots, no clothes, no bread!' he thundered. 'But the stores of the enemy are crammed to bursting point; all yours to take, to conquer! If you *wish* it, we can do it! Let us go!'

But the Little Corporal knew better than to rely on loot; he sent peremptory dispatches post-haste to Paris, demanding immediate supplies of food, uniforms, boots, weapons and ammunition, savagely pointing out that no army could march to victory armed with nothing but patriotic good wishes from well-fed politicians in Paris. And the five velvet-clad 'Directors' scurried to carry out his orders. They could hardly do otherwise for the Little Corporal was outwitting, out-fighting the bewildered Austrians in the most un-orthodox surprise-attacks, quick-marching his men here, quick-marching them there, making them snatch catnaps as they went, intoxicated with the heady taste of victory.

Moreover the Little Corporal was taking no notice whatever of the 'Directors'' orders to leave all peace treaties to them. He speedily concluded his own peace treaty on the spot with every wealthy Italian state or city he liberated from the Austrians. And again the 'Directors' could not look other than delighted as into jubilant Paris rolled load after load of the trophies of victory: millions in gold currency, priceless paintings, statues, a host of the art treasures of Italy, all showered, or so one said, by the grateful Italians on their liberators.

Eight months of victory upon victory in Italy, and the Little Corporal was poised to quick-march his triumphant army across the Alps and on to Vienna. It was then that the Emperor of Austria swiftly asked for peace.

That December, General Napoleon Bonaparte, garlanded with most profitable peace treaties, triumphantly returned to Paris. But as the Parisians celebrated victory, it was his wife, Josephine, as well as Napoleon, they toasted again and again. She was their idea of a woman: elegant, charming, kind and friendly. Napoleon himself had declared, 'I win battles, Josephine wins hearts.' She had certainly brought Napoleon and France the most spectacular of good fortune, so fill up the glasses and drink again to 'Josephine our Lucky Star'.

This good fortune, and above all those profitable peace treaties meant that soon there was far more money about. And one Sunday Monsieur Desfontaines, who had long been one of the small circle of Monsieur L'Héritier's friends, announced that he had welcome news for Pierre-Joseph. Not only had he found the very botanist to write the Latin text for Pierre-Joseph's collection of paintings of succulent plants, but he had found a publisher, Monsieur Garnery, who was interested enough to risk publishing it.

Before Pierre-Joseph could find words to thank him, Monsieur Desfontaines was explaining that the botanist was a young Swiss, not yet twenty, with the splendid name of Augustin-Pyramus de Candolle. Monsieur Desfontaines had been very impressed by his work when he was a student in the Jardin des Plantes. A most amiable and talented young man, Pierre-Joseph would certainly like both him and his work.

A few days later Monsieur Desfontaines brought the young botanist to take a look at Pierre-Joseph's paintings of succulent plants, and as he studied them, his young face positively shone.

'They are superb,' he breathed, and then all his delight seemed to fall from him.

'But . . . but . . . ' he stammered.

'But what?' exclaimed Monsieur Desfontaines, very taken aback.

The young botanist began to stammer that it was an honour to be asked, a real honour, but he was still so inexperienced, he doubted his ability to do justice to Pierre-Joseph's paintings.

Whereupon Monsieur Desfontaines quietly assured this engagingly modest young botanist that he had only to ask, and he, Monsieur Desfontaines, and Monsieur L'Héritier too, would willingly help him in every possible way, give him the benefit of their own long experience. And thus encouraged, Augustin-Pyramus de Candolle began work the very next day on the Latin and French text to accompany Pierre-Joseph's paintings of succulent plants.

It was infuriating! Everyone said so. France had subdued all her enemies in Europe, but there, across the narrow Strait of Dover, glowered the old enemy, England, still exasperatingly defiant, not even politely requesting the privilege of having peace-talks with victorious France.

The 'Directors', with the full approval of the 'Ancients' and the 'Five Hundred', therefore decided that General Napoleon Bonaparte should now have the honour of bringing England to her knees, and appointed him 'Commander in Chief of the Army of England'.

It was strange but it was now that quiet Henri-Joseph Redouté was startled to receive a most mysterious offer of work. He had been tranquilly earning a living, sometimes helping Pierre-Joseph to paint flowers, plants and trees for some botanical publication, though he still preferred to accept offers to paint snakes, fishes, shells, sticklebacks, and any other animal zoologists needed to illustrate their work. Pierre-Joseph now saw to it that he signed his name to all his work, but even so, he had a way of signing everything 'Redouté jeune' – 'Young Redouté' – as if he deliberately chose to live in the safe shadow of cheerful, easy-going Pierre-Joseph.

His work, however, must have spoken for itself for he came to see them one evening, his eyes bright with excitement. He began by swearing Pierre-Joseph and Marie-Marthe to secrecy, and this in itself, coming from Henri-Joseph, was enough to take their breath away. He then disclosed he had been approached by a famous scientist who said he had been given the mission of finding a team of eminent scholars, botanists, zoologists, artists, historians, writers, engineers and archaeologists who would be prepared to embark on a secret and most ambitious mission, one never before undertaken by any nation. Even its title was deliberately vague and mysterious: The Artistic and Scientific Commission.

'By the way,' the famous scientist had then said, as casual as you please, 'General Napoleon Bonaparte will be with us.'

Apart from this, Henri-Joseph had not been given the slightest hint of just where this commission would take him, or how long he would be away. But Henri-Joseph, very gratified by this flattering invitation to take part in so unusual and mysterious a mission with so distinguished a company, had at once accepted. He was now to make his own way, unobtrusively, to the port of Toulon where he would join the other members of the Commission.

Pierre-Joseph looked at his quiet retiring brother in amazement, and then slapped him on the back, crying 'Bravo, this will be a wonderful experience!' And proudly added that no Redouté ever lacked courage.

'Courage! For pity's sake!' cried Marie-Marthe. 'One would imagine Henri-Joseph was about to become the second Crusader in the family, off to fight a horde of ferocious Saracens!'

Nevertheless she warmly kissed Henri-Joseph. She was very fond of him but to Marie-Marthe's mind he was far too diffident, far too retiring. This Commission was precisely what he needed. She saw him coming home, crowned with laurels, and full of a new assurance.

Then, being Marie-Marthe, she at once secretly planned a marriage for this new, assured, successful Henri-Joseph – to the right wife, of course. No need to worry about that however. Sensible happy marriages, like painting, ran in the family.

As soon as Henri-Joseph had set off for Toulon, clothes neatly packed by Marie-Marthe, Pierre-Joseph took pen and paper, stared at the blank sheet before him, and wished to heaven he could *talk* to their brother, Antoine-Ferdinand. Talking was so much easier; letter-writing was hard labour to Pierre-Joseph. But Antoine-Ferdinand was decorating a fine mansion many miles away and he would be angry and hurt not to have a letter now from Pierre-Joseph. Moreover Henri-Joseph had made him promise to write.

Antoine-Ferdinand would be glad to learn that Henri-Joseph's work had been officially recognised but there was no shaking off the feeling that Antoine-Ferdinand would also be glad to know that those two brothers of his were in no danger of starving in a garret. It was still plain that to Antoine-Ferdinand's mind there was no lasting security in painting flowers for botany books or animals for books on zoology. Whereas, as he had so often told them, there were always rich men with town or country houses who employed expert decorators.

Presently Pierre-Joseph gave up staring at that blank white sheet of paper, summoned up his courage, and scrawled his letter to Antoine-Ferdinand underlining the sentence that ran: 'All news of this Commission must be kept a close secret.'

On 19 May 1798, a fleet of French ships quietly sailed out from Toulon and was as quietly joined by more ships from other Mediterranean ports.

On board those ships were not only all the members of the Artistic and Scientific Commission and General Napoleon Bonaparte, there was also an army of 34,000 men and 16,000 sailors. Away they sailed as if on some pleasure cruise – destination, purpose, still a well-kept secret.

On the flagship, L'Orient, was Captain Louis Casabianca and his son, aged ten, very proud and happy to be with his papa on so glorious an adventure.

Early that July, the news broke. Napoleon, in the name of the Republic of France, had seized the island of Malta, freed all the slaves, set up a provisional government, commandeered all the weapons and ammunition of the arsenal there, together with a choice selection of the richest treasures of the ancient Church of Saint John, worth at least 6,000,000 francs, so one said. All this with astonishing speed and efficiency, and then sailed away leaving the island of Malta still reeling from shock.

Hard on this came even more sensational news. Napoleon and his army, and the Artistic and Scientific Commission, had successfully landed – in Egypt! Napoleon had taken the port of Alexandria, and then promptly marched his sweating army across the desert towards Cairo. And at the foot of the ancient, awe-inspiring Pyramids he had addressed his men:

'Soldiers, from the summit of these Pyramids, forty centuries of history look down on you!'

And there, with the Pyramids apparently looking down with approval, the French had fought and won their first victory over the Mamelukes, the fierce professional warriors who had long tyrannised and exploited the down-trodden Egyptians.

Egypt, explained the newspapers, was a rich province of Turkey and these Mamelukes were supposed to collect the tribute due to His Turkish Majesty, the Sultan. But very little of the tribute they squeezed from the unhappy Egyptians was ever received by the Sultan. In fact His Turkish Majesty was eternally having trouble with the Mamelukes who not only terrorised the Egyptians, but often fought fiercely between themselves.

His Majesty, the Sultan, would certainly welcome France as an ally, a friend, and be grateful that these troublesome, arrogant Mamelukes were being taught a well-deserved lesson. As for the Egyptians, they would welcome the French as liberators sent by Allah himself.

The French nation was also informed that before Napoleon triumphantly marched on to Cairo, he had given that battle a fine dramatic name, one calculated to stir the imagination of men not only all over Europe but in far-away America as well. It was to go down in history as the 'Battle of the Pyramids'.

Very gratifying to national pride of course, but Pierre-Joseph and Marie-Marthe were naturally wondering what was happening to that Artistic and Scientific Commission and quiet Henri-Joseph. So little was then known of Egypt apart from hair-raising tales told by travellers who had narrowly escaped dying of thirst in the desert or being tortured and hacked to pieces by blood-thirsty Christian-hating Arabs.

Then came a most reassuring official announcement. Napoleon had given precise details of that vaguely named Artistic and Scientific Commission. It was to be called the Institute of Egypt and it was to have palatial headquarters in Cairo with a well-equipped library, laboratories, studios, everything that a band of experts could possibly desire.

Between them they were to make a detailed survey of Egypt, the flora, fauna, people, history, customs, crops, and monuments – in short, every facet of Egypt, past and present, was to be studied, recorded and illustrated. For the first time in history there was to be a vast and comprehensive encyclopaedia of everything Egyptian – thanks to General Napoleon Bonaparte. And far from dying of thirst in the desert, the members of the Institute were to be magnificently lodged in the palaces abandoned by the tyrannical Mamelukes and other immensely wealthy and corrupt Egyptians.

'Splendid residences, immense gardens marvellously planned, everywhere the gentle murmur of rippling streams, and the voluptuous shade of many wonderful varieties of trees', wrote one of the fortunate scientists.

Not that Henri-Joseph mentioned any of these wonders in a short letter he managed to send Pierre-Joseph and Marie-Marthe. He said he hoped all was well with them, that he was well, and his first commission was to paint the many varieties of fishes that swam in the Nile – lovely, magnificent fishes. These paintings were to be on finest vellum and a number of them would ultimately be included in the 'Vellums'. And Henri-Joseph ended by sending kisses to his two nieces, and his assurance that he was ever Pierre-Joseph and Marie-Marthe's loving brother, Henri-Joseph.

'No letter-writers, these Redoutés,' grumbled Marie-Marthe, and added that it was nevertheless a pleasure to imagine Henri-Joseph, happy as a king, painting fishes to his heart's content, and then returning to some palatial abode and strolling of an evening in beautiful gardens with the murmur of streams rippling about him, and no doubt whole choruses of nightingales singing away in the voluptuous shade of those splendid trees.

Yes, one could feel happy about Henri-Joseph.

Late that June, there was a special mention of Henri-Joseph in the well-known journal, *Le Moniteur Universel.*

It stated that Citizen Redouté had given a report on his study of the fishes of the Nile to the members of the Institute of Egypt in Cairo and at the same time he had shown them a number of the sketches and paintings he had already executed.

'The exactitude of these sketches and the accuracy of the paintings are so perfect that one believes one can *see* these animals. The beauty of his work makes it truly regrettable that forty of the paintings by this citizen when he was at Alexandria, Rosetta, and in the Delta, have been lost. He let them fall in the Nile when his horse suddenly bolted and carried him into the river.'

'Thank God he was not drowned!' cried Pierre-Joseph. 'But he must have been heart-broken to lose those paintings.'

'Never mind about the paintings,' said Marie-Marthe. 'Henri-Joseph can easily paint forty more. All that matters is that he is safe and well and that his work is so highly praised by these learned gentlemen in Cairo.'

Pierre-Joseph decided not to tell Marie-Marthe that Monsieur L'Héritier was not at all happy about this invasion of Egypt. One Sunday he had abruptly said that his friends must be well aware that he never indulged in facile optimism, and he could not persuade himself into believing that England would obligingly sit back and permit Napoleon to make a French colony of Egypt.

'It would be too dangerous for her,' said Monsieur L'Héritier. 'Egypt would make a splendid base from which to strike at England's trade with her richest colony, India.'

Moreover Napoleon had not included first-class engineers in his Artistic and Scientific Commission for nothing. He had definite plans to cut a canal through the Isthmus of Suez, and so create a new and far shorter shipping route to the fabulous Far East. This was no new idea, but Napoleon was determined to add this ambitious engineering achievement to the glory of France, for France would, of course, have full control of this strategically important Suez Canal.

'No,' said Monsieur L'Héritier, 'England will not stand idly by and permit all this.'

Monsieur L'Héritier's dark forebodings were soon to prove well-founded. When August came, the French fleet, having brought Napoleon and his army, and the Artistic and Scientific Commission, safely to Egypt, lay peacefully at anchor in the Bay of Aboukir. Not an English ship had been sighted. All was so quiet, so reassuring, that one-third of the crew had been given shore leave.

Suddenly, literally out of the blue, a squadron of English ships under the command of Rear-Admiral Horatio Nelson appeared, and all hell was let loose in that tranquil bay.

At ten that terrible night the French flagship, *L'Orient*, was set ablaze, some said deliberately by Captain Casabianca to avoid capture. All that is certain is that there was suddenly a terrific explosion and that proud ship and all aboard her were literally blown sky-high into eternity. Among them was that ten-year-old boy.

All accounts of this battle, both French and English, state that there was then a desolate silence. For all of ten minutes not a gun was fired. But war is war and the battle, the slaughter then began again.

By two the following afternoon it was all over. The French fleet had been destroyed or captured; only a few fast frigates had managed to escape to take the disastrous news back to France.

The French newspapers reporting the battle made a brief mention that the ten-year-old son of Captain Casabianca had lost his life when his father so heroically set his flagship ablaze. That was all. No French poet or writer thought the fate of that ten-year-old boy worth recording.

And this was ironical, if you please. In the years to come it was an English poet who immortalised that boy. Beautiful, high-minded Mrs. Dorothy Hemans had been very moved to read an account of the tragic death of that boy and she wrote a poem that began:

The boy stood on the burning deck . . .

Little did Mrs. Dorothy Hemans dream that as the years went by, her uplifting poem would become the most hackneyed, the most parodied poem in the English language, for the simple reason that no guffawing comedian ever paused to discover that there had indeed been a 'boy on the burning deck'. And that he had been only ten years old.

When news of the disastrous battle in Aboukir Bay arrived in France, it was hard to accept the cold truth: Napoleon, his army, and the Artistic and Scientific Commission were 'bottled up' in

Egypt; the French fleet had been wiped out; and English ships were keeping a vigilant, constant blockade to see there was no escape. And the young English Rear-Admiral, Horatio Nelson, had delivered a resounding 'quid pro quo' to Napoleon's 'Battle of the Pyramids', he had given *his* victory the immortal name: 'The Battle of the Nile'.

Pierre-Joseph was distraught. Their quiet Henri-Joseph was also 'bottled up' now in Egypt and he bitterly reproached himself. Without giving it any serious consideration, he had applauded Henri-Joseph's decision to take part in this mysterious mission. The very name of Napoleon Bonaparte ought to have warned him that this would be no peaceful mission. But no, he had at once cried 'Bravo!' – a fine irresponsible way to behave.

Marie-Marthe would have none of this. 'Henri-Joseph is thirty-two!' she cried. 'Thirty-two!' He had led far too sheltered a life. He had sensibly realised this, and he had been right to summon up the moral courage to accept the invitation to take part in this mysterious mission – without consulting anyone, not even Pierre-Joseph.

And why see everything in black, demanded Marie-Marthe. One had only to listen to the talk all about one to realise that people were quickly recovering from this terrible shock. Mark their words, the sages of the cafés and market-places were saying, the Little Corporal would again stagger the world.

The news that presently began to trickle in from Egypt, in spite of the blockade, certainly did much to confirm this consoling optimism. The Little Corporal had haughtily declared that this 'event' – the 'Battle of the Nile' indeed! – with never an English ship sailing on that river – this 'event' simply meant that he and the victorious French army would have to achieve even more than at first planned.

As for the Institute of Egypt, that was still carrying out all its schedules of work, precisely as planned.

Marie-Marthe, very relieved to hear this, said that they must now have the faith to go on picturing Henri-Joseph blissfully painting the beautiful fishes of the Nile and many other strange Egyptian animals too no doubt. In any case pessimism helped no-one. On the contrary it poisoned the blood, any sensible doctor would tell one this.

Pierre-Joseph agreed, but in his heart he prayed heaven to bolster his faith. Please God, Henri-Joseph was indeed safe and sound, peacefully painting away, not in the least dismayed at the prospect of being 'bottled up' in Egypt. And God alone knew for how long.

One day in January 1799, Pierre-Joseph came home and reverently set a slender volume on the table.

'Behold!' he cried, 'Instalment One of *Plantarum Succulentarum Historia* – "The Story of Succulent Plants".' When Marie-Marthe opened this slender volume, there on the title-page it proclaimed bold and clear that the illustrations in colour were the work of Pierre-Joseph Redouté, and the text in Latin and in French was by Augustin-Pyramus de Candolle.

True, it was a very slender volume, this Instalment One, only six pages of text and six illustrations, but there was also a Foreword by Monsieur Garnery stating there would be fifty instalments in all, and botanists and others interested were therefore advised to wait until all fifty were available before they bound them together and so secured for themselves a complete 'Story of the Succulent Plants' which undoubtedly would make botanical history.

That first instalment was an immediate success, and presently instalment followed instalment. Never before had any botanical publication had such illustrations, and time and again Pierre-Joseph was to remember his early days in Paris when the work on the Italian theatre had come to an end, and Antoine-Ferdinand had been delighted to receive other excellent offers of work. He had been so dismayed when Pierre-Joseph showed no eagerness whatever to go on working with him, and had chosen instead to work as an apprentice for a time in the workshop of the eminent engraver, Monsieur Lemarteau, because he wished to learn a new skill, the art of engraving and colour reproduction. Now Pierre-Joseph was not only reaping the reward of that apprenticeship, he had devised an even better way to reproduce illustrations in colour.

Above all, Pierre-Joseph would recall a certain day when he had silently made a solemn vow to himself in Monsieur Lemarteau's workshop, and had then laughed aloud thinking that the chance to keep that vow was never likely to come his way.

But that golden chance *had* come. He was now able to take every one of the colour reproductions of his paintings of succulent plants, and with swift, deft strokes of his brush make each one glow with life, as fresh, as delicately accurate as on the day he had dropped everything to paint it.

As for the text by Augustin-Pyramus de Candolle, Marie-Marthe declared it was worthy of Pierre-Joseph's illustrations. She could think of no higher praise than that. Admittedly she couldn't make head or tail of the Latin text, but the French text was so lively and interesting that a woman could read it with pleasure – not, to be truthful, the instructive details about sepals, petals and all the botanical rest, it was the footnotes, the incidental information this young Swiss botanist had spared no trouble to collect, that fascinated Marie-Marthe.

He too had been amazed at the extraordinary punctuality of these succulent plants. He gave the exact times at which this or that one opened and closed its petals. There was one, for instance, that opened as the sun went down, remained open all night long, and then resolutely closed its petals as dawn broke. A veritable nightingale of a succulent plant, decided Marie-Marthe.

Then there was one that grew in the freezing wastes of Siberia but when one dug it up, what a surprise! That succulent plant had roots that smelled of roses!

On the other hand there was one that came from the sunny Canary Islands. But did it have a sunny disposition? It most certainly did not! One day Augustin-Pyramus had taken a small experimental bite of one of its leaves, and not only did it taste atrociously but his tongue had been swollen for days. On another day he had accidentally brushed his hand against it and it had viciously retorted by giving him a nasty rash that had lasted for days. A malicious menace to any botanist, that succulent plant.

Marie-Marthe did not even try to memorise the names of these succulent plants – one could always find them, if necessary, in one or the other of the instalments of *The Story of Succulent Plants*. There was one exception, however, the one called 'The Candle of Peru'.

It wasn't only that this was so easy and poetical a name to remember, but it seemed this succulent plant had such long sharp thorns that the women of Peru carefully cut them off and *used* them – for knitting needles! Imagine it, cried Marie-Marthe, a thrifty Peruvian wife and mother setting off, armed with a sharp knife, to gather a supply of knitting needles. A very useful succulent plant, that 'Candle of Peru'.

In short, Marie-Marthe was fascinated by all the incidental information collected by young Augustin-Pyramus de Candolle, though she was not in the least surprised when that modest young botanist declared that the success of *The Story of Succulent Plants* owed everything to the beauty, the accuracy of Pierre-Joseph's illustrations, and if his text had added to this success, it had been a case of learning as he went.

Now that, said Marie-Marthe, explained the secret of those footnotes. One shared the young botanist's wonder and surprise as he discovered so much unusual and lively information.

But delighted as Pierre-Joseph was at the success of *The Story of Succulent Plants*, there was that one dark nagging worry at the back of his mind – what was happening to quiet Henri-Joseph, 'bottled up' in Egypt?

No, try as he might, Pierre-Joseph could not feel happy about Henri-Joseph.

11

Malmaison

All this while Pierre-Joseph's two daughter, Josephine and Adélaïde, were fast growing up. In 1798 when their quiet uncle Henri-Joseph had suddenly set out on the mysterious mission that was to take him to Egypt, Josephine reached the important age of twelve. At least, she considered it was important.

Next year she would be thirteen and if she had been a boy, she could have taken brushes and paints, a bundle of clothes, kissed her papa and maman and little Adélaïde, and set off to lead a wandering life, earning her supper and a bed for the night by painting pictures and portraits – just as her papa had done when he was thirteen.

It would be so romantic to be a wandering painter, strolling along the country lanes on a warm summer morning with all the birds singing.

Then that sensible twelve-year-old reminded herself that her papa had once said that one should always remember the old saying: 'There are two sides to every medal,' and that poets could sing themselves hoarse declaring 'a wandering life is all delight, warm sun by day, bright stars by night' but one also had to go wandering, teeth chattering, in the cold bleak days of winter. And many a time he had been glad to have a supper of black bread spread with bacon fat or a bowl of soup for his supper. He had also known what it was to sleep in a barn with an icy wind straight from Siberia blowing through all the cracks of the door. And outside in the starless darkness, owls would hoot and bats would fly.

No, Josephine would not have enjoyed that side of the medal. So it was just as well that she was a girl since girls were never permitted to become wandering painters. And she was far more fortunate than most girls. Home was not only warm and comfortable, it was also very interesting, always delightfully cluttered with papa's lovely paintings. And other people's paintings too, for to her maman's dismay, papa's artist friends would sometimes present him with one of their paintings. And up on a wall, somewhere or another, it had to go since one could not stack one's friends' paintings in some dark corner.

Then papa was the best of company. She and Adélaïde never grew tired of his stories, especially of Saint Hubert and good Dom Hickman and how they had wandered through the forests looking for the wild plants and herbs Dom Hickman needed for his medicines to cure the sick. And how once they had come across a patch of delicate white flowers, such an enchanting sight that papa had only to close his eyes to see them again. And papa would cry 'Look!' and snatch up pencil, paper and paints, and as they watched him, those lovely flowers began to bloom before their eyes.

Yet no French botanist had come across those flowers, though papa now knew many well-known botanists. He would sometimes bring some of them home, without a word of warning, and maman would fling up both arms as she and Josephine fled into the kitchen to prepare a meal for them. Papa would also sometimes bring home tired, grey-faced men who weren't well known, only very hungry. But they too were his friends and papa and maman knew how to make them feel at home, the most welcome of visitors.

Then when spring came, they would sometimes spend a whole day in the countryside outside Paris, and she and little Adélaïde would pick wild flowers very carefully and gently so as not to bruise or hurt them. Papa said that flowers were the stars of this world, a gift of the good God, and one should always handle them with tenderness, gratitude and love.

So they would wrap those wild flowers in moist grass or moss, and when they came home, before they took off their bonnets, they would carefully place them in a vase or jug full to the brim with water. And it was wonderful to see them next day, looking as fresh as when they had picked them.

Then came the great moment when papa would teach them to paint one of these flowers. He was a wonderful teacher; he never grew cross or impatient when the colours ran and nothing went right. He would wipe their eyes with his big handkerchief and say, 'Look, my treasure, I will show you.'

It was always breathtaking to watch papa painting a flower, his big hands moving so delicately, so very swiftly. Indeed it was nothing short of miraculous, and Josephine knew in her heart that she would never paint like papa. Never.

Marie-Marthe would sometimes look at her two daughters and think that Josephine was the living image of her papa – apart, thank heaven, from her hands. Pierre-Joseph never gave a thought to his enormous hands, he simply did not care, but a girl, even a sensible girl like Josephine, would be eternally trying to hide them.

As for little Adélaïde, Marie-Marthe had long decided that from all she heard, she must be very like Pierre-Joseph's mother, very gentle and quiet. And just as Pierre-Joseph had always protected his quiet brother, Henri-Joseph, so Josephine cared like a mother for little Adélaïde. It was touching to see them together, all the more so as Adélaïde was very frail and delicate, and needed much care and love.

Then thinking again of Henri-Joseph, Marie-Marthe offered up yet another State-forbidden prayer to heaven to keep an eye on delicate Henri-Joseph, still 'bottled up' by the English in far-away Egypt.

The *Story of Succulent Plants* was being so warmly received, and selling so well, that Pierre-Joseph now began to consider another family of flowers that also gave botanists a constant headache – 'Les Liliacées', the Lily Family.

As one querulous authority complained: 'No botanist can successfully conserve them in his herbarium to consult at his convenience – a very grave inconvenience.'

This alone went to Pierre-Joseph's heart. He always winced to see flowers dried and pressed to make a useful herbarium for a botanist to consult at his own convenience. He could do far better. He could begin to paint these flowers and so truly conserve them, show a botanist how they look when they grow and bloom in gardens, hothouses, or meadows. And it would be fascinating work for the Lily Family was enormous, with a bewildering variety of flowers of all colours and sizes, often looking very different, and yet all belonging to one family.

One Sunday, Pierre-Joseph began to speak of his new idea to Monsieur L'Héritier. An excellent project, said Monsieur L'Héritier, it would make a handsome and very informative publication. But beware, added Monsieur L'Héritier, not all French botanists agreed with Linnaeus, the Swedish naturalist who had spent his life setting down hard and fast laws on how plants and animals should be classified, described, and given a correct and informative Latin name. It was highly likely that some contentious gentlemen would begin to argue that Pierre-Joseph ought not have included this or that flower in *Les Liliacées*, and so spark off one of those interminable and tedious controversies so relished by dry, pedantic botanists.

Pierre-Joseph said he would be happy to allow the botanists to argue away uninterrupted by him. He was content to accept all he had learned from Monsieur L'Héritier who wholeheartedly accepted the rules set down by brilliant, orderly Linnaeus. Not only this but he himself had the honour to be a Founder Member of the Linnean Society of Paris, though for many a year meetings of any kind had been regarded as politically dangerous. They could easily become a convenient cloak for anti-government intrigues. So the Linnean Society of Paris prudently rarely met. A pity, for Pierre-Joseph much enjoyed listening to talk of flowers.

As he walked home that Sunday, Pierre-Joseph forgot the troubles of the Linnean Society of Paris, and began to see in his mind the flowers of the Lily Family he would paint. The Madonna lily, of course, the wild lily of the valley, the charming narcissus of the poet, the bluebell, the jacinth, the spring crocus, so many of the flowers he had loved to paint, when given the chance, in the days when he had trudged along the roads of his native land.

Then he would paint more than one stately amaryllis, the pride of many a hothouse; and he would wait until a strange and fascinating asphodel came into bloom in a hothouse of the Jardin des Plantes. It had been brought to France from Greece where asphodels had bloomed since time began. Monsieur L'Héritier said that legend had it that they were the favourite flower of the gods of Ancient Greece and that they bloomed perpetually in the Elysian Fields, the Abode of the Blessed after death.

Then in sharp contrast to this Elysian flower he would paint the flower of the homely garlic plant; and Pierre-Joseph recalled how his mother had always grown garlic in one corner of that small well-kept garden behind their Third-Class house. His mother, and knowledgeable Dom Hickman too, would have been staggered to learn that the homely garlic flower also belonged to the Lily Family.

Yet when he considered it, Dom Hickman, in his own way, had classified plants, herbs and flowers every bit as conscientiously as famous Linnaeus – but all according to their healing qualities of course. In one class he would include all those he had proved to be good for the stomach; in another, those that made soothing infusions for hacking coughs, or sore throats. In another he would list the ones that helped poor souls suffering from palpitations of the heart, and so on, and so on.

All most unorthodox, of course, yet just as conscientious and meticulous as the laws set down by Linnaeus. Indeed one might argue that Dom Hickman's classification was far more worth while. Then Dom Hickman had dearly loved flowers, and at times Pierre-Joseph wondered if some botanists ever paused to exclaim and wonder at the beauty of a flower before they settled their spectacles on their noses and began to dissect and classify it before they ruthlessly dried and pressed it to include it in yet another herbarium.

Tomorrow then, no later than tomorrow, Pierre-Joseph would begin work on *Les Liliacées*. He would do as he had done for the succulent plants. The moment he saw one about to come into bloom, he would forget everything else and prepare to sketch and paint it.

How pleasant too to think that he need not give a thought to finding an interested publisher. He was now earning excellent money, he was asked to contribute to every major work on botany, and it still staggered him to realise that botanists were positively eager to pay handsome sums for the privilege of illustrations by Pierre-Joseph Redouté.

From now on, he, Pierre-Joseph Redouté, would become his own publisher. He would superintend every step of the production of each instalment of his new work. As for the Latin text, there would be no difficulty about that. Augustin-Pyramus de Candolle had become his friend; he would surely be delighted to supply that. And if Candolle hadn't the time, Pierre-Joseph now knew other botanists to whom he could safely entrust the Latin and French text for *Les Liliacées*.

Pierre-Joseph, hurrying along as if he hadn't a moment to waste, pictured in his mind the first handsome instalment, with the title in capital letters:

LES LILIACEES

And walking on air, literally considering 'the lilies of the field', Pierre-Joseph at last came home, flung open the door and cried, 'Listen, Marie-Marthe, listen!'

To understand what happened next to Pierre-Joseph, we must return now to the days immediately before General Napoleon Bonaparte had set out so mysteriously for Egypt. Napoleon's wife, Josephine, had persuaded him to spare a few hours to go with her to look at a rambling old house near the tranquil village of Rueil some sixteen kilometres from Paris.

It had the most unattractive of names – Malmaison. Moreover it had been badly neglected for years and the gardens and parkland all about it had become a veritable wilderness. Napoleon, it seemed, looked at all this in stony silence, but Josephine had cried, 'We could renovate it, and lay out lovely gardens! It would be wonderful to come here from time to time away from Paris. It's what I have always longed to have – a house, a home in the countryside.'

'Anything you wish, anything,' said Napoleon. 'But later on, not now.'

But still Josephine tried to convince him that she could transform this ramshackle house into the most delightful residence, that the wilderness about it could become the most enchanting of gardens where she would grow the loveliest of flowers, trees and shrubs.

Talk as she might, all Napoleon could see was that tumbledown badly planned house surrounded by acres of wild neglected land.

He agreed that it would be pleasant to have a country house conveniently near Paris. Indeed he had already asked his brother, Joseph, to look around for a suitable small estate at a reasonable price. So let Joseph find a country house for them, one that would not need a fortune spent on it before they could live in it.

Josephine, however, had no intention whatever of allowing someone else to choose that longed-for house in the country, least of all her brother-in-law, Joseph. It was common knowledge by now that Josephine had done her charming best to win the affection of Napoleon's family but maybe she had tried too hard, for Napoleon's mother, his three sisters and four brothers, had resented her from the very start. To them she was the scheming woman whom their Napoleon had married without a word to them until it was too late – an unforgivable affront to a Corsican family. They were convinced that this elegant woman had trapped their Napoleon into marrying her.

To make the marriage even more undesirable in their eyes, Josephine had been a widow with two children by her first marriage, a boy, Eugène, and a girl, Hortense. Napoleon was absurdly fond of them both, and behaved as if he were their real father, not a step-father.

Then Josephine had no means of her own, yet before she trapped their Napoleon she had contrived to live in considerable style and comfort; she had given her two children an excellent education. How had she managed to do all this? The scandalmongers of Paris had plenty of solutions to this mystery.

The Bonapartes' admirable mother had also been left a widow, and with eight children. But she had toiled all the hours God gave to feed, clothe and educate them. She had known what it was to go down on her knees to scrub and wash their clothes in the cold water of a river. One had only to look at Josephine's delicate white hands to know she had been brought up on a tropical island, waited on hand and foot by slaves. And there in Paris, when she became a penniless widow, who had 'protected' her? Yes, who?

Ah no, this was not the woman a good Corsican son ought to have married. And she was not even pregnant yet, she was as wantonly slim as a young girl. And she was outrageously extravagant, squandered money, their Napoleon's money, like water. But their successful Napoleon doted on her, worshipped the ground she walked on, so this was not the time to open his eyes, they would have to wait. And the Bonapartes, always swift to quarrel among themselves, closed their ranks. They now had one common enemy – Josephine.

Josephine was well aware of their cold, implacable hostility, and once Napoleon had sailed away to Egypt, Paris became unbearable to her. All the Bonapartes were settling there, his brothers in excellent jobs dutifully found for them by Napoleon, and his mother and three sisters lavishly provided for, also by Napoleon. Not that they were warmly grateful. Heavens, no! Napoleon was only doing his duty to his family as a successful good Corsican son and brother was expected to do.

And now, in Napoleon's best interests, they began to spy on Josephine, lap up all manner of malicious gossip. So Josephine raised the money to pay a deposit on Malmaison – she had no difficulty at all in borrowing money now she was the wife of successful General Napoleon Bonaparte. She also pawned her jewellery and in record time she had an army of builders, decorators and gardeners, hard at work on that dilapidated house and the wilderness all about it.

The two eminent architects she engaged to carry out her plans were aghast as they listened to her. Their hair had stood on end when they made their first professional survey, and they had courteously but bluntly informed Josephine it would be far better to tear the whole place down, build a country house on the site that would be worthy of famous General Napoleon, not 'restore a badly planned, tumble-down house, a house which had been built for someone very ordinary'.

Josephine waved all this aside, she knew just what she wanted to do with Malmaison, and in an incredibly short time, and admittedly at enormous expense, that 'ordinary house' became a charming and most unusual residence, a country house after Josephine's own heart.

As for the wild neglected acres about the house, Josephine also knew just what she wanted. She loved all she had heard of great English gardens where one exclaimed with delight as one came across a rustic bridge over a little stream, or saw against the sky in the distance a grove of beautiful trees, or a lovely lake with swans sailing upon it. Nothing in the least stiff and formal about those English gardens.

Regardless of all expense she planned just such a garden. She too would have streams of clear water meandering here and there, crossed by charming little rustic bridges. Then in the right artistic setting she would have graceful marble statues, some of the many that Napoleon had brought back from Italy; and here and there she would have little summer-houses where one could sit and contemplate her idyllic garden.

Josephine also decided she must have a ruin in some secluded spot – ruins were then all the rage. But Josephine was not accepting some counterfeit ruin no matter how genuinely ancient it looked. No, Josephine had an authentic ruin removed from some derelict estate and set up again, stone by stone in Malmaison, and soon it looked as if it had been there for centuries, romantically smothered in tangles of honeysuckle and ivy.

Then she must have a hothouse in which she could grow rare and beautiful flowers – Josephine adored flowers. But her hothouse must be as unusual and elegant as the rest of her house, with marble statues and lovely velvet divans set artistically here and there so that one would feel as if one was stepping into a charming drawing room with the warm air scented with exotic, brilliant flowers that would bring back memories of her happpy, carefree childhood in the sunny island of Martinique.

When Napoleon came home from Egypt, victoriously of course, he would be astonished, delighted, full of praise for all she had achieved whilst he had been away and there would be no stormy scenes when she had to mention, at the right moment, the bills, the monumental bills awaiting settlement.

And Josephine, head full of wonderful plans for Malmaison, forgot the Bonaparte family in Paris who daily grew more righteously infuriated to learn of the lavish restoration of that 'badly planned, tumble-down house, a house which had been built for someone very ordinary'.

It was now that Pierre-Joseph stepped into the story of Malmaison, and once again this was thanks to, indirectly to be sure, but definitely thanks to his excellent friend and benefactor, Monsieur L'Héritier.

Monsieur L'Héritier had always made a point of introducing Pierre-Joseph to his friends, and among these friends was the dedicated garden-lover, Monsieur Cels. It was in the garden of Monsieur Cels that Pierre-Joseph had met the well-known botanist, Etienne Pierre Ventenat, who was working on a publication to be entitled:

DESCRIPTION OF NEW AND LITTLE KNOWN PLANTS
CULTIVATED IN THE GARDEN OF J. M. CELS

Pierre-Joseph had contributed many of the illustrations for this work, so he was not in the least surprised when Ventenat called in to see him one evening. But this time it was not to discuss more new plants in the garden of Monsieur Cels.

'I have had the honour', he announced, face shining with pride, 'to be appointed the official botanist of Malmaison! I am to describe and classify all the flowers that grow there.'

But Josephine, it seemed, also wished to have paintings of her flowers. She had heard of Pierre-Joseph, she had seen some of his work, and in a nutshell, she would be delighted to employ Pierre-Joseph Redouté.

'Think of it!' cried Ventenat, 'between us, we could bring out the most accurate and beautiful records of the flowers of Malmaison. I assure you no expense will be spared.'

Pierre-Joseph did not need to think. The very next morning, his coat well-brushed by Marie-Marthe, he set out for Malmaison.

When he returned that evening, Marie-Marthe threw up both hands imploring heaven to grant her patience for there sat Pierre-Joseph saying oh yes, he had seen Josephine, in fact they'd had a long and friendly conversation – about flowers, of course. And it was crystal-clear that she really did love flowers.

But was she really beautiful? How was she dressed? In white, thought Pierre-Joseph, yes, in white, and she had asked him a thousand questions about the famous Kew Gardens near London and all the flowers Pierre-Joseph had admired there. And it was amazing how many varieties of flowers already grew in Malmaison. Indeed Pierre-Joseph could see Malmaison becoming another Kew Gardens – but not with a pagoda for Josephine had preferred that romantic ruin.

So began the busiest, the most successful years of Pierre-Joseph's life. His days were overflowing, every one of them a delight. At times he was called upon by the friendly Dutchman, van Spaendonck, to paint another rare flower in the Jardin des Plantes. And now he would sign his name to this and be filled with a warm deep satisfaction to think that he, Pierre-Joseph Redouté, was adding to the unique collection of paintings begun so long ago by Gaston, Duke of Orleans.

He had made a start on *Les Liliacées*, and realised more and more that this had been an inspiration straight from heaven. Then from time to time he went to Malmaison to paint yet another of Josephine's flowers.

Now Josephine, like everyone else, must have been startled when she first set eyes on Pierre-Joseph. One expected to see a man who *looked* as if he painted flowers. One simply did not expect to see this thick-set man with the homeliest of faces, and an accent straight from the Belgian Ardennes. It had obviously never entered his head to think he ought to cultivate any other way of speaking. Above all she must have been staggered to see his hands. People who had never seen Pierre-Joseph, poetically decided, on seeing his flower-paintings, that he must have long, tapering fingers – 'the fingers of a fairy' as one imaginative journalist had put it, much to Pierre-Joseph's amusement.

So when they first beheld his enormous, mis-shapen hands, his stumpy fingers, they could not believe their eyes. How could one possibly paint flowers with hands like this? It was unthinkable – until they saw Pierre-Joseph at work.

Josephine was far too kind, too well mannered to show her surprise when she first met Pierre-Joseph, and now as she watched him at work she knew she had found the very artist to paint her beloved flowers. And as the days, the months sped by, Marie-Marthe declared that Josephine was also Pierre-Joseph's 'lucky star' for never before had he been so well paid and all for the joy of doing what he most loved to do. He painted every hour of daylight – and spent as fast as he painted.

Marie-Marthe and his two daughters must have all the comforts they deserved. Moreover he was still forever bringing home hungry and hard-up friends, lending them money and promptly forgetting it. No matter what he earned, money always slipped like sand between his un-fairylike fingers. But as Marie-Marthe thought that everything Pierre-Joseph did was right, Pierre-Joseph was truly the happiest of men both at work and at home.

There were, however, two dark clouds on Pierre-Joseph's sunny sky. He was very worried about Henri-Joseph, 'bottled up in Egypt', and Monsieur L'Héritier was again sorely troubled about the fate of France.

In the absence of Napoleon, their foolhardy government had sent armies to 'revolutionise' – in plain words, to annex Switzerland, the north of Italy and Holland. They had even occupied Rome and 'exiled' the Pope. His Holiness was now virtually a prisoner in France, in the small town of Valence on the banks of the Rhone.

All this had again roused the anger of the great European powers and their armies were once more on the march. France was again in grave danger of invasion.

But Monsieur L'Héritier was not only distraught at the folly of the politicians of France, he was lonely, completely lost without his wife. And his oldest son, Jacques, never came to see him, never wrote him an affectionate line. So Pierre-Joseph grieved for Monsieur L'Héritier, and never once failed to pay him the long-established Sunday visit.

Then came news that flew like wildfire from one French village to another and from town to town. Napoleon had eluded the English ships! He had escaped from Egypt on a fast French frigate and had safely landed at Fréjus, a small Mediterranean port. All the triumphant way to Paris, he was cheered, welcomed with wild enthusiasm, and the uneasy 'Five Hundred' and the 'Ancients' decided it would be prudent to meet now in the Palace of Saint Cloud near Paris.

One short month later, Napoleon, escorted by a squad of grenadiers, drums rolling, bayonets at the ready, sent the quarrelling politicians flying for their lives, some through the windows, and as they ran they hurriedly tore off the majestic Roman togas designed for them by the painter, David, and left them behind in the shrubbery.

Then General Napoleon Bonaparte was proclaimed First Consul of France and took over full charge of the government – to put it bluntly – an all-powerful dictator.

A far cry this from the free and democratic France that Monsieur L'Héritier and so many other liberal-minded men had dreamed, and died, to establish. But people everywhere were sick and weary of ten years of war and corruption in high places. The heroic armies of France were fighting magnificently in foreign lands but there at home, highwaymen were holding up innocent travellers, arrogantly robbed them before permitting them to go on their way, guffawing that they believed in equality and freedom, especially freedom – to do as they pleased.

Napoleon was 'the man of the hour', the only man who could be counted upon to restore law and order in France, and vanquish her enemies abroad.

So *vive* Napoleon, First Consul of France!

At first it seemed to Pierre-Joseph as if everyone was so busily rejoicing and celebrating the return of Napoleon that no-one spared a thought for the French army, and the Artistic and Scientific Commission he had left behind in Egypt, 'bottled up' even more vigilantly now by the disconcerted English.

Then came official and reassuring bulletins. The First Consul had left the army in the capable charge of General Kléber. As for the members of the Commission they were doing excellent work, collaborating, as planned, on the magnificent and unique work to be entitled:

DESCRIPTION OF EGYPT

So Pierre-Joseph prayed that quiet Henri-Joseph was still palatially lodged and, forgetful of time and captivity, was still happily painting the fascinating 'living creatures of Egypt'.

Then came a thunderbolt, a black and tragic day for Pierre-Joseph. Late on the evening of 16 August 1800, Monsieur L'Héritier was walking, as always, back to his home when he was suddenly set upon a few steps from his own door.

Not a cry, not a sound was heard, and presently his children who were waiting for their papa to come home, had their evening meal and were sent to bed. 'Papa must have been detained,' said the housekeeper.

As dawn broke next day, Monsieur L'Héritier's body was discovered. He had been brutally murdered, savagely hacked to death – with a sabre, the police decided.

When Pierre-Joseph heard this terrible news, he was numb with shock and grief. Who could find it in his heart to murder so upright, so honest a man?

Who? And why?

The police had no evidence, no clue whatever, but there were appalling rumours that he had been murdered by his own son, Jacques, who had suddenly left Paris and no-one knew where he had fled. Pierre-Joseph could not bring himself to believe this. It would be too cruel, too unspeakably cruel.

Monsieur L'Héritier was buried in the garden of his home in Paris, and Pierre-Joseph stood at his open grave among the many learned men, botanists, scientists, lawyers, who had come to pay their last respects. And as is the custom even today in France, they made many moving speeches. They paid tributes to Charles Louis L'Héritier de Brutelle; they spoke of his fearless and dedicated work as a lawyer, his love of botany, and the esteem in which he was held by all civilised men.

Pierre-Joseph was the last to leave that garden. He was forcing himself to face the truth. This was no nightmare. His friend was lying there, dead, buried in the garden he had loved. His children had been mercifully taken to the home of close relatives. His home now stood desolate, empty.

Never again would Pierre-Joseph come here to spend a few hours with his friend. Never again would he listen to that dry authoritative voice, encouraging, advising him.

Never again would he listen to his friend 'unpacking his heart with words', troubled and disillusioned, as one after the other, his high ideals for a democratic France were betrayed.

In the silence of the darkening garden, Pierre-Joseph recalled the red-letter day in the Jardin du Roi when Monsieur L'Héritier had first spoken to him. He relived the many hours he had spent in the library of this house where Monsieur L'Héritier had talked to him, opened wide the world of botany, and taught him to paint flowers with meticulous accuracy.

He remembered the hours they had spent together in the warm hospitable house of Sir Joseph Banks in Soho Square, London. Monsieur L'Héritier had never been a man to show his feelings but those days in England had been truly happy days for him. And Pierre-Joseph thanked God for that excellent Englishman, Sir Joseph Banks.

So many memories came crowding back and presently the moon, the stars came out and began to shine over that desolate garden.

It was late. Marie-Marthe would be growing anxious. So Pierre-Joseph turned away and began to make his way home. And behind him he left the best, the most upright of friends.

That night, Pierre-Joseph searched among his papers and found a letter he had carefully put away. It was from Monsieur L'Héritier who had been studying a new family of plants which he intended to call REDOUTEA, a great compliment to Pierre-Joseph, of course.

Pierre-Joseph was to illustrate this work and Monsieur L'Héritier had written:

> You are the inseparable associate in the task I have to accomplish. Dear Redouté, the truth of your brush, even more than its magic, will make me share perhaps the celebrity our work together will one day earn for us both.

Now their work together was over and done. And Pierre-Joseph reading that letter swore that one day he would look at some work he had done and know that this was his 'magnum opus' – the highest peak to which he would ever climb.

In that work he would acknowledge all he owed to Charles Louis L'Héritier de Brutelle.

In the days that followed Pierre-Joseph often thought how Monsieur L'Héritier had always planned to study in close detail the herbarium and notebooks which Joseph Dombey had managed with so much difficulty to bring back from Peru and Chile, and to publish at his own expense an account of the collection of new and interesting plants, so expertly dried and pressed by that enthusiastic but most unfortunate traveller.

That herbarium from Chile and Peru, thought Pierre-Joseph, already had a history that made fiction look pale. What would happen to it now? And to Monsieur L'Héritier's treasured collection of books, his pride, and his solace in many a black hour?

Pierre-Joseph later learned that the Directors of the National Museum of Natural History would have liked to acquire them all, but Monsieur L'Héritier's family refused to accept the price they offered. And his vast collection of books, second only to that of Sir Joseph Banks, was sold in lots by public auction and who can say now where Monsieur L'Héritier's well-loved books can be found?

Monsieur L'Heritier's family, however, recognised that the French government had paid the cost of Joseph Dombey's travels in Chile and Peru, and presently that herbarium was safely stored in the Museum of Natural History in Paris. There it is to this very day, and professional botanists from all over the world still come to consult it with the greatest interest.

Gay, courageous Joseph Dombey, who had died in that oven of a prison cell in Montserrat, had not risked his life in vain in Chile and Peru. The stormy story of the herbarium he had brought back with him had at last come to a happy and peaceful end. He would have asked for nothing better.

12

Les Liliacées

At times when Pierre-Joseph was painting in the garden or hothouse of Malmaison, he would hear the sound of the church bells of the nearby village of Rueil, and think no music could sound more lovely, above all when it rang across the quiet green countryside.

Not that the bells of Rueil were calling on men to pause and reflect that 'man shall not live by bread alone'. The bells of Rueil rang out to tell the time of day, nothing more. Religion had been abolished for ever in France. But no governmental decree, thought Pierre-Joseph, no power on earth could silence the call of bells to the human heart.

However, Pierre-Joseph was uncharitably astounded when it became known that Napoleon had also been moved on hearing the bells of Rueil ringing across the garden of Malmaison.

'I was taking a solitary walk,' Napoleon was later to write, 'surrounded by the silence of nature when suddenly the sound of the church bells of Rueil struck my ear. I felt very moved, so great is the influence of early habits and our education. I thought, "What an impression bells must make on simple, credulous people! Let your philosophers and theorists reply to that! The people *must* have a religion".'

Having decided this, Napoleon silenced all opposition, and promptly restored religious freedom in France. He also settled the terms of a peace treaty, the 'Concordat', with the captive Pope. And all the while, with ruthless speed and efficiency, he was also setting in order the chaotic affairs of France, everything from civil and criminal law to education.

In fact it would seem to Pierre-Joseph that the moment he stepped out of his quiet world of flowers, he heard nothing but excited comments on the latest decrees, the latest reforms of the Little Corporal, now First Consul of France.

One said he was a genius in peace as well as war. He had the most surprising, and to some the most intimidating, of long memories. And heaven how he worked! Eighteen hours a day, and not content with that he would often summon his secretaries in the middle of the night and dictate still more orders – all at the gallop.

Pierre-Joseph would cheerfully agree with Marie-Marthe that he too worked all the hours of daylight, but how tranquil was his small world! And no-one could say he ever insulted Marie-Marthe by bolting his meals in double-quick time. Whereas even when Napoleon came to spend a few days of respite at Malmaison, there was always a hurrying, a scurrying of government officials, to all of whom he rapped out commands as if they were so many grenadiers.

At times Josephine would persuade him to have a picnic under the trees by the side of one of the delightful little streams, or play a popular game such as 'prisoner's base' at which Napoleon always cheated, or so one said. Rules were for others, not for him. And one observant gardener remarked one day to Pierre-Joseph that it seemed to him that even when Napoleon joined in a game, he would be uttering an impatient if silent command to their guests: 'Enjoy yourselves! Enjoy yourselves! Don't waste time! Enjoy yourselves!'

Then back he would go to the planning of victorious peace and establishing law and order from one end of France to another.

No, Pierre-Joseph would not have thought that Napoleon would pause one day to listen to the bells of Rueil. Which, said Pierre-Joseph, showed how mistaken and uncharitable one could be.

Marie-Marthe said she thanked the good God for religious freedom as fervently as any of the cardinals singing *Te Deum* – with two orchestras playing away – on that Easter Sunday in Notre Dame. But what she could not stomach was the way speculators had immediately moved into another money-making market – the sale of prayer-books!

Satan alone knew where or how these cunning scoundrels had managed to store them against such a day, but they alone had prayer-books for sale, and poor Christian souls had to dig deep into their pockets to find the prices they demanded.

Marie-Marthe therefore congratulated herself on obstinately remaining 'simple and credulous'. She had always had the unshakeable belief, now rediscovered by Napoleon, that people *had* to have religion. So she had been deaf as a post to orders to patriotic citizens to make a bonfire of their prayer-books and thus demonstrate their belief in 'liberty, equality and fraternity'.

Now she triumphantly brought out the prayer-books she had hidden away, and among them was one that Henri-Joseph had brought with him from Saint Hubert. It was the one their mother had saved, sou by sou, to buy. Pasted on the inside cover was a naïve picture of Saint Hubert on his knees, his eyes fixed on a shining cross between the antlers of a stag – the kind of picture always carried in the packs of 'les marchands du Bon Dieu', or sold to pilgrims to Saint Hubert.

Pierre-Joseph, looking at that prayer-book, saw again his mother's face, remembered his promise to her to look after Henri-Joseph. And hoped with all his heart that his quiet brother would soon come home, safe and well, from Egypt.

But here now was Marie-Marthe saying he hadn't been listening to a word she had been saying, so she would say it all over again. One also had to be grateful to their First Consul for restoring courtesy as well as religion in France. One could now drop this bleak Citizen and Citizeness, and again teach one's children to address their elders as Mademoiselle, Monsieur, or Madame.

1802 was a memorable year. Napoleon had won such resounding victories over all the European enemies of France that England, left with no ally anywhere, and also much impressed by Napoleon's reforms, at last made peace with France. Here was a man who had restored religion, law and order in France. Travellers were safe as never before on French roads. One could respect a republic directed by such a man. As one admiring poet wrote:

He has known how to restore to France,
Her altars, her high principles, her laws,
All good and noble things.
The Universe recognises his power,
His genius is a lesson to kings.

And into Paris came crowds of visitors, all eager to see this new, orderly France. Pierre-Joseph was delighted to see so many English gentlemen and ladies drinking coffee, a glass of wine, or relishing French ice-cream in the cafés of Paris. He also saw them strolling around the Jardin des Plantes, or paying a visit to Malmaison, hoping no doubt to catch a glimpse of that remarkable First Consul, or better still for the ladies, to see his elegant wife, Josephine.

Pierre-Joseph would also notice little crowds standing on the Place de la Concorde where the heads of King Louis XVI and Queen Marie-Antoinette and so many others had fallen into the bloody basket of the guillotine. And wonder what they were thinking.

He also wondered what English visitors thought when they beheld French high-school boys being marched into their 'Lycées', every boy in military uniform, every boy a future soldier dedicated to the glory of France. Into their class-rooms they would smartly march, left-right-left-right; and begin and end every school-day to the rat-tat-tat of drums.

Such order! Such discipline! All as laid down by Napoleon, First Consul of France.

Pierre-Joseph was presently interested to learn that one woman in Paris had decided this was the opportune moment to shake the dust of orderly France from her feet and travel in the reverse direction – to England. With her she took a couple of caravans carefully packed with unique life-size wax figures and the original plaster moulds from which other unique figures had been made.

Yes, the plain, gifted niece of Doctor Curtius. She'd had enough of slaving to pay the gambling debts of her unsatisfactory husband. Her uncle was now dead, she had inherited the exhibition, lock, stock and barrel, and she felt she had every right to ship it where she pleased.

Before she went, however, she had a wonderful stroke of luck. Napoleon was always far too busy, far too impatient, to sit for any portrait. Unhappy artists had to snatch any opportunity to sketch him, positively galloping behind him so to speak. Yet at six sharp one morning, there, in the Palace of the Tuileries, sat Napoleon resigned to having his head modelled in wax.

Warm-hearted Josephine had not forgotten the plain little woman who had tried to comfort her in that crowded prison cell in the dark days of the 'Terror'. It was thanks to Josephine that she was now to have the honour of modelling a wax head of Napoleon.

That sensible little woman lost no time. She at once politely but firmly stuck two straws up Napoleon's nose, one in each nostril, explaining that this was to enable to First Consul to breathe. Then as she prepared to cover his face with plaster, she courteously assured him he need not be alarmed – it would not hurt him.

That did it! 'Alarmed!' barked Napoleon, as ferociously as he could with two straws up his nostrils. 'I would not be alarmed if you were to surround my head with loaded pistols!'

The wax head was a masterpiece – even Napoleon nodded approval. And now, off to England, packed in one of those caravans, went the original plaster mould from which it had been made. Moreover that plain little woman had organised her departure with such speed and secrecy that it was only days later that a journalist commented on the disappearance of that popular exhibition of wax figures.

When it became known that it was touring the cities of England, Marie-Marthe said she had no doubt whatever that the English would go in crowds to see that dramatic collection of wax figures. But little did Marie-Marthe, or anyone else for that matter, dream how successful that exhibition would become.

Still less did anyone dream that the name of that plain little woman would become world-famous. She was, as you must have guessed by now, Madame Tussaud.

Best of all to Pierre-Joseph, of course, the peace treaty with

England meant that the French army and the members of the Artistic and Scientific Commission, 'bottled up' so long in Egypt by the English fleet, were at last being shipped home.

Typically, almost the last to arrive was Henri-Joseph, and as they hugged and kissed him the tears came to Marie-Marthe's eyes. This was not the new confident traveller she had expected to see come swaggering in. Henri-Joseph was quieter than ever, he looked ill, he was as thin as a rake, and his eyes were in a lamentable state, very red and inflamed. He had caught, like thousands of others, the infection dismissed by Napoleon as the Egyptian Eye Disease.

Napoleon had issued instructions that those afflicted must bathe their eyes as frequently as possible and discipline themselves to stop worrying about them. Nature would do the rest.

Unfortunately ill-disciplined Nature took no orders from Napoleon, and one out of every three of the returning army and the members of the Commission came home still suffering from acute and painful inflammation of the eyes.

It was only little by little that Henri-Joseph began to talk about his three years and eight months in Egypt. Oh, yes, he had counted the days, the months, the years. Then he would hurriedly say that the work of the Commission had been admirably planned. It would certainly make history when the results were published in a magnificent book under the title of *Description of Egypt*.

All this might have been lost to France, however, Napoleon, said Henri-Joseph, had misjudged His Turkish Majesty, the Sultan. He had not been a friend and an ally; on the contrary he had resented the French 'liberation' of his rich province of Egypt. The Egyptians too had been so hostile that the members of the Commission had to go everywhere under armed escort.

Then before Napoleon slipped through the English blockade, he had left the army in the capable charge of General Kléber. But this gallant officer had been assassinated and General Menou had assumed command.

No military genius, General Menou! And to cut short an inglorious story, a combined army of Turks and English had defeated the army Napoleon had left behind in Egypt.

To the consternation of the Artistic and Scientific Commission the English demanded that 'all the Collections made by the French Republic' were to be handed over to them. The English obviously wanted to have the pleasure of displaying this 'French Collection' in their own great Museum in London. And to the Commission's horror, General Menou was quite prepared to oblige. The Sultan, by the way, wasn't in the least interested in Egyptian antiquities; he had plenty, and to spare, in Turkey. As far as he was concerned, the English could help themselves to what they pleased.

Fortunately the English commissary sent to arrange the transport of the 'French Collection' was a polite and cultivated gentleman. He was plainly taken aback when he was told that rather than hand over the results of their work, the French were prepared to burn, to destroy the lot.

'If this is the celebrity you have in mind,' said the French spokesman, 'then you can indeed count on going down in history.'

Very embarrassed by so dramatic an ultimatum, and also by the unspoken reminder that their own scientists, led by Sir Joseph Banks, had a reputation for being scrupulously fair-minded, it was decided that the English commissary should select the items which interested him most, and all the rest should be shipped to France.

Among the items shipped to England, said Henri-Joseph, was an ancient slab of black basalt unearthed at a place called Rosetta in the delta of the Nile. All its interest lay in the three inscriptions upon it. One was in Greek, the experts recognised this, but the others were in two types of Egyptian writing. The experts hoped that by studying and comparing these inscriptions, they would solve one of the world's oldest mysteries – the meaning of the inscriptions on the walls of the magnificent tombs of long-dead Egyptian kings, queens and high dignitaries. These were in hieroglyphics, a strange and beautiful kind of picture-writing. One could only stare at these hieroglyphics and wonder what message they were meant to convey.

Thanks to that slab of black basalt, now stored no doubt in some British museum, the mystery might at last be solved.

And yes, agreed Henri-Joseph, suddenly tense as if reliving a nightmare, it was a pity he had lost forty of his paintings. It seemed he had been jogging peacefully along the bank of the Nile, thinking with quiet satisfaction of the work he had done in Alexandria and Rosetta when his horse suddenly reared high on its hind legs and bolted. Startled by some sudden noise maybe, or stung by some vicious insect – there were plenty of them in Egypt – and the next moment there was Henri-Joseph floundering in the muddy waters of the Nile. When he managed to scramble to dry land again, his forty paintings were fast disappearing, carried away by the swift running current.

As Henri-Joseph's quiet voice trailed away into silence, Pierre-Joseph could see him, soaked to the skin, head between his hands, sitting on the sun-baked bank of the Nile. But all Pierre-Joseph could find to say was, 'Marie-Marthe, what about some coffee?'

Presently Henri-Joseph agreed – with a singular lack of enthusiasm – that he had at times lived in one of those palatial houses in Cairo. But he had spent most of his time far from that luxurious city. He had been sent to paint Egyptian landscapes, or some ancient ruin, or the animals and plants that struggled to exist in the sandy wastes of the desert.

Then by way of a change, he would be commissioned to sketch the pots and pans being unearthed that had been used by Egyptian women countless centuries ago. He had also sketched the ones they used today and it was remarkable how little they differed from the ones in use centuries ago.

It moved Marie-Marthe to see how patient and kind Henri-Joseph was to Josephine and Adélaïde. It was not every day that an uncle came home from the mysterious land of Egypt, and tired and ill as he was, Henri-Joseph tried to answer all their eager questions. And they listened wide-eyed, above all when he told how he had once gone with a division of the army making its way to the ruins of the ancient city of Thebes – Henri-Joseph's duty was to paint and sketch any new discovery, of course.

When dawn broke one day, they saw before them the ruins of that fabulous city – mighty columns soaring to the sky and colossal statues, their backs to the steep cliffs behind them, facing the sacred waters of the Nile. So tremendous, so awe-inspiring a sight, that the whole division had burst into loud cheers and as the bands struck up a triumphant march, every man presented arms.

A spontaneous salute to the sculptors of ancient Egypt who had known how to create those magnificent monuments, still standing there, royally defying time, sun and the scouring of sandy winds.

Some months later, Henri-Joseph, in recognition of the work he had done in Egypt, was made an associate-member of the Institute of France, given a very small pension, and presented with a silver medal. Silver, not gold.

That was all the recognition Henri-Joseph was ever to receive. Other members of the Commission knew how to be fittingly rewarded with handsome pensions, have *gold* medals pinned on their chests to fanfares of trumpets, receive the gold star of Napoleon's new Legion of Honour which was awarded not only to soldiers for outstanding bravery but also to civilians who had rendered distinguished service to France.

But not to Henri-Joseph, not quiet retiring Henri-Joseph. No-one seemed to notice how many of his paintings and sketches illustrated that history-making *Description of Egypt*. He was the only one of the Commission who was not made a member of the Legion of Honour.

This did not seem to anger him. He was too ill, too tired, to be resentful. It was as if he wanted to forget Egypt, though he did as Pierre-Joseph suggested – he kept all the originals of his sketches and paintings, wearily agreeing that they might increase in value as time went on. But by the way he agreed he seemed to be saying: 'And now, for pity's sake, let me forget Egypt!'

So Pierre-Joseph and Marie-Marthe let him forget. By now they had learnt something of the dangers, the hardships he had endured, the terrible sights he had seen – soldiers maddened with thirst trampled to death in a sudden rush to reach a well, men dying of plague tortured with evil flies, and most desolate of all, the fear that they had been abandoned, forgotten, were 'bottled up' for ever in the hostile sandy wastes of Egypt.

One can talk lightly of being homesick but no-one can understand if one has not known the misery of longing, thirsting for the cool skies, the green fields of home. To add to this mental misery there had been the physical misery of that Egyptian Eye Disease.

No, Henri-Joseph had found no happiness in Egypt, no happiness whatever, and Pierre-Joseph and Marie-Marthe saw to it that Josephine and Adélaïde asked no more questions.

Fortunately Henri-Joseph was soon offered work, and he slowly began to find peace of mind as he sketched and painted snakes, worms and snails and other animals to illustrate the publications of leading naturalists. Then at times he would be called to the Jardin des Plantes by kindly Monsieur van Spaendonck to paint another interesting animal to add to the 'Vellums'.

Pierre-Joseph thanked heaven that Henri-Joseph was kept so busy though it was heart-breaking to see him at work, his head bent so low, his eyes straining to catch every minute detail, every subtle change of colour. The Egyptian Eye Disease had obviously done grave damage to his sight.

Marie-Marthe also noticed that Henri-Joseph still signed his work:

H. J. Redouté (jeune)

He always added this 'young' as if he still wished to live in the shadow of Pierre-Joseph. Ah well, thought Marie-Marthe, if this made Henri-Joseph feel safer – even at his age – a woman had better hold her tongue. It would be wrong to nag at him, righteously telling herself it was for Henri-Joseph's own good. Nothing was more hateful than being told that unwelcome advice was for 'one's own good'.

The only 'good' she could do for Henri-Joseph was to accept him as he was, even if she did wish he would learn to stand on his own two feet. Heaven knew he too was gifted. What Henri-Joseph really needed was a good sensible wife. But these Redoutés always took their time before risking matrimony. Jeanne-Marie, Pierre-Joseph's sister, for instance, had been all of thirty-five before she made up her mind to marry.

Now when Pierre-Joseph had decided to become his own publisher, he was well aware he would have to begin by sending out a prospectus to people who might be interested in subscribing to his new work. Subscriptions to *Les Liliacées* were essential or he could end up bankrupt.

So Pierre-Joseph sat down one day to compose his Prospectus, one he would include in his first instalment under the title of 'Preliminary Discourse'.

It took Pierre-Joseph hours to compose that 'Preliminary Discourse'. He was ill at ease with formal words so he used far too many to say he alone was the proprietor of this new work, and assured subscribers that every plant in *Les Liliacées* would be 'drawn, engraved and coloured with all the fidelity science could desire'.

He pointed out that his new work would supply a much-needed want since *Les Liliacées* were the despair of botanists, naturalists and everyone else who tried to dry and press them to make a herbarium.

It would also, he felt, be of value to artistic manufacturers who liked to embellish their wares with floral decorations.

Every illustration would be accompanied by a page of text in French, which would give each flower its correct name, its history, its uses – if any – together with other necessary botanical information.

At last Pierre-Joseph decided he could not improve on that wordy 'Preliminary Discourse'; he was also heartily sick of the sight of his pen, and he briskly concluded by stating that an instalment of *Les Liliacées* would be published every six weeks, cost thirty-six francs, and each instalment would contain six illustrations and six pages of informative text. He then gave a list of addresses at which subscribers would be able to obtain their instalments, and threw down his pen with a mighty 'Ouf!' of relief.

Josephine Redouté was sixteen and Adélaïde ten when their papa began to publish instalment after instalment of *Les Liliacées*. Every instalment was so enchanting that Marie-Marthe wiped her eyes and said it made her forget the money Pierre-Joseph was lavishing on publishing his own work, though she would admit she'd had nightmares at times of the family sleeping on beds of straw, not of lilies.

Sixteen-year-old Josephine affectionately decided her poor maman need not have worried, indeed need never worry. There was no flower-painter on earth who could hold a candle to her papa. And it wasn't the money, it was the infinite love he lavished on his work that mattered.

Her papa was keeping the solemn vow he'd made when he hadn't two francs in his pocket. With swift sure strokes of his brush he gave life to all his illustrations of *Les Liliacées*, gave each flower a subtle 'something' so that it looked as if he had that moment painted it.

Josephine never tired of watching her papa at work. It was as if some unerring instinct, some inward eye flashed a message to his great powerful hands. And as Josephine watched him, she'd remembered the story told by her grandfather to his three sons, how the great painter, Chardin, had once said one used colours, but one *painted* with feeling. This 'feeling' shone in all her papa painted.

Les Liliacées was at once acclaimed a major artistic and botanical success. Naturally Pierre-Joseph was also delighted that it proved financially successful, especially when it became known that both the First Consul and his wife were subscribers, very generous subscribers. Napoleon ordered copies of a regally bound volume of sixty-two instalments to be sent to important museums and libraries all over France and Europe, and also to every European monarch, ambassador and distinguished artist.

Marie-Marthe said she too was delighted, but she had a feeling this was very clever of their First Consul. He was demonstrating that victorious France had once again become the leading patron of all the Fine Arts.

To Pierre-Joseph the best compliment of all came when Madame Josephine Bonaparte ordered copies to be sent to Sir Joseph Banks of Soho Square, London – this was how Pierre-Joseph always thought of Sir Joseph. His name was linked for ever in Pierre-Joseph's mind with that warm hospitable house in Soho Square. And Pierre-Joseph wished that Monsieur L'Héritier had lived to see the day when a copy of *Les Liliacées* stood on a shelf of the library of that friendly house.

· · ·

In 1803 Sir Joseph Banks received another beautifully bound book from Madame Josephine Bonaparte. It was the first instalment of *The Garden of Malmaison*, illustrations by Pierre-Joseph Redouté, text by Etienne-Pierre Ventenat.

Ventenat had written a 'Foreword' to this book, and Pierre-Joseph was much impressed by the eloquent way Ventenat dedicated this and all future instalments to Madame Bonaparte:

Madame,
   You have thought that a love of flowers ought not to be a sterile study . . .

How right, cried Pierre-Joseph, thinking of the dry-as-dust botanists he sometimes met.

Therefore, went on the Foreword, Josephine had brought together the rarest flowers now growing on French soil. Some had never before left the Arabian deserts or the burning sands of Egypt. But now, naturalised, classified in orderly fashion, and growing in the beautiful Garden of Malmaison, they were the kindest, the most gentle souvenirs of the conquests of her illustrious spouse, and the most amiable proof of her own studious leisure hours.

Pierre-Joseph said he had no doubt that those naturalised Egyptian flowers, now growing in Malmaison, and classified for the first time in their disorderly lives, would meet with Napoleon's full approval. But he doubted if they would go down in botanical history as 'kind and gentle souvenirs' of Napoleon's conquests.

Those Arabian deserts, the burning sands of Egypt were still there – unconquered, unconquerable.

Napoleon must have been impressed by the first instalment of *The Garden of Malmaison* for one day when Pierre-Joseph was absorbed in painting another of the flowers from the 'burning sands of Egypt', he was aware that someone was standing beside him, silently watching. And when he looked up, there stood Napoleon.

Pierre-Joseph, brush in hand, wondered if one was permitted to speak first, or if one had to wait respectfully until the First Consul saw fit to begin a conversation. However, as always, Napoleon had no time to waste. He stooped to look more closely at Pierre-Joseph's work, then barked: 'You paint well. Why do you choose to spend your time painting flowers? With your talent, and those hands, you should be painting heroic moments of history – not flowers.'

Pierre-Joseph glanced down at his enormous hands and to his amazement, heard himself say: 'Historical scenes! Ah, no! I'd have had no success whatever at that. I lack the necessary education, I wouldn't do history justice. Early on in life I agreed with Caesar that it was far better to try to be first in something one *can* do in some less exalted sphere.'

Napoleon gave him so searching a look that Pierre-Joseph had a sinking feeling that the First Consul of France did not relish great Caesar becoming a source of handy quotations for a painter of flowers. Then he must have realised Pierre-Joseph had blurted out the simple truth, and he nodded, and strode away.

Pierre-Joseph, brush still in hand, watched him go and suddenly he seemed to hear his father's voice again. This is how he had spoken, urging Pierre-Joseph to paint great scenes of history.

And it was as if Pierre-Joseph had at last found the words to defend himself, not to Napoleon, but to Charles-Joseph Redouté, his father. Then Pierre-Joseph ruefully told himself that here he was, over forty years old, and still wishing his father had lived to approve of his work, to understand that he had become a painter of flowers because this was where his heart lay.

He also remembered how good Dom Hickman had said he had but one gift – he was able, when God willed it, to heal the sick, or failing that, to give them some blessed relief from their suffering. And Dom Hickman daily prayed that heaven would never regret bestowing this one gift on so unlettered a monk.

As Pierre-Joseph saw it, he too had but one gift, and he too trusted heaven would never regret bestowing it upon him. Honours, money, were welcome indeed, he would be an ungrateful liar to deny this, but nothing could compare to the exultation of spirit he felt when he saw some lovely flower in bloom.

It was then that he knew what it was 'for that time to be lifted above earth'.

13

Painter to the Empress Josephine

It was now that fashionable ladies in Paris began to think it would be very 'high-life' if Monsieur Pierre-Joseph Redouté could be persuaded to give private lessons to them or their daughters.

Flower-painting was a ladylike and charming pursuit, 'de rigueur' in fact, if one wished to be considered accomplished. This Belgian artist was very well known, his work was altogether admirable and one said that Josephine, the wife of their all-powerful First Consul, was enchanted with his paintings of the flowers she loved to grow at Malmaison.

'Heavens above!' cried Marie-Marthe when Pierre-Joseph began to receive flattering requests to give private lessons, 'How will you find the time?'

But as usual Pierre-Joseph found the time, and began to give lessons in flower-painting, mostly to young ladies chaperoned by their richly dressed mamans. It always amused him to sense how taken aback they were when they first saw his homely face, his enormous hands, and how when he began to speak, Mesdames, their mamans, would raise their eyebrows. One simply did not expect a famous flower-painter to retain so rustic an accent.

Then, suddenly, he would know that he had them there, in the hollow of his powerful hands, as he taught them to look closely at a flower, study it, pay homage to its beauty before they dared to put pencil to paper. It was as if his own love of flowers reached out and captivated them so that they hung on his every word.

His successful friends, earning fat fees for painting portraits or

horrific battle-scenes, emphatically told him he must ask high fees
for these lessons.

'They expect it!' they insisted. 'The higher the fee, the better
value they think they receive. So why disappoint them?'

Pierre-Joseph soon recognised the cynical truth of this advice.
He also decided that even if he could never hope to make artists of
these young ladies, he at least could teach them to look at flowers
with wonder and respect.

But he achieved more than that. A few, admittedly only a few,
showed they had real talent and as time went by, Pierre-Joseph
could feel justly proud of their work.

The fees he was paid for these lessons, without a murmur of pro-
test, together with the money coming in from all his other work,
meant that Pierre-Joseph was now earning a great deal of money.
But it was always the same story, the more he earned, the more he
spent, lent, and gave away. No-one in need ever came to Pierre-
Joseph and went away empty handed.

One day Marie-Marthe decided that she really ought to convince
this generous happy-go-lucky husband of hers that it was time they
began to save some money, but on that very day he came home with
a surprise for her. It was a beautiful set of silver table-ware, everything from salt-cellars to soup ladles.

How could a woman preach economy with Pierre-Jospeh standing there, face beaming with pride to be able to buy her such a
present! Marie-Marthe's face shone too. This silver-ware would look
wonderful shining in the candle-light when she served up a meal.
So she flung her arms about Pierre-Joseph, and away flew all her
stern resolve to reform him. It was she who needed reforming. A
woman couldn't wish for a better, kinder husband.

By the end of May 1803, there wasn't an English visitor left in
Paris. They had all packed their bags and hurried back home.
France and England were again at war; peace had lasted just thirteen
months and three weeks. Pierre-Joseph found it hard to understand
why it had been necessary to declare war again – a question of who
was to occupy the island of Malta it seemed.

The French newspapers vehemently denounced 'perfidious Albion' of course. She had not kept her solemn promise to evacuate that island, hand it over to France.

But Napoleon would soon teach these English a lesson, have them down on their knees begging for peace, and life in Paris went on undisturbed – except on one bright, cold morning in December 1804.

From dawn that day the streets were lined with excited people, the cafés were packed, everyone jostled for a place from which to watch an historical procession pass on its way to Notre Dame.

Pierre-Joseph, entreated by Marie-Marthe and his two daughters, had hired a room with a window that would give them a good view of this unique procession. They arrived early and as they sat there, watching the crowds grow more and more closely packed along the route, Pierre-Joseph thought that men did indeed have obligingly short memories.

Twenty years ago it had been declared to thunderous cheers that 'Royalty was abolished for ever in France!' and off with the unpatriotic head of anyone who dared to disapprove, or was even suspected of disapproving.

Yet now the French had given a thunderous 'Oui!' when asked, by plebiscite, if they desired their First Consul, Napoleon Bonaparte, to become their Emperor with the right to leave the Crown of France to his heirs in perpetuity.

Napoleon had decided to dazzle the world with all the ancient pomp and ceremony dating back, so one said, to the coronation of the great Emperor Charlemagne, and Notre Dame had been redecorated for the occasion, restored to such splendour that one irreverent wit declared that 'God Himself would now lose His way inside.'

The procession was greeted with rapturous cheers. First came the mounted troops, men and horses glittering with splendid accoutrements. Behind them came one magnificent coach after another, each drawn by six horses, all the occupants dressed in resplendent style, and last and most regal of all came a coach that made everyone gasp. It was all glass and gold and drawn by eight horses decked in white, crimson and gold – a coach straight out of some fairytale.

Inside sat Napoleon dressed as sumptuously as any fairytale prince, in crimson velvet embroidered with gold and sparkling with diamonds, and on his head a hat adorned with superb white ostrich feathers.

By his side sat Josephine in a low cut gown of white satin, also embroidered with gold thread and sparkling with diamonds. Her white velvet cloak, gloves, and stockings were gold-embroidered too and on her head she wore a lovely diadem of pearls and diamonds.

Royalty was being restored to France in a blaze of splendour and how the crowds loved it!

That night, and for days after, a thousand tales were told of that coronation. Everything had been conducted with utmost ceremony as in the days of old – apart from two startling differences. Napoleon had not humbly prostrated himself flat on his face before His Holiness, the Pope. Neither had he given His Holiness time to set the Crown of France on his head. No, Napoleon had imperiously taken the Crown from the hands of the Pope and in one regal gesture, set it firmly on his own head.

Napoleon with his own two hands had crowned Napoleon I, Emperor of the French.

All this was fact, seen by everyone in that packed Cathedral. But one had to take with a pinch of salt the many other stories that swept Paris. The ancient solemn ceremony had seemed so interminable that even Napoleon had been seen to yawn, and then prod his nodding uncle, the Cardinal Fesch, with his sceptre. Napoleon had been heard to whisper to his brother, Joseph, 'If only our father could see us now!' Madame, Napoleon's mother, had not been there, and one wondered why. And one could not help admiring the way enterprising hawkers had managed to slip furtively and silently between the rows of shivering spectators, selling hot sausages and rolls at an outrageous price, and the way the two orchestras had managed to play away non-stop, though their teeth must have been chattering in their heads with the cold.

But all rumours aside, it was a dazzling, most theatrical coronation and everyone agreed that Josephine had looked ravishing, not a day over twenty-five though she was now forty-one. She had been dressed and 'made-up' by artists, under the watchful eye of Isabey, the famous miniature painter.

Everyone also agreed that the Bonaparte family had positively glowered to behold *their* Napoleon, the Crown of France on his head, stoop to crown Josephine as she knelt before him. On her arrival at Notre Dame, she had put on a mantle of purple velvet, lined with ermine. It was so heavy that as she rose from her knees, she could not move forward until it was lifted by the three train-bearers, Napoleon's sisters. And they maliciously and deliberately let the full weight fall on Josephine's shoulders. For a moment she was seen to stagger and Napoleon had hissed something so savage in Corsican, that his three sisters had hastily picked up the heavy train of that ermine-lined cloak and Josephine, Empress of the French, had gracefully taken her place by the side of Emperor Napoleon I.

Pierre-Joseph, thinking of all this, hoped that Monsieur L'Héritier was not turning in his grave. What would he have made of Napoleon I!

The great composer, Beethoven, made no secret of what he thought. Like many other idealists all over Europe and in Britain too, he had warmly admired Napoleon as the 'man of the hour', the man who would carry out the noble liberal ideals of the first days of the Revolution. Beethoven had therefore dedicated his new work, the 'Eroica' Symphony, to Napoleon. But when he learned of Napoleon's decision to have himself crowned, he had burst into angry tears and savagely crossed out that dedication.

Not that the new Emperor turned a hair when he heard of this. He contemptuously brushed it aside; he had far weightier matters on his mind – the invasion and conquest of England.

Pierre-Joseph could never be drawn into commenting on the new Emperor of the French, but he made no secret of the fact that he had the warmest regard and admiration for Josephine. To his mind she would make the best of empresses. She was kind, generous, gracious to everyone, and she loved flowers.

So Pierre-Joseph and Pierre-Etienne Ventenat had worked harder than ever to bring out Instalment Two of *The Garden of Malmaison* to commemorate this coronation year for Josephine. It too was acclaimed a superb botanical masterpiece. One eminent critic wrote: 'France can cite with pride the description of *The Garden of Malmaison*, in which the talents of the botanist, Ventenat, and those of the artist, Redouté, have competed to raise a worthy monument to the munificence of the Empress Josephine and the enlightened protection she gives to the sciences.'

The new Empress was swift to show her appreciation. Pierre-Joseph came home one day, kissed his wife and two daughters and then solemnly said:

'Take a look at me! Kindly take a good look at me!'

'M'm,' said Marie-Marthe, 'you don't look a day older than when you had breakfast this morning.'

Pierre-Joseph drew himself up, and said:

'Here stands Pierre-Joseph Redouté, one-time painter to Her most unhappy Majesty, Queen Marie-Antoinette, and now . . . '

'And now what?' cried Marie-Marthe. 'Don't keep us suffocating with suspense!'

'And now,' said Pierre-Joseph, 'Painter by Appointment to Josephine, Empress of the French! And this time it will not be all honour, and no pay. Ah no, from now I am to receive a most handsome yearly salary.

'So on Sunday next, we will again spend the day in Meudon, but this time we will buy a house.'

'Buy a house!' cried Marie-Marthe, unable to believe her ears.

'Buy a house,' repeated Pierre-Joseph. 'A house, with a garden and an orangery. Just as I promised you sixteen years ago.'

At dawn the following Sunday, Pierre-Joseph and Marie-Marthe set off again to spend a festive day in 'charming, amiable' Meudon, and with them went Josephine, now nearly nineteen, and Adélaïde, a frail thirteen-year-old.

Pierre-Joseph had set his heart on everything being as on that sunny day sixteen years ago. On that day, so he declared, he had worn his new title: 'Painter to Her Majesty Queen Marie-Antoinette' like a gay peacock feather stuck in his hat. Invisible to everyone else of course but he had been blissfully aware of it, even if he was also well aware that Her Majesty Queen Marie-Antoinette regarded her royal painters as so many superior lackeys necessary to the dignity of her royal household. And right royally forget to pay them.

The Empress Josephine was altogether different. She made her painters feel they were her friends, she warmly appreciated their work, and always paid them most generously. The salary that went with Pierre-Joseph's new title was to be no feather-weight. He was to be paid 18,000 francs a year. 'Think of it!' cried Pierre-Joseph, '18,000 francs a year for the joy of painting the flowers of Malmaison!'

Marie-Marthe did her best to think of it, but those 18,000 francs a year together with all the other money Pierre-Joseph was now earning made her head spin. At times she had a secret sympathy for Napoleon's thrifty, level-headed mother. It was said that on one occasion on beholding her family, decked in royal fashion, and spending as to the manner born, she had been heard to mutter, 'Pourvu que ça dure' – 'Provided it lasts.'

Pierre-Joseph had no such dark doubts. To him those extra 18,000 francs a year meant they could now buy a house in Meudon with a garden and an orangery, just as he had promised on that sunny day sixteen years ago. Moreover he was convinced that they would find this dream-house that very day.

Marie-Marthe hated to cast a shadow on his rosy optimism. She told herself that it certainly would be wonderful to have a house in Meudon where they could spend the summer months. The clean country air would be good for them all, especially for frail little Adélaïde.

Heaven preserve her though, thought Marie-Marthe, from some grand house in which she would always feel an intruder, never truly at home. No, give her something pleasant and unpretentious with a large garden about it. And never mind about an orangery as long as there was one spacious room for a studio for Pierre-Joseph, for he not only liked to keep the originals of all his own paintings, he would also cheerfully buy a painting now and then, often to help a hard-up friend, not to mention those which other artists would give him from time to time.

Yes, the Redouté family certainly could do with a roomy studio in which Pierre-Joseph could work, give lessons, and display his collection of paintings.

And what, thought Marie-Marthe, if Meudon now disappointed them; it was always a risk to 'go back on one's steps'. They might well be seeing Meudon through rose-coloured spectacles.

But Meudon was as 'charming and amiable' as ever. The sun shone in the blue sky and Pierre-Joseph sang and laughed as they climbed high in the forest, and to Marie-Marthe's relief, he never uttered a word about that house. Once again they looked down on the valley of the Seine far below, and the air was full of the scent of the fir-trees, the pines; and under their feet the grass and moss grew soft and warm.

They enjoyed an excellent meal in the same modest inn, and this too had not changed. And again Pierre-Joseph invited the innkeeper to sit down and have a friendly glass of wine with them. It was then that Pierre-Joseph casually asked if there were any vacant properties for sale in Meudon or in the tiny nearby village of Fleury.

But, said Pierre-Joseph laughing, but most emphatic, he was *not* looking for one of those fanciful, comic-opera 'cottages' with a thatched roof, and imitation cracks painted on the walls outside, all time-worn poverty without, and luxurious draught-proof rooms within. Very fashionable this type of 'cottage' just now, especially with successful actors and actresses who loved to fly from the hurly-burly of Paris to a romantically rustic retreat in the country where they could enjoy a few days' respite with every comfort.

The innkeeper guffawed, and said ah yes, there were one or two of these 'cottages' in the neighbourhood, and a sour joke they were too to poor devils with the north wind whistling on a cold winter's night through the genuine cracks of their cottage walls. But what kind of property, asked the innkeeper, had Monsieur in mind?

Monsieur said he was thinking of an older type of house, solidly built, set in a large garden, something he could turn into a comfortable home for his family. And if there was some big outhouse, all the better, as he would like to try his hand at growing a few orange trees.

The innkeeper said now let him think, and Pierre-Joseph poured him out another glass of wine to assist his thinking. And presently the innkeeper said, wait a moment, there was a property up for sale on the hillside half-way between Meudon and Fleury. Indeed one always spoke of it as Fleury-Meudon. This might possibly interest Monsieur for there was already an orangery there with a house and a coach-house, all in a convenient huddle so to speak. This was because the house had once been the living quarters of the gardeners employed on the estate of the Marquis of Mirabeau who naturally preferred these domestic quarters well out of sight of his château. A nobleman liked to have an uncluttered view from his windows.

With the house, the orangery and the coach-house went the six acres or so of land about them. But it would need money spent on it, said the innkeeper, for there hadn't been a gardener in the house, a coach in the coach-house or an orange tree in the orangery for many a long year. As for the land, well, that was now a wilderness. To be honest, would-be buyers had so far taken one look at that huddle of buildings and decided it was hopeless as it was, and that it would cost far too much to demolish it and build a suitable house on the site. And the innkeeper had heard that the lawyer in charge of the sale was now prepared to accept 18,000 francs, which was reasonable enough with land eternally soaring in value.

18,000 francs! Pierre-Joseph's face lit up like a lamp, but Marie-Marthe's heart sank like lead. She knew what Pierre-Joseph was thinking. 18,000 francs was precisely the amount of the yearly salary he was to receive from the Empress Josephine. To Pierre-Joseph, this was an omen, an indisputable, good omen. And when the time came to take the boat back to Paris that day Pierre-Joseph had a piece of paper carefully stowed away in a pocket. On it was written the name and address of the lawyer in Paris in charge of the sale of that vacant property in Fleury-Meudon.

Marie-Marthe, sitting by Pierre-Joseph's side as they sailed back to Paris, thought how fast the hours had flown as they inspected that derelict house, coach-house and orangery, and how swiftly and with what mounting excitement Pierre-Joseph and Josephine had seen the most ingenious of possibilities. They would knock down walls; they would have extra doors here and there; they would put in corridors and an extra staircase. They'd decided where the kitchen should be, the bedrooms, the sitting-room and the dining-room.

They would have two terraces, they decided, on which to sit and enjoy the air. One, outside the sitting-room, would look out on the garden but the other would be far more dramatic. It would be on the flat roof of the orangery with a charming little footbridge leading into one of the upstairs rooms.

And Pierre-Joseph was already seeing the beautiful roses he would train to climb on trellises on either side of those two terraces so that they could revel in the scent of roses as they drank their coffee on a warm summer evening.

And wasn't it fortunate that Pierre-Joseph was friendly with so many professional gardeners! They would gladly give him advice, help him to make those six acres 'blossom as a rose'. Such flowers Pierre-Joseph would grow – roses, whole beds of roses, and masses of irises, yellow, purple and blue, and a hundred other gay and lovely flowers.

Then how touching it was to think, said Josephine, that beyond one wall of the courtyard stretched the grounds of the royal château where the little Dauphin had once suffered so cruelly and died. The grounds and the château were in a sad state, abandoned, neglected for many years. But there was a door in their courtyard, push it open on its rusty hinges and one could wander for hours in those neglected grounds, discover a thousand flowers blooming wild and free.

Then think how fortunate it was that in a corner of the courtyard was a well fed by an underground stream, an endless supply of pure refreshing water.

Presently Marie-Marthe was also carried away on the bright wings of imagination and she too began to see that dream-house, the two terraces, the six acres tamed and beautifully laid out with smooth green lawns with tall trees, well-trained bushes here and there, and bed upon bed of beautiful flowers.

Then suddenly they awoke to reality. They were back again in noisy, dirty Paris.

On the Saturday of the following week Pierre-Joseph signed a contract with the lawyer in Paris and came triumphantly home, the proud possessor of a house, a coach-house, an orangery and six acres of land in 'charming and amiable' Fleury-Meudon, all for the sum of 18,000 francs.

Daylight robbery, exclaimed some of their hard-headed friends. Happy-go-lucky Pierre-Joseph had spent, in advance, every franc of his first year's salary as 'Painter to the Empress Josephine'. And for what? Three derelict buildings and six acres of wilderness, waist deep in weeds and brambles.

As the months went by, those hard-headed friends began to change their tune. In record time, Pierre-Joseph transformed those three derelict buildings into an attractive and most unusual house. True, the alterations cost a small fortune, and no professional architect in his senses would have designed such an oddly shaped house, but there was no denying that Pierre-Joseph's country house *was* delightful.

Then Pierre-Joseph's garden-loving friends readily came to his assistance and soon, though at considerable expense, those six acres became equally delightful with smooth stretches of green lawn, lovely trees, well-trimmed bushes, and beds brimming over with bright and sweet-smelling flowers. And on either side of the two terraces, roses were soon climbing, and these were Pierre-Joseph's special delight.

To Marie-Marthe it was nothing short of a miracle how everything Pierre-Joseph had imagined became reality. It was almost as if that forlorn huddle of buildings, those six wild acres, gratefully responded, and became a dream come true.

One lovely summer day two years later, when the garden was at its best, the house spick and span, and the fine new windows wide open to let in the air, a very special visitor came to that house in

Fleury-Meudon. It was the Empress Josephine, and from that day on, Marie-Marthe shared all Pierre-Joseph's warm regard for their new Empress. She admired everything, above all the garden, saying she too had known the delight of transforming a weedy wilderness into the garden of her dreams.

When she returned to Malmaison, the Empress ordered two young trees to be sent to Pierre-Joseph, a chestnut and a cedar. Both quickly took root and flourished but Pierre-Joseph was especially proud of the cedar. Year after year it grew in majesty, an evergreen souvenir of the Empress Josephine and that red-letter summer day.

And there it still grows, in Fleury-Meudon, to this very day.

14

Monsieur Renou

❈ ❈ ❈

In 1805 all the artists living rent-free in the obscure quarters of the Palace of the Louvre were requested to find forthwith other accommodation. Napoleon had given orders that the Louvre was to be converted into a vast treasure house in which to display the thousands of priceless pictures, statues, vases and a host of other rich trophies of his victorious wars.

Pierre-Joseph quickly found an expensive apartment in Paris with one enormous room he could use as a studio. This was easy enough as Pierre-Joseph did not give a thought to the cost. However, as he viewed it, he suddenly remembered his first room in Paris. High under the roof it had been with a couple of hooks on the door for his few clothes, and just space enough for a narrow bed, a table and a chair. But he had asked for nothing better. He was in Paris, he was twenty-three, and he hadn't a care, or a sou to his name. He had been happy, gay as a lark, in that small room.

But one can never recapture the heady happiness of one's shining twenties, it vanishes like dew on grass. And in this Pierre-Joseph knew no sense of loss or regret. He now knew a different happiness. He was doing the work he loved, he had a dearly loved wife and two daughters, and it gave him a warm satisfaction to surround them with every comfort, see them so spaciously lodged.

As always in these rare moments of introspection, Pierre-Joseph thought of his father and wished he had lived to see his house and garden in Fleury-Meudon, and now this fine apartment. All made possible by painting flowers with these two great ugly hands of his.

And surely also by his love of flowers. This had been no acquired love, it had stirred within him even when he was a child. And suddenly Pierre-Joseph seemed to see himself in the quiet herb gardens of the Abbey of Saint Hubert.

Ten years old, clogs on his feet, lost in enchantment before a rose-bush in full bloom and solemnly agreeing with Dom Hickman that roses were a gift from heaven, both for their beauty and the remedies one could make with them.

Then Pierre-Joseph realised that there he was smiling to himself in that spacious empty room. But there was no shaking off the strange feeling that he had been promising his solemn ten-year-old self that one day he would paint roses, all the roses that grew.

When Marie-Marthe first viewed their expensive new apartment in Paris she again resolutely suffocated the impulse to echo Napoleon's mother: 'Providing it lasts.' And thought instead of Pierre-Joseph's vast output of work.

He was now helping to illustrate a magnificent work to be published by wealthy Monsieur Duhamel whose one passion in life was trees and bushes. This work was to come out under the title, *Treatise on the Trees and Bushes that are Cultivated in the Open Air in France*. It too would be published in instalments, and take years to complete.

Then there was Pierre-Joseph's work painting the flowers of Malmaison; and a call from time to time from Monsieur van Spaendonck to paint another new flower in bloom in the Jardin des Plantes to add to the 'Vellums', not to mention the well-paid lessons he found time to give.

It amused Marie-Marthe to realise that these lessons had become 'le dernier cri', the height of fashion. Ladies loved to say nonchalantly, 'Ah yes, I adore painting flowers. I take lessons, of course, from Monsieur Redouté, Painter to the Empress.'

And all the while, Pierre-Joseph was publishing regular instalments of *Les Liliacées*, each one as successful as the last.

There was one member of this vast family of lilies that particularly interested practical Marie-Marthe. It had been discovered by a botanist in South Carolina and no-one could say its orange-yellow flowers were remarkable for their beauty, but their seeds and roots more than made up for this. When steeped in water they made a rich vermilion dye. The botanist who had discovered it had dedicated it to Monsieur L'Héritier and called it: 'L'Héritiera des Teinturiers' – 'Héritiera of the Dyers'. Not poetical maybe but the very name for this useful plant from South Carolina.

Pierre-Joseph had promptly seized this chance to pay a tribute to Monsieur L'Héritier, but he'd thought it only right and proper to phrase it as if it came not only from himself but also from the botanist who had discovered it as well as the one who would be writing the text to accompany the illustrations. So it ran:

> This plant has been dedicated to celebrated and unfortunate Héritier whose premature and tragic death was a grievous loss to his friends and the science which he cultivated with so much success. May we be permitted to seize this occasion to express our gratitude to the distinguished scholar who guided and encouraged one of us in the study of natural science and in his first attempts to paint in a way that won the approval of botanists and the approbation with which the public today honour him.

Very stately and formal, to be sure, but that was how one was expected to express one's sentiments in those days.

Marie-Marthe, thinking of all this, would again tell herself she had the best of husbands. He worked long hours every day, yet he was always so good-humoured, so generous in every way. Their house in Fleury-Meudon, their spacious apartment in Paris were most comfortably, indeed beautifully furnished. Best of all, she knew that Pierre-Joseph now met many an elegant and fascinating lady. They all liked him, but she was the only woman in his life.

Her own days too were full to overflowing. Their home was always wide open to Pierre-Joseph's many friends and to every Belgian who came on a visit to Paris. Marie-Marthe loved to keep a well-stocked larder, and prided herself that she could set a good meal on her beautifully polished table at any hour of the day and often late at night.

Yes, life was kind and good so why be a Doubting Thomas and think ungratefully: 'Providing it lasts.'

Pierre-Joseph was soon to discover that no-one could live long in Fleury-Meudon without hearing tales of that controversial writer and philosopher, Jean-Jacques Rousseau.

He had been dead these twenty-seven years, but country-folk have long memories and there were some who delighted to tell how they recalled seeing Jean-Jacques Rousseau prowling around the countryside of Fleury-Meudon – 'botanising' so they said.

There was no mistaking him, his dress had been so peculiar. He always wore a fur cap planted firmly on his head and a long robe tied about his waist with a wide belt. This bizarre attire was said to be Armenian. All Armenians were reported to enjoy the most robust of health, often living to well over a hundred, as hale and hearty as you please. And as Jean-Jacques Rousseau was exceedingly concerned about his own health, he had obviously decided that being dressed as an Armenian would be salutary for him too.

When he came to Fleury-Meudon he had just returned from England where he had a very good friend, an English 'Milady', the Duchess of Portland. A very agile 'Milady', this Duchess of Portland, who was as crazy about botany as Jean-Jacques Rousseau. Together they would tramp miles up hill and down dale in the cold damp English countryside, 'botanising' to their hearts' content.

And it wasn't the chilly English climate, the fog, the rain, that had sent Jean-Jacques Rousseau suddenly flying back to France. No, he'd had another of his terrible obsessions, convinced that he was again going to be the victim of some mysterious and sinister plot. And he couldn't set foot in Paris, the police there would have been enchanted to arrest him, throw him in jail, teach him to proclaim, 'Property is theft!'

So he had taken refuge in Fleury-Meudon in the château of the Marquis de Mirabeau, a very liberal-minded and hospitable nobleman.

Strange, when one came to think of it, the way Jean-Jacques

Rousseau for all his revolutionary views, had no scruples whatever about accepting the hospitality of the landed gentry. And who could blame him, the poor unhappy man? He was so convinced he was going to be persecuted again that he even assumed a false name during his stay in Fleury-Meudon but he couldn't make up his mind which one to adopt. At first he called himself 'Monsieur Jacques'; later on he decided to become 'Monsieur Renou'.

The secret soon leaked out. This strange gentleman, the mysterious guest of Monseigneur the Marquis, was no Armenian. He was Jean-Jacques Rousseau the writer and philosopher, now turned botanist.

The good people of Fleury-Meudon kept the secret, and not only because it would not have been wise to offend Monseigneur their Marquis. No, they'd felt a certain pride in seeing 'Monsieur Jacques' prowling over their countryside. They felt sympathetic towards a man hounded from pillar to post, forever haunted by the dark shadow of persecution because he dared to speak his mind and upset the self-righteous.

All this began to intrigue Pierre-Joseph since their house in Fleury-Meudon had once been the gardeners' quarters, the coach-house and the orangery of that liberal-minded nobleman, the Marquis de Mirabeau. So it was more than likely that Jean-Jacques Rousseau had wandered, 'botanising' over Pierre-Joseph's own six acres of land.

This made Pierre-Joseph remember the day when Monsieur L'Héritier had talked to him of Jean-Jacques Rousseau, shown him his unpretentious botany book, offered to lend it to him, saying it was very lively and unconventional, and suggested that he might like to read it and maybe illustrate it one day. But Pierre-Joseph had only been able to think of the unhappy fate of Jean-Jacques Rousseau's five illegitimate children, how he had left them, one after the other, on the steps of the Foundling Hospital. And he had made some lame excuse not to borrow that botany book, and had never given it another thought.

Now Pierre-Joseph remembered how Monsieur L'Héritier had quoted Jean-Jacques Rousseau's 'cri-de-coeur':

'My dialogue with plants came only after humanity had refused me its companionship.'

He also recalled how Monsieur L'Héritier, who was never given to easy sentimentality, had quietly added that the only peaceful, happy hours Jean-Jacques Rousseau had ever known were those he spent 'botanising' in the countryside. And now it moved Pierre-Joseph to imagine that unhappy, quarrelsome man, in whom heaven had short-sightedly packed far too many gifts, wandering and finding peace and contentment as he 'botanised' in tranquil Fleury-Meudon.

It was still a penance for Pierre-Joseph to make himself read any botany book, but he obtained a copy of *Letters on Botany* and began to read it.

Monsieur L'Héritier had been right. It certainly was the most lively and unusual of botany books. In fact it was not a conventional textbook at all; it was precisely what the title said – a collection of letters written from time to time by Jean-Jacques Rousseau, some to a lady who wished her young daughter, Madelon, to take an intelligent interest in botany, some to Madame, the agile Duchess of Portland, and some to other botanists whom Rousseau had met at one time or another. And finally, as an afterthought, he had tacked on what he correctly called:

FRAGMENT FOR A DICTIONARY OF TERMS USED IN
BOTANY

Definitely the most haphazard of botany books. But as he read on, Pierre-Joseph began to have an unexpected feeling of sympathy, even admiration, for outspoken Jean-Jacques Rousseau. He never minced his words, especially when expressing his opinion on botanists who wrote exasperatingly learned books to impress other botanists, and never deigned to spare a thought for the eager would-be botanist.

Jean-Jacques also caustically dismissed learned botanists who only thought a plant or flower worthy of consideration if it was mentioned by Aristotle or some other long-dead Greek or Latin authority. He was equally contemptuous of erudite botanists who when asked to name a flower took a deep breath and began to recite a long litany of Latin names, for all the world as if uttering some magic incantation. These same botanists, declared Jean-Jacques Rousseau, could chant their way around the Jardin des Plantes, declaiming litanies of the Latin names of all the exotic or rare plants growing there, but set them down in a meadow or forest and they would not be able to recognise, much less give an everyday name to any wild flower growing there.

And this went straight to Pierre-Joseph's heart – Madelon was instructed 'to read nature, not books'. She was to take country walks and learn to recognise flowers and plants, and only then, begin to learn their simple, everyday names.

'Take a lily', commanded Jean-Jacques Rousseau, and went on to give clear instructions on what Madelon was to observe in this first study of a flower.

'Take a lily. . . . ' How strange to read these three words at the very time Pierre-Joseph was bringing out instalment after instalment of *Les Liliacées*, because he too had said one day:

'Take a lily. . . . '

Then Jean-Jacques Rousseau had an engaging way of mixing botany with news of himself, his aches and pains, together with inquiries about his friends and their aches and pains, not to mention a sprinkling here and there of condolences or congratulations, as well as details of his struggle to improve his knowledge of botany.

Such disasters befell poor Jean-Jacques Rousseau! He had once spread some precious seeds on a table to dry, and a satanic rat had eaten the lot. Another time he had spread some tiny, valuable seeds on a sunny window-sill to dry in the sun, and a sudden treacherous breeze had come dancing through the open window and sent them flying, together with all the papers on his desk.

Jean-Jacques Rousseau also gave Madelon precise instructions on how to dry and press flowers – he obviously took a great pride in his own herbarium. But he mourned the lazy, reprehensible way he had of slipping some interesting flower he intended to study one day between the pages of a handy book.

'I have found the secret,' he wrote, 'of ruining nearly all my books in this way and of losing my plants as well for they tumble out without my even noticing them, as I hastily turn the pages, only concerned to find some information I need to know.'

Then more than once Pierre-Joseph would roar with laughter at the abrupt way Jean-Jacques Rousseau would end a letter.

'Goodbye! No more writing paper!' or 'I fear you won't be able to read all this and I haven't the time to rewrite it. Goodbye!'

On the other hand, Pierre-Joseph would be moved to pity to realise how bitter was Jean-Jacques Rousseau's resentment of bigoted, savage criticism and his haunting fear of persecution. In dark moments like this, he would begin a letter with:

> *Poor men that we are! And blinded!*
> *Heaven, unmask the impostor!*
> *Force open their barbarous hearts*
> *To the gaze of mankind.*

Jean-Jacques Rousseau gave no explanation for this outburst, he did not name the barbarous 'impostors', but went straight on writing his letter.

Sometimes he was in too much of a hurry to write all four lines of his appeal to Heaven to unmask these 'impostors' and he would write:

> *Poor men that we are! And blinded!*

And follow this with 'ETC.' in large capitals.

When Pierre-Joseph had finished reading these letters, he felt shaken, chastened. How easy it had been to be self-righteous. Maybe this tormented genius had truly believed that he was doing the best possible thing for the five children he had abandoned. Maybe he had indeed believed they would grow up uncorrupted, close to nature, loving the tranquil countryside as much as he did. Who knew if he imagined he saw a son or a daughter when he passed some farmer's boy, whistling merrily as he planted cabbages, or a milkmaid calling to the cows in a meadow. Sentimental, but possible, for who can read the heart of any man?

This was not all that chastened Pierre-Joseph. Monsieur L'Héritier had made him well aware of the value, indeed the necessity of a good herbarium for any serious botanist. Nevertheless Pierre-Joseph still winced to see flowers dried and pressed in the interests of botany.

But to Jean-Jacques Rousseau a herbarium had meant far more than an interesting, instructive collection of dried flowers. He had only to look at them and he would be back in some meadow or wandering through a forest or climbing up a mountain track. He not only saw each flower blooming again, he seemed to catch again its very scent.

When he had finished reading *Letters on Botany*, Pierre-Joseph decided to make amends. He would illustrate the book he had once refused to borrow, and he would begin by obeying Jean-Jacques Rousseau's first instruction: 'Take a lily.'

As he painted a lily and then many others of the flowers mentioned in the *Letters on Botany*, it would seem to Pierre-Joseph that he was young again, snatching any chance to stop and 'consider the lilies of the field', the flowers growing in the hedgerows, the meadows, and cottage-gardens. But now close on his heels was the shade of Jean-Jacques Rousseau, stooping to look and sniff appreciatively when Pierre-Joseph painted honeysuckle, wallflowers, sage, fennel and chevril.

Jean-Jacques always had to stoop to look closely at any flower, his sight was very poor, but heaven had compensated for this, he had a wonderfully acute sense of smell.

The new edition of *Letters on Botany* by Jean-Jacques Rousseau with sixty-five illustrations in colour by Pierre-Joseph Redouté, was an immediate success. But Jean-Jacques was not there, of course, to share the acclaim or the money coming in from the sale of the book.

This was a real regret to Pierre-Joseph. He now knew that in his lifetime Jean-Jacques Rousseau had bitterly complained of the lot of any successful writer. As soon as a book he had slaved to write was published, down would swoop the birds of prey and bring out hundreds of copies of his book without as much as a by-your-leave, much less a grateful share of the easy profits they made.

But Jean-Jacques was dead and buried. As for Thérèse, he had married her in a belated fit of remorse when he was fifty-six and she all of forty-seven. At least she thought she might be forty-seven. And Pierre-Joseph now discovered that when Jean-Jacques died, Thérèse, then a haggard fifty-seven, had thrown herself into the arms of a detestable ostler aged only thirty-four.

This gentleman had seen a profitable investment in poor Thérèse. He treated her with far less consideration than he bestowed on the horses he tended. He turned her out in the streets in all winds and weathers – to beg. And unlike his horses, the older Thérèse grew, the better the day's takings. So it was a real financial blow to that gentleman, when Thérèse, aged eighty and looking most profitably pathetic, decided to lie down and die in a gutter.

No-one could now help poor Thérèse. But Marie-Marthe, knowing her Pierre-Joseph, thought it highly likely that he had left all the money he would have gladly given to Jean-Jacques Rousseau or poor Thérèse, on the doorstep of the Foundling Hospital one dark night. If so, Marie-Marthe hoped to heaven he'd had the sense to ring the bell or hammer on the door, and then hide in a doorway to make sure this windfall was safely taken inside.

But Pierre-Joseph never let his right hand know what his left hand did, and who was Marie-Marthe to question this?

She trusted, however, that if Jean-Jacques Rousseau was now 'botanising' in those Elysian Fields, he would learn of this new edition of his *Letters on Botany* and be satisfied with those sixty-five illustrations.

All this while as Pierre-Joseph painted his flowers or gave well-paid lessons, Paris was again buzzing with rumours of coming events that would shape the course of history, not only of France but of all Europe.

Napoleon, one said, was definitely going to invade England. A fleet of flat-bottomed boats was already assembled in Boulogne waiting to take the invading army across the Channel – precisely as William, Duke of Normandy, had successfully done in 1066. Napoleon even had the famous Bayeux Tapestry brought to Paris and put on show. If William of Normandy could invade and conquer England, so could Emperor Napoleon I.

Some said that Napoleon already had medals struck to commemorate the success of the coming invasion.

Others said that the down-trodden English working class would welcome their French 'liberators', shower them with flowers.

But Pierre-Joseph confided in Marie-Marthe that from all he'd seen of the English when he was in London, they'd be far more likely to shower any foreign 'liberators' with brick-bats, not flowers.

Marie-Marthe said she trusted Pierre-Joseph was keeping this opinion to himself or he might well be accused of 'failing in his duty to the Emperor'. She'd seen with her own two eyes a copy of the new Catechism drawn up by Napoleon for the compulsory religious instruction of young French Christians, and it had made her hair stand on end. For example:

Question: What should one think of those who fail in their duties to our Emperor?

Reply: According to the Apostle Saint Paul, they would be resisting the order established by God Himself, and thus make themselves deserving of eternal damnation.

Pierre-Joseph said to his mind the Apostle Saint Paul would have been outraged at the way he was quoted to support the most un-Christian of arguments. And it was a sad pity that this authoritative, much-quoted apostle had not forestalled the great philosopher, Voltaire, and ordered all quarrelling Christians 'to go and work in the garden'. Pierre-Joseph had yet to hear a gardener threaten another with 'eternal damnation'.

By the end of October 1805, all the rumours of the coming invasion of England were abruptly silenced. Napoleon would have needed the French fleet to protect that flotilla of flat-bottomed boats across the Channel, and a terse paragraph in the French newspapers informed the nation that their fleet had suffered heavy losses in a sea-battle against the English fleet just off the Cape of Trafalgar to the north-west of Gibraltar.

Nobody admitted it, of course, but Nelson had chalked up another victory – Britannia still ruled the waves.

After the first shock no-one seemed unduly concerned, except of course the sorrowing new widows and orphans. And the sages of the cafés soon decided that Napoleon might have to postpone for a while his invasion of 'perfidious Albion' but the English had lost their brightest hope – their invincible little Admiral Nelson. He had won that Battle of Trafalgar but he now lay cold and dead in their Abbey of Westminster – killed in action.

Moreover Napoleon soon showed he had other urgent matters to settle. An Anti-French Coalition had been drawn up and signed by England, Austria, Sweden and Russia. And Paris woke up one morning to find Napoleon and his army had gone. At dead of night they had marched away – eastwards, at incredible speed, sparing neither men or horses.

Then up again surged wave after wave of patriotic pride as news came in of one brilliant victory after another. In a nutshell, by 1809 all Europe was dominated by Emperor Napoleon I, and by imperial decree, no European port was henceforth to trade with England. This blockade would spell death to England's prosperity. She would be starved, ruined, forced to her knees.

Then Napoleon, who had set the crown of France on his own head, also set the crown of this and that European kingdom or principality on the heads of his brothers and sisters, apart from his brother, Lucien.

Lucien, it seemed, was the rebel of the Bonaparte family. He had married a wife of whom they all disapproved and he refused to be bribed by the offer of a kingdom if he agreed to divorce this unsuitable woman. Lucien said, 'No!' and meant it, even when Napoleon was magnanimous enough to say he could keep his divorced wife as his mistress if he agreed to marry as befitted the Imperial Bonaparte family.

Lucien still said 'No!', and chose to reside in Italy but he obviously had the same exalted views as the rest of his family for he bought himself the title of Prince of Canino together with the principality, though nobody seemed to know just where this was. All one knew was that Lucien, Prince of Canino, lived in considerable luxury. Napoleon might be furious with his brother but he could hardly permit him to live as a pauper.

And to think, said Marie-Marthe, that Napoleon had come to France, a poor proud little scholarship-boy! And look where he and all his family were now! Truly history was stranger than any fiction.

But this wasn't all. The Empress Josephine's two children by her first marriage, Hortense and Eugène, also toed the imperial line. Napoleon looked upon them as his adopted son and daughter – much to the fury of his family, and Hortense had dutifully, but most reluctantly, married Napoleon's brother, Louis. The bridegroom had been equally unenthusiastic. But 'noblesse oblige' and on their heads went two crowns – they became King and Queen of Holland, and never before had the Dutch beheld so dejected a newly-wed, royal couple.

Eugène, Josephine's son, was more fortunate. He married a comfortable, likeable Bavarian princess and to his mother's delight they soon became devoted to each other.

Again Marie-Marthe's heart warmed to Napoleon's mother, who declined to be dazzled, and refused any title except 'Madame Mère', 'Madame Mother'. And 'Madame Mère' was reported to have said on viewing her royal family that no mother in her time could have slapped so many future kings, queens, princes and princesses. And that it was just as well she had the sense to save most of the money Napoleon lavished on her, for who knew? One day she might have to foot the bread-bills for the royally spendthrift lot of them.

Napoleon also created his own nobility, thirty-one dukes, five hundred counts and five hundred barons. And no recognising any of the nobility of former days.

Napoleon was also determined that his imperial court should have all the pomp, the glitter, the pageantry, the rigid ceremony of the royal days before the Revolution. And just as in those days, the press was muzzled, rigorously censored, and the theatres only permitted to give performances of suitably expurgated plays.

Back again now to Pierre-Joseph's mind came memories of his first years in Paris when he would sit in a café of an evening, making a cup of coffee or a glass of wine last as long as possible as he listened to his young friends. How eagerly, how fervently, they had set the world to right, reaching out to the stars, singing of democracy, liberty, fraternity and equality for all mankind, with France leading the way.

Back too came the memories of the hours spent every Sunday with upright, dedicated Monsieur L'Héritier and his friends. They, too, had reached for the stars, saw their beloved France 'regenerated', an example to all the civilised world.

But where were they now, those shining 'snows of yester-year', the dreams of freedom, equality and fraternity for all mankind?

All swept away by Napoleon I, victorious Emperor of the French.

Ironically enough, Pierre-Joseph's work had never before been in such demand. It had become part and parcel of the evidence to convince the world that France, under Napoleon I, was the centre of civilisation, leading the way in all branches of the arts and sciences.

Handsomely bound albums of the latest instalments of *Les Liliacées* and *The Garden of Malmaison* made splendid gifts to distribute to anyone whom Napoleon wished to impress.

But it was not only for all this that Pierre-Joseph was to remember the victorious year, 1809. He and Henri-Joseph were shocked and grieved to learn one day of the sudden death of Antoine-Ferdinand.

Antoine-Ferdinand had done his conscientious best to be a good brother to them both. He bore them no grudge for refusing to listen to his advice, and join him in a lifetime of safe and well-paid decorating. They had always known he would be ready to help them at any time. Antoine-Ferdinand had also been a good husband and father. He had worked twenty-three years in France and had been recognised as a skilled and competent decorator of fine houses.

Unlike Pierre-Joseph he had given prudent 'thought for the morrow', so his widow was left in no want of money. He had also carefully trained his sons to become competent decorators, and they and his daughters had taken their time, but were all now sensibly and happily married.

Marie-Marthe, wiping her eyes, said to her mind, Antoine-Ferdinand Redouté well deserved to be greeted at the gates of heaven with an approving 'Well done, good and faithful servant.'

That same year, 1809, Pierre-Joseph was much troubled about the fate of the Empress Josephine. He knew, everyone in France knew, that over the years she had consulted the most famous of doctors, she had often travelled to the spa of Plombières in the Vosges Mountains to 'take the cure', swallow endless draughts of the water there which was reputed to cure sterility.

All in vain. Josephine could never hope now to give Napoleon the son and heir whom they both passionately desired. And Napoleon, they said, was growing more and more inclined to listen to smooth deferential voices urging him to do his patriotic duty. Never again, they said, must prosperous victorious France fall into the hands of quarrelling, bungling politicians. Napoleon *must* have an heir, a rightful successor. And leading the chorus, the ever increasing pressure, were the Bonapartes of course. France owed everything to a Bonaparte. It was therefore just and right that a Bonaparte should be Heir to France. Napoleon must divorce his barren and ageing wife and marry again.

It was now, of all times, that the most cruel of historical portraits made its appearance. It was pompously called *The Reunion of the Monarchs.*

There, in this portrait, in an imposing chair sits Napoleon, tricorne hat adorned with magnificent ostrich feathers on his head, one hand outstretched as if majestically acknowledging the five lesser monarchs seated in lesser chairs to his right.

To his left, sit Josephine, Madame his Mother, and five of his royal sisters or sisters-in-law.

Not one of them looks in the least enchanted to be thus regally united. Josephine alone looks truly dignified, as graceful, as elegant as ever. Yet her heart must have been breaking at that 'Reunion of the Monarchs' for ten short days later she stood in the Palace of the Tuileries, hand in hand with Napoleon, before all the high dignitaries of France, the Bonapartes, and mercifully her own two children, Eugène and Hortense. She heard Napoleon say that only God knew how much it had cost his heart to take such a decision; he could only congratulate himself on the attachment and tenderness of his most dearly loved wife but he was now forty and in the sacred interests of France, by the desire of his people, he must leave behind an heir to the Throne on which Providence. . . .

On and on went that lofty plausible speech; and then it was Josephine's turn to read the speech carefully written for her, saying that as she could no longer hope to bear a child it was her wish to give the Emperor, her dearly loved husband, the greatest proof of affection ever given by any woman on earth. . . .

They said that at this point her voice died in her throat. And it was the Grand Chamberlain who had to take the speech from her, and read aloud that she was willing to give Napoleon a divorce.

Then came the formal signing of those cruel documents, and Napoleon kissed his ex-wife's hand and led her from the room. And promptly returned and ordered Hortense to go at once to her mother.

Some hours later Josephine, with Hortense at her side, crossed the courtyard of the Tuileries and, giving no backward glance, mounted the steps of her carriage, and with all the blinds drawn, drove through the driving December rain to her beloved Malmaison.

The Parisians sitting in their cafés that evening gloomily shook their heads. Josephine had been their 'lucky star'. Who now would bring France such luck? And who could be counted upon to present Napoleon with a son and heir in the minimum of time?

One said that Napoleon had already been considering the relative merits of every eligible blue-blooded princess in Europe. And one wouldn't have to wait long, the Emperor was not the man to let the grass grow under his impatient feet.

At dawn the next day Pierre-Joseph set off for Malmaison. The lovely park was silent, rain-swept, deserted, and he at once made his way to the magnificent hothouse where a black marble fountain splashed and played and graceful marble statues and tall vases stood here and there among a wealth of beautiful exotic flowers. Usually Pierre-Joseph would stand for a momement admiring all this, but on that day he did not hesitate. He was going to paint a sweet-smelling heliotrope which should now be in full bloom.

He was not disappointed. The heliotrope was at the peak of its beauty and he at once set to work. As always, as he painted he forgot time and place until some instinct made him aware that he was no longer alone. And when he turned, she was standing there, watching him – the Empress Josephine. She looked exhausted, ravaged with grief.

'Majesty. . . . ' stammered Pierre-Joseph, and began to stumble to his feet.

Josephine was swift to sense his emotion. 'No, no, Monsieur Redouté, don't let me disturb you,' and she stooped for a moment to smell the heliotrope, and then she looked at Pierre-Joseph's painting.

'It is one of my favourite flowers,' she said.

'Yes . . . Majesty . . . I knew.'

And not another word could Pierre-Joseph utter.

Josephine looked at him for a moment, her lovely eyes brimmed with tears, but she smiled.

'Thank you, Monsieur Redouté!' she said. 'Thank you!'

Then she turned and was gone as silently as she had come.

15

Au Printemps Perpetuel

Everyone recognised that Napoleon did his best to make life as easy as possible for the wife he had divorced. Josephine was to retain her rank and title; appoint whom she pleased as her chamberlain, chaplain, ladies-in-wating, major-domo, every member of her own household.

Napoleon also made it known that he expected everyone to treat her with the utmost deference and courtesy, visit her just as in the past. And he sharply reprimanded any sycophant who showed signs of turning his back on Josephine now she no longer wore the crown. In short, there was to be no further humiliation.

So whenever Pierre-Joseph went to Malmaison, there would be as many visitors calling on the Empress Josephine as before, and everyone admired the way she received them. She was as kind and charming as ever but she seemed to have acquired a touching new dignity – born of grief.

One of her ladies-in-waiting told Pierre-Joseph that Her Majesty had given strict orders to her household that everything was to remain just as it had been when Malmaison was also the country home of the Emperor. Day after day his room was dusted and aired, the furniture polished, the linen he had left behind newly laundered and his clothes brushed, as if Her Majesty hoped against hope that one day, please God, the Emperor would return to Malmaison and to her.

Josephine had always loved roses and Pierre-Joseph was delighted when she now began to take more and more interest in her rose-beds.

She wanted to see every variety of rose blooming there, and botanists and travellers all over the world, learning of this, began to send her seeds and cuttings of roses not yet known in France. And generous Josephine was always ready to send cuttings and seeds of her own roses to other rose-lovers.

Pierre-Joseph would sometimes arrive at Malmaison soon after dawn on a warm summer day and before he began the work planned for the day, he would stroll for a while around Josephine's beds of roses. And think Dom Hickman and great Saint Benedict had been right. There was no lovelier, no more God-given sight than a rose-bush in bloom. And he would promise himself yet again that he would one day begin to paint roses, every known variety of roses.

Presently Napoleon presented Josephine with the estate and château of Navarre in Normandy. To get her out of the way, said the gossips. His future Empress might well object to his first wife holding her own court at Malmaison – it was far too near Paris.

Josephine quickly showed she had no love for that estate in Normandy. The château was so ugly, so lacking in charm that the villagers derisively called it 'The Pot'. It was also draughty, atrociously decorated and furnished and, to add to all this, it had been empty, neglected for years.

But Josephine did her best. She set an army of gardeners to work on the grounds of the château, but no matter how she tried to improve the château, it still remained obstinately ugly, a most unlovable place. A 'Pot' it was, and a 'Pot' it seemed determined to stay.

It then became known that Napoleon had lavished still more money on Josephine, conscience-money maybe. And he had written: 'Now you can plant all you wish,' as if he knew her gardens, her flowers now meant more than ever to her. She dutifully spent a great deal of this money on the grounds around the 'Pot', and soon many new and beautiful flowers began to bloom in the new hothouses there.

From time to time Pierre-Joseph would travel to Navarre to paint these new flowers to include in another magnificent work to be published under the title *Description of Rare Plants Cultivated at Malmaison and Navarre*. The text for this had been entrusted to the botanist, Aimé Bonpland, and Pierre-Joseph much enjoyed working with this knowledgeable man.

The flowers, of course, delighted Pierre-Joseph but one look at the 'Pot' made him understand Josephine's dislike of that gaunt ugly château, and why she always quickly and discreetly returned to Malmaison.

Whenever Pierre-Joseph returned from a visit to Navarre or Malmaison, Marie-Marthe and both their daughters loved to hear him talk of Josephine's new flowers.

There was, for instance, the lobelia that had come from Mexico, a splendid deep red lobelia. Another beautiful deep red flower was a single but handsome peony and that, if you please, had been found blooming in Siberia.

Then there was a white magnolia that grew in Virginia, Carolina, Pennsylvania and the West Indies, and Aimé Bonpland said that a certain Professor Richard had assured him that there was a lady called Madame Amphon, who was celebrated not for her beauty or charm, but for the exhilarating liqueurs she made from that magnolia.

Naturally Madame Amphon was not prepared to disclose how she made her famous liqueurs, but they were definitely far superior to any Professor Richard had ever had the pleasure of drinking in France.

'I've come to the conclusion', said Marie-Marthe one day, 'that it would be a good idea to include a map of the world in that *Description of the Rare Plants Cultivated in Malmaison and Navarre*. Then one could improve one's geography as well as one's knowledge of botany. I ask you, flowers from Mexico, Siberia, Carolina and the West Indies! It's enough to make one's head spin.'

France was not kept waiting long for her new Empress. Three months after the divorce, it was announced that the Emperor was to marry the Archduchess Marie-Louise, the nineteen-year-old daughter of His Imperial Majesty, the Emperor of Austria. The very bluest blood in all Europe ran in her veins – the Hapsburgs could trace their dynasty right back to great Charlemagne.

The Archduchess, one said, had been most carefully educated, trained to obey her father in all things. She also enjoyed excellent health and could confidently be expected to present Napoleon with one royal child after another. Her mother had borne thirteen children, her grandmother had done even better, she had borne twice that number, yes, twenty-six little Archdukes and Archduchesses.

But as Marie-Marthe remarked to Pierre-Joseph, nobody commented on the fact that their future Empress was the great niece of Queen Marie-Antoinette.

Marie-Antoinette had been only fourteen when she had travelled from Vienna to Versailles to marry the Dauphin of France aged nearly sixteen. She had made the journey in a magnificent coach lined with rich velvet. And she had gone to her death, hair shorn short, hands tied behind her back, sitting on a rough plank slung across a dung-cart.

But all that was forty years ago. So forget the past, and cry welcome now to the Emperor's young Austrian bride.

Nevertheless, the crowds that lined the streets of Paris to catch a glimpse of their future Empress did not precisely shout themselves hoarse as she passed by. One guardedly said that this rosy-cheeked Austrian Archduchess looked harmless enough.

This, it seemed, was also the opinion of Madame, Napoleon's mother. She took one look at her new daughter-in-law and summed her up in one devastating word: Insipid.

But rosy-cheeked, insipid Marie-Louise came up to all expectations. In exemplary time she presented Napoleon with a son. A salvo of one hundred guns welcomed him into this world, and Napoleon, shining with paternal pride, promptly set a crown on his new-born head and made him: King of Rome.

It was now that Pierre-Joseph admired Josephine more than ever. She was truly delighted that Napoleon at last had a son. She longed to see the baby, and some even declared that Napoleon had arranged for his nurse to be at some discreet spot one day, and Josephine had been able to take his little son in her arms for a moment.

Nobody dared to do more than whisper this. Everyone knew by now that prim and proper Marie-Louise would have been outraged, wept for hours at the very idea. She was understandably jealous of the graceful, elegant and well-loved lady of Malmaison. She resented the very mention of her name, so one learned to be discreet, very discreet, when one had the honour to be in the company of the Empress Marie-Louise. One also had to learn to stifle one's yawns. Her Imperial Majesty was not a gifted conversationalist.

Pierre-Joseph, as always, made no comment on these 'one says', but Marie-Marthe sensed he felt sorry for the young Empress. She probably knew how Napoleon had once declared 'I win wars. Josephine wins hearts.' No doubt the new Empress felt that now she had presented Napoleon with a son and heir, it was she who ought to have won the hearts of the French. And her blue eyes would instantly become cold and hostile if someone was foolish enough to make some harmless mention of Malmaison.

Then out of the blue one day a letter arrived for Pierre-Joseph, a letter with the royal crest of the Empress Marie-Louise.

For a moment, Pierre-Joseph stared at it till Marie-Marthe cried 'But open it, do!'

When Pierre-Joseph opened and read that missive, it was a royal invitation, though as Marie-Marthe rightly put it, it was more of a royal command:

Her Imperial Majesty, the Empress Marie-Louise, desires Monsieur Redouté to give her lessons in flower-painting.

'Heavens!' cried Marie-Marthe, seeing the look on Pierre-Joseph's face. 'One would imagine you were reading your own death sentence!'

And she hustled Pierre-Joseph into the coat he wore for special occasions, and packed him off to catch the diligence – for Malmaison.

'Ask to speak urgently to the Empress Josephine,' she insisted. 'She will see you. Show her this letter. She will put your mind at rest.'

When Pierre-Joseph came home that evening, Marie-Marthe looked at him and cried, 'The Empress understood, of course?'

'She did more,' said Pierre-Joseph. 'She read the letter and said she was delighted.

' "Don't you see, dear Monsieur Redouté," she said, "this is also a very real compliment – to me!" '

Marie-Marthe would naturally have liked Pierre-Joseph to come home from the Palace of the Tuileries after giving his first lesson in flower-painting to their new Empress, ready to answer a few questions any woman would have asked.

How was the young Empress dressed, for instance.

Was it true that she had such bright blue eyes and rosy cheeks – almost like one of these expensive dolls?

Did she really speak with so flat an Austrian accent?

But infuriating Pierre-Joseph would shrug his shoulders and say he had gone to the Tuileries to give the young Empress a lesson in flower-painting, not a head-to-foot inspection. And Marie-Marthe would indignantly say Pierre-Joseph had a positive gift at times for making a woman feel uncharitable.

As for the lessons Pierre-Joseph gave the young Empress, all Marie-Marthe, or anyone else ever learned, was that he was always shown into one of the smaller drawing-rooms of the Palace of the Tuileries where there would be a vase of freshly picked flowers on a table. Her Imperial Majesty, attended by two ladies-in-waiting, was always punctiliously punctual. She would greet him politely, select the flower she wished to paint, and the lesson would begin.

Marie-Marthe had no doubt whatever that from that moment on, Pierre-Joseph would forget the high rank of his new pupil and patiently try to teach her to use her blue eyes and any artistic talent heaven had bestowed on her. But as he never came home elated with the progress the young Empress was making, Marie-Marthe drew her own conclusion. The Empress was probably not in the least artistic; she wished to be taught to paint flowers because that was the highly fashionable thing to do, and Pierre-Joseph had been given this honour and privilege because he was the most famous flower-painter in Europe. And also because he was impeccably respectable – this too would be imperative in the eyes of the young Empress.

The two Empresses had never met of course. Marie-Louise would have had a 'crise de nerfs' at the very idea. Yet it was Pierre-Joseph of all people, who was responsible for bringing them face to face one day.

There had been some unforeseen delay that year and they had not yet gone to spend the summer in Fleury-Meudon. A pity, for the weather was exceptionally warm, and the sun was shining in a cloudless sky when Pierre-Joseph set off one morning to spend a day painting in Malmaison.

Now he always caught a certain 'coucou', one of the small, two-wheeled public coaches that drew up outside the Palace of the Tuileries and waited there for ten minutes or so for passengers to Malmaison.

To his surprise he had to push his way that morning as best he could through a crowd of people, all craning their necks, obviously hoping to see someone emerge from the Palace.

It was then that Pierre-Joseph accidentally jostled a young woman with a baby in her arms.

'Oh, pardon, Madame!' said Pierre-Joseph, and was shocked to see how thin and ill this young woman looked.

'I am truly sorry. So very sorry!'

But the young woman assured him she hadn't been aware that he had jostled her.

'Perhaps you can tell me, Madame,' said Pierre-Joseph, 'why is there such a crowd here today?'

'They are waiting to catch a glimpse of the Emperor's little son,' she said. 'And so am I, though heaven knows why!'

She looked down at the baby sleeping in her arms and said it was perhaps because he had been born on the same day as the Emperor's son. Some people even said he looked like him. But *her* son would never have crowds waiting to catch a glimpse of *him*. Her son would never have servants to wait on him. Ah no, her son would be fortunate if he had enough bread to eat.

She gave a bitter little laugh and added, 'Yet, Monsieur, my son's father died on the battlefield fighting for the Emperor and France.

'And I am left destitute to die of grief and want.'

There was such despair and bitterness in her quiet voice that at first Pierre-Joseph could find nothing to say. Then he found his voice again.

'Madame, I assure you that if the young Empress knew of this, she would certainly help you.'

'Help me! You are mistaken, Monsieur. The Empress takes no notice of the letters I write. Maybe she never sees them. All I know is that no-one ever troubles to reply.'

'Give me your name and address,' said Pierre-Joseph. 'I promise you I will do all I can to see you receive a reply.'

He hastily took paper and pencil from one of his pockets, and jotted down her name and address, and as he put the paper back, he pulled out his purse and placed it between the baby's hands. Then not waiting to be thanked, he hurried on through the crowd; he would just have time to catch that 'coucou'.

It was only when he was about to climb the steps of the 'coucou' that he realised he had no money now to pay the fare. And as he stood, fumbling in this pocket and that, hoping to find some loose cash, the 'coucou' rattled off on its two wheels, dead on time, and left him stranded, penniless, on the pavement.

Should he hurry back home for some money? No, it was a lovely morning. He would walk to Malmaison. It would do him good. Remind him of the days when he strode along the roads of his native land, whistling merry as a bird.

He could easily walk to Malmaison. And off he went.

The sun grew high in the cloudless sky as Pierre-Joseph walked on and on. But surely the kilometres were longer than they used to be. Far longer. And the roads dustier, far dustier.

Presently Pierre-Joseph, mopping his brow, faced the truth. Forty years or so ago, he would have thought nothing of walking from Paris to Malmaison. But he was now all of fifty-five and here he was, puffing and blowing, feeling every day of those fifty-five years. And with every long kilometre, his satanic boots were growing tighter and tighter.

When he came at last to Malmaison, he was told the Empress wished to see him. She was wondering where he was, he was always so punctual.

'Why, my poor Monsieur Redouté,' she cried as he came limping in, boots thick with dust. 'You look exhausted!'

Pierre-Joseph apologised for being so late, something had detained him, he'd missed his usual 'coucou', and it was such a fine day that he'd decided to walk.

And never had an apology sounded so lame.

'Walked! You walked all the way from Paris! On so warm a day! Come, come, Monsieur Redouté, why not tell me what happened to you?'

Ten minutes later Josephine knew precisely what had delayed Pierre-Joseph.

'The poor young woman!' she cried. 'There is nothing more desolate than feeling that no-one cares if one lives or dies.

'Listen, you must take me to see her, but she must not know who I am. Not tomorrow. I know you cannot go then. But the day after tomorrow, definitely the day after tomorrow.'

Kind-hearted Josephine had remembered that the next day Pierre-Joseph would be giving his weekly lesson to the young Empress Marie-Louise.

The following day, spick and span in the ceremonious clothes he was expected to wear on these royal tutorial occasions, Pierre-Joseph came limping into the Palace of the Tuileries. His blistered feet were still protesting and even after a night's sleep, he still looked tired, so tired that the young Empress abruptly demanded to know if he felt ill. No? Was he sure? And why was he limping like this?

She asked such direct questions that Pierre-Joseph, trying to sound casual, said it had been such fine weather yesterday morning that he'd walked from Paris to Malmaison. And it had been, well, a little exhausting.

'Walked!' said the young Empress, and now there was something acidly malicious in her voice. 'Ach! So this is how the "lady" of Malmaison treats her painters!'

'No, no, Your Majesty!' protested Pierre-Joseph, and before he gave himself time to think, he'd told her how he had come to miss his usual 'coucou'.

The young Empress then began to ask so many more direct questions, all in her flat peremptory voice, that it did not take her long to learn the young widow's name and where she lived.

As Pierre-Joseph limped home that day he felt cosily complacent. He felt that the young Empress Marie-Louise would now order the authorities in charge of awards to war widows to reply at once to the letters of that young widow and see she received the state pension to which she was surely entitled. And kind-hearted Empress Josephine would certainly be generous to her and her little son.

The next day, Josephine dressed very simply, with Pierre-Joseph at her side, drove away from Malmaison in a carriage with no royal crest, no outward sign of rank painted on it.

The young widow had a dark airless room in a dismal house in one of the dirtiest and oldest districts of Paris. Her face lit up when she saw Pierre-Joseph but she obviously had no idea who the simply dressed lady with him could be. And she began to cry when this sympathetic lady took her little son in her arms and said, 'What a beautiful baby! You are right. He certainly resembles the King of Rome.' And before she gave the baby back to his mother, she put a purse between his little hands, and said she would see to it that someone came the next day and rented a far better and cleaner room for her and her adorable baby.

At this moment, the door flew open, and into the room came the young Empress Marie-Louise, escorted by Monsieur her Chamberlain.

For one endless moment, the two women looked at each other. It was Josephine who recovered first. She politely and quietly said that she had been distressed to learn of this young widow's plight and had been glad to offer to be of some help to her and her child.

The young Empress Marie-Louise, back stiff as a poker, flat voice cold as ice, retorted, 'Perhaps, Madame, *my* protection will be far more effective.'

It was the insufferable way she said this, every syllable a studied insult.

The atmosphere in that dismal room grew positively explosive, and Monsieur the Chamberlain, pretending not to recognise Josephine, grabbed Pierre-Joseph's arm as if to hustle him and this officious lady through the door and out of the presence of Her virtuous young Majesty, the Empress Marie-Louise.

Pierre-Joseph was never able to explain how he managed to collect his wits and escort the Empress Josephine to the door before the Empress Marie-Louise, rosy cheeks now crimson with anger, blue eyes blazing, had the time to add yet another insult. And never would he forget the incomparable dignity, indeed the elegance of Josephine's departure. She stooped to kiss the baby, gave his mother one of her warm smiles, and swept out.

Pierre-Joseph returning home that day, blamed himself for this disastrous encounter. He had never dreamed his good intentions would end like this. When would he learn to think before he spoke!

Marie-Marthe briskly said she'd never heard such nonsense. How could Pierre-Joseph be held responsible? The two Empresses must know by now how honest he was. Nevertheless perhaps Pierre-Joseph would now stop to think before he gave away every sou he had in his pocket. Indeed she would make sure he did. She would never again permit him to go through the door without two purses, one for immediate use, the other for emergencies only. She'd sew this second one in a tight little pocket so that Pierre-Joseph would be obliged to think before he managed to bring it out and give that away too.

But though Marie-Marthe made light of that encounter, she was also very relieved when it became clear that Pierre-Joseph was not going to be held responsible by either Empress. He went on as before, giving his lessons to the young Empress Marie-Louise, and delighting the Empress Josephine with his paintings of her flowers in Malmaison and Navarre.

It was good too, to think that the young war widow would now be receiving the pension to which she was entitled, and that Josephine would certainly keep her promise to help her and her little son.

So life for Pierre-Joseph went on as smoothly as before, and as profitably, for his work was always in demand. As one journalist put it: 'The palette of Monsieur Redouté is an inexhaustible gold-mine,' which made Marie-Marthe tartly observe that it was a pity that this journalist was not better informed. It was Pierre-Joseph's love of flowers, the long hours he worked to perfect his work, it was this that was 'inexhaustible'. Loyal as she was, Marie-Marthe had to admit to herself that it was small wonder that this journalist had decided that Pierre-Joseph's palette was an 'inexhaustible gold-mine'. She would take a look at times around their apartment in Paris and grow cold to think how much gold their beautiful furniture must have cost.

Their delicate Adélaïde had always loved books; she was, so Marie-Marthe declared, a 'devourer of books'. Pierre-Joseph had therefore bought handsome walnut bookcases with leaded glass doors, and spent a small fortune on books to go in it, and Adélaïde would sit hour after hour 'devouring' volumes of poetry, philosophy, botany, and all manner of other books.

Then Pierre-Joseph had been as pleased and happy as a child to buy equally handsome furniture for every other room in their apartment. As for the very large room he used as a studio, Marie-Marthe would declare it would take a miracle to find a space to hang another painting or print on any of the walls.

And one was obliged to thread one's way between a maze of easels, mahogany chests of drawers, cupboards, desks, with every drawer full to overflowing with paints, brushes, palettes, saucers for mixing colours and all the other clutter a painter finds so necessary. To add to this artistic confusion dozens of portfolios were stacked against the walls – Pierre-Joseph still liked to keep the originals of all his paintings.

Then Marie-Marthe would look around the other eight tidy, beautifully furnished rooms of their apartment and thank merciful providence for that spacious studio.

•　　　•　　　•

Now sometimes Marie-Marthe would glance at the clock of an evening and say, 'Ah, supper will be somewhat delayed. My faithful husband has been painting in the Jardin des Plantes today and on the way home he will be paying one of his little visits to the Palais-Royal.'

And she would laugh and so would any friends who happened to be there.

The Palais-Royal, you must understand, had the most curious, indeed dubious, reputation. An English gentleman, Mr. Edward Planta, who had brought out a *New Guide to Paris*, had done his conscientious best to describe it: the dance halls there, not at all the place to take one's wife or daughters; and strolling round the gardens, ladies of the very easiest virtue; and apartments that were nothing but dens of debauchery and vice.

Yet in sharp contrast to this, there were also apartments where learned societies held their meetings, and where lectures on philosophy, and, to quote Mr. Planta, other 'scientific pursuits' were given at almost every hour of the day. But next door to these cultural centres there might well be the luxurious apartments occupied by – and here one could almost hear Mr. Planta give an embarrassed little cough – the luxurious apartments occupied by the 'fashionable impure'.

Mr. Edward Planta also informed his readers that under the arcades at one end of the Palais-Royal was a double row of little shops in which ladies could find a beautiful display of jewels, china, prints, books, ribbons and every other Parisian luxury.

Mr. Planta had then summed up the Palais-Royal in one comprehensive sentence: 'It has everything to inform the understanding, and everything to corrupt the heart.'

The Palais-Royal was therefore the very last place in Paris to which one would expect Pierre-Joseph to pay regular little visits. But Mr. Planta had not mentioned that one of those small luxury shops was the most fashionable florist's shop in Paris and that the sign swinging over the door read:

AU PRINTEMPS PERPETUEL

And spring – and all the other seasons of the year – certainly bloomed perpetually, and most expensively, in that small shop.

It was owned by Madame Widow Prevost who thought nothing of keeping her wealthy and fashionable clients in an orderly line outside her shop while she attended to the requirements of the one or two clients who were graciously permitted to step inside. There wasn't space to admit more.

Moreover it was always Madame Prevost who decided what each client required and no-one dared to question her decision. Madame had impeccable taste, she could arrange flowers, always the freshest and choicest of flowers, in the most appropriate way for any occasion.

Madame Prevost was also infinitely discreet; one could confide in her. Madame was therefore extremely well informed. She knew where all her bouquets and nosegays were going, and why.

Madame charged the highest of prices, but she had a soft spot for any stammering young man who clearly ought not to be indulging in the expensive luxury of sending his true love a few flowers from 'Au Printemps Perpetuel'. She would modify her prices but not too dramatically, just enough not to empty his pockets. She had no wish to send him off, rapturous, but without the price of his supper.

Madame Prevost, like Pierre-Joseph, worked long hours among flowers. It was the fashion then for any elegant woman to wear flowers in her hair, or carry a delightful nosegay, and delicately hold it to her nose from time to time whenever she went to a theatre. Young ladies often wore crowns of flowers on their heads and of course the nosegays that Madame created for them would be delicately virginal. Their mamans could wear or carry more sophisticated and heavily scented flowers.

Now Pierre-Joseph had been very friendly with Madame's late husband. The Prevost family had long-established nursery-gardens and hothouses near Paris and Pierre-Joseph had often been glad to paint the flowers blooming there.

When Monsieur Prevost died, Pierre-Joseph had paid a visit of condolence to Madame, his widow. They liked each other from the start and they soon became the best of friends. But don't jump to uncharitable conclusions! Madame Widow Prevost, as Marie-Marthe and everyone else knew, was a woman of impeccable virtue. The most innocent of affection and respect made Madame Prevost and Pierre-Joseph such excellent friends – they both loved flowers.

As soon as Pierre-Joseph appeared outside the 'Perpetual Spring-time', the door would be opened and, ignoring the waiting clients, he would be invited to come in and he'd at once go through the small shop into a cool room behind it. It was here that Madame, and her son, Eugène, prepared the bouquets and nosegays. But on one small table there was always a special vase, and in this would be Madame's 'flower of the day', the loveliest of the flowers that had been cut at dawn that morning in the Prevost gardens or hot-houses.

No-one else was ever invited to step inside this room, it was Madame's 'holy of holies'. So Pierre-Joseph was privileged indeed.

Presently Madame would leave the shop for a while to Eugène and come in to join Pierre-Joseph. And they would stand, side by side, united in delight before this pearl among flowers.

Marie-Marthe knew this, and though she would naturally exclaim for pity's sake didn't Pierre-Joseph see flowers every day of his life, enough to satisfy any man, she never resented his little visits to the Palais-Royal. She knew he didn't go there to 'improve his under-standing', and most certainly not to 'corrupt his heart'. He went to shake hands with the widow of his old friend, the impeccable Madame Prevost, and to see the 'flower of the day' she always kindly set apart for him to admire.

Presently in would come Pierre-Joseph often carrying that 'flower of the day', a gift from Madame Prevost to Marie-Marthe to set on her table; and more often than not he would bring young Eugène Prevost home with him.

Eugène had inherited his mother's gift for flower-arranging but he also longed to know how to paint flowers, and Pierre-Joseph would often give him a lesson. Marie-Marthe would welcome young Eugène and begin to order everyone to sit down, do, or her omelette would be ruined, fit only to sole one's shoes. But quiet Adélaïde would take Madame Prevost's 'flower of the day' and put it in a vase of water.

She knew that tonight when everyone else was in bed, her papa would not be able to rest until he had painted that flower, another of the 'stars of this earth' he loved so dearly.

16

Le Roi d'Yvetot

As you can imagine, everyone in the family was always delighted when the time came to spend the summer months in Fleury-Meudon.

They could afford expert help now to keep the garden in order but Pierre-Joseph loved to work there too and plant with his own two hands new varieties of flowers, above all of roses. He would even try his hand at cross-pollinating them and sometimes stand proudly in front of some new rose and say, 'Ah, now this one's papa is that red one over there, and the pink one is its maman.'

'In that case,' would say Marie-Marthe, 'it must resemble some distant great grandmama or grandpapa for it certainly doesn't look like either of them.'

But that it seemed made it unique. Every tiny rose-seed was a fascinating mystery. No-one could ever foretell what colour rose it would decide to be.

Marie-Marthe, too, could afford help in the house, but she was queen in her own kitchen. She would permit others to prepare vegetables, scrub the tables, keep them white as the driven snow, wash up the dishes, scour the pans, but do the cooking? Never!

On certain days when they were at Fleury-Meudon, Pierre-Joseph would declare a man risked his life if he dared to step inside Marie-Marthe's kitchen. On those days a delicious smell would come drifting out – the time had come to make Marie-Marthe's speciality, her 'gelée de groseilles framboisée', her raspberry-flavoured white-currant jelly.

They had choice white currants and raspberries growing in the garden and Marie-Marthe would select the finest ones in perfect condition. Then she'd roll up her sleeves, put on a large white apron and set to work. From that moment on, no idle conversation, no interruptions were permitted.

Marie-Marthe would mix equal weights of sugar and white currants in a thick-bottomed pan and set it over a clear hot fire. And wait and watch in religious silence until she saw bubbles begin to appear around the edge of her pan.

Attention now! Josephine and Adélaïde, when permitted to assist, would hold their breath until bubbles appeared in the centre and presently covered the whole surface. Then OOP-LA! Marie-Marthe would whisk that heavy pan off the fire and pour the boiling contents over a sieve covered thick with ripe raspberries. And down into the big pan beneath the sieve a clear, transparent liquid would slowly filter, and presently set into a delicious jelly.

Marie-Marthe always made an ample supply of her raspberry-flavoured white-currant jelly to take back with them to Paris. But this wasn't the only jelly Marie-Marthe made. Heavens no! She also made apple, plum and quince jellies, and delicious strawberry jam, peach jam, pear jam, plum jam, lemon-flavoured apple jam, pots and pots of jam all tied down with clean white paper soaked in brandy.

Marie-Marthe would also have long earnest conversations with a certain farmer's wife, a woman after her own heart, one she could trust. When the time came to return to Paris, they always took succulent hams cured and smoked to perfection by that reliable countrywoman. But it was the raspberry-flavoured white-currant jelly that was Marie-Marthe's speciality. As one of Pierre-Joseph's friends rapturously said every spoonful was a 'taste of summer itself'.

Oh yes, Marie-Marthe had her triumphs too.

Marie-Marthe would sometimes ask why on earth their Adélaïde had to get up so early of a summer morning, go quietly down the stairs, cross the courtyard, push open that door in one wall and disappear for hours on end in the neglected grounds of the empty, desolate royal château – it now belonged to Napoleon of course but he had never shown the slightest interest in it.

'Botanising again', would say Marie-Marthe, and agree that it was a healthy, harmless, pastime but why go 'botanising' at crack of dawn? Those wild flowers would still be there when the sun had had the time to take the dew off the morning. But Pierre-Joseph would laugh and say one learned never to argue with any determined botanist.

Both Josephine and Adélaïde were proud to be Associate Members of the 'Linnean Society of Paris' and loved to go with Pierre-Joseph whenever it was considered safe to hold one of their rare meetings. It seemed that Adélaïde always sat there, rapt and attentive, even when other members began to cough or shuffle their feet as some erudite naturalist droned on and on, endlessly quoting the laws laid down by Linnaeus, by which one should determine to which family this or that flower or animal belonged. It always staggered Pierre-Joseph to think that Linnaeus had also found the time, the patience to classify animals as well as flowers. And to be honest his attention would often wander when some enthusiastic entomologist, for instance, would hold forth on the latest insects he had observed and classified in the interests of science.

One evening Adélaïde astonished them by confessing she would sit there wishing she could have met Linnaeus, not when he became famous, but when he was a student and so poor that he had to repair his one and only pair of boots with soles made of the bark of a forest tree.

She also liked to think how Linnaeus had scraped together the money to travel to England and how one sunny day he had suddenly seen a bank of English gorse, so golden and glorious a sight that he had fallen on his knees and kissed the ground on which it grew.

Adélaïde did not add that she too had known just such a poignant surge of emotion. Those wild neglected grounds about the ruined royal château of Fleury-Meudon had become her secret domain. As she pushed open the heavy door in the wall of their courtyard, it would seem to be waiting for her, enchanted, silent, until a lark would go soaring high in the sky, trilling and singing till she thought her heart would break with sudden delight. Or she would come across a tangle of honeysuckle, so lovely a sight, and with a scent that filled the air about her.

At moments like this Adélaïde did not kneel down and kiss the ground, but stood motionless, and obeyed the Psalmist: 'Be still and know that I am God.'

Then there was one fallen tree on which she would sit for a while and look at the ruined, desolate château, and think of the little Dauphin who had died there on a hard billiard table surrounded with pots of scented flowers to comfort him on his agonising path to God.

She would also think of his younger brother who on the execution of his father had legally become King Louis XVII of France. And she would pray that the latest story about him was true – that he had been rescued from prison and smuggled away to America. It was terrible to believe that this child-king had been most cruelly treated by his jailers who made him swallow so much coarse, strong wine that he would stagger and fall down. Then they would pull him to his feet, make him swallow still more, and command His Most Christian Majesty, King Louis XVII of France, to sing the vile songs they had made him learn until at last that wretched child would fall down in a drunken stupor to the loud guffaws of his jailers.

Two royal children of France, both so unmercifully doomed to suffer. And it would seem to Adélaïde that high in the tall green trees the wind would be sighing 'Miséricorde, miséricorde', and she would be lost in a strange gentle melancholy, and only scramble to her feet when she heard the voice of her sensible sister, Josephine, calling to her, asking where she was, saying that maman had said she was to come home at once before she caught her death of a cold in that damp wilderness.

Then came the summer when an army of builders, carpenters, decorators and gardeners suddenly invaded the long-neglected château and the grounds about it.

Napoleon had made another of his lightning decisions. The château, the grounds, were to be restored to their former grandeur. The château was to become a 'School for the Sons of Kings and

Emperors'. The eldest son and heir of every monarch in Europe was to come there as soon as he was five years old and be educated with his own son, the King of Rome. In this way France would train all future kings and rulers, teach them to recognise from their childhood on that Paris was the capital city of Europe, and as Napoleon put it, teach them that 'there must be a superior power that dominates all other powers with enough authority to force them to live in harmony with one another, and that France was best fitted for that high purpose'.

Napoleon's orders, as always, were obeyed with astonishing speed and efficiency. The ruined château was renovated, the stately rooms were regally decorated and furnished, and the long-neglected grounds were ruthlessly tamed into trim and irreproachable formality.

But when everything was completed, no future little monarchs arrived to be educated in the château of Fleury-Meudon. Napoleon had decided to postpone this privilege; but as the château had once been the official residence of the Dauphins of France, he decided it should now become the imperial country mansion of his own small son, the King of Rome.

The little King arrived in 1812 and was often seen riding in his small carriage up and down the wide terrace in front of the château – just as the little Dauphin had once done. Not that anyone openly mentioned this. The past was dead and gone; Fleury-Meudon again enjoyed royal and profitable patronage, and everyone agreed that the little King of Rome was the most lovable of children.

But Adélaïde would lie in bed of a night and grieve to think that never again would she be able to push open that door in the wall of their courtyard. It was now securely barred and bolted on the other side.

Her secret enchanted domain had gone, gone for ever.

In June that year, 1812, Napoleon at the head of the largest army Europe had ever seen, set off to teach the Czar of Russia a resounding lesson.

The French newspapers stated they were now able to disclose that the Czar had secretly been negotiating with the English, and breaking his solemn promise to block all Russian ports to English ships, and so help to ruin the trade of that stubborn 'nation of shopkeepers'.

Even Pierre-Joseph was aware that there was a singular lack of enthusiasm for yet another of Napoleon's glorious campaigns. There was an unfinished war dragging on and on in Spain. Napoleon had made his brother, Joseph, King of Spain, but no matter how he tried to win over the Spaniards, they still resisted all attempts to make peace. One said that even the poorest Spaniards were as proud as Lucifer and savagely fought the French like tigers, helped of course, by the perfidious English. It was heart-breaking to see the crippled veterans of the war in Spain straggling along the roads, hoping to die in peace at home in France, and bitterly asking why Napoleon had turned his back on Spain.

The newspapers, rigorously censored by Napoleon's 'Literary Police', foretold another brilliant campaign crowned with so decisive a victory that Russia, Spain and the rest of Europe would recognise that France was the 'superior power', the one 'with enough authority to force them to live in harmony'.

The newspapers made no comment on the fact that the nations already dominated by France were not in the least enthusiastic about enforced harmony, or the conscription of all their able-bodied young men. Dutch, German, Polish, Italian, Swiss and Croatian, they were all marched off to swell the ranks of Napoleon's 'Grande Armée'.

Now it often happens at times like this that a song with no pretentions whatever will catch in homely words the unspoken cry from many a heart.

Just such a song, written by a penniless poet and song-writer called Pierre-Jean Béranger, began to be whistled and sung all over Paris, and soon all over France.

Pierre-Joseph had never met this poet and song-writer but both Adélaïde, Josephine, and Marie-Marthe too, had learnt a great deal about him. This was because the wife of one of Antoine-Ferdinand's sons sometimes came to see them, and they would eagerly listen to all she could tell them about a cousin of hers, a young woman called Judith Frère.

Judith, she said, was a saint on earth, an angel of goodness to penniless Pierre-Jean Béranger. It seemed he lived in an attic under the roof of one of the tall dark houses in the heart of Paris – just as Pierre-Joseph had once done. From the tiny window of his attic he too had a splendid view over Paris, but there all splendour ended.

In that attic there was a narrow hard bed, one old blanket, a table and two chairs. No fire-place, no stove, and on his door hung two shirts carefully patched and darned by Judith. The poet song-writer had to wear the rest of his wardrobe and a pair of boots that made his heart sink whenever he remembered to clean them. There was always something or the other threatening to leak next time it rained, and his one coat was so old and had been so often beautifully patched and darned by Judith that he had grown to love it, and had even written a poem about it:

> *Be faithful, oh poor coat that I love,*
> *Together, old friend, we grow old.*

This threadbare poet had already composed many a popular song but he was still as poor as a church mouse for the simple reason that as soon as he had written a song he would merrily sing it the next time he met his friends in their favourite café. At the end of every verse there were always a few lines for everyone to sing. And sing they all did at the top of their voices.

In next to no time before happy-go-lucky Béranger remembered he ought to try to sell this new song, astute publishers who preferred not to *buy* a song, would print and sell thousands of copies of his latest song with never a franc of the easy profits they made going into Béranger's empty pockets. So Béranger went on living and shivering in that attic, and faithful saintly Judith went on patching and darning his two shirts and his one coat.

The idea of his latest song had come to Béranger when he noticed a gay, painted sign hanging over the door of a country inn. It showed the merriest of monarchs, crown askew on his head, face beaming with jovial bonhomie. And the sign proclaimed:

LE ROI D'YVETOT

Béranger then recalled the legend of this merry monarch. In the days of long-ago some black-hearted scoundrel had wronged the jovial Lord of the Manor of Yvetot, a very modest manor in a small village lost in the orchards of Normandy. The King of France, a worthy monarch, had come to hear of this and he decided to make amends by declaring the Lord of the Manor the 'King of Yvetot'.

And Béranger sat down at his table and wrote verse after verse in praise of that legendary king, with a refrain at the end of every verse that went:

> *Oh, oh, oh, oh! Ah, ah, ah, ah!*
> *What a good little king was he!*
> *La, la!*

The verses all in easy rhyme told how this good little king got up late, went to bed early, ate four good meals a day in his thatched 'palace'; and peacefully ambled around his 'kingdom' on a donkey, his only escort his dog.

To keep his people happy, a king also needs to feel happy but every time he downed a mug of wine, down too went the taxes.

He never once sought to increase the size of his 'kingdom', he was the best of neighbours, an example to all monarchs. And it was only when he died, that his people knew what it was to weep.

Fortunately, said the last verse, there was still a portrait of this good little king hanging as a sign over the door of an inn well-known in the countryside. And on high days and holidays, people would drink to him, singing:

> *Oh, oh, oh, oh! Ah, ah, ah, ah!*
> *What a good little king was he!*
> *La, la!*

When Pierre-Joseph heard this song, and one could hardly *not* hear it unless one was stone-deaf, he understood why it had become the 'song of the day'. People everywhere dared not say so aloud but they were sick and weary of years and years of victorious wars, weary of weeping for husbands, sons, sweethearts, maimed, mutilated, or lying dead on some distant battlefield.

This was a cry from all their hearts. It was anti-war, anti-ambitious monarchs, anti-Napoleon.

Napoleon's 'Literary Police', always so ready to pounce on anyone daring to criticise the Emperor, turned a deaf ear to that popular song. They were growing increasingly worried about far graver matters. There was disturbingly little news of Napoleon and his 'Grande Armée', there were no glorious victories to reassure them, so people went on whistling and singing Béranger's latest song. But no-one, least of all Béranger himself, ever dreamed that the children of France would take that good little king to their hearts and that generation after generation of French children would go on singing 'Le Roi d'Yvetot' down to this very day.

17

The Rose-garden of Malmaison

One day late in July 1812, Pierre-Joseph returning home from working in the Jardin des Plantes, paid one of his little visits to the Palais-Royal and declining honeyed invitations from ladies of easy virtue strolling in the gardens there, made his way to that exclusive shop 'Au Printemps Perpetuel'.

As usual he was at once admitted and shown into the cool room behind the shop when Madame Prevost soon joined him, and together they admired a graceful spray of red and purple fuchsia which Madame had decided was the pearl of the day's flowers.

Madame Prevost then surprised Pierre-Joseph by saying she was not given to quoting the scriptures though in her distant youth she had chanted whole litanies of quotations suitable for the young when she sat with rows of other small girls, arms neatly folded across their flat little chests. There had been a stern nun, ironically called Sister Benignus, who seemed to stand ten feet tall, and have eyes like a hawk ready to swoop down and smack any little girl beginning to fidget. Sister Benignus did not believe in sparing the rod and spoiling the child.

Strange to remember all this now! But lately Madame Prevost had been reminded of one of those quotations:

*As cold water is to a thirsty man so is good news from a
far country.*

No good news was coming to a very thirsty France from that far country, Russia. Madame had some important government officials among her clients and she gathered that the Russians had their own way of dealing with foreign invaders. They set fire to their crops, their villages, buried or carried away their stocks of grain – and disappeared.

One said Napoleon was furious. His 'Grande Armée' was meeting with no resistance. Indeed where were they, those elusive Russians?

On and on across the empty sunbaked plains, deeper and deeper into the heart of Russia, marched the 'Grande Armée' – which was precisely what the Russians, it seemed, intended them to do.

One could only trust, said Madame, that Napoleon would again pull a victory from his black felt hat as dramatically as an adroit conjurer pulls out strings of silk scarves or pigeons from the most unlikely of places.

And on this dubious note of hollow optimism, Madame Prevost shook hands with Pierre-Joseph, and escorted him to the door.

Newspapers were now not only rigorously censored, they were also very dear. But in any good café, one could count on finding the day's editions, and usually one gentleman would read aloud the latest news to a small group of other gentlemen, with many a noisy interruption, of course.

One chilly September evening when Pierre-Joseph decided to have a cup of coffee in his favourite café, everyone was jubilant.

At last, at last, the 'Grande Armée' had come face to face with the Russians! Both sides had fought like lions, but the 'Grande Armée' had of course been victorious.

The jubilation did not last long. It was then reported that the infuriating Russians had swiftly retreated, in excellent order, and again vanished into thin air.

On 13 September 1812, the 'Grande Armée' marched into Moscow, the 'holy city' of Russia – a menacingly silent city of empty streets. And that very night the city was set ablaze.

Nevertheless, in the nick of time, stores of food had been discovered. Napoleon could afford to wait. Surely now the Czar would ask for peace. But day after day dragged by and Napoleon, simmering with rage, waited for a message from the Czar. None came.

Then appeared the most sinister of enemies – the Russian winter.

It set in early that year and the shivering 'Grande Armée' was short of boots and warm greatcoats; and those stocks of food were fast dwindling.

On 19 October Napoleon, face black as thunder, ordered the retreat.

That retreat from Moscow! In the months, the years, to come it made one's blood freeze to listen to some gaunt survivor tell of the piercing winds, the short dark icy days, the long bitterly cold nights when starving men froze to death as they slept.

As the 'Grande Armée' straggled in an endless file across the sinister, silent plains of frozen snow, men threw down their arms, their haversacks, their weapons, the useless loot of gold and precious stones stolen from the charred ruins of houses and churches of Moscow, and on and on they stumbled, past abandoned cannons, carriages, dead horses and the frozen bodies of their comrades in arms. And all about them was a deadly silence broken only when a band of Cossacks came galloping down on them, yelling and cracking their terrible whips and dealing death to left and right with their long curved Turkish sabres before they galloped away again singing wild songs of triumph as they went.

No more whitewashing the truth now in any French newspaper. Napoleon's invasion of Russia had proved an appalling disaster. And before he had time to recover, the nations of Europe he had so long dominated forgot their incessant quarrelling and, at last, united and defeated him.

When April came in 1814, Napoleon was on his way to rule the little Mediterranean island of Elba – his 'cabbage patch' he called it, where Marie-Marthe, and everyone else, trusted he would have the sense to live now like a 'stay-at-home' good little king, another Roi d'Yvetot.

But Marie-Marthe and Pierre-Joseph were amazed to see how thousands of Parisians warmly welcomed the occupation forces of Russia, Prussia, England and Austria.

Yes, Austria too! On the defeat of Napoleon, his royal father-in-law, the Emperor of Austria, had been only too happy to forget the vows of eternal friendship he had made with Napoleon when he had given him the hand of his dutiful and most obedient daughter, Marie-Louise.

One said that Marie-Louise had wept floods of tears when she'd heard of the defeat and then the abdication of Napoleon. She had made the most touching show of longing to join him on his 'cabbage patch', help him to make two ends meet on the 2,000,000 francs a year granted to Napoleon under the surprisingly generous terms of the treaty he had been obliged to sign.

Marie-Louise, however, had been brought up to obey her imperial papa in all things and some were uncharitable enough to say she was infinitely relieved when she was told she was to have a 'cabbage patch' of her own – the Duchy of Parma. Her wily papa then saw to it that she had the most charming of escorts, the General Neipburg. One said the gallant General had received secret instructions to make Marie-Louise forget France and Napoleon, console her, wipe away her tears.

General Neipburg had lost one eye in battle but the black satin patch he wore to conceal this, added something very dashing and romantic to his handsome face. He could have stepped straight from the pages of a romantic novel. He had such perfect manners, he was so attentive, and he could play the piano so divinely on a moonlit night, and presently Marie-Louise forgot to weep for Napoleon and the gallant General forgot his wife and five children.

And that neatly disposed of dutiful Marie-Louise, once Empress of France.

As for her little son, the King of Rome, Napoleon had at first abdicated in his favour, proclaimed him Napoleon II. All in vain. Never again was Napoleon's little son seen riding in his carriage along the terrace of the royal château of Fleury-Meudon. His royal grandfather, the Emperor of Austria, soon whisked him away to be brought up as a high-born Austrian. One said they even took away his dearly loved French toy soldiers and replaced them with others in Austrian uniform and that he was firmly discouraged to ask questions, above all about his papa who had loved to spoil him. And no, they told him, he was not Napoleon, King of Rome, he was Franz, the high-born Duke of Reichstadt.

And God have pity on him, cried Marie-Marthe. The poor child would not be crying for lost crowns and empires. No, he would be waking in the night and it would not be a nightmare. His papa and maman had gone, left him in a strange land, and no-one would tell him where they had gone and when they would be coming back for him. And he hated his new name. He was not Franz, Duke of Reichstadt, he was Napoleon, King of Rome. His papa had told him he was.

The third of May 1814, was a perfect spring day. Nobody in Paris went to work except the patrons and waiters of cafés who were up at dawn and at once began to do a roaring trade. And out from the windows floated white sheets which one trusted looked like the white flag adopted by the Royal House of Bourbon. The streets were decorated with white garlands, the church bells began to ring, and bands began to play, to welcome back King Louis XVIII of France. He had spent twenty-five years in exile.

Pierre-Joseph as usual made no comment but he again thought how amazingly convenient were the short memories of men. Nobody now chose to remember that this smiling, and very corpulent, monarch was the brother of King Louis XVI who had lost his head in the bloody days of the Revolution, or the uncle of the pitiful little boy who had then legally become King Louis XVII. Nobody knew what had happened to that unhappy little king. There had been many wild rumours to be sure, but he could now safely be assumed dead.

So forget the past and cry: 'Vive, vive le Roi, Louis XVIII of France.'

One also cheered the weeping lady sitting by the King's side. She was his niece, Madame Royale, and from time to time the royal carriage drawn by eight white horses would come to a halt so that yet another bevy of young ladies, attired in white, could offer her bouquets of white flowers, and sing her a chorus written by the famous composer, Gluck, for Queen Marie-Antoinette. And no wonder Madame Royale then wept even more – she was the only daughter, the only living child, of Queen Marie-Antoinette.

Elegant Parisiennes also compassionately remarked that one could tell poor Madame Royale had been so long in exile in England. Heavens! That dowdy dress, that frightful hat! Ah, yes, the sight of weeping Madame Royale simply wrung one's heart.

Pierre-Joseph was again to remember his early days in Paris when the popular opera-singer, Madame Thible, had decided to become the first woman balloonist in history, and had sailed high over Paris singing at the top of her powerful voice:

Oh, to travel in the clouds!

Another intrepid lady balloonist, Madame Blanchard, was now determined to outshine Madame Thible. She couldn't sing but she was going to immortalise the arrival of King Louis XVIII by soaring over Paris in a snow-white balloon and let loose a whole flight of snow-white doves. A most poetical gesture, chorused the newspapers.

There was one moment, however, when the crowds craning their necks to see Madame Blanchard's snow-white balloon, gasped to see it 'recline for a moment' on the statue of King Henri IV of France. Pious spectators swiftly made the sign of the cross. Was this a bad omen? No-one ever forgot good Henri IV who had declared he would not be content until every peasant in France had 'une poule au pot' – a chicken cooking in the iron pot slung over his fire.

But huzza! In the very nick of time resourceful Madame Blanchard managed to pull the right rope, or maybe good Henri IV gave her balloon a royal push, for away sailed Madame Blanchard letting loose her white doves which all seemed enchanted to fly poetically in the blue sky to the cheers of the admiring crowds on earth below.

In this way, white doves flying, bands playing, maidens singing, and guns firing salvoes of welcome, King Louis XVIII, and Madame Royale, Marie-Antoinette's daughter, came back to Paris.

That evening Madame Prevost told Pierre-Joseph she was exhausted, absolutely exhausted. She had been working non-stop for twenty-four hours making bouquets of white flowers, garlands of white flowers, nosegays of white flowers.

Every flower had to be white of course, said Madame Prevost, white being the chosen colour of the royal House of Bourbon, and one had to demonstrate one's joy to see France again ruled by a Bourbon king.

No call for violets now, said Madame Prevost, violets being a Napoleonic emblem, though to be candid, this had always baffled her. Napoleon, of all men, to favour violets! One said there were violets woven into the very carpets on which he trod, violets engraved on his bath-taps. And of course there had been hundreds of signs with violets painted on them, swinging over the doors of fashionable shops. These had hastily been taken down, repainted, she supposed, but one would have one's work cut out to obliterate all those other Napoleonic violets.

No call either now for the golden fritillary Pierre-Joseph had painted so beautifully for his third instalment of *Les Liliacées*. Madame Prevost said she supposed that one could imagine, if one tried hard enough, that its circle of golden drooping flowers looked like some fairytale crown. No doubt that was the reason it had become known as the 'Imperial Crown' and thus linked for ever with Napoleon.

Yet her husband, God rest his soul, had told her it had come to France years ago, via Vienna from the mysterious East. But adieu now to the 'Imperial Crown', adieu the modest violet! Both were now banished for ever from France.

And she supposed that Pierre-Joseph knew that the rose named after Napoleon had become 'Great Alexander' in honour of the Czar of Russia. But that was life, wryly said Madame Prevost, even the names of flowers could become politically suspect at the drop of a crown.

There was one consolation however; she could now safely display the lovely white lily of France. That too had once been banished for ever. Quite a habit, this banishing for ever!

Then abruptly changing the subject, Madame Prevost asked if Pierre-Joseph had seen a certain newspaper that day and read the translation of a leading article in that most English of newspapers, *The Times?*

No? Madame Prevost opened a drawer and pulled out a newspaper cutting.

'Listen to this,' she said.

'1814 will rank among the most memorable year in history. It has seen the downfall of the most formidable despotism that ever threatened the security of the civilised world.

'It has witnessed the restoration of a paternal government to the country which for five and twenty years passed through the greatest variety of conflicting revolutions.

'In Vienna it has beheld all the Sovereigns of Europe assembled, personally, or by their representatives, in peace, to lay the foundation of permanent tranquillity. . . . '

And so on, and so on, said Madame Prevost, and she trusted heaven would keep a sharp eye on all those monarchs and their representatives, now assembled in peace in Vienna. She herself found it difficult to imagine them, suddenly transformed, becoming a band of benevolent angels chanting 'Peace on Earth' as they laid the foundations for permanent tranquillity.

Ah well, one could only hope for a miracle. And Madame Prevost said here was one weary woman who was going to banish herself, take a good night's sleep to recover from the joyous return of King Louis XVIII. So good-night, dear friend, good-night!

As she opened the door of her shop, however, she said he must forgive her, she was not herself these days.

At home Marie-Marthe was also not herself. She was stalking around, tight-lipped but inwardly fuming.

They had a Prussian officer billeted on them, the Secretary of His Majesty, the King of Prussia. He was impeccably correct, clicking his heels and bowing whenever he came in or went out. But did he ever show any sign of appreciation at being so comfortably lodged and well fed? Ach, nein! He never uttered an unnecessary word. It was plain to Marie-Marthe that this Prussian disliked, distrusted, despised everything French.

Pierre-Joseph, trying to pour oil on troubled waters, said one had to remember that Napoleon in his time had treated Prussia very harshly, bled their country white. It was understandable that the Prussians had no brotherly love for the French. This young officer was not precisely amiable but he had been ordered to be correct, and he was obeying. That was all that mattered.

Marie-Marthe was to be far more upset when they returned that summer to Fleury-Meudon. Bands of soldiers, returning from Russia, had broken into their house, smashed windows, mirrors, Marie-Marthe's best china plates, and stolen silver candlesticks and other valuable ornaments. And they'd ended their frenzy of wanton destruction by tearing up or trampling down the plants and flowers in the garden and, even more heart-breaking, they had torn up Pierre-Joseph's orange trees, tossed them out to wither and die.

Ah no, wept Marie-Marthe, it was all the more terrible to think it was French soldiers who had done all this. French!

Never did Josephine admire her father more than she did that day. His own face too was white with shock and dismay but he took Marie-Marthe in his arms and said they should try to understand. Those soldiers returning from that terrible campaign in Russia were angry men. All they had suffered had been in vain. Their Emperor, their 'Little Corporal', had been exiled, foreign troops occupied Paris, and here was a house where some family had lived in comfort, endured no cold, no hunger. They would give that cosy family something to remember.

And one should remember that this, and far worse, had happened to a million and more families all over Europe, so many had been left with no roof at all over their heads, so many men lay dead and their widows and children left destitute.

All this damage to their own house and garden could be put right.

There was so sad a look on Pierre-Joseph's face that Marie-Marthe mopped her eyes and said she had better make a start on restoring order. But as she worked she soberly told herself that it was far too easy to lament the damage done to one's own cherished possessions. Pierre-Joseph was right. One could always replace possessions. She ought to be down on her knees thanking God for Pierre-Joseph and her two daughters. Countless other women had lost their husbands, their children, all they owned in this world.

When would men come to their senses, recognise the cruel folly of war? It had never solved any quarrels, and never would.

The royal château of Fleury-Meudon had been taken over, much to everyone's alarm, by a company of Cossacks clad in enormous sheepskin coats, bright blue baggy trousers and belted tunics, all armed with those notorious whips and Turkish sabres. They would come riding along the roads on their small lean horses that were said to be able to gallop like the wind and never show a sign of fatigue, no matter how long the distance.

The Cossacks certainly looked ferocious but to everyone's surprise and relief they were remarkably well behaved, showed astonishing discipline, and never once stooped to loot, not even a hen or a pig, though of course they at once clapped an official tax on the inhabitants of Fleury-Meudon, a contribution to the price of peace.

Soon everyone was repeating the true story of the Cossack who had come striding into a farm kitchen one day, pulled some money from a pocket, slapped it on the table, and managed to make the farmer and his wife understand that he wished to buy some eggs, *buy* them, and no crack of his whip to indicate he did not intend to be swindled.

Suddenly the farmer and his wife froze in their wooden clogs. The Cossack had spotted a picture of Napoleon on the wall over the fireplace. They waited for him to tear it down, stamp on it, hurl it on the fire.

But no. He stood there looking at it, one would almost say with respect. Then he turned and said:

'Napoleon, not good. But great soldier, da! Great captain, da!'

In Paris too, to everyone's relief the Czar of Russia was amazingly magnanimous. He saw to it that the Jardin des Plantes was left undisturbed, unoccupied by troops. And as the weeks went by, Pierre-Joseph realised more and more how fortunate he was. Apart from the damage done to their garden and house in Fleury-Meudon, and the 'amiable' Prussian officer billeted on them in Paris, life went on as peacefully as before. He was still bringing out instalments of *Les Liliacées* and so far each proved as successful as the last. Monsieur van Spaendonck, still in charge of the 'Vellums', would ask him from time to time to paint another new flower now blooming in the Jardin des Plantes, and it was always a delight to add a painting to that priceless collection.

Pierre-Joseph had of course lost his royal pupil, the Empress Marie-Louise, but aristocratic families now fast returning to France to his surprise had not forgotten that he had also been patronised by Queen Marie-Antoinette. And as it was still highly fashionable, still 'de rigueur', for a young lady to have lessons in flower-painting, who better to teach them than this Pierre-Joseph Redouté who had become so famous.

He was such a character, too, with his enormous ugly hands, his amusing Belgian accent and always at ease with everyone, no matter how aristocratic.

Then he positively hypnotised one into taking flower-painting seriously, though of course one paid handsomely for the privilege of being taught by Monsieur Redouté.

Yes, Pierre-Joseph was undoubtedly fortunate in many ways but poor Henri-Joseph was again far from fortunate. The meagre pension awarded him on his return from Egypt was now discontinued. The occupying forces were not in the least concerned about the members of Napoleon's Artistic and Scientific Commission.

But Pierre-Joseph quietly saw to it that his diffident brother always had some work to do for one or the other of friendly and sympathetic naturalists who appreciated the delicate accuracy of his work, and allowed him to take his time over it. His eyesight was slowly, steadily, growing worse.

Now none of the occupying forces bore the ex-Empress Josephine a grudge. To them she was the charming, elegant woman whom Napoleon had heartlessly divorced in order to marry the youthful Marie-Louise who could be counted upon to give him a son and heir.

So they left the ex-Empress undisturbed in Malmaison, no troops were ever billeted there, and they generously continued to allow her the princely yearly income settled on her by Napoleon.

This meant of course that Josephine was able to retain all her staff, that Pierre-Joseph remained her official painter, and still continued to paint the flowers Josephine delighted to grow at Malmaison and Navarre, above all at Malmaison.

Pierre-Joseph was therefore staggered to arrive one day at Malmaison and see a company of Cossacks on guard in the courtyard. One of Josephine's ladies-in-waiting, stiff with excitement, told him that the Czar had come to call on Josephine. He had been most courteous, a perfect gentleman, and Josephine, not in the least flustered, had received him with her customary tact and charm.

From that day on, Czar Alexander of Russia often came to visit Josephine at Malmaison, and Pierre-Joseph would sometimes see them strolling in the grounds, deep in conversation, Josephine in one of her simple but elegant white dresses, the tall Czar in a magnificent uniform tightly belted about his astonishingly slim waist, and with his astonishingly wide shoulders blazing with gold epaulettes. As for his beautifully polished black leather boots, they fitted his long legs like gloves right up to his knees. Pierre-Joseph would wonder how on earth he managed to pull them on and off. A couple of Cossacks no doubt had this honour.

The Czar set the fashion. Soon the King of Prussia and his son came to pay their respects to the ex-Empress Josephine, so did the rulers of other kingdoms and principalities. It was only the Emperor of Austria who did not pay a courtesy call – one could understand this of course.

One day that summer Pierre-Joseph arrived at dawn at Malmaison. He was going to give himself the delight of looking at some of Josephine's new roses before he began the work planned for the day. It was then that he was greeted by an old gardener already at work weeding one of the rose-beds.

One friendly word led to another and presently that shrewd old man was telling Pierre-Joseph that these monarchs and other highborn foreigners were not all enthusiastic botanists or even knowledgeable garden-lovers. He could tell that. So it wasn't only to see the rare orchids and other flowers in the hothouse or even these magnificent beds of roses that they came to Malmaison.

No, every man enjoys talking to an elegant and gracious lady, strolling with her around a beautiful garden, and no doubt they all wondered how Napoleon could have been such a fool to divorce so charming a wife.

They all admired the rose-garden of course, it was now the finest in Europe, and mark his words, in the years to come – and God only knew what they would bring – one thing was certain, whenever men spoke of the Empress Josephine they would remember her garden of Malmaison, and for ever link her name with roses. She loved all her flowers, but she now loved her roses more dearly than all the others.

And say what one liked, said the old man, there wasn't an orchid that could compare with a lovely rose.

'No,' said Pierre-Joseph. 'No.'

And suddenly it blazed within him again, his long-cherished dream to paint roses one day, every rose that grew.

No more dreaming now! Tomorrow, early tomorrow, he would go to see his friend, Monsieur Thory.

18

Les Roses

Monsieur Thory was a conscientious civil servant but once his day's work was done, he pulled down a shutter in his mind and became Monsieur Thory, Member of the Linnean Society of Paris, and an enthusiastic gardener as well as a botanist.

He too loved to grow roses and he and Pierre-Joseph had often exchanged cuttings and seeds. Pierre-Joseph not only admired the roses growing in Monsieur Thory's well-kept garden, he also admired the way Monsieur Thory never meekly accepted the opinions of professional botanists as if they were Holy Writ. He liked to make his own observations and then agree or disagree and give excellent reasons for his decisions.

Monsieur Thory would be the very man to write the text for *Les Roses* – this of course was the only name for Pierre-Joseph's new work.

Monsieur Thory needed no persuasion. He immediately said it would be work after his own heart. And to listen to Marie-Marthe, from that day on all her family and Monsieur Thory ate and drank talking of nothing but roses, and probably dreamed of them all night as well.

Heavens, the kilometres those two men covered travelling to other people's gardens to consider the roses growing there! They visited the grounds of professional horticulturists, they went to royal parks, to the gardens of all their friends, always hoping to come across another variety of rose to include in *Les Roses*. And this was pleasant – people soon heard of their quest and they began to receive polite invitations from complete strangers who had roses growing in their gardens that might interest Messieurs Redouté and Thory.

One day, for instance, they received an invitation from a horti-culturist, Monsieur Dupont, who had gardens and greenhouses some kilometres from Paris. He took them to inspect a bed of sturdy little rose-bushes in full bloom. Some were single but others had a double circle of rich crimson petals with the soft sheen of velvet, and within the crimson petals was a wealth of golden yellow stamens.

And its name? 'Portland' after the Duchess of Portland, the agile English Milady who had trudged up hill and down dale in the damp English countryside, 'botanising' with Jean-Jacques Rousseau! One could not have thought of a better name for that sturdy rose.

Young Monsieur Dupont said his grandpapa had once visited England and he may well have been given a couple of bushes, or some good cuttings of this rose from Milady, the Duchess, herself. But all he knew for certain was that 'Portland' roses had been bloom-ing in the Dupont gardens since 1809. And of course he'd be de-lighted, indeed honoured, to permit Monsieur Redouté to paint them. He and Monsieur Thory would be welcome any day in the Dupont gardens.

Then he invited them to step inside his house, and he brought out a bottle of excellent wine and they drank a toast to *Les Roses*.

While Pierre-Joseph and Monsieur Thory visited gardens and greenhouses in and around Paris, Josephine and Adélaïde, armed with a tin box filled with damp moss, went for long walks in the countryside and forests of Fleury-Meudon in search of wild roses.

One day on a hillside they saw some wild roses as yellow and bright as daffodils in spring. They soon discovered that though the flowers could not be said to be sweet-smelling, the leaves when gently rubbed in their fingers, had a delicious smell, rather like russet apples. They carefully cut off a couple of sprays, wrapped them in the damp moss in their tin box, hurried back home, and at once set them in a tall glass of water.

Pierre-Joseph and Monsieur Thory were delighted with their

find. No botany book had yet described this wild rose, it had therefore been given no name. Monsieur Thory decided to call it 'Eglantine', and he set to work and discovered that this daffodil-yellow wild rose was a determined Spartan. It detested being pampered. It flourished far better on the poor soil of a hillside than in any carefully prepared, luxurious rose-bed.

Quiet Henri-Joseph also caught the 'rose fever' as Marie-Marthe chose to call it. When he spent a holiday in Saint Hubert he too had gone wandering for days on end along the mountain tracks of the Ardennes looking for wild roses. One day he was well rewarded. On a sunny hillside in the Marienbourg district, he saw a thicket of ragged little white wild roses with so wonderful a scent that he had taken a rest flat on his back to revel in the air of that sunny hillside.

The following day Henri-Joseph returned and carefully sketched some of those ragged bushes of wild roses. He also cut off some sprays and wrapped them in a blanket of wet moss.

On his return the whole family waited breathlessly whilst Monsieur Thory took a close look at Henri-Joseph's sketches of those sprays of wild white roses. And Henri-Joseph's face shone when Monsieur Thory declared that he had never before set eyes on this rose, nor had it yet been mentioned in any botany book. He solemnly announced that he would call it 'Rose of Marienbourg', and in his text he would write that it had been first discovered by Monsieur Henri-Joseph Redouté, Painter of Natural History, and brother of Monsieur Pierre-Joseph Redouté.

Quiet Henri-Joseph was delighted with this acknowledgement. In the world of botany it always added lustre to one's name to be the first to discover any flower. As for Pierre-Joseph, he was equally delighted to paint this scented mountain rose from his native land.

Then came a triumphant day when Marie-Marthe declared one would imagine Monsieur Thory had crowned the whole Redouté family with roses – though she was obviously the proudest Redouté of them all.

There, in their own garden of Fleury-Meudon, two rose bushes were blooming that Pierre-Joseph had grown from seeds. On close examination, Monsieur Thory exclaimed they were both unique.

One he named 'Rosier Redouté à feuilles glauques' – 'glauques' being the ugly French adjective to describe the sheen of the leaves of this charming single rose with its five white petals tinged here and there with a delicate pink.

The other he named 'Rosier Redouté à tiges et épines rouges' for its stems and thorns were as red as a robin's breast. It was also a single rose, a pink one with a faint but sweet scent, and as Adélaïde pointed out, its petals were romantically heart-shaped. In summer its leaves were as green as those of a holly bush but in autumn they became a vivid red. Then with its red stem and thorns and its lovely red foliage, that Redouté rose had, as Monsieur Thory wrote in the text, a 'most picturesque aspect'.

Now you must keep in mind that all this was done by Pierre-Joseph and Monsieur Thory in their free time. Day in, day out, Monsieur Thory went on being a conscientious civil servant, and Pierre-Joseph went on painting the flowers of Malmaison and Navarre, bringing out instalments of *Les Liliacées*, giving those well-paid lessons, and from time to time painting a new flower to add to the 'Vellums'.

But in every free moment, back would go Monsieur Thory and Pierre-Joseph, searching, thinking, talking only of roses, both as happy as kings. The age-old enchantment of roses had them both in its spell.

Then Adélaïde, the studious one of the family, the 'devourer' of books, became fascinated by the history of roses and the names bestowed on them. It filled her with wonder to learn that since time began, men have always loved roses, how 2,000 years ago, the Greek poet, Anacreon, had written:

> *Thou art the smile of the gods,*
> *The pure joy of mortal man,*
> *All grace adorning.*

Centuries later, the troubadours went from one castle to another, singing tender love songs and stories, always comparing a gentle lady to a rose. In those romantic days the very name of a rose had to evoke some tender emotion, some idyllic scene. The 'Rose of Love' – now there was a name, thought Adélaïde, that would win the heart of any lover in any age.

Then there was the 'Rose of the Seraglio'. This made Adélaïde dream of some enchanted moonlit garden in Persia where all night long a nightingale declared its passionate love for a rose growing there. To be tiresomely accurate, this nocturnal bird was a bulbul but all the old stories called him a Persian nightingale and swore he trilled and sang all night of his undying love for that 'Rose of the Seraglio'.

Then there was the 'Rose of York and Lancaster'. Now that name set Adélaïde 'devouring' books of history, the ones that told of a civil war in England that broke out in 1399 and dragged on until 1485. The English had given that savage war the most ironic of names: 'The War of the Roses'. On one side were the forces of the 'White Rose of York', on the other those of the 'Red Rose of Lancaster'.

The 'Rose of York and Lancaster' symbolised the peace that at last united those two quarrelling noble families. Adélaïde had seen bushes of this rose in the Jardin des Plantes. On one and the same bush, there could be white roses, pale red roses, white ones tinged with red, and red roses with streaks of white.

Poor rose! Forever linked with memories of a cruel and savage war.

Then Adélaïde had often heard how Dom Hickman made soothing lotions, ointments and medicines from the roses he loved to grow in the herb garden of Saint Hubert. She was fascinated to discover that even the most unpoetical of the herbalists of old had agreed with Dom Hickman. Seventeen hundred years ago the Roman naturalist, Pliny, had recorded no less than thirty of the rose-remedies favoured by his countrymen.

To the astonishment of the rest of the family, their quiet Adélaïde began to grow lyrical about the most remarkable of these ancient rose-remedies, until Pierre-Joseph would cry yes, yes, but wait a moment, a sufferer also had to have a good supply of faith, and patience. Even the time-honoured concoction of roses boiled in pure

water, with a generous dose of honey added, could not be expected
to cure overnight a hacking graveyard cough.

However, on the sad day when he looked in the mirror and saw to
his horror that he was growing bald as an egg, he would certainly
fly to the lotion of roses that would encourage a luxurious crop of
new hair to spring up on his aged head. He'd also be grateful to try
the one guaranteed to fasten his teeth when they became loose in his
poor old jaws.

Early one morning in April, Pierre-Joseph went to Malmaison to
paint a new and rare species of orchid that was about to bloom in a
well-heated hothouse there.

He again decided to stroll first around the rose-garden. Monsieur
Thory had assured him he would see a rose-bush there that might
already be in flower. It had the reputation of eagerly rushing into
bloom at the very first breath of spring. In fact one could buy
sprays of it in early April in the flower markets of Paris. And it
truly was the most obliging of roses for if one gave it a little encouragement and attention, watered it well in the cool of the evening, it would continue to bloom the summer long.

When autumn and winter set in, one had only to shelter it under
glass, and that obliging rose would still go on blooming. It had
therefore been given a name that spoke for itself: 'Rose of Four
Seasons'.

It was sweetly scented, said Monsieur Thory, and each stem bore
a cluster of charming white roses. Altogether, a most faithful and
delightful friend to many a rose-lover.

Presently Pierre-Joseph came to a halt. There it was, a joy to see,
the 'Rose of Four Seasons', blooming beneath the cool April sky.

As he stood there, he saw the Empress Josephine coming towards
him. She smiled as she greeted him, so warm and friendly a smile
that Pierre-Joseph began to tell her he was hoping to paint every
variety of rose that bloomed in France.

'Monsieur Redouté,' cried the Empress, 'this is wonderful news!
I know it will be your greatest success. You must come here and
paint my roses whenever you choose.'

Then she added very quietly, 'Monsieur, my roses are . . .'

She hesitated for a moment, and then even more quietly said: 'very dear to me now'.

She smiled again and walked away, but not before Pierre-Joseph had seen the tears that had come to her eyes.

Pierre-Joseph, very moved, still stood there before the 'Rose of Four Seasons' until a voice called a jovial good-day. It was one of the gardeners, laughing, and saying well, to be sure, he'd never seen Monsieur Redouté looking so melancholy and on an April morning too, not even seeming to see the first rose of spring.

Pierre-Joseph laughed and said he'd been resisting the temptation to dawdle there in the spring sunshine and that it was high time he hurried now to the hothouse or he'd never finish the work he'd planned for the day.

A month later, on May 27, when Pierre-Joseph arrived at Malmaison he was alarmed to see everyone looking very worried, talking in subdued voices as if some tragedy was in the air.

He was told that Josephine was ill, very ill. She had caught a chill and had not been able to shake it off. She had at last been persuaded to rest in bed, and now she had a high fever and her throat was so inflamed and painful that she had all but lost her voice.

However, kind as ever, as soon as she knew Pierre-Joseph was there, she asked to see him. She was propped up on pillows in her bed, and Pierre-Joseph was aghast to see how ill she looked, and how worn with pain. But she smiled and held out her hand. And then gently drew it back.

'No, no,' she croaked. 'You must not come near me. You might catch my terrible throat.

'But I'll be better in a few days, then I'll come . . . and watch you . . . painting . . . my roses.'

The effort to speak proved too much for her. She sank back on her pillows, exhausted, but she managed to smile again. And Pierre-Joseph bowed, and blindly followed a lady-in-waiting from the room.

Two days later the Empress Josephine died of her 'terrible throat'. She had the last comfort of seeing her two dearly-loved children, Hortense and Eugène, at her bedside as she lay dying. And the last words they heard their mother whisper were:

'Bonaparte . . . Elba . . . Little King of Rome . . . '

Even in her last agony, warm-hearted Josephine was grieving for Napoleon and the little son he had so passionately desired, and would never see again.

Pierre-Joseph, hearing the news, sank heavily down on the nearest chair and buried his face in his hands. He had lost the kindest, the most generous of friends who loved flowers as dearly as he did, and Marie-Marthe understood his grief. This was how he looked when he'd heard of the tragic death of Monsieur L'Héritier who had also been the best of friends.

The world grows dark indeed when one loses such friends.

For three days, the roads to Malmaison were choked with people coming to pay their last respects to Josephine. They filed silently past her coffin lying in a candle-lit room, the walls shrouded with black draperies, and filed out, weeping, into Josephine's garden where the first roses of summer were in bloom.

On June 2, Russian and French soldiers lined the road from Malmaison to the church of the village of Reuil. High overhead, swallows wheeled and dipped in the blue sky, and over the green countryside tolled the church bells of Reuil as the representatives of all the occupying forces followed the coffin of the lady who had once been the Empress of France. Behind them came a vast number of people from kilometres around, mourning the 'Lady of Malmaison' who had always been kind and generous to everyone.

And lost among them, walked Pierre-Joseph Redouté, heart heavy as lead within him.

The staff, the gardeners, everyone in Malmaison truly mourned the death of Josephine but understandably they were also very worried about the future.

What would happen now to Malmaison?

Everyone knew that Josephine had left everything she owned to her son, Eugène and daughter, Hortense. This included the ugly château of Navarre, a house in Switzerland, a small plantation in her native island, Martinique, some government securities, and, of course, Malmaison.

To their dismay they discovered that their generous mother had also left an alarming pile of debts. She never had the heart to dismiss any of her staff, to say 'No!' to anyone, to economise in any way.

Eugène was happily married but his wife and family were in Bavaria. Hortense, once the unhappy Queen of Holland, was caught up in a long, bitter legal wrangle with her estranged husband, Louis, Napoleon's brother, who was now demanding the sole custody of their two little sons. She, too, had her own estate at Saint Leu where she loved to grow violets and roses.

In short, neither Eugène nor Hortense wished to reside in Malmaison and they would simply have to find the money to settle all those bills as quickly as possible. They therefore decided to engage business experts to advise them, and these hard-headed gentlemen began by suggesting it would be highly profitable to dispose of Malmaison, put it up with all its contents for sale by public auction. People would come in crowds, they said, to bid for the château, the land about it, and souvenirs, such as tables, chairs, lamps, ornaments, anything that had once belonged to the Empress Josephine or the Emperor Napoleon.

But Hortense and Eugène could not bear to think of the home, the treasures, the gardens their mother had loved being offered for sale in this way. They decided to sell everything *except* Malmaison, but they had to consider the cost of maintaining this for they both wished to leave everything as it was in their mother's lifetime. So they left it in the charge of a few faithful servants, and did the best they could for the rest of Josephine's staff.

As for the gardens, the hothouses their mother had also loved so dearly, these too were to be maintained just as their mother would have wished.

Pierre-Joseph was naturally glad to learn this, and he was deeply moved when Hortense gave him full permission to come to Malmaison, paint the flowers there, whenever he chose.

'The Empress, my mother,' she said, 'would have wished it. She had the warmest regard for you and your work.'

Pierre-Joseph heard himself stammer he was truly grateful but he could not find words to express the deep regret that was always to tug at his heart. He would never have the joy of showing his paintings of her roses to the Empress Josephine.

How could he ever forget that morning when she saw him in her rose-garden?

How could be forget her quiet voice:

'My roses . . . are very dear to me now.'

19

Le Marquis de Carrabas

It was now that Pierre-Joseph met the successful young journalist, Jules Janin. It was Madame Prevost who introduced him to Pierre-Joseph and this, in itself, was most unusual for Madame Prevost was not given to easy introductions. But it does not explain why Pierre-Joseph, to listen to Jules Janin, stood there at first and glowered at him, not in the least enchanted to make his acquaintance.

Pierre-Joseph later admitted he might well have scowled for he had been very taken aback to be introduced to Jules Janin in Madame Prevost's 'holy of holies', that cool room behind the shop where nobody, but nobody, except Pierre-Joseph, was ever permitted to enter. And there stood that young man, smiling with all his teeth, as he held out the hand of friendship to Pierre-Joseph.

What if this meant the end of those delightful moments when he and Madame Prevost would stand, side by side, both lost in love and admiration before her 'flower of the day'?

But Pierre-Joseph soon recovered from that moment of resentment for Jules Janin was the most tactful of young men and as Madame Prevost explained he greatly admired Pierre-Joseph's work and had implored her to introduce him.

Pierre-Joseph then made amends for scowling so resentfully at Jules Janin. He took him home to introduce him and to have a meal with the rest of the family. They all liked him, and soon he was telling them he had been born in a small house, oh, the smallest of houses, on the Place du Peuple in the mining town of Saint Etienne. 'My good town of Saint Etienne' he called it and said it was the friendliest of towns where even the poorest would share their last crust, their last bottle of wine with others. But naturally with all that coal right under their feet, and mines to left and right, one had to wash far more frequently than in the nearby oh-so-clean and oh-so-stiff-and-proper city of Lyons.

Jules had come to Paris to seek his fortune as a journalist, and he had been lucky. He now wrote for one of the most important journals of the day, *Le Journal des Débats*, and he quickly showed he genuinely admired Pierre-Joseph's work. He lost no opportunity to write glowing articles praising it to the skies and he certainly had a gift for words. People enjoyed reading the articles of Jules Janin.

But it was not for this alone that he so rapidly won their friendship and affection. He had so pleasing a way of showing how much he appreciated spending an evening with them. And they certainly enjoyed listening to his racy comments, especially on the latest plays – Jules was also the theatre critic for that important journal.

Nobody could better describe how an audience reacted to some new play, how some would indignantly jump to their feet and yell aloud their opinion of both the play and the actors. Others would immediately try to drown these vociferous protests in a storm of applause. Whereupon a lively 'free-for-all' would erupt and the rest of the audience would either join in, or sit back and forget both the play and the unfortunate actors as they gleefully watched the opposing sides emphasising the argument with fists and walking sticks.

On the other hand there were unforgettable nights at the theatre when one could have heard a snowflake fall. Some famous ballerina, for instance, would hold them all spellbound, and at the end of the ballet, up would jump the cheering spectators and down on the stage about her feet would come a deluge of bouquets. The ladies would even tear out the flowers entwined in their hair, and toss them as well as their scented nosegays at the feet of the ballerina. They even threw jewels, diamond necklaces and bracelets, so great was their rapturous delight.

'M'm,' said Marie-Marthe, 'one wonders if they were so delighted the next day, that is if those diamonds and other jewels were genuine.'

Madame Prevost, as one could expect, was not enthusiastic about this rapturous tossing on a stage the flowers she had taken hours to arrange but then she would shrug her shoulders and say well, that was life.

One evening Marie-Marthe found herself alone with Jules Janin for ten minutes or so, and he astonished her by suddenly becoming very serious. He said he did not wish Marie-Marthe to misunderstand him. He loved his work as a journalist, he realised he had gifts for nothing else. But he sometimes wondered if he, and so many others, were not eternally caught up in what Shakespeare had called 'a tale told by an idiot, signifying nothing'.

No, no, let him go on, cried Jules Janin. In his opinion Pierre-Joseph was the happiest of men. His dedication to portraying the beauty of truth in his gentle world of flowers had given him an inward tranquillity. Everyone sensed this happy tranquillity and felt all the better for spending an evening in the kind and sane hospitality of their home. And this, said Jules Janin, gallantly kissing her hand, was also the best of tributes to Marie-Marthe.

Jules Janin did not know it, but he couldn't have chosen a better moment to speak like this to Marie-Marthe.

She, too, had been deeply grieved by the sudden death of the Empress Josephine, but to be honest she had also been fretting over the sudden loss of the 18,000 francs a year the Empress paid Pierre-Joseph. It still made Marie-Marthe's hair stand on end when she considered the cost of maintaining their beautiful flat in Paris and their house and garden in Fleury-Meudon. Not to mention the satanic taxes, which always went up, but never, never went down. It had been a solid comfort to rely on that 18,000 francs a year.

But Marie-Marthe would again sternly take herself to task, reminding herself how everyone was staggered at Pierre-Joseph's vast output of work, how it was always in demand and so highly paid.

Jules Janin was right. Pierre-Joseph was the happiest of men. He deserved to be. And this was all that mattered.

.   .   .

Fortunately for Marie-Marthe's peace of mind, she did not know that for the first time in his life Pierre-Joseph was secretly feeling far from being the 'happiest of men'.

One evening Marie-Marthe sent Josephine to summon Adélaïde and Pierre-Joseph to their evening meal. Josephine knew just where to find Adélaïde – curled up in a chair, 'devouring' another book, but when she opened the door of his studio, Pierre-Joseph was not painting, but seated, pen in hand, looking most mournfully at a half-finished letter.

'Poor papa!' thought Josephine. It was always such a penance for him to write any letter. However, he looked up, smiled, and said letters could always wait, whereas suppers and tempers never improved with waiting.

Before he followed her through the door Josephine saw the envelope on his desk. The address on it ran:

> à Monsieur
> Monsieur De Candolle,
> Proffesseur de botanique et de
> Medecine, a la Chaire de Montpellier,
> a Montpellier

'Monsieur, Proffesseur de botanique et de Medecine', in Montpellier, smiled when he received this oddly addressed, ill-spelt letter.

Dear Pierre-Joseph Redouté! Always the same sublime disregard for the correct, accepted way to address and write a letter, scattering his capital letters where and how he pleased. And his spelling, grammar and punctuation were as original as ever.

The friendly 'Proffesseur' was none other than Augustin-Pyramus de Candolle who sixteen years ago had been so hesitant about writing the Latin and French text for *The Succulent Plants*. He had been afraid he was too young, too inexperienced to do justice to Pierre-Joseph's superb paintings of those strange and punctual plants.

But Augustin-Pyramus de Candolle had come a long way in those sixteen years. He was now an eminent Professor of Botany at the University of the pleasant city of Montpellier, and he had written and published some excellent botany books of his own. He and Pierre-Joseph had remained the best of friends, exchanging letters from time to time, mostly about the work they were doing and hastily concluding with a polite greeting such as: 'My salutations to you dear wife and children'.

This letter from Pierre-Joseph was very different. Professor de Candolle read it twice and decided it was not at all like Pierre-Joseph to write in this way.

Pierre-Joseph began by saying he had been glad to learn that in spite of the troubled times in which they lived, de Candolle had continued to be so busy. But that year, everything had conspired to discourage Pierre-Joseph – the occupation of Paris, the 'amiable' Prussian officer they'd had billeted on them in Paris, the way his house and garden in Fleury-Meudon had been 'ravaged', and most grievous of all, the death of the Empress Josephine.

As for the monarchs of Europe now assembled in Paris, if de Candolle thought they encouraged the Arts and Sciences, then Pierre-Joseph must disillusion him. They hadn't spent six francs between them on anything except having their portraits painted by Gerard. They had even cancelled their subscriptions to *Les Liliacées*.

Then came the real reason that had goaded Pierre-Joseph into writing this letter. The publisher, Garnery, was '*tormenting*' him. He wished to complete *The Succulent Plants*, and Pierre-Joseph also thought that they ought to bring this work to a close. Garnery was in England at the moment, but Pierre-Joseph had promised to write on his behalf.

So would de Candolle now let him have news of himself, and send him something to pacify Garnery.

All Pierre-Joseph's family joined with him in sending sincere salutations to de Candolle's dear wife and family, and he was ever his friend, Redouté.

Pierre-Joseph had then added a dejected PS. As he was about to seal this letter, he had received an official notification that the Ministry for the Fine Arts was cancelling half of their subscription to *Les Liliacées*. But he would go on, as planned, to publish the remaining instalments.

Now much as de Candolle sympathised with Pierre-Joseph he was not astonished that the monarchs now assembled in Paris were not prepared to lavish money encouraging French artists and scientists.

As for having their portraits painted by Gerard, this too was not surprising. Gerard might be French but he was universally known as 'King of Painters and Painter of Kings'. Naturally every monarch now in Paris wished to take this opportunity to have his portrait painted by so famous an artist. In the years to come, that portrait on his palace wall would recall the glorious year, 1814, when he, and the other monarchs of Europe had defeated Napoleon and triumphantly occupied Paris.

Some critics acidly declared that Gerard's fame as 'Painter of Kings' was easily explained. He flattered them all, made them look magnificently regal, story-book monarchs.

Professor de Candolle smiled as he recalled that Gerard was a friend of Pierre-Joseph and that he loyally maintained that this was how the 'King of Painters' saw the people he painted. And how when he'd painted a flattering portrait of Pierre-Joseph, he'd given it a startled look and exclaimed that if this was how Gerard saw him, then he must be a friend indeed.

Professor de Candolle then considered the rest of Pierre-Joseph's letter.

The death of the Empress Josephine must certainly have been a blow. She had paid Pierre-Joseph a handsome yearly salary; she appreciated his work and had always generously subscribed to all his lovely but costly publications and set the fashion for others to subscribe as well. A painter can ill afford to lose so generous a royal patron and friend.

The loss of those subscriptions for *Les Liliacées* must also have been a blow, and not only financially. Pierre-Joseph had always had such immediate and enthusiastic support for his work. He must find this humiliating. He had planned, indeed announced in his 'Preliminary Discourse' that there would be eighty instalments of *Les Liliacées*; he had completed seventy-two so he still had eight more instalments to publish. They might well be a financial risk now, those eight last instalments.

Professor de Candolle frowned to think that the publisher, Garnery, had chosen this moment to 'torment' poor Pierre-Joseph. It was Garnery, of course, who had agreed in 1799 to risk publishing, in instalments, *The Succulent Plants*. All had gone well until 1805 when he and de Candolle had quarrelled, and the instalments had come to an abrupt end. Very annoying and frustrating for Garnery as all the instalments to date had been so successful, and profitable.

Indeed, in spite of not being completed, *The Succulent Plants* was regarded as an outstanding achievement, an artistic botanical masterpiece.

Now Garnery wished to complete the work. He already had Pierre-Joseph's paintings, all he needed was the text for the remaining instalments from Professor de Candolle. And Pierre-Joseph was entreating him to send something, a few pages or so, to pacify Garnery.

Professor de Candolle decided he would find the time, one of these days, to write the text of those final instalments. At the moment he had far more urgent work on his hands. Garnery, whom he heartily disliked, would have to wait.

Professor de Candolle also decided there was no need to worry about dear old Pierre-Joseph. He *knew* him. He would soon be his old self again.

The Professor was right. Pierre-Joseph was soon his old carefree self again, as busy as ever, though it was 1816 before he published the last of those eight final instalments of *Les Liliacées*. The eighty instalments made eight magnificent volumes, with 503 coloured illustrations. This work is now priceless, acknowledged to be one of the world's finest and loveliest botany books.

Unfortunately Professor de Candolle was never to find the time, or maybe the inclination, to write the text for the final instalments of *The Succulent Plants*. Nevertheless, though unfinished, it too is still regarded as one of the world's most beautiful botany books.

Some months later, Professor de Candolle sent Pierre-Joseph a copy of his own latest publication, *Flore Française*. In this, de Candolle had comprehensively listed the flowers to be found growing in France.

Among them there was one he had named 'Trientalis Europea', a shy delicate white flower on a slender stem, which had been found growing in pine forests and heathlands in France, and in many other parts of Europe as well.

In his text, however, Professor de Candolle stated it had been first discovered by Monsieur Pierre-Joseph Redouté in the forests of his native Ardennes, not far from his birth-place, Saint Hubert.

At last, there it was, listed and described in a botany book, the lovely little flower Pierre-Joseph had discovered so long ago when he had wandered in the forests with good Dom Hickman, the flower he had so often described and painted from memory when Josephine and Adélaïde were children and had loved to hear him tell stories of the days when he was a boy in Saint Hubert.

But what a name to give so dainty a flower, exclaimed Adélaïde. And yes, yes, she knew that she was an associate member of the Linnean Society and was therefore aware that every flower must be given an accurate Latin name so that botanists of all nations could identify it.

But the common everyday names of flowers were often so apt and poetical, said Adélaïde, though it seemed that the unpoetical English, heaven forgive them, had dubbed that dainty little flower: 'Chickweed Wintergreen'. But then they had also dubbed the scented wild roses of their hedges: 'Dog Roses', though there was some excuse for this. They had an old belief, dating back to the Romans, that a remedy made from the roots of their wild roses could cure hydrophobia, a terrible and unnatural dread of water that afflicted any poor soul who had been bitten by a mad dog.

But 'Chickweed Wintergreen'! What possible excuse could the English have for that name?

Ah no, said Adélaïde, she agreed with good Dom Hickman who was of the opinion that one couldn't improve on the name given to that charming flower by the pilgrims who came to Saint Hubert. They called it: 'The Star Flower'.

Once the family had admired Professor de Candolle's new book and glowed to see Pierre-Joseph officially awarded the honour and glory of being the first to discover 'Trientalis Europea', Adélaïde gave *Flore Française* pride of place in their most handsome book-case.

To her, this was a triumph for the boy who loved all the wild flowers of the forests and fields, and had grown up to be the most famous flower-painter in Europe, Pierre-Joseph Redouté, her papa her kind and gifted papa.

One January day in 1815, Jules Janin came to spend the evening with them, and he was plainly feeling far from cheerful.

More and more men, he said, were now regretting Napoleon. They had forgotten the long cruel years of war, they only remembered the honour, glory and wealth he had brought to France. They were growing sick of the sight of foreign troops, and above all they were furious at the way the veterans of those victorious wars had been treated. They had fought so long, endured so much, and they had all been put on half-pay or even more heartless, no pay at all. Above all they were bitterly angry that the tricolour under which they had fought, had been banished, and the white flag of the royal House of Bourbon now floated all over France.

As for their king, Louis XVIII, he was well meaning but he was far too fat, and he suffered with gout in both his feet. Not at all an heroic figure. No-one actively disliked him but everyone was beginning to detest the swarm of aristocrats who had fled from France in the early days of the Revolution, and were now fast returning arrogantly demanding the return of their vast estates, their châteaux and all their old privileges.

Many of them, said Jules Janin, had never lifted an aristocratic finger to help France and it infuriated even the mildest of men to behold their airs and graces.

Again that penniless poet, Béranger, still shivering in his garret, had caught the mood of the moment. He had composed another of his satirical songs, one that went something like this:

> *See how this old marquis*
> *Treats us as vanquished foe!*
> *He returns to us from far away,*

Le Marquis de Carrabas

On his war-horse, scraggy and grey,
Back to his castle see him go,
Brandishing sword as in days of old
This noble gentleman proud and bold.

Hats off, bow low!
Hats off!
Glory to the Marquis of Carrabas.

There was another verse in which the noble Marquis of Carrabas ranted and raved:

People! Animals that you are!
You will feel our feudal whip once more
On your backs bowed and bare
And all our ancient rights restored
Our noble heirs will rule for evermore.

Poetical exaggeration of course, said Jules Janin, and no-one dared to publish or openly sing Béranger's new song. But it *was* being sung in dimly-lit cellars packed with battle-scarred veterans who remembered the flaming passion of their youth when they fought for 'Liberty, Equality and Fraternity', not only for France but for all mankind. And the taste of defeat, the betrayal of all their high ideals, was bitter indeed.

Jules Janin said that even well-meaning peace-loving Louis XVIII had his 'Literary Police' but when they brought 'Le Marquis de Carrabas' to his notice and demanded that this outrageous poet must be given a salutary lesson, spend a year or so in prison to cool his dangerous republican ardour, the King had smiled.

'No, no, Messieurs,' he said, 'one must forgive the author of "Le Roi d'Yvetot".'

Hearing this, Pierre-Joseph rose to his feet, filled Jules Janin's glass, and cried 'Then we must drink to the health of His Most Christian Majesty, King Louis XVIII of France!'

This, as Jules Janin later said, literally took away his breath, especially when Marie-Marthe inconsequently but charitably added, 'And he suffering too, poor monarch, with his gout.'

Yes, an evening with the Redoutés was just what Jules Janin needed from time to time.

Late in February 1815 it seemed as if a tremendous clap of thunder echoed and rang from one end of France to another. Could it be true, this sensational news fast sweeping north from the Mediterranean?

It was true. Napoleon, with a band of seven hundred sunburnt men who had shared his exile, had escaped from Elba. They were marching straight towards Paris, and as they marched, more and more men were flocking to join them, crying 'Vive l'Empereur!' and triumphantly carrying aloft the tricolour flags they had hidden away in attics and cellars.

Napoleon had landed, so one said, safely and undramatically on the shore of the Gulf of Juan, at a spot between Fréjus and Antibes. Twenty days later he arrived in Paris. A cold wind was blowing, the rain was pouring down from a grey and sullen sky but there were thousands of excited men massed around the Tuileries roaring a welcome to 'Père Violette', their 'Little Corporal', who would bring honour and glory back to France. And they carried, literally carried, Napoleon into the Palace.

The elderly King Louis XVIII was not there. He had fled to Belgium, suffering from an acute attack of gout in both feet, hardly able to hobble out to the carriage waiting for him, and mourning, so one said, the comfortable old slippers he had left behind. His arrogant younger brother, Charles, had also fled, so had all the Court and government officials. And over rain-swept Paris, down came the white flags of the House of Bourbon and up again went the ragged, triumphant tricolour of Republican France.

Some days later, Pierre-Joseph on his way home from the Jardin des Plantes, called to see Madame Prevost. At times like this Madame Prevost always had her own shrewd opinions, and she knew she could safely pay Pierre-Joseph the compliment of airing them to him.

She at once requested Pierre-Joseph to follow her into her 'sanctum sanctorum', the cool room behind the shop.

'Ah, my dear friend,' she said, 'once again our world has turned over, and I am exhausted, positively exhausted, making garlands, posies, bouquets, this time of violets. Nothing but violets.

'But that's history for you. One only interprets it as it affects oneself. To me, this dramatic moment of history means my clients again adore, will have nothing but violets. Did you know that Napoleon was moved to tears to learn he had been given the secret name of "Père Violette"?

'Or so one says. But that again is history for you. Nothing but a long, long litany of "one says" or "one said". Select and string together the ones you prefer and voilà! Solemnly call this history.

'I need not tell you, of course, that the white "Lily of France" has again been banished for ever. How fortunate you are, my dear friend! You can safely paint any flower you choose, whereas if I am to keep a roof over my head, I must use political floral discretion.'

Madame turned and wearily poured cups of coffee for Pierre-Joseph and herself from a pot steaming on a little stove. As she sipped her coffee, she said Pierre-Joseph must have noticed how all those lily-decked signs over the doors of fashionable shops had been repainted at the gallop. Violets again blossomed all over them.

Madame had heard there were some astute merchants who had simply turned their signs round, and lo, on the other side was a wealth of Napoleonic violets. The lily-decked sides now had their backs to the wall.

And what was going to happen to France now, asked Madame Prevost; and not awaiting or expecting a reply, she poured them more coffee and said those monarchs or their representatives assembled in Vienna must have had the shock of their lives. They had been having a right royal time. Such pinning on of medals and decorations on one another's chests, such glittering balls at night! Vienna had never revelled in such magnificent festivities.

But between these festivities, those monarchs had undoubtedly been quarrelling in the time-honoured way as they carved up the map of Europe between them.

Then hop-là! Napoleon had taken their imperial breath away, and hey presto, they had at once united again, refusing to believe one word of Napoleon's admirable speeches and letters, declaring he had returned to create a free, orderly and liberal France, one that could be counted upon to live on excellent terms with all her neighbours.

Not a noble sentiment would they believe, said Madame. And who could blame them? They could hardly be expected to believe in an enduring 'Pax Napoleonic'. Their armies were already on the move. God forbid that France should again be invaded.

But enough of this, said Madame, and abruptly set down her cup, went to a corner of the room, and returned with a bunch of primroses.

'For Mademoiselle Adélaïde,' she said. 'I hear she is not well.'

In that cool little room, those primroses seemed a breath of spring. Pierre-Joseph, as he thanked Madame Prevost, held them to his nose, and thought there was something delicate and touching about the scent of primroses. One could not explain it any more than one could explain why some gentle little melody will move one to tears.

But Madame was taking the primroses from him and slipping them into a paper bag lined with damp moss. As she held it out to him, she said, 'Ah, well, we'll both have to follow Voltaire's advice again – "go and work in the garden." Just as well, of course, otherwise one would go crazy speculating on the fate of France. So au revoir, my dear friend. Come again soon. My compliments to Madame your wife, and Mesdemoiselles, your daughters.'

As Pierre-Joseph hurried home, he forgot how the quarrelling world had again turned over, and thought only of how delighted Adélaïde would be with this posy of primroses. She would know just how to arrange them, and she would not rest until she had painted them before they faded. She had real talent, she would have made a name for herself if only she were more robust. She was still so delicate and fragile in spite of all the care Marie-Marthe lavished on her.

They never had to worry about Josephine, thank God. She enjoyed the best of health. But even her fond papa could not claim she had inherited the Redouté gift for painting. Fortunately she had been the first to recognise this. She had even laughed and said what would poor maman have done if one of her daughters hadn't inherited her gift for cooking and making preserves.

Not that Josephine wasn't interested in flowers. She was a faithful member of the Linnean Society, and she thoroughly enjoyed working in their garden at Fleury-Meudon.

And thinking only of all this, Pierre-Joseph at last came home with that bunch of primroses.

20

October 1818

❈ ❈ ❈

As the weeks went by, Napoleon might well have cried with the Psalmist, 'I am for peace: but when I speak, they are for war.'

If it had to be war, in spite of all his eloquent efforts to convince the world he was for peace, then he would oblige his enemies. It would not be the first time he had gambled, staked his future and that of France, faced 'fearful odds' and won resounding victories. And Napoleon, with a fast-growing confidence in his destiny, prepared for war.

One hundred days later, Napoleon's last gamble was over and done; and ever since men have never wearied of writing, arguing, quarrelling over those 'Hundred Days' and the bloody battle fought on the mournful plain of Waterloo.

But defeat it was, and those 'Hundred Days' ended most ingloriously for Napoleon – a prisoner of war, on his way to the Island of Saint Helena, lost in the vast Atlantic Ocean. This time, the victors were taking no chances. Napoleon, closely guarded, would remain on that remote island from which death alone could release him.

Meanwhile France was to pay dearly for Napoleon's last gamble – 700,000,000 francs to be paid in hard cash, and an army of occupation, 150,000 men, to be maintained until the last franc was paid.

Jules Janin summed it all up one evening when he said that in the last twenty-two years of incessant war, France had lost 2,000,000 men. And for what? She had been stripped of all her conquests, humiliated, defeated. The Kingdom of France was now smaller in extent than in the days before the Revolution. But her enemies had come out of the struggle with even vaster empires, their ancient dynasties more powerful than before.

And to think, cried Jules Janin, that it all began with those first burning ideals to establish liberty, equality and fraternity, not only in France but the wide world over.

What had gone wrong? Who could hope to unravel this tangled, terrible tragedy?

Now Madame Prevost was undoubtedly right when she said the world can turn over, but what does one best recall? The way it affects oneself. And there were two of those 'Hundred Days' that Pierre-Joseph was never to forget.

The first began when he arrived early one morning in Malmaison and was greeted by the old housekeeper in a frenzy of excitement. Mademoiselle Hortense – they still called her this – had arrived unexpectedly at midnight to warn her that Napoleon would be coming to Malmaison that very morning. Mademoiselle Hortense wanted to be there to welcome him back to France.

But no, cried the housekeeper, there was no need whatever for Monsieur Redouté to hurry away. Mademoiselle Hortense would not wish it.

Pierre-Joseph decided to paint in a discreet corner of the elegant hothouse, well out of sight. There was a lily from China there that should now be in bloom. He was fortunate. The lily, newly opened, seemed to be waiting for him, and as he painted it, he completely forgot Napoleon was in Malmaison. It was only when he had finished painting the lily from China and turned to look at a splendid stately amaryllis, that he caught sight of Napoleon.

It was a lovely spring day and he was strolling with Mademoiselle Hortense along a path in the silent garden. It must seem like a dream to him, thought Pierre-Joseph, the smooth green lawns, the beautiful trees bursting into leaf, the drifts of spring flowers coming into bloom. Maybe he was remembering the days when he was First Consul and Josephine had to implore him to come to this tranquil place to take a few days' rest.

Late that evening when Napoleon had returned to Paris, the old housekeeper, wiping her eyes, told Pierre-Joseph that Napoleon could not bring himself to believe that Josephine was no longer there, and that before he went he'd said he wished to spend some time in her room – alone.

He would have found everything in Josephine's room just as she had left it, everything dusted and polished, said the old housekeeper with great dignity.

When Napoleon rejoined Mademoiselle Hortense, it was plain that he had been weeping. And before he drove away, he'd asked Mademoiselle Hortense to paint him a small copy of his favourite portrait of Josephine. She had been his 'lucky star' in the old days. It was as if he needed that small portrait as a talisman for the days that lay ahead.

The second of the 'Hundred Days' that most affected Pierre-Joseph came soon after the disastrous battle of Waterloo. When he arrived that day at Malmaison, the old housekeeper, again in a frenzy of excitement, told him Napoleon was there. He was sleeping in his old bedroom where everything was just as he had left it, linen freshly laundered and ironed, furniture dusted and polished, just as the Empress Josephine had wished.

But this was strange. Napoleon gave the impression that he'd come to Malmaison to await a miracle. He thought his generals, the government, would send for him, beg him to renew the campaign against the combined armies of the enemy now fast advancing on Paris.

Mademoiselle Hortense, catching sight of Pierre-Joseph that morning, insisted he must come when he pleased, go on painting her mother's roses now in full bloom. Sometimes Napoleon would stride past him, deep in thought, not seeing him. And the old housekeeper confided in Pierre-Joseph that Mademoiselle Hortense had told her that Napoleon had said:

'Poor Josephine! I cannot get used to living here without her. I keep seeing her appearing at the end of one of these paths, stooping to pick one of the roses of which she was so fond. She was the most graceful woman I ever saw.'

At dawn on 29 June 1815, Napoleon startled everyone by appearing dressed in the uniform of a colonel of the Light Cavalry Guard, his hat ready to put on his head. He sent a messenger post-haste to Paris to say he was now ready to fight the invading armies, as a French officer, not as Emperor of France.

He feverishly paced up and down his study, waiting for a reply. When it came, it curtly stated that the government would have no more of him. He was going to be handed over as a prisoner of war.

Napoleon read it twice, tore it up, and then returned to his bedroom. When he came back, he had taken off his uniform and was dressed in the plain dark clothes of a tradesman. Again he told Mademoiselle Hortense that he wished to spend an hour in Josephine's room – alone.

Then pale as death, he climbed into a waiting carriage, and this time his journey was to end on the island of Saint Helena lost in the grey waters of the Atlantic Ocean, a prisoner for the rest of his life.

To Pierre-Joseph the fate of Malmaison was a tragedy. Louis XVIII, safely back again on the throne of France, was not going to tolerate the presence now of any member of Napoleon's family in France. Mademoiselle Hortense escaped to Switzerland, and her mother's beloved house was occupied for a time by German troops.

Then came the day when Pierre-Joseph came home with a sale catalogue from a well-known auctioneer. It advised the public that on 24 March 1819 and for several days afterwards there would be a sale of valuable pictures, antique statues, vases and columns, beautiful furniture and numerous 'objets d'art' and 'curiosities' –

All the Contents
of the Château de la M. . . . .

An astute gentleman, that auctioneer! He well knew that everyone would realise that 'M. . . . .' meant Malmaison.

Into Malmaison on those March days poured a jostling noisy throng, some genuinely interested in the valuable pictures, furniture, and marble statues, others eager to secure one of the 'curiosities', anything that had belonged to Josephine or Napoleon, and others who had come just to enjoy themselves as spectators of this unique sale.

When it was over, Josephine's well-loved home had been stripped bare – apart from a forbidding grey granite obelisk that stood in the library and which nobody was willing to buy, even at a knock-down price. And that night a cold March moon looked down on the empty house and the desolate garden of Malmaison, trampled by hundreds of careless feet.

This was not the end. Later on a Swedish banker bought Malmaison. He intended to redecorate and furnish it to please his own sober taste. But he did not wish to maintain so extensive a garden. All he required was a much smaller, more manageable garden, so he sold, at a handsome price, all the land he did not require.

The Swedish banker then had a high fence erected about his new property with two formidable gates that were always kept locked and barred. No-one was permitted to set foot inside without his written permission.

Needless to say, Pierre-Joseph never once asked for this.

Adélaïde would often think of Malmaison as she lay awake at night. It was as if another enchanted domain had vanished, leaving only the stiff formal garden of that Swedish banker.

She would hear an owl hoot or some other night-bird plaintively calling, and imagine she saw the forlorn ghost of the Empress Josephine wringing her hands to see her home, her garden, despoiled.

Then Adélaïde would be comforted to think how many of Josephine's roses had been painted by her papa, every rose as lovely and true to life as on the day he had painted it. Surely in the years to come, people, seeing them, would think kindly of Josephine and the roses she had loved to grow in Malmaison.

Adélaïde would remember how rose-lovers everywhere were welcoming each instalment of *Les Roses*, how their friend, Jules Janin, always led a fanfare of praise from all the journals, and how botanists said that Monsieur Thory's text was masterly. A botanist who had unfortunately lost his sight could have it read aloud to him and see each rose in his mind's eye, learn where it had first bloomed in France, and other interesting details of its history. *Les Roses* was a triumph for her kind gifted papa and for their good friend, Monsieur Thory.

Pierre-Joseph was naturally gratified at this chorus of praise and approval, but he also fervently hoped this would encourage more subscribers to *Les Roses*.

In the past, the Empress Josephine had so liberally subscribed to his work, sending copies to all her friends, and Napoleon had been equally open-handed, ordering copies to be sent to all the important people he wished to impress.

His Majesty, King Louis XVIII had no wish to impress anyone, and the Minister of Home Affairs no longer had regal funds at his disposal. He had decided that as the great libraries and museums of France already had albums of the beautiful work of Pierre-Joseph Redouté on their shelves, he could only afford a limited number of subscriptions to this very costly new work.

Of course *Les Roses* was costly, indignantly cried Marie-Marthe. Pierre-Joseph was sparing neither time nor money on every instalment. And mark her words, in the years to come, people would be amazed to learn he had found it difficult to find subscribers to so lovely a work.

'But take a look at this', she cried one day and showed Pierre-Joseph a poem printed on the back page of a newspaper, a poem by a poet who obviously loved to embellish his verse with erudite references to the classics.

On beholding the first instalments of *Les Roses*, this poet had been moved to compare the hands of Pierre-Joseph Redouté to those of Aurora, Goddess of the Dawn, scattering roses as she opened the pearly Gate of Morning.

Pierre-Joseph read the poem and laughed aloud. Monsieur this poet, said Pierre-Joseph, could never have set eyes on him, and he feared Aurora would not be flattered to have her delicate tapering fingers compared to his.

He had been just as amused when he'd had the honour to be elected a member of the learned society of the 'Children of Apollo'. Apollo, he explained to Marie-Marthe, was the God of Light and of all the Arts. But he was also divinely beautiful, so Pierre-Joseph trusted Apollo had the customary paternal blindness when he beheld his children.

Pierre-Joseph was not only one of the 'Children of Apollo', he was now a member of many other learned societies as well. Marie-Marthe had been proud to see him thus recognised and honoured, but now she began to think again that there was truth in the old saying that there was another side to every medal. All those learned societies expected a yearly subscription from their members and it was amazing how much these subscriptions cost Pierre-Joseph.

But so far, so good, thought Marie-Marthe. Pierre-Joseph was still earning an excellent income from one source or another. He was far too busy to waste time giving thought to a most unlikely penniless tomorrow.

And he was right, Marie-Marthe fiercely told herself. Of course he was right.

Pierre-Joseph was always to remember the October of 1818. It was a red-letter month for France for she had managed to pay that gigantic bill for Napoleon's last gamble, and back to their homelands marched the occupying armies, all 150,000 of them. But it seemed ungrateful to Pierre-Joseph that not a French poet had rushed into verse singing of the beauty of that autumn, so idyllic that the fruit trees burst into bloom again, gardens everywhere were bright with flowers, and the birds carolled away as if they believed it was spring, and were calling on the world to sing, sing, sing.

Pierre-Joseph was wrong. When he next called on Madame Prevost she told him that the incorrigible penniless poet, Béranger, had written of the beauty of that autumn in a new song he'd written to celebrate the departure of the occupying forces.

In the first verse, said Madame Prevost, Béranger saw Peace descending on the world and crying aloud:

> *French, English, Belgians and Germans*
> *From now on form a sacred band*
> *One to the other*
> *Offer a friendly hand.*

In the last verse Béranger sang of the beauty of that autumn, decked with flowers, and the good wines of France flowing gay and free over all the frontiers as people everywhere, one to the other, offered a friendly hand.

But when would that penniless poet learn a little discretion, asked Madame Prevost, for in the other verses of his new song he made Peace denounce insolent potentates, grasping monarchs, and heartless conquerors who were to blame for the hatred that had divided men. And that verse too was followed by the chorus, to be sung *fortissimo* no doubt:

> *English, French, Belgians and Germans,*
> *From now on form a sacred band*
> *One to the other*
> *Offer a friendly hand.*

Béranger must have known that the Czar of Russia, the Emperor of Austria and the King of Prussia had formed a 'Holy Alliance', solemnly swearing to be brothers, and to remember they were the Delegates of Providence, entrusted to rule over their people.

Béranger had plainly shown what he thought of that 'Holy Alliance'. He had called his new song: 'The Holy Alliance of the People'.

That reckless poet would be marched off to jail one day, said Madame Prevost. And then added she too had her doubts about the 'Holy Alliance' of Russia, Austria and Prussia. Then she abruptly changed the subject as she so often did and said, 'Well, what do you think of *this* holy alliance?'

There in a vase on the little table was a beautiful bouquet of camellias, narcissi and pansies. They too had all rushed into bloom thinking this idyllic October must be sunny spring or summer.

.   .   .

When the tenth instalment of *Les Roses* was finished, Monsieur Thory suggested it would be a good idea if Pierre-Joseph painted a frontispiece, a wreath of roses to encircle some lines written by the Greek poet, Anacreon. Centuries ago Anacreon had sung the praises of wine and love – in that order, it seemed, no penitential high-thinking for wine-loving, amorous Anacreon. But Monsieur Thory had come across some lines he'd addressed to Bacchus, the god of wine.

> *Crown me then, o Bacchus,*
> *And playing on a lyre before thy altar,*
> *Accompanied by a snowy-breasted young virgin*
> *I will dance, crowned with roses.*

A wreath of roses, said Monsieur Thory, encircling that quotation, would add an attractive note of classical erudition to mark their tenth instalment. Marie-Marthe tartly said she could well imagine that tipsy young pagan with his wreath of roses askew on his head, playing his lute and capering with his snowy-breasted young virgin before the altar of Bacchus.

But Marie-Marthe promptly forgot this when Pierre-Joseph painted this frontispiece. It was a miracle of joyous innocence, a wreath of wild roses most exquisitely painted. Everyone thought it was delightful and it certainly helped to bring in more subscriptions. The first ten instalments, bound, and with this frontispiece, together with a list of all the roses pictured in this volume, made a most handsome New Year gift to give one's friends.

However, when instalments fourteen, fifteen and sixteen were completed, one of those carping critics who all down the ages think it is their high duty to find something acid to say, wrote that these instalments were up to the standard of the previous ones, but Monsieur Redouté did well to continue to paint in water-colour. His oil-painting lacked a certain vigour and delicacy.

Well, one must expect a thorn or two among roses, said Monsieur Thory. But easy-going Pierre-Joseph bristled. So his oil-paintings lacked vigour, delicacy, did they! Well, one day he'd make that critic eat his words. But not now. He and Monsieur Thory must think only of future instalments of *Les Roses*.

Sometimes of an evening they would find it convenient to meet in a favourite café in Paris to discuss some problem. It was often difficult to identify a rose, discover if it had already been given a name, and if not, agree on the one to give it.

One bleak February evening in 1820 Pierre-Joseph arrived early in this café, ordered some coffee and took a newspaper from the rack. All the best cafés now kept a rack of newspapers for the convenience of their patrons. No-one expected them to swallow their coffee and vanish. Gentlemen were welcome to linger over their coffee and read a newspaper as they waited for a friend.

An article in the paper Pierre-Joseph had taken at random made him sit bolt upright. He had suddenly been reminded of the days he had spent in the Gardens of Kew on the banks of the Thames, and as Marie-Marthe had complained, had never found the time to see a single English sight, not even the Tower of London, not even a glimpse of the English King George III.

Now staring at him was an article announcing the death of His Majesty George III. The article said he had been a good man, impeccably faithful to his wife, and he'd had the sound good sense to abandon the pretence that English monarchs were still, legitimately, Kings of France. For four hundred years, the 'fleur de lys' had been displayed on their royal coat of arms – they simply could not forget their Henry V and the Battle of Agincourt fought four centuries ago. But George III had at last swept away that lingering illusion.

One infinitely regretted, went on that article, the sad close to His Majesty's long life. He had become blind, deaf and afflicted with fits of madness. One day, however, he'd had a blessed moment of sanity and the Queen, his wife, had entered his room and wept to see him playing his harpsichord and singing a hymn though he could not hear his own voice or the sound of the music.

Then he went down on his knees and prayed aloud for the nation, his beloved wife and their fifteen children. Last of all he earnestly entreated heaven to lift his heavy cross from him, or give him the courage to submit. But at the thought of so desolate and silent a future, he burst into tears and that brief moment of sanity fled.

Pierre-Joseph was deeply moved to read this. It was a sad, cruel way for any man to die. He remembered how Monsieur L'Héritier had always had the highest regard for this English king, a friendly unpretentious monarch who'd say good-day and stop to chat to anyone he met. Moreover he and Sir Joseph Banks had been the best of friends.

But someone was now slapping Pierre-Joseph on the back and demanding to know if it was a bout of satanic indigestion that was making him sit there looking so melancholy.

It was Monsieur Thory, and Pierre-Joseph pretended to laugh, and called for more coffee, his own had grown cold; and Monsieur Thory immediately began to tell him of a conversation he'd had with a gentleman who had recently returned from the Island of Bourbon in the Indian Ocean.

The islanders there had a genius for making excellent rum, this gentleman had told Monsieur Thory, and they had an artistic way of growing whole hedges of roses, pink ones, delicately scented and with evergreen foliage. He thought seeds of this rose and maybe cuttings had been sent to France but apart from this, he had been infuriatingly vague. He had no idea to whom those seeds or cuttings had been sent.

If this rose from the Island of Bourbon was now growing in France then Monsieur Thory would not rest until he had the pleasure of seeing it, studying it, and then introducing it to Pierre-Joseph with a triumphant 'Now paint me this one. Another variety worthy of a place in *Les Roses*!'

When Pierre-Joseph came home that evening he began to tell Marie-Marthe and his daughters of the cruel death of King George III.

Marie-Marthe, very moved, crossed herself and said: 'God rest his soul.'

It was then that Adélaïde surprised them. She quietly said that death had not been cruel, it had been his friend, his last kind friend.

And in the years to come they were to remember Adélaïde's gentle voice, the look on her sensitive face as she said death had been that English king's 'friend, his last kind friend'.

Parma Violets

It is strange how often in life one memory of the past is fast followed by another. In June that year Pierre-Joseph was again to remember the months he and Monsieur L'Héritier had spent in London. Just as on the previous occasion he was waiting in their favourite café for Monsieur Thory to arrive, and he had again taken a newspaper at random from the rack.

This time his attention was caught by an article announcing the death of Sir Joseph Banks. It went on to pay Sir Joseph the warmest of tributes, saying it was regrettable that for so many years of his life, England had been at war with France.

But if an English ship captured a French one and found it carried a botanist's herbarium, seeds or living plants, these were always sent to Sir Joseph Banks. But did he keep these scientific spoils of war as a lesser man would have done? Never! He invariably found some way to send them on to those for whom they were intended. He had returned no fewer than ten important collections to the Jardin des Plantes, and with the first to arrive was a letter from Sir Joseph, saying he had not even glanced at it, that he would 'not steal a single botanical idea from those who had gone in peril of their lives to get them'.

This was typical of Sir Joseph. He had held out the hand of friendship to men of science, regardless of race and creed. He made them all welcome in his fine residence in Soho Square, London, where they could study at their leisure his unique herbarium and his vast collection of books on all manner of learned subjects. One could justifiably say that Sir Joseph's house had been a 'gathering place of science'.

The article conclued by offering, on behalf of the readers of the newspaper, their respectful condolences to Milady Banks, the widow of this upright man – distinguished scholar and true gentleman.

As Pierre-Joseph read this article the years seemed to roll back and he saw himself and Monsieur L'Héritier in that 'gathering place of science' in Soho Square, London.

There they would sit in comfortable English armchairs before a glowing fire, deep in talk about the flowers of Kew Gardens.

He saw the silent discreet servants who politely offered them tea or coffee and delicious hot rolls and English butter.

He saw the walls of that splendid room lined from floor to ceiling with books, hundreds of books, all meticulously classified by faithful 'Old Dry'.

He remembered the happy hours he had spent in the Royal Gardens of Kew, sketching and painting the flowers to illustrate *Sertum Anglicum*, the *English Garland*, Monsieur L'Héritier's tribute to the English, his offering of gratitude for the help and hospitality he had received in England.

Monsieur L'Héritier's *English Garland* was surely above all a grateful memorial to Sir Joseph Banks.

Now call it coincidence or what you will, but as soon as Monsieur Thory arrived and the waiter had set coffee before them, he began to talk about a remarkable rose which one of his friends, Monsieur Boursault, had invited him to come and see.

Monsieur Boursault had led him to his temperate greenhouse, and he certainly had every reason to pride himself on this greenhouse. It was enormous with a very high roof, but the rose which Monsieur Boursault was so proud to show Monsieur Thory had climbed, with a little support here and there, right up to the lofty roof. It was a veritable mountaineer of a rose, said Monsieur Thory, and a very attractive one. Its name? 'Lady Banks'.

Yes, yes, 'Lady Banks'.

Monsieur Boursault had told Monsieur Thory that he thought it had first been discovered growing in China but he couldn't swear to this. All he knew was that a traveller had brought it to England and given it the honourable name: 'Lady Banks'.

Monsieur Boursault had been in England two years ago and he'd managed to bring back a frail little bush of 'Lady Banks', so frail that he'd planted it in the shelter of this temperate greenhouse. 'Lady Banks' had gratefully responded for see how she had grown and flourished! And yes, Monsieur Boursault would be delighted if Monsieur Redouté cared to come and admire and paint his 'Lady Banks' now she was in full bloom.

The very next day Pierre-Joseph was led by Monsieur Boursault to his vast greenhouse. He flung open the door and cried 'There she is! The only successful "Lady Banks" growing in France!'

Pierre-Joseph could hardly believe his eyes. Cluster upon cluster of 'Lady Banks' roses looked down on him from the lofy roof. But thank heaven 'Lady Banks' had been considerate enough to send out any number of rambling side branches each of them bearing an enchanting bouquet of roses. So Pierre-Joseph wouldn't have to borrow a high ladder and risk breaking his neck to paint a spray or two of this mountaineer of a rose.

The roses were small but dazzlingly white; they all had four or five rows of petals, the inner ones crumpled as if to hide and protect the stamens, and they had a soft gentle scent that reminded Pierre-Joseph of another flower but he couldn't think which one.

Monsieur Boursault, talking away, said he'd given excellent cuttings to several well-known rose-growers who had carefully planted them in pots, hoping to plant them out later on in their gardens. But 'Lady Banks' had declined to flourish for any of them.

And well, yes, agreed Monsieur Boursault, it would be excellent if 'Lady Banks' could be persuaded to become acclimatised and grow out of doors. She would look wonderful climbing over a summer-house, and to his mind, her scent was far sweeter, more subtle than any honeysuckle.

At last Monsieur Boursault left Pierre-Joseph to select a flowering side branch of 'Lady Banks'. Swiftly, lovingly, he sketched and then began to paint it, and time flew on scented wings until he had finished, and there was Monsieur Boursault at his elbow exclaiming, 'Unbelievable! I'd swear I'd only have to stoop to smell it!'

'Monsieur Boursault,' said Pierre-Joseph with mock severity, 'you forgot to mention another admirable virtue of "Lady Banks". She has no thorns, no thorns whatever!'

That evening Pierre-Joseph brought back a couple of flowering sprays of 'Lady Banks' for Adélaïde. Without a word she took them and set them in a slender vase of water, and then stood back to look at them.

'Thank you, papa,' she said. That was all, but the look on her face told Pierre-Joseph she could not have been better pleased if he'd brought her back a diamond necklace.

'It has a lovely scent,' she said. 'Something like Parma violets.'

'So it has,' cried Pierre-Joseph. 'I've been wondering all day which flower had just such a scent.'

'But this is far more delicate,' said Adélaïde. 'It's as enchanting as Lady Banks herself.'

That same week Pierre-Joseph paid one of his regular visits to Madame Prevost. She greeted him and at once led the way into the cool dark room behind the shop.

'I was hoping you would come today. Take a look at my "flower of the day". Did you ever see so golden a rose? But it is the despair of even the most experienced of rose-growers here in France. It declines to bloom to perfection even if they plant it in the most favourable of places, protected by a wall from all the winds that blow and where it can have the maximum of sunshine. A pity, for it is surely the queen of all yellow roses.'

Pierre-Joseph looked and looked at that golden-yellow rose, and as he looked he knew that somewhere he had seen that rose. But when? And where?

At last it came to him. Amsterdam!

Fifty years ago it must have been when he'd stood, lost in awe one day before one of the masterpieces of famous Jan van Huysum. It was a superbly painted bouquet and there, among the flowers, was this golden-yellow rose.

'You must have it, of course,' said Madame Prevost. 'I haven't a client who would appreciate it as you do.'

'Madame,' said Pierre-Joseph, 'you are the kindest, most generous of friends.'

'Nonsense,' said Madame briskly. 'I just happen to like pleasing someone who loves flowers as much as I do, even if I do have to earn my bread by selling them.'

With that she held out her hand, but this time, Pierre-Joseph stooped and kissed it, and Madame turned, saying, 'Au revoir, my dear friend. Come again soon.' And Pierre-Joseph hurried away carrying that golden rose in one of Madame Prevost's elegant little paper bags as if its petals were indeed of pure gold.

Monsieur Thory was also enchanted with that beautiful yellow rose but he insisted it was sulphur-yellow, definitely sulphur-yellow. 'Gold' was too vague; it covered a whole gamut of shades from palest gold to a deep rich gold.

No, no, this lovely rose was the colour of sulphur. So the 'Sulphur Rose' it became, and Adélaïde was appalled to learn that so beautiful a rose had been shackled to so unlovely a name. And it was small comfort to think that great Shakespeare had declared 'a rose by any other name would smell as sweet'.

Some weeks later a large canvas, eight feet high, was delivered to Monsieur Redouté's apartment in Paris.

Marie-Marthe groaned as it was carried into Pierre-Joseph's studio. What on earth did her happy-go-lucky husband intend to paint on that enormous canvas?

The mystery was solved that evening when Pierre-Joseph brought three friends home to have a meal with them: Monsieur Percier, the well-known architect, Monsieur Thibault, the grandson of the famous painter, Poussin, and a distinguished artist himself, and Monsieur Gerard, the 'King of Painters and Painter of Kings'.

They had merrily decided to give the artistic world the sensation of the century – a magnificent oil-painting, the combined work of all four of them.

Monsieur Percier, the architect, was to paint a stately portico with marble pillars, as noble and imposing as any in ancient Greece.

Monsieur Thibault was to be responsible for a Grecian landscape, with groves of stately trees, and a charming little stream meandering across it, and overhead, of course, the bluest of Grecian skies.

But Monsieur Gerard, the 'King of Painters and Painter of Kings', now chose to put on a fine show of reluctance to paint his share of that future masterpiece.

'What!' he groaned, 'you want me to paint two ravishing nymphs dallying by that stream? Ah no! I know just what Pierre-Joseph will do. He'll have flowers blooming everywhere. He'll have them climbing up all the marble pillars, growing along that little stream, and probably have water-lilies floating upon it as well, and he'll certainly, most certainly, have them blooming all about the lily-white feet of my nymphs.

'I tell you they would be overcome by the scent of all those flowers.'

This was met with a roar of derisive laughter and presently the 'King of Painters' agreed that two ravishing Grecian nymphs would expect, indeed be affronted not to have, a carpet of flowers about their lily-white feet.

Then they all drank to the success of the oil-painting that would leave the critics speechless – for once – at the sight of their combined artistic genius.

In the years that followed Marie-Marthe was often to look at that unfinished masterpiece. The noble portico, the marble pillars, the shady groves and the two graceful nymphs dallying on the banks of the little stream had all been painted.

But not a flower bloomed anywhere and Marie-Marthe would fancy those two nymphs were beginning to look outraged to dally so long, waiting for this Pierre-Joseph Redouté to find the time to paint a few flowers about their lily-white feet.

When tackled, Pierre-Joseph would say of course he would complete this masterpiece, just give him time, and he would confound the critic who'd decided he did well to paint flowers in watercolours. This oil-painting would make him change his tune.

Then came the day when Marie-Marthe noticed that the unfinished masterpiece had its face to the wall. No doubt those ravishing nymphs were beginning to look reproachfully at Pierre-Joseph whenever he came into his studio.

In March 1821, quiet Henri-Joseph summoned up his courage to face the future, his ever-darkening future.

Twenty-two years had slipped away since he'd returned from Egypt suffering from the Egyptian Eye Disease. He faced the truth, his sight was slowly, but relentlessly growing worse, his work was taking him longer and longer. The naturalists who valued his illustrations were always kind and tolerant, so was the Dutchman, Monsieur van Spaendonck when he gave him the privilege of painting another 'Vellum'.

Pierre-Joseph and Marie-Marthe were both unfailingly good to him but Henri-Joseph had his pride. As long as he could see, he would with the help of heaven, be self-supporting. But it would be a godsend if he had a little more capital behind him, enough maybe to buy a small annuity.

Henri-Joseph was very like his quiet mother who had been the soul of thrift. The small pension he'd been awarded for his work in Egypt had come to an end with the downfall of Napoleon, but he'd always put aside some part of what he earned. But prices were always rising and as fast as they rose, down went the value of his careful little capital, and now his work took so long, he was earning less and less.

The monumental work, *Description of Egypt*, the combined work of the members of the Artistic and Scientific Commission had long been published and among the many illustrations were fifty-four by Henri-Joseph. Pierre-Joseph had advised him to keep the originals saying they would increase in value as the years went by, and as always Henri-Joseph had done as Pierre-Joseph had advised him to do.

Parma Violets

But this was not the only reason that Henri-Joseph was now glad he had kept those fifty-four sketches and paintings.

It is strange how often as the years go by men seem to develop a selective memory of even the most terrible of wars. They begin to recall not the miseries, the suffering, the appalling way so many had died, all of which they had thought they would remember with bitter resentment to the end of their days. They begin to remember instead with wry affection and even pride certain days and experiences of those days.

This had happened to quiet, peace-loving Henri-Joseph. He now recalled the wondrous sights he had seen, the Pyramids, the ancient monuments, the strange and beautiful fishes of the Nile, the fascinating reptiles he'd love to paint, even the cooking pots that had been unearthed – and so much beside.

He had also brought back with him an interesting herbarium of the plants he had seen, and among these carefully dried and pressed Egyptian flowers there were some that at the time had made him sick with longing for the cool skies of home. It seemed unbelievable to find flowers and weeds growing near Cairo that also grew in the countryside around Saint Hubert, wild convolvulus for instance, stinging nettles and scarlet poppies.

For some time now, at the back of his mind, Henri-Joseph had been cherishing a dream to publish a book of his own one day, with a title such as, *Historic Journal of Observations and Research during the Expedition to Egypt.*

True, the monumental work, *Description of Egypt*, had been published but his *Journal* would be altogether different. It would be a record of all he himself, one man alone, had seen and discovered.

But the years had gone by and not one chapter of his *Historic Journal* had he managed to write. He faced the truth, the bitter truth. He would never now write his *Journal*, his eyesight was too precarious.

However, he still had the originals of those fifty-four illustrations. The time had come to sell them, and he knew the very man who would appreciate them, give him a good price for them – Monsieur the Count of Chabrol.

Monsieur the Count of Chabrol had also been a member of the Expedition to Egypt, and he now held the important post of Prefect of the Department of the Seine. He would have funds at his disposal for the acquisition of work of scientific value; and he would certainly remember how highly he had praised Henri-Joseph's fifty-four sketches and paintings.

Head bent low over his desk, Henri-Joseph composed a draft of a polite and formal letter to the Count of Chabrol. When he felt he could not improve on it, he began to make a fair copy:

Monsieur the Count,

Inspired by the love you have for the Sciences and Art, and for those who cultivate them, makes me hope you will consider the offer I have the honour to propose to you – to acquire for the Library of the Hôtel de la Ville of Paris the fifty-four original paintings and sketches that I brought back from Egypt, which now illustrate the great work of the Commission to which, as you know, Monsieur the Count, I too had the honour to belong.

Here Henri-Joseph hesitated. He had a horror of making his appeal sound like a begging-letter. But he steeled himself to continue, dipped his pen in the ink and slowly, painstakingly wrote:

In acquiring these for France you will also come to aid of an unfortunate artist who is no stranger to you.

I therefore dare to hope, Monsieur the Count, that you will consider this request and honour me with a favourable reply.

I am, with respect, your humble and obedient servant,

H. J. Redouté, jeune.

One cannot be sure that the Count of Chabrol, busy with endless functions as Prefect of the Department of the Seine, found time to consider Henri-Joseph's letter, or that it was even brought to his notice. All that is certain is that days later some careless hand scrawled across it:

Library cannot make this acquisition. Reply expressing regrets and thanks for offer.

The days dragged on but at last it came – the eagerly awaited letter from the Prefecture. Henri-Joseph tore open the imposing official envelope, and read and reread the reply. It could not have been more brief. Some clerk must have been told to write this cold, insultingly curt letter, express these hollow perfunctory regrets.

Henri-Joseph sat down, his legs seemed to be giving way under him, and stared blindly before him. His dream of publishing a book of his own one day, and now his hope of selling his long treasured paintings and sketches, they had all been a mirage, nothing but a mirage such as some desperate and thirsty man sees before him in the sandy wastes of the Sahara.

Now he must struggle on as best he could, pray earnestly to heaven to save what was left to him of the priceless gift of sight so that he might earn enough to pay the rent of his modest room, and never, never, please God, have to eat the bread of charity.

One look at Henri-Joseph's pale face when he next came to see them was enough to tell Pierre-Joseph and Marie-Marthe that he'd had a bad shock. But when he showed them a copy of his letter to Monsieur the Count of Chabrol and that curt official reply, they knew it was far more than a shock, it was a cruel, most humiliating disappointment.

'But they are fools, I tell you,' cried Marie-Marthe, 'all that swarm of self-important officials earning fat salaries at the Prefecture. Ask anyone who has ever tried to squeeze an intelligent reply from them. They toss a letter from one desk to another for days on end. They don't even bother to open and read it carefully, I'll be bound, unless it bears an important crest upon it.'

Marie-Marthe, still raging at the crass stupidity of the Prefecture and all employed therein, went off to make her panacea for all shocks, a pot of strong coffee. But as she made it, she felt there were times when she could shake Henri-Joseph until the teeth rattled in his head.

Why emphasise eternally that he was only Henri-Joseph, 'jeune', the younger brother of Pierre-Joseph, give the impression that he forever lurked in his protective shadow. He was so gifted an artist.

When would he realise this and sign his work 'Henri-Joseph Redouté'? And no more nonsense about this feeling that he must add 'jeune'.

But when she carried in the coffee she slammed it down and continued her tirade: 'The Prefecture? Huh! I tell you, Henri-Joseph, your work will be remembered, admired when the whole pack of those officials are dead, buried and forgotten.'

In her anger, Marie-Marthe was speaking the sober truth. One hundred and fourteen of the priceless 'Vellums' stored today in the Library of the Jardin des Plantes in Paris are signed: 'Henri-Joseph, jeune', and date both before and after his return from Egypt.

No-one studying the latter ones would believe for a moment that Henri-Joseph had then been afflicted with the grim handicap, the Egyptian Eye Disease. Everyone is amazed at the admirable and meticulous accuracy of every one of those 114 'Vellums'.

On 5 May 1821, a violent storm broke over the island of Saint Helena. The wind howled and shrieked as it savagely uprooted trees, and the sky suddenly seemed to be rent apart and down in torrents poured the rain.

On his bed, on that day in May, Napoleon lay dying in agony of a cancer of the stomach, and as the tempest raged outside, he most mercifully died.

As soon as the news of his death was known in Paris, a thousand and one rumours began to fly around. One said that as he lay dying Napoleon had pleaded, begged like a child to be given a sip of coffee. But the doctors attending him had forbidden it, saying it would be bad for him.

Bad for him! When they knew that nothing he swallowed would now be bad or good for him!

Others said those English must have hearts of cold stone not permitting any one of his family to be with him, hold his hand, close his eyes in death, not even Madame Mère, his mother. Everyone respected Madame Mère. Hadn't Napoleon once declared that the only woman he had both loved and respected was Madame Mère?

Others denied this. They said that Madame Mère refused to believe in any news coming from Saint Helena. She was sure her son would soon elude the English again and return, safe and sound.

Then one evening Jules Janin dumbfounded Pierre-Joseph by thoughtfully saying that in all justice to Napoleon, one had to have the honesty to remember that he did not begin the wars that had ended so disastrously at Waterloo. Their revolutionary government had started this warfare, their lofty aim at first had been to liberate, not conquer the people of Europe.

Success had soared to Napoleon's head, their wars of liberation had become wars of conquest. Napoleon, to his mind, had 'confiscated' the Revolution to further his own ambitions and now as Shakespeare had put it: all 'his conquests, glories, triumphs, spoils, shrunk to this little measure' – a narrow grave in the Valley of Geraniums in that island lost in the grey vastness of the Atlantic Ocean.

Madame Prevost too had heard many conflicting rumours all claiming to be the truth, the solemn truth, of every detail of Napoleon's last agony and death.

'I suppose you've heard', she said when Pierre-Joseph next visited her, 'that one swears Napoleon had a locket about his neck when he died, and inside were some Parma violets from Josephine's grave, and that his last words were "Poor Josephine! I truly loved her."

'Others say he rambled on about his "Grande Armée", the brilliant victories he had won. But why go on? Why believe in any of these "one says. . . . "? As I've so often said to you, endless gallons, a sea, of ink, will be needed by historians, busily selecting the "one says" they prefer and no doubt there will be an avalanche of ponderous volumes all claiming to be the veritable, the only veracious history of the rise and fall of Napoleon.

'Ah, my dear friend,' sighed Madame Prevost, 'what times we have known in our day.

'By the way,' said Madame, abruptly changing the subject – she had quite a talent for this – 'tell Mesdemoiselles, your daughters, not to be distressed to learn that the imprudent poet, Béranger, has at last landed in jail. I'm told he wrote another of his songs, a most touching one this time, about a poor old soldier, mutilated in the wars, who'd hidden away the tricolour flag he'd proudly carried in many a battle. And the refrain is being sung in many a dimly lit cellar packed with veterans of Napoleon's wars.' It went something like this, so Madame Prevost had gathered:

> *Oh, when shall I shake off the dust*
> *That now dims thy noble colours?*

This had proved too much for the Royal Literary Police, and that incorrigible poet had been arrested and sentenced to three months in the prison of Saint Pélagie.

But Pierre-Joseph had to tell his daughters that Béranger was dumbfounding his jailers, assuring them that he was thoroughly enjoying his stay in Saint Pélagie. After forty years in his garret, he now had every comfort, the roof over his head didn't leak, he had a good thick blanket on his bed, and luxury of luxuries, he had regular meals brought in to him!

In fact he was afraid that Saint Pélagie might spoil him, make him used to this carefree way of life.

'Ah, well,' said Madame Prevost, 'it's comforting to know someone is enjoying life today.'

And with that, she turned to show Pierre-Joseph her 'flowers of the day' – a vase of Parma violets.

22

Adélaïde

❈ ❈ ❈

For weeks the talk in the cafés of Paris was still of nothing but the death of Napoleon, and whenever Pierre-Joseph and Monsieur Thory arranged to meet in their favourite café, they were assailed with more and more conflicting rumours.

But soon they would be oblivious of the heated arguments raging about them, they would be discussing another variety of rose that had been brought to their notice – often by friendly rose-lovers they had never met. They were still devoting every free hour to their work on *Les Roses*, determined as ever to make it the most beautiful, accurate and comprehensive record of the varieties of roses then growing in France.

So imagine Pierre-Joseph's pleasure one evening when Madame Prevost showed him her 'flower of the day' – an enchanting branch of a rose-bush. It bore a cluster of three roses and a charming bud, but it would be well-nigh impossible to find the precise words to describe its subtle, unusual colour, a soft pink that became almost violet when the petals caught the light. Its foliage was also unusual for both sides of its leaves had a soft green sheen.

For a long moment Madame Prevost and Pierre-Joseph stood in silence sharing the same delight, the same veneration for this miracle of loveliness.

Madame, as always, was the first to speak, bring them both down to earth again.

'Now that is a rose you simply must paint.'

'Yes,' said Pierre-Joseph. 'Yes.'

'As far as I know', said Madame Prevost, 'it hasn't a name, but of course I'm no botanist. You must show it to Monsieur Thory. He'll know its name if anyone does.'

She took the branch of roses, expertly and swiftly wrapped it and handed it to Pierre-Joseph, shook hands and escorted him to the door with the customary 'Au revoir, my dear friend. Come again soon.'

Now Pierre-Joseph had not told Madame Prevost, indeed she hadn't given him the time to tell her, that he had already decided to paint that rose. A small number of rose-lovers were already growing bushes of it in their gardens or greenhouses, but not one of them knew its name. Monsieur Thory had closely examined it, noted all the botanical details, made his usual exhaustive inquiries and had come to the conclusion that it had definitely not yet been given a name. They would have to decide on a fitting name for this fascinating rose.

When Pierre-Joseph brought home that spray of roses, he gave it to Adélaïde. She filled a slender vase with water and in it set that graceful spray of roses. Only then did she stand back, looking at it, lost in thought.

Presently she said, 'Papa, it's exquisite! And it's not only its colour, it has something else, something I can only call distinguished.' Then she laughed and said: 'It's ridiculous I know, but I sometimes think that roses are like beautiful women. Each has a beauty of its own, from the great generous cabbage of a rose to the dainty, most fragile of wild roses. But this one has an elusive "something" as well, something very special.'

It was then that Pierre-Joseph made a lightning decision. He knew that *Les Roses* was his finest work, and in this there was no arrogance only the intuitive certainty that he would never surpass it. The moment had come to keep his vow. It was in *Les Roses* that he must pay his tribute to the man to whom he owed so much. This outstandingly lovely rose must bear the name:

'Rose L'Héritier'

Pierre-Joseph sensibly left it to Monsieur Thory to put in his excellent French all that he wished to say, and after much thought, Monsieur Thory wrote:

> We have given this rose the name of L'Héritier (Charles-Louis), the distinguished and erudite botanist, born in Paris in 1746, dead, assassinated, during the troubles of the Revolution on April 16, 1800.
>
> The painter of this work, in dedicating this modest monument to the memory of Monsieur L'Héritier, has wished to make a public recognition of his gratitude to the illustrious Academician who in entrusting him with the illustrations for his *Sertum Anglicum* as well as the greater part of much of his other work, directed his steps into a new career, taught him to perfect his talent, and thus enabled him to win the approval with which the public today honour him.

One was expected to frame a tribute like this in formal phrases, but it was, of course, the exquisite painting of the 'Rose L'Héritier' that truly expressed Pierre-Joseph's gratitude and affection for upright L'Héritier.

January 1822 was the blackest month of all their lives. Their quiet gentle Adélaïde began to suffer agonising headaches, and not one of the eminent doctors in Paris was able to do anything but dose her with more and more pain-killing drugs. Relentlessly, cruelly, their effect grew less and less, and back again would come the agonising pain in her head, and day by day, hour by hour, she grew weaker, less able to endure it.

It was heart-breaking to be told that they must have the courage to face the inevitable, accept that Adélaïde was dying of a 'pressure on the brain', probably an inexplicable pressure of water, or a tumour. But diagnosing the cause made no difference. An operation was out of the question: it would be fatal.

It was heart-rending to see her in such agony, and be able to do nothing, nothing at all, but sit by her side, hold her hand and pray.

When the end came and Adélaïde at last lay in peace, they remembered her gentle quiet voice saying that death had been the last friend of King George III of England, his kind and merciful last friend.

Death had released their Adélaïde from her agony; quiet death had also been her last merciful friend. They would not have wished her to live another hour in such anguish.

All that night, Pierre-Joseph, his heart breaking within him, toiled at his desk to write the epitaph for Adélaïde. No-one else could express their love for her, and their sorrow.

When dawn broke, Marie-Marthe came into his studio with a cup of hot strong coffee.

'Drink it,' she pleaded. 'Please drink it.'

The floor was littered with crumpled sheets of paper which Pierre-Joseph had thrown aside, but now he looked up, face grey and haggard, and pushed aside his last attempt to write that epitaph.

Marie-Marthe picked it up and read it. 'My love,' she said, and put her arms about him, 'no need to try again. No need at all.'

Pierre-Joseph's last attempt read:

UNDER THIS MONUMENT REPOSES

MARIE-LOUISE-ADELAÏDE

REDOUTÉ

ASSOCIATE MEMBER

OF THE LINNEAN SOCIETY

OF PARIS

BORN IN THIS TOWN

15 APRIL 1792

DIED

22 JANUARY 1822

TO THE NOBLE QUALITIES OF HER SEX

SHE KNEW HOW TO UNITE

A GREAT GIFT

KNEW WELL HOW TO PAINT NATURE

PURE OF SOUL

BEAUTIFUL, BEST OF DAUGHTERS

LOVING SISTER, DEVOTED FRIEND,

SHE WAS LOVED BY ONE AND ALL.

SHE HAS LEFT TO EVERYONE
THE EXAMPLE OF HER VIRTUES,
AND ETERNAL GRIEF
ON HER DEPARTURE
FROM THIS EARTH.

'It's perfect', choked Marie-Marthe, 'Perfect.'

Letters of sympathy came pouring in and it deeply moved them to realise how their quiet, gentle Adélaïde had won the affection of all who had known her.

At the next meeting of the Linnean Society of Paris there was one tribute they were to cherish all their lives long. One member spoke for the others when he said:

'The lovable daughter of a painter whose brush has immortalised the most beautiful of flowers, Adélaide Redouté whose youth, loveliness, talents and virtues were powerless to save her from a destiny so like the fate of the roses so beautifully painted by her father which nature destines to live but a day.'

Josephine had always been devoted to Adélaïde. It was desolating to realise that never again would she see her sister curled up in a chair, 'devouring' another book, and scold her, tell her to come out with her and enjoy the fresh air and sunshine.

Josephine was not imaginative; she had no gift for words, but she had the deepest sense of duty to God and her family. And she was convinced that heaven inspired her when she found her mother weeping bitterly in the kitchen one day.

'Maman,' she said quietly, 'Adélaïde is not dead. She is with God.'

'Yes,' sobbed Marie-Marthe, and took a towel and dried her eyes.

From that day on they began to talk freely about Adélaïde, not as dead, but as if they knew she was indeed with God. And in this, they found consolation and peace of mind.

Pierre-Joseph and Marie-Marthe were never to know that Josephine had now decided she would never marry. In days past Marie-Marthe had often been exasperated to see what little interest her two daughters showed in marriage though they had every opportunity to meet many a suitable young man. And very vexed Marie-Marthe would be when neither of them ever exchanged a romantic smile with any young man. Polite? Oh, yes. Interested? Again yes, especially when some exasperating young man was holding forth on the Roman monuments of Nîmes or some other frustrating topic.

Level-headed Josephine knew she was not beautiful, but neither was she ugly and unattractive. She'd decided she might well marry one day but so far no young man had ever made her dream of walking hand in hand with him in a moonlit garden of roses with nightingales singing rapturously of love. Much less marry him.

Life at home was happy, full of interest, for both Pierre-Joseph and Marie-Marthe loved to have visitors. They made even the most unexpected of them welcome, insisted that they stay and eat a meal with them. And this was always possible for Marie-Marthe prided herself on her well-stocked larder and loved to hear compliments on her excellent cooking.

'Now, taste me this!' she would say as she triumphantly brought in a magnificent soufflé, golden brown, done to a turn, and ordered their visitors to take up their forks and do immediate justice to that culinary masterpiece.

Josephine had always made herself useful in a hundred practical ways, and she realised that her parents now had great need of her. She dearly loved them. In future they must always come first in her devotion and loyalty. It would be a good way to spend her life. To Josephine it was as simple, as uncomplicated as that, and no self-righteous halo ever quivered over her sensible head.

So thanks to Josephine, they presently flung back the dark shutters of grief and let in the sun and air, and their home again became a warm and hospitable place where their many friends loved to visit them, just as before.

Just as Adélaïde herself would surely have wished.

23

Fête Champêtre

Early in May that same year, 1822, the genial Dutchman, Monsieur
van Spaendonck, died. He was seventy-six and for almost thirty
years he had held the post once pompously called: 'The Chair of
Natural Iconography or the Art of Drawing and Painting all the
Productions of Nature'. But this had now been abbreviated to
'Professor Administrator of the Jardin des Plantes'.

His duties, however, remained as before; it was he who had full
charge of the 'Vellums', he who decided when to add another
'Vellum' to that priceless collection, and who should be given the
privilege of painting it. It was also he who gave the popular public
lessons in the magnificent library of the Jardin des Plantes. For all
this, he was paid a yearly salary of 5,000 francs.

Pierre-Joseph had always worked so closely, so harmoniously,
with Monsieur van Spaendonck that it was generally assumed that
he would now step into his shoes. He had never painted better, and
he could teach. What more natural than that Pierre-Joseph should
also think that he would be the one to take on the work of Monsieur
van Spaendonck?

But to Pierre-Joseph's horror, the death of Monsieur van Spaendonck became the signal for all manner of petty intrigues. Pierre-
Joseph had no weapons against this. He loathed all intrigues and
when some malicious gossip would buttonhole him and with the
time-honoured device of all trouble-makers, begin to say how much
he regretted to have to tell him . . . but . . . in Pierre-Joseph's best
interest of course . . . he felt he ought to know. . . .

At this point, Pierre-Joseph would say, 'Forgive me, Monsieur, but I have an urgent appointment,' and hurry away, leaving the gossip, mouth still open, gaping at this ungrateful Belgian.

Now the Linnean Society of Paris had always liked to make a red-letter day of 24 May, the birthday of great Linnaeus. This had not always been possible in the stormy past when suspicious official-dom had seen danger in meetings of any kind. They could be so convenient a cloak for anti-government agitators. But times had changed. Louis XVIII had no liking for his Literary Police and the Linnean Society of Paris was again flourishing.

It was unanimously decided to make May 24 that year a most memorable occasion. They would hold their first 'Fête Champêtre' in the lovely forest of Fleury-Meudon.

Now the very name 'Fête Champêtre' conjures up the romantic pictures the artist, Watteau, painted in the days when Louis XIV reigned over his magnificent pleasure-loving court of Versailles. They depict ladies, young and beautiful of course, in elegant low-cut gowns, and handsome young gentlemen, also elegantly dressed, lounging gracefully in some forest glade or dancing a stately minuet on the smooth green turf of a wooded glade.

The first 'Fête Champêtre' of the Linnean Society of Paris was going to be altogether different, a birthday celebration worthy of great Linnaeus.

There were the kindest of reasons behind this decision. They were all very fond of Pierre-Joseph and his family, and they had been truly grieved to hear of the death of Adélaïde. They were also aware of the underhand petty intrigues now simmering in the Jardin des Plantes, and they knew how Pierre-Joseph must be feeling about this.

When Pierre-Joseph and Marie-Marthe were discreetly approached, they both thought a 'Fête Champêtre' a wonderful idea, and Marie-Marthe added it would be just the tonic they needed.

At crack of dawn on 24 May 1822, the members of the Linnean Society of Paris arrived with exemplary punctuality at an agreed meeting place in the forest. For days the weather had been unusually warm and though it was so early, it was already so warm that one would think it was noon in high summer. However a welcome sight met their eyes – light refreshments awaited them on long trestle tables set out under the trees.

They merrily made short work of this and then divided, as planned, into small groups, and away they went, the botanists in search of flowers, plants and ferns they had not seen before, the entomologists, armed with nets, in search of interesting butterflies and other insects.

Presently the less diligent among the young lady botanists began to dawdle and to pick flowers to make festive garlands to hang about everyone's neck. And never before had the lovely forest of Fleury-Meudon echoed and rung with such cries of delight and joyous laughter.

Then came the signal to assemble. The younger botanists gathered around the more erudite, older ones, the young entomologists about the more learned authorities on insects. And what a rewarding search it had been for the botanists! They had discovered a number of rare forest orchids, a strange little pink, and joy of joy, three wild roses unknown to Pierre-Joseph and Monsieur Thory.

No-one recorded if the young entomologists had been equally successful. Insects on the wing always seem to take a positive delight in eluding the nets of all eager amateur entomologists. However, the learned, more experienced entomologists patiently gave them the correct names of any insects which had obligingly flown into their nets, and information gathered in a forest is infinitely more interesting than any indoor lecture.

The time had now come to meet the wives, mothers and daughters of these nature-lovers, every lady among them exclaiming heavens, how hot it was! They all made themselves as comfortable as possible in the shade of the trees and their Annual Meeting began.

Monsieur their President opened the proceedings with an official statement of the progress made during the past year by the Society, followed by a solemn assurance of its unswerving high moral and scientific aims.

One member after another then rose to make a speech but some of the ladies were now beginning to look apprehensively up at the darkening sky, and start when from far away came the roll of thunder. More ominous still, the birds had ceased to sing.

Then came a vivid flash of lightning and a mighty roll of thunder. This was truly unfortunate for the lady poet who at that very moment was declaiming an ode she had composed for the occasion. Head thrown back, clasping her hands in a veritable transport of poetical verse, she was announcing she was gazing into the 'vault of heaven above', and 'invoking Apollo, the God of the Arts'.

But alas, Apollo must have been deafened by the roar of thunder for down from the 'vault of heaven above' came the rain, a deluge of rain, and led by Pierre-Joseph away they fled to his nearby house.

What a welcome awaited them there! Piles of towels in every room, and pots of hot coffee to restore them. The whole house rang with exclamations of grateful relief and as one gentleman later put it, there was 'a most amiable disorder'.

All this thanks to Josephine, who had seen the storm gathering and discreetly slipped away to help her mother prepare to welcome their rain-soaked friends. Once dry and refreshed, they inspected Pierre-Joseph's greenhouses and exclaimed again and again at his wonderful collection of rare and lovely flowers.

Then the sky cleared, the sun shone out again, and they strolled around Pierre-Joseph's garden, admiring his beds of flowers, above all the roses already in bloom. Pierre-Joseph's homely face shone. This was how a home, a real home should be – all these friends sharing his delight in his comfortable house, his beautiful garden and greenhouses.

At five o'clock they assembled again in Pierre-Joseph's large sitting-room, gay with vases of flowers, and in place of honour a bust of Linnaeus crowned with a wreath of 'immortelles' – everlasting flowers, we call them in English. Everyone admired the pictures on the walls, idyllic Greek and Italian landscapes and many a superb flower-painting. Most of all, for by now they were very hungry, they admired the table in the shape of a horseshoe laden with dish upon dish of delicious food and a festive array of bottles of wine. And to a chorus of appreciation, the Annual Banquet began.

No-one expected such a feast to be devoured at the gallop. Heavens, no! There was much lively conversation and every now and then a gentleman would rise to his feet and make a speech. There was one witty speech for instance by one of their members who had sailed around the world, and en route had landed in Gibraltar. It had been a real pleasure to meet the English governor there, one Milord Don, a genuine philanthropist, benevolent to one and all and with only two passions in life: peace, and potatoes.

But the Ile de France, now that was deplorably different. That small island off the coast of Madagascar had suffered from three major disasters: a raging fire, a howling hurricane and Monsieur their Governor. Of the three, Monsieur their Governor was undoubtedly their greatest disaster. The fire and the hurricane had died away, but Monsieur their Governor remained, a permanent disaster.

As always on such occasions there were some earnest gentlemen who weren't going to miss the chance to deliver an edifying speech that droned on and on. The ladies were therefore doubly grateful that they had been presented with beautiful fans, decorated with the Floral System of great Linnaeus. A lady could fan her face and delicately hide a little yawn now and then.

Then there were two gentlemen who had both written long poems instead of speeches, very long poems, but between the poems, the speeches, they could all relax and join again in lively conversation – until another gentleman rose to his feet.

To conclude their Annual Banquet their treasurer had written new words to the tune of an old song they all knew and soon they were all singing the chorus:

> *Let us sing a joyous refrain*
> *To Linnaeus, flowers, and science.*
> *Decorum will not hide her face*
> *As we our dear love loud proclaim.*

After this coffee was served on the two terraces and Marie-Marthe, flushed and triumphant, was besieged by ladies begging to have the recipe for that most delicious jelly, the raspberry-flavoured white-currant one.

Then away they went to a nearby forest clearing and began to dance. Yes, dance. It's easy to dance when one is happy and well fed. And with a couple of local fiddlers delighted to play away non-stop, and earn a little money adding such gaiety to this unusual 'Fête Champêtre'. And if the older members grew a little breathless, they could sit down, backs against a tree and watch the younger ones.

Meanwhile their conscientious Secretary had remained behind to record the events of that red-letter day, everything from the meeting at dawn to the speeches, the poems, the songs that enlivened their Annual Banquet, and finally this most enjoyable of rustic balls in a forest clearing.

At the time agreed, there was a call for silence, and as Monsieur their Secretary read out his report, the forest rang to loud applause especially when he came to this sonorous and splendid conclusion:

Let dour rigorists dare to criticise, condemn our spontaneous joy, and we shall pity them. The sciences have been created to civilise men, to make life more beautiful, not increasingly tedious and boring.

This was signed 'in the forest of Meudon' by Messieurs their President, their Vice-President and their Secretary, and as a distant clock in a church steeple struck nine, Monsieur their President declared their 'Fête Champêtre' had come to its end. Then with many a cordial handshake and gallant kissing of ladies' hands they said 'Au revoir!' and presently that forest clearing lay still and silent under the moonlit sky.

That night Pierre-Joseph, Marie-Marthe and Josephine surveyed the 'amiable confusion' about them and Marie-Marthe said it had all been worthwhile, so worthwhile.

But Pierre-Joseph and Josephine had seen the tears that had come to her eyes, and Pierre-Joseph kissed her and said, 'Yes, my love. It was what Adélaïde would have wished.'

'Yes,' said Marie-Marthe, and blew her nose and said it was high time they went to bed. All this 'amiable confusion' could wait until tomorrow.

24

Legion of Honour

At last came an official announcement that for reasons of economy, the post held so long by Monsieur van Spaendonck was to be abolished. It was to be replaced by two posts, one for 'all matters to do with botanical illustrations', the other for 'all matters relating to the science of zoology'. The yearly salary of 5,000 francs received by the late Monsieur van Spaendonck was to be divided equally between them.

Pierre-Joseph had been given the first of these two posts. He would be in full charge of the 'Vellums', and would be required to give thirty lessons a year, each to be three hours long, and to be given on Mondays, Wednesdays and Fridays in the library of the Jardin des Plantes.

Two thousand five hundred francs a year! This was a real blow. Pierre-Joseph had been counting on twice that amount. Even this would have been a pittance compared to the yearly 18,000 francs paid to him by the late Empress Josephine. Each instalment of *Les Roses* was costing so much to produce and though critics praised the excellence of the illustrations and Monsieur Thory's text, the number of subscriptions was still disappointing. Great libraries, museums, patrons of the arts were still short of money.

And for the first time for many years, so was Pierre-Joseph. But happy-go-lucky as ever he saw no real difficulty in making two ends meet. The first edition of *Les Roses* would soon be completed, then he would bring out other editions on less costly paper, and these would surely sell, and he'd have the ready money to meet all expenses.

It never entered his head that he was now over sixty, that the time had come to stop and think before he spent, lent, and gave away as generously as ever. Moreover he already had a wonderful idea for his next major work, one that would surely be successful in every way. He had even thought of the title: *Choice of the Most Beautiful Flowers*.

But first he must devote all his free time to those final instalments of *Les Roses*.

Now Henri-Joseph had been hoping against hope that he might be given the post of Professor of 'all matters relating to zoology'. But he soon learned that he had not even been considered. Everyone knew his eyesight was very poor and not in the least likely to improve. Then one could not imagine so diffident a man having the assurance to teach, to command attention. The post had therefore been given to a zoologist with excellent sight, and admittedly excellent qualifications as well.

He too would be required to give thirty lessons a year, each to be three hours long, on Tuesdays, Thursdays and Saturdays in return for his annual 2,500 francs. But if he considered some new species, a strange or lovely bird or animal ought to be painted to add to the 'Vellums' then he had to defer to Pierre-Joseph who would decide which artist was most worthy of this honour. And as there was no doubting Pierre-Joseph's integrity, his ability to choose the right artist, life in the Jardin des Plantes became as harmonious as in the days of Monsieur van Spaendonck.

Sometimes when Pierre-Joseph thought of the 'Vellums' he would be filled with wonder. Who would have dreamed as he set out from Saint Hubert, aged thirteen, snatching every chance to paint a flower as he went, that he would one day be in full charge of so priceless a collection! And he would devoutly hope he would not be 'weighed in the balances', and 'found wanting', either by heaven or the critical shade of Gaston, Duke of Orleans.

High officialdom, having engaged two eminent men for the price of one, now took its leisurely time to settle all the final details.

Month after month went by until at last at nine sharp on the morning of 24 April 1824, Pierre-Joseph walked into the spacious library of the Jardin des Plantes and was staggered to see so many would-be painters of flowers awaiting his arrival. Why, there must be well over a hundred of them!

Curiosity, decided Pierre-Joseph. And he greeted them, and at once began to arrange a few spring flowers in vases of water he had arranged to have ready for him. They watched him as he selected a flower and at amazing speed began to sketch it lightly in pencil and then paint it, explaining all the while why he was doing this or that.

He heard it of course, the first familiar amused murmur at his Belgian accent, the homely way in which he spoke, but it rapidly died away and he knew he had them in the hollow of his great ugly hands; all one hundred of them were watching and listening in rapt silence.

His students were then requested to split up into small groups around a vase of flowers, and to select and study the flower they wished to paint. And Pierre-Joseph began to go from group to group, pointing out with unerring precision what was wrong, emphasising that they must sketch a flower with absolute accuracy, and then, only then, attempt to capture in paint its delicate colouring.

He was naturally flattered when his lessons continued to be attended by a record number of students, but he was taken aback when his old friend Madame Prevost greeted him one evening at the door of 'Au Printemps Perpetuel' and ushered him with elaborate ceremony into the small room behind her shop.

'Well! Well!' she exclaimed, 'I knew you were, rightly, considered to be the most gifted of flower-painters but did I ever imagine you would also become the rage of the most elegant women in Paris?'

'No, my dear friend, I did not!

'It's those lessons you give at the Jardin des Plantes. They afford an elegant woman such an opportunity to be seen in the latest of gowns and bonnets. And those well-dressed gentlemen who have become so interested in flower-painting, can it be that they are also interested in this or that one of your beautifully dressed lady students?'

'Ah, no!' cried Pierre-Joseph. 'And I have been deluding myself that they were genuinely interested in learning to paint flowers.'

'Oh, but they are. I assure you they are,' said Madame Prevost. 'I hear you hypnotise them into listening to you to the point of forgetting the latest in high fashion and even the latest intriguing affair of the heart!'

'Well, thank heaven for that,' said Pierre-Joseph. 'I'd hate to think I am wasting my time, talking myself hoarse in the interests of high fashion and romantic attachments.'

'But wait,' said Madame Prevost, 'it's obvious you never see fashionable journals for ladies. You have become, my dear friend, a benefactor, a gift to their editors. They now have weekly material for fascinating articles giving details of the gowns worn by ladies of fashion who flock to be taught flower-painting by famous Monsieur Redouté. And being truly feminine, they are also able to give discreet hints on the progress of some budding romance or an equally fascinating scandal. No names, of course, just professionally discreet and titillating hints.

'Now, now,' cried Madame Prevost. 'Don't stand there looking so aghast. They also write of the deep respect, the admiration, indeed the warm affection your students have for you. Such excellent publicity, my dear friend!'

Madame Prevost, who was usually so well informed, did not know, however, that a certain gentleman had been closely observing Pierre-Joseph. He too was a gift to editors, not of journals for ladies, but of newspapers with a lively 'gossip column'. He wrote under a variety of names and could be relied upon to supply the most amusing and informative article on any topic of the day, seasoned with a piquant pinch of malice.

He was also far-seeing. He made copious notes and filed them for future reference. Among this gentleman's notes was an eye-witness description of the famous flower-painter, P. J. Redouté. He would be able to sell this at a high price – if Pierre-Joseph suddenly died for instance. He was already over sixty.

'A short, thickset, sturdy body,' wrote this gossip-writer. 'Limbs like an elephant's. Face flat and interesting as a Dutch cheese. Thick lips. An unmusical voice. Crooked, enormous fingers. Altogether not an attractive, indeed a repellent figure.

'Yet under this unprepossessing rind there is the most delicate of tact, exquisite taste, a dedication, a fidelity to his art, everything necessary to develop his undoubted genius.

'Such was Redouté, the painter of flowers who had as his students all the pretty women of Paris.'

You can imagine how Marie-Marthe would have blazed if she had read this gentleman's notes. Pierre-Joseph was certainly not the most handsome of men. But repellent? No, definitely no. His generous homely self shone through that 'unprepossessing rind', and he was not in the least embarrassed by the 'crooked, enormous fingers' the good God had seen fit to give him. He would have roared with laughter to learn his face was 'as flat and interesting as a Dutch cheese', and probably said he loved good Dutch cheese, a generous chunk of it had often been a godsend to him in the days he spent long ago in Holland. As for his voice, it was far better than 'musical', it was warm, friendly and completely unpretentious. As his father had said on that day when he set out to trudge the roads looking for work, Pierre-Joseph 'had so pleasant a way with him. Everyone liked their Pierre-Joseph. Everyone.'

Fame had not corrupted him. Everyone still liked Pierre-Joseph. They saw what was behind that 'unprepossessing rind' and liked him all the more.

In 1824 *Les Roses* was completed. It had taken Pierre-Joseph and Monsieur Thory every moment of their free time for seven years but now the thirty instalments could be bound into three volumes of which they could be justly proud.

One enthusiastic journalist even proclaimed that Pierre-Joseph Redouté was the 'Rembrandt of Roses'. Pierre-Joseph decided this was very flattering but he had a feeling that this journalist had never stood before the masterpieces of great Rembrandt. Then he would have known that here was the work of a giant among painters. His paintings were like the music of Beethoven which made one's hair stand on end, even on Pierre-Joseph's own unmusical head.

No, no, he was no Rembrandt, he had a more modest gift, but if his work opened the eyes of men to the miracle of flowers, the 'stars of this world', then he would be well content.

Pierre-Joseph suddenly laughed aloud. It was not often that he was moon-struck, thinking so poetically. And there was nothing in the least poetic about his present shortage of money.

Then up again soared his spirits like boiling milk. He had come to a major decision. It cost far too much both in time and money to be his own publisher. He would ask Monsieur Panckoucke to become his publisher, leave all future editions of *Les Roses* in his competent hands.

Now Monsieur Panckoucke was a wealthy and successful publisher. Not only had he brought out many a beautiful book but he also had a vital flair for publicity. It was a hard inescapable fact that in those days no matter how successful a publisher, or how excellent a book he wished to publish, he could not risk such a venture without an adequate number of advance subscribers. In short he *had* to have a gift for persuasive publicity.

Pierre-Joseph had no gifts whatever for this preliminary spade-work. In the old days it had been so easy. The subscriptions had come rolling in, thanks to the magnificently generous example set by the Empress Josephine and Napoleon. Moreover he had no need to give a thought to cost when he had that generous yearly salary of 18,000 francs.

Now everything was different, altogether different. But having decided to give up being his own publisher, it seemed to Pierre-Joseph that the future shone safe and carefree. It would be very pleasant to have competent Monsieur Panckoucke as his publisher. He too had a country house in Fleury-Meudon, Pierre-Joseph had given his wife lessons in flower-painting, and they had become friends as well as neighbours. Oh yes, Monsieur Panckoucke was just the publisher Pierre-Joseph needed.

Meanwhile to tide Pierre-Joseph over any urgent lack of ready money, there was obliging Monsieur Mercier.

Obliging, far too obliging Monsieur Mercier! It was a black day when that astute gentleman managed to be introduced to Pierre-Joseph and then hint very discreetly that he would be only too happy to 'accommodate' Monsieur Redouté with a loan at any time. In these difficult days, sighed Monsieur Mercier, a gentleman could so easily become short of ready money for a while.

But by the way, added Monsieur Mercier, he must, with his customary integrity, make it clear that the interest on any 'accommodation' he made would not be acceptable in paper money. Monsieur Mercier had learnt to distrust paper money. Come some national upheaval – and one had seen so many, alas – and an obliging financier could find himself left with sacks of worthless paper. Whereas gold or silver currency kept its value, more or less, as Monsieur Redouté would agree. But he must apologise for rambling away like this, and Monsieur Mercier, having cast his bait, politely left Pierre-Joseph to reflect on how convenient it would be to count from time to time on the services of so obliging and discreet a financier.

Now Monsieur Mercier chose to call himself a financier, but in plain words he was a money-lender. He had his nose close to the ground and he must have discovered that *Les Roses* when viewed in the cold light of financial success, had not been a gold-mine, that this famous painter was generous to a fault, that he had no head for business, that he had an expensive apartment in Paris to maintain as well as a house in the country, and most interesting of all, he was now short of money. And interesting meant financially interesting, of course, to obliging Monsieur Mercier. It would be a pleasure to 'accommodate' so eminent, and unbusinesslike an artist. He could be counted upon to pay the interest on any 'accommodation', and if the worst came to the worst, which was not likely, there was always his property in Fleury-Meudon, a cast-iron security.

It is sadly ironical to admit that astute Monsieur Mercier had accurately assessed the financial success of *Les Roses*. It certainly proved to be no gold-mine. Yet Pierre-Joseph's paintings of roses still live on, still go to millions of hearts the wide world over.

Pierre-Joseph would have been delighted to have known this but there he was now, in the Year of Our Lord 1824, aged sixty-five and he had spent so much on publishing *Les Roses* that he was short, indeed very short of money. And presently he began to borrow from obliging Monsieur Mercier – just to tide him over temporary difficulties, of course.

Then having settled the most urgent bills and tax demands, Pierre-Joseph began to spend all his free time selecting and painting his *Choice of the Most Beautiful Flowers*.

Madame Prevost, who had been selling arrangements of the 'most beautiful flowers' for many a year, was silent for a moment when Pierre-Joseph enthusiastically told her he planned to paint a 'choice' of sixty of them.

'M'm,' she said, and added she didn't envy him. One would need to be Solomon himself to judge between one beautiful flower and another. But from that day, whenever Pierre-Joseph paid her a visit he would always hurry home carrying Madame's most beautiful flower of the day, a branch of a scarlet fuchsia for instance, a superb white camellia, or just as lovely in its simplicity, a golden snap-dragon. Every one of them was a token of Madame's warm affectionate regard for Pierre-Joseph, who loved flowers as much as she did.

He painted them, she sold them. Well, 'c'est la vie.' And Madame was enchanted to learn that just as she expected, those lessons Pierre-Joseph gave three times a week in the Jardin des Plantes were proving excellent publicity. He was receiving requests to give private lessons to ladies who moved in what the gossip-writers called 'the highest society', and he was showing sound common sense in asking the highest fees for this private tuition, just as she asked the highest price for the flowers they respectfully lined up outside her exclusive shop to buy from her.

Marie-Marthe and Josephine were also grateful that Pierre-Joseph was giving those well-paid private lessons. They knew that they now needed that extra money, every franc of it, to pay the taxes and household bills. But of course all worries would vanish like snow when Pierre-Joseph completed his *Choice of the Most Beautiful Flowers*. He confidently believed this, so they too loyally smothered all dark doubts about the future. Nevertheless they did their best to economise, unobtrusively. They also knew of Monsieur Mercier and they both disliked, distrusted this obliging 'financier' who was always so ready, far too ready to 'accommodate' Pierre-Joseph.

Then came a most gratifying and unexpected request from Monseigneur Louis-Philippe, the Duke of Orleans, cousin to the King. He wished Monsieur Redouté to give private lessons to two of his daughters.

Now the very name of Louis-Philippe, Duke of Orleans, brought back memories of the dark days of the Revolution. It made one recall that the Duke's father had enthusiastically become a red-hot revolutionary who believed in the equality of all men to the point of insisting he was called 'Philippe-Egalité'. But in the blackest days of the Terror, he too was denounced and as he could not deny the crime of coming of a family of hated aristocrats, the guillotine had sliced off his head.

His son, the present Duke of Orleans, had also been fired by the first high ideals for the 'regeneration' of France. When the King's two brothers and many other aristocrats had taken to their heels and fled to safety abroad he had remained in France and fought valiantly with the ragged ill-equipped French army when they startled the world by triumphantly defeating and driving back the proud invading armies of Prussia and Austria.

However when his father, for all his revolutionary fervour, was executed, he saw no point in losing his own head as well. He managed to escape, and eventually landed in America. But now, in 1824, he was back in France with his wife and large family of children and he wished Monsieur Redouté to give private lessons to two of his daughters.

'Ah now, this will be interesting!' cried Jules Janin who had come to spend the evening with them on the day Pierre-Joseph received this invitation. 'From all I hear, the Duke knew poverty, face to face, in America, the Land of the Free, when duke or no duke, he was expected to work if he wished to eat. I gather he wasn't at all successful when he tried to teach mathematics so he turned to giving lessons in painting.

'Now he and his family spend the summer on their estate in Neuilly, and the winter in the Palais-Royal here in Paris, just as his noble ancestors always did. But from all I hear, Philippe-Egalité would have approved of the way his son lives "the simple life", and when I say "the simple life" I mean precisely that. In fact his plebeian ways outrage our high-born aristocrats. He actually gets up early, lights his own fire, and swears his favourite food is soup. As if he were of peasant stock!

'But as there would be no sense in raking up the muddy past, and also no denying that his ducal blood is bluer than theirs, they have to acknowledge his existence, but icily, of course.

'You'll like him,' said Jules Janin. 'And he'll certainly like you.'

The following week Pierre-Joseph took the diligence to Neuilly and gave his first lesson to Mesdemoiselles Louise-Marie-Thérèse-Caroline-Elisabeth, aged fourteen, and her sister Marie-Christine-Caroline-Adélaïde-Françoise-Léopoldine, aged thirteen.

It was Marie-Marthe who took the trouble to be so well informed about the names of Pierre-Joseph's new pupils. Then she had the pleasure of flinging up both arms and exclaiming at the long litany of Christian names inflicted on children of royal blood, even if their grandpapa had been a red-hot revolutionary.

Pierre-Joseph came home from that first lesson saying his two new pupils were charming, very eager to learn to paint flowers. It would be a pleasure to teach them. But could he answer any harmless questions that any woman would ask, such as: were they pretty, how were they dressed? Oh no! infuriating Pierre-Joseph hadn't the least idea. All he ever knew was they were always delighted to see him, and were model pupils, listening attentively to his every word. And that the elder one, the Princess of Orleans, to give her formal title, showed a real gift for flower-painting.

One evening, however, Pierre-Joseph came home with more interesting and amusing news. He'd had the pleasure of meeting their papa, Monseigneur the Duke of Orleans. He'd apologised for interrupting the lesson but he'd come to see for himself the progress his two daughters were making. He was the most affable of men, and as he looked at some of their paintings he complimented Pierre-

Joseph; and then jocularly complimented him on the fees he was able to command.

He said he had spent some years in America during the Revolution but the most he'd ever been able to ask for giving lessons in painting was one dollar an hour, never a cent more. But those one-dollar-an-hour lessons at least paid for traditional American breakfasts, piles of hot buckwheat griddle cakes that looked like so many flat round pieces of flannel, but swamped in butter and maple syrup, they were enough to sustain a hungry Frenchman for a day.

Monseigneur the Duke chuckled and said he believed he was artistic, at least he liked to believe he was, but he had no delusions whatever about those dollar-an-hour lessons. He'd frequently thanked his stars that his dollar-an-hour pupils weren't in the least critical. It was ladylike to have lessons in painting, and their republican papas had no doubt been talked into agreeing. But pay him more than one good American dollar an hour for his daughter or wife to be considered ladylike? No, sir, no.

But to be serious, said Monseigneur the Duke, he was very pleased that his two daughters enjoyed their lessons so much and were making excellent progress. And on that note of approval, he shook hands with Pierre-Joseph and left him to get on with the lesson to Mesdemoiselles, his daughters.

As Jules Janin predicted, the Duke certainly liked Pierre-Joseph and he began to invite him from time to time to have dinner with him and his family. Always a simple meal, said Pierre-Joseph, no fuss, no ceremony, for the Duchess Marie-Amélie obviously shared all her husband's views. She was a devoted wife and mother, very gentle and quiet, and she always made Pierre-Joseph feel welcome.

All in all then, Pierre-Joseph had every reason to feel optimistic. He even began to say he'd confess now that he'd always had one regret, their well-loved house in Fleury-Meudon had no extensive view. . . .

'View!' cried Marie-Marthe, instantly alarmed, and said they already had the most attractive views of the garden from their two terraces. Pierre-Joseph said yes, but think how wonderful it would be if they had a view from which they could look down on the valley, see the Seine flowing far below, just such a view that had enchanted the Roman, Julian, centuries ago.

And how, demanded Marie-Marthe, did Pierre-Joseph propose to acquire this view? Pray for a miracle to transport their house and garden overnight high up the hillside?

'Marie-Marthe,' said Pierre-Joseph, 'I once promised you a house, a garden and an orangery in Fleury-Meudon. Well, I'm now promising you that one day we'll have an extensive view as well.'

Marie-Marthe's heart sank like lead. Could Pierre-Joseph be dreaming of buying more land? Then she remembered that this was how she had felt so many times in the past, and in the end had felt ashamed to have been another Martha, 'careful and troubled about many things'. So why cast a gloom now on Pierre-Joseph's happy assurance that the future was going to be as successful as the past.

In September that year, 1824, King Louis XVIII died. Everyone said it was a merciful release, he had been suffering agonies of gout, there was even a rumour that gangrene had set in.

He was childless, and this, declared Jules Janin, was a national disaster, for his brother, Charles, now became His Majesty, His Most Royal Majesty, King of France. He boasted, openly boasted – as if this were a virtue – that he had not changed since the day he had fled from France to save his head.

He decided to be crowned in Rheims as if he were great Charlemagne himself. He even expected his obedient subjects, said Jules Janin, to swallow, without comment, the story that the phial of sacred oil last used at the coronation of Charles III, rightly called the Simple, had been discovered. It had not been broken in the year of Our Lord, 93, as one had always believed. No, it had been miraculously discovered intact, seventeen centuries later, just in time for the coronation of Charles X!

As if this wasn't wondrous enough, Charles X had decided not to be outshone by Charles the Simple who had ordered a host of singing birds to be brought into the Cathedral and let loose from their cages to fly around and sing joyously to celebrate his coronation. Charles X had also had hundreds of singing birds brought into the

Cathedral and set free to fly overhead, singing away, most royally one trusted, all through the endless ancient rites of his coronation.

This crowning of their new king, said Jules Janin, had proved costly for that reckless song-writer, Béranger. He had promptly composed new verses to an old melody and called it 'The Coronation of Charles the Simple'. Every verse ended with the people crying warnings to those heedless birds flying and twittering in the Cathedral of Rheims.

> *The people cry: 'Birds, your wings we envy,*
> *Keep, oh keep secure your liberty!'*

Charles X was not tolerating dangerous songs such as this, and Béranger was sentenced to nine months, not in Saint Pélagie, but in the far less hospitable prison, La Force. He was also fined 10,000 francs, but as he wryly complained he also had to pay the legal fees for the privilege of being sent to jail so the bill came to 11,250 francs. Fortunately, said Jules Janin, Béranger's poems and songs were now selling well and he had many generous friends.

And believe it or not, said Jules Janin, but one sycophantic priest had been all unaware of the cold, hostile silence of his congregation when he confidently assured them that nine months in prison and a fine of 11,250 francs was nothing compared to the punishment awaiting Béranger . . . in hell!

Yes, hell. Poems, songs, like his insulted the Royal Family, and had a corrupting influence on all who read, or more sinful still, sang them.

One could feel a certain respect, said Jules Janin, a liking for Louis XVIII. One even said he had a book of Béranger's poems on the table by his bed. He had done his best to rule in peace – and when possible in his comfortable carpet slippers. But his brother, His Most Royal Majesty, King Charles X, was already alarming many liberally minded men. He was sixty-eight and surely it showed a singular lack of intelligence to boast he had not changed in any way in the thirty-five years he had spent in exile. He *should* have changed, learnt a salutary lesson or two. But no, he seemed determined to bring back all the suffocating ceremony of the old days when the aristocrats danced attendance on the King, and the peasants bowed low before their lords and masters.

So, clad in military uniform, blazing with gold epaulettes and magnificent decorations, white-plumed hat on his head, he was eternally prancing around as if proclaiming: 'Behold me, as elegant and dashing as ever!'

And as narrow-minded and frivolous as ever, added Jules Janin. One could only trust His Most Royal Majesty would soon come down from the moon and face the fact that France had changed in the last thirty-five years, and that no-one, except the ultra-royalists, longed to return to the old days just as they were before the Revolution.

Pierre-Joseph, as usual, made no comment and presently Jules Janin turned to Marie-Marthe and Josephine who had been obviously very interested in all he'd been saying, and cried, 'Look at him! There he sits and if he's silently thinking of our new King – which I doubt – then all he's been hoping is that His Majesty will at least appreciate flowers.'

'Well,' said Pierre-Joseph, 'there's always hope for a man who takes an interest in flowers.'

Five months later Jules Janin said he had had to admit that Charles X occasionally had a moment of common sense. He detested the very name of Napoleon but he had decided to follow the example of his brother, Louis XVIII, and retain Napoleon's famous Legion of Honour, the award for distinguished services to France, both civil and military.

On 14 January 1825, His Majesty, King Charles X, most regally attired, stood before his throne in the splendid salon of the Louvre, and gazed for a moment at the one hundred and one high officials and other eminent men assembled there. To the King's right was a gentleman holding an ornate basket in which lay twenty-seven decorations, the crosses to be awarded to men deserving to become members of the Legion of Honour, though one much preferred to call them Chevaliers, members being so bleak a word.

To the King's left stood another gentleman, armed with a list of twenty-seven names. On that list were the names of artists famous for their scenes of history, others who specialised in landscapes; there were also the names of well-known sculptors and engravers, and of one Englishman, Sir Thomas Lawrence, painter of portraits to the King of England.

But there too on that list of names was that of Pierre-Joseph Redouté, painter of flowers. When he heard his name called, he came forward and stood before the King who took the Cross of the Legion of Honour handed to him by the gentleman to his right, and bestowed it on Pierre-Joseph, saying as he did so:

'I compliment you on the outstanding pupils you have taught. Mademoiselle d'Orléans will be an honour to you.'

The next name was called and back to join the distinguished assembly of spectators retreated Pierre-Joseph, without falling over his feet, thank heaven.

Strange that at such a moment Pierre-Joseph should suddenly think of Napoleon, how on the great day of his coronation, he had been heard to say to one of his brothers: 'If only our father could see us now!'

Pierre-Joseph was also thinking if only his father could see him now – Chevalier of the Legion of Honour of France.

25

Visitor from America

On his way that January evening to congratulate Pierre-Joseph, Jules Janin decided he would have to suffocate his own angry reaction at the lofty, condescending way His Majesty, Charles X had complimented Pierre-Joseph when he handed him his Cross of the Legion of Honour.

His Majesty could not be expected to be liberal enough to compliment Pierre-Joseph on his illustrations of *Letters on Botany*, the work of that detestable revolutionary, Jean-Jacques Rousseau. One could also understand why he had made no mention of Pierre-Joseph's beautiful paintings of the flowers grown by the Empress Josephine – that would have evoked memories of Napoleon whom he loathed and despised. But how mean-spirited of him not to compliment Pierre-Joseph on his illustrations of the work of so many eminent botanists. Not one word of praise either for *The Story of the Succulent Plants* or *Les Liliacées*, not a complimentary mention of *Les Roses*, when all three were acknowledged to be among the world's most beautiful botany books.

A royal compliment paid to *Les Roses*, and in would have come the most welcome of subscriptions to the future editions which Monsieur Panckoucke was now to publish.

But no, His Majesty had complimented Pierre-Joseph on the outstanding pupils he had taught with a special mention of his niece, Mademoiselle d'Orléans. This, in his eyes, was obviously honour enough for any painter of flowers.

Jules Janin knew however that Pierre-Joseph would be as

pleased and happy as a child, and that evening began most festively with Jules Janin congratulating Pierre-Joseph, warmly embracing him, Marie-Marthe, Josephine, and quiet Henri-Joseph who was also there, and then slapping a bottle on the table with a rollicking, 'Champagne! Finest vintage, though I say so myself. We must drink to the health of Pierre-Joseph Redouté, Chevalier of the Legion of Honour of France. And no doubt when they learn of this, the village of Saint Hubert lost among those forests of the Ardennes will also be raising their glasses to the Pierre-Joseph they knew as a boy, and who has shown those French how a Belgian can triumph in the city of Paris.'

Now a royal mention of *Les Roses* would certainly have made all the difference to the subscriptions needed for future editions. But Pierre-Joseph was as optimistic as ever. He still worked so hard and joyously that, as one journalist reported, one would imagine Monsieur Redouté was still in his twenties. This was the simple truth. Pierre-Joseph never considered for a moment that in July he would be sixty-five. Come rain, come shine, he never missed giving his lessons in the library of the Jardin des Plantes, and these continued to be astonishingly popular. He was also giving more private lessons for which he could ask high fees, and yet he found the time now and then to paint another flower to include in his new work.

Pierre-Joseph had no dark shapeless fears of the future. Monsieur Panckoucke would successfully bring out new editions of *Les Roses*, and the money for these, together with the advance subscriptions to his *Choice of the Most Beautiful Flowers*, would work the miracle. He would be able to pay in full the bills, the taxes and everything else that so bedevil a man with no head for business.

Meanwhile the high fees Pierre-Joseph received for those private lessons were more than welcome to Marie-Marthe and Josephine. It was becoming increasingly difficult, indeed at times impossible, to pay the bills, the taxes, and the interest most promptly requested by obliging Monsieur Mercier on the money he had lent Pierre-Joseph. And Josephine would often have to write a polite letter of apology for not settling some account with the assurance that it would be paid as soon as money due to her father came in. Then she would persuade Pierre-Joseph to write to some absent-minded pupil, courteously reminding her – it was always 'her' – of unpaid fees for the private lessons he had given her.

But both Marie-Marthe and Josephine were resolutely determined to show a brave face to the world. Their expensive apartment in Paris must be maintained. Distinguished people came there, very interested to meet Pierre-Joseph and to see the studio of so famous a painter of flowers. This, as Marie-Marthe would say, was gratifying and sound business as well, for these visitors often bought a flower-painting, signed 'P. J. Redouté'.

There was however one memorable day for Marie-Marthe herself when the richly dressed First Lady of Honour to the King's daughter-in-law, Madame the Duchess of Berry, called and asked if she might have the pleasure of seeing Madame Redouté. Yes, Madame Redouté – if she was at home.

Of course Madame Redouté was at home, and with Josephine's help, she hastily put on the dress she kept for special occasions and walked with splendid dignity into Pierre-Joseph's studio, Josephine lost in admiration, walking behind her.

Josephine saw the twinkle in Pierre-Joseph's eyes on beholding dignified Marie-Marthe, and hoped to goodness he would not be tempted to say, 'Permit me to present *my* First Lady of Honour!'

But the First Lady of Honour to the Duchess of Berry immediately began to tell Marie-Marthe that Madame the Duchess had gladly accepted Monsieur Redouté's kind offer to paint a bouquet of pansies and a branch of her favourite camellia to go in her album of flower-paintings. Madame the Duchess was so enchanted with these two paintings that she would like Madame Redouté to accept this token of her appreciation.

With this, she handed Marie-Marthe an artistically wrapped parcel, said a polite farewell and drove away in a magnificent carriage, leaving Madame Redouté still searching for the ceremonious words with which she ought to have expressed her thanks.

When Marie-Marthe opened the parcel, the 'token' was a teapot. Yes, a teapot, but a very beautiful one of solid silver encrusted with gold. Marie-Marthe at once gave it place of honour in a special display cabinet, but did she ever make tea in it? What a question! Risk denting it? Never.

So there it stood in all its splendour, undented, unused, and Marie-Marthe would proudly say that no English Milady, not even Milady Joseph Banks of Soho Square, London, could have had a finer teapot. Marie-Marthe was firmly convinced that all English 'Miladies' drank tea non-stop and must therefore own countless teapots. Practical Josephine however would sometimes wonder if they could make superlatively good tea in that treasured teapot, but this of course was unthinkable.

On another memorable day, Madame the Duchess of Orleans, Marie-Amélie, and her two daughters, came to see Pierre-Joseph's studio, and Marie-Marthe and Josephine were also presented to them. The Duchess Marie-Amélie was the gentlest, the most unpretentious of ladies, and her two little daughters were charming, obviously very fond of Pierre-Joseph, and so respectful, as if they were deeply grateful to be taught by so understanding and excellent a master-painter. As they should be, proudly thought Marie-Marthe.

In the summer of 1825, Pierre-Joseph carefully cut and arranged a bouquet of the finest roses blooming in their garden at Fleury-Meudon, and set out for the village of Reuil.

No Bonaparte, by birth or marriage, or anyone with close ties with their family, was now permitted to set foot in France, but after much pleading, Eugène and Hortense, the son and daughter of the Empress Josephine by her first marriage, had been given permission to commission a marble monument to their mother in the quiet church of Reuil.

It is still there. It shows graceful Josephine kneeling, head bowed, hands folded as if in prayer, looking precisely as the artist, David, had painted her in his famous *Coronation of Emperor Napoleon I*. This was how she had knelt before Napoleon as he was about to place the Crown of France on her head.

The inscription below this monument is a masterpiece of cold brevity:

Visitor from America

Not a word more had been permitted to express their deep love for their mother, only those five words and the date.

But just as David's cruel sketch of Marie-Antoinette on her way to the guillotine, hands tied behind her back, seated on a plank slung across a dung-cart, had given her a touching dignity and courage, so those five curt words seem to add to the poignant dignity of that marble monument.

Pierre-Joseph was not the only one who faithfully remembered how dearly Josephine, once Empress of the French, had loved flowers. Never a day passed but flowers, often from some cottage garden, were laid before that monument to the 'Lady of Malmaison'.

On 20 September 1828, a most unusual visitor, carrying a large and battered portfolio called to see Pierre-Joseph.

Pierre-Joseph who rarely noticed the clothes on a man's back, was interested to see that this visitor was wearing the fringed buckskin jacket of an American woodsman, as depicted in tales of settlers in America.

This was soon explained. His visitor introduced himself as Jean-Jacques Audubon, or John James Audubon as he was known back home in America.

'Home in America!' exclaimed Pierre-Joseph. 'But you speak such excellent French, Monsieur!'

'That isn't difficult, Monsieur,' said the visitor. 'Both my parents were French. But permit me to show you my letters of introduction.'

From a capacious pocket of his buckskin jacket he pulled out a number of letters.

'A little the worse for wear, I'm afraid,' he said. 'I have been carrying them around with me for almost three years.

'They are signed, I assure you, by eminently respectable Americans in New York, New Orleans and Philadelphia. This, however, is the one I'm hoping will interest you.'

He handed Pierre-Joseph a letter, written in French, and signed: 'Charles Alexander Lesueur'.

'Monsieur Lesueur urged me to call on you if I had the good fortune to survive the journey and arrive one day in Paris. He asked me to express his great admiration for your work and that of Monsieur, your brother. As you probably know Monsieur Lesueur is now in America studying and painting the fishes of our rivers, just as Monsieur, your bother, did so admirably in Egypt.'

'Why yes, of course,' said Pierre-Joseph. 'He is sending back the most interesting paintings and notes to the Department of Zoology. Forgive me whilst I read his letter.'

It was not a letter to Pierre-Joseph alone. Monsieur Lesueur warmly recommended Jean-Jacques Audubon to all those interested in the arts and sciences. It stated he was a first-class naturalist and above all an authority on the wild birds of America. He was now engaged on an outstanding work to be called *The Birds of America.*

The letter concluded with the earnest hope that Jean-Jacques Audubon would find encouragement and financial help in the form of advance subscriptions to this work which would undoubtedly be a 'chef d'oeuvre' of a kind never published before, beautifully illustrated and with an impeccably accurate text.

Pierre-Joseph gave back the letter, shook hands with his visitor and said he would certainly do all he could to help him. Then looking at his visitor's large portfolio he laughed and said Audubon had obviously brought some of his paintings with him.

'Yes, Monsieur', said Audubon. 'I was hoping you would allow me to show a few to you.' And he began to untie the tapes of his portfolio.

'No, no, wait a moment,' cried Pierre-Joseph. 'My brother is spending a few days with us. He and my wife and daughter too would never forgive me if they did not have the pleasure of meeting you.'

So Henri-Joseph, Marie-Marthe and Josephine were introduced to Jean-Jacques Audubon, and Marie-Marthe of course insisted he must lunch with them – if he had no other engagement. Audubon said, well no, and Marie-Marthe said splendid, it was not every day they met an artist from America.

Jean-Jacques Audubon proved to be the most interesting of visitors; he was very handsome, he looked so distinguished in his buckskin jacket, and he had the most charming way with him. Moreover the story of his life surpassed any fiction.

He had been born in Haiti in the West Indies where his father had a plantation. He had been barely four years old but he could dimly remember the terrible days when the black slaves there rose in rebellion, yelling abuse, letting loose centuries of pent-up hatred and began to murder their white masters. They had heard of the Revolution in France and they too were going to be free, rid themselves for ever of tyranny.

And, said Audubon, his father who was a kindly liberal-minded man, would sadly say it was a miracle this had not happened before. Many of the plantation owners thought only of their rich crops of coffee, cocoa and sugar and treated their slaves abominably as if they were animals, not human beings.

The Audubon family had been fortunate – their own slaves did not hate them, and they had escaped. After what seemed an eternity of tossing up and down on the ocean they had safely landed at Nantes. His father had a small estate in the countryside some miles from the port itself. But as Pierre-Joseph would remember, Nantes had been a royalist stronghold and soon his father was saying they had escaped from one bloody massacre to face an even more vicious one – Frenchmen were murdering Frenchmen. Thousands of the citizens of Nantes were put to death, or thrown to drown in the river, accused of being loyal to the King.

So it was indeed fortunate that the Audubon house was lost in the quiet countryside, and to tell the truth Jean-Jacques had only pleasant and peaceful memories of those dark and terrible days – thanks to his stepmother and their family physician and friend, Doctor d'Orbigny.

Oh yes, he had a stepmother. He had no recollections whatever of his natural mother but this had never troubled him. His stepmother had been a true mother to him in every way. And so understanding! She did not say so but it was clear she had no opinion whatever of the local school. Not surprising, for in those chaotic days village schoolmasters were forever arriving and disappearing. And not one of them ever remarked how often young Audubon played truant.

His stepmother turned a blind eye, she knew that Doctor d'Orbigny would be truanting with him. Together they would wander in the fields and forests and Doctor d'Orbigny was the best of companions. He was an enthusiastic naturalist and he taught young Audubon to stand very still to watch and listen to the birds, note how and where they built their nests and fed their young.

But Doctor d'Orbigny wasn't only interested in wild birds, he also taught Audubon to look and admire the beauty, the endless variety of trees and wild flowers. And Audubon began to gather flowers and branches of trees and take them home and try to paint them.

All this led of course to Pierre-Joseph remembering his young days when good Dom Hickman had been just such a friend to him. Ah yes, said Aubudon, but Pierre-Joseph had also had the good luck to be taught to paint by his papa. Aubudon's papa was no artist and when he realised his young son seemed bent on painting, he decided he must go to Paris and study seriously under the master-painter, David.

Oh, dear heaven, that terrible, that tyrannical David! Audubon had hated every moment spent in his studio. He even had the youthful audacity to detest great David's famous masterpieces, especially the one depicting Socrates swallowing the hemlock. In fact he was delighted when his father decided in 1803 to send him post-haste back to America to manage, so he said, a small estate he owned in Pennsylvania. The real reason was that he was now eighteen and this would save him from being conscripted into Napoleon's army. Great David probably never noticed his absence, and if he had, he would have shed no tears over losing so unsatisfactory a student.

At this point, Marie-Marthe rose to her feet and said they must eat and Monsieur Audubon was not to speak of anything except maybe the weather, for she did not wish to miss a word of all that then happened to him.

Presently they were seated around the table and Marie-Marthe was quick to notice their visitor was very hungry and was much enjoying her excellent cooking. And they certainly enjoyed listening to him.

He said he had been only eighteen at the time but this was no excuse – he had been the most reprehensible of young managers. He had neglected his ledgers and everything else to go wandering in the forests and along the river banks, watching, listening to the wild birds, and fascinated too by the many wild flowers he had never before seen.

But it was the birds that captivated him more and more, the amazing variety of the wild birds of America. And well, they wouldn't be surprised to learn he'd made a dismal failure of managing his father's small estate. He'd also been a failure in every other venture he undertook from being an ill-paid clerk to running a 'backwoods store' – the name spoke for itself. Always the same reason. He had been the eternal truant, forever escaping to some nearby forest or lake-side to watch, sketch, and paint those fascinating wild birds. Sixteen years of one inglorious failure after another and he landed in jail – a bankrupt.

However, he had a splendid memory of one of his failures. He'd had legal difficulties with a pugnacious American, one Samuel Adams Bowen. Sam, being big and brawny, believed that might was right and decided to kill Audubon, that being far quicker and far more economical, to Sam's mind, than paying a lawyer. Moreover he knew Audubon had injured his right arm.

So Sam grabbed this golden opportunity for instant justice and attacked Audubon with a murderous club. All Audubon had been able to do was snatch a knife and stab Bowen in self defence, not fatally, thank God, but enough to put an abrupt end to Sam's bid for instant, economical backwoods justice.

They were both brought before the local court of justice and when he'd heard all the evidence, the learned judge rose in all his majesty and walked to the dock where Audubon stood, quaking at the knees.

'Mr. Audubon,' he said, 'you have committed a serious offence – an exceedingly serious offence – by failing to kill this rascal.'

'You see,' said Audubon, spreading both hands in mock dismay, 'I failed even in this.'

But to return to his stay in jail as a bankrupt. Some very good friends had paid his debts and once he was free he had decided of course he must pay them back and keep the wolf from the door, by doing the one thing he had been disciplined to do well. He was now, most belatedly, grateful to relentless, terrible David who'd taught him to draw and paint with accuracy.

Famous David would have shuddered, however, at some of the work Audubon now did. At times he'd help to decorate the walls of some great mansion, just as Pierre-Joseph had once done, but he'd also decorate the walls, not of theatres, but of the gaudy parlours of the pleasure boats that plied up and down the River Ohio. He'd also, when given the chance, teach Art, heaven forgive him, in schools for young American ladies.

But it was always a 'nip-and-tuck' existence as they said back home in America, a life of bread and cheese and not always enough of the cheese. Then he began to sketch portraits, in black chalk at first, that being cheaper than paints. As he became better known he invested in paints and was able to put up his fees.

However, again just like Pierre-Joseph, he hated the thought of a lifetime of painting portraits. His heart was always out there in the forests, on the lake-sides or river banks, watching, studying, sketching, painting those wild birds.

It was his wife, Lucy, who persuaded him to risk devoting his life to this absorbing passion. Oh yes, he had the good fortune to have the best of wives, an Englishwoman. She had the courage to have faith in him in spite of all his years of chronic failure.

Audubon pulled out a locket he wore on a silver chain around his neck, opened it and showed them a miniature of his wife, Lucy. Pierre-Joseph, as he looked at it, thought Lucy had lovely and intelligent eyes and he could well believe it when Audubon declared he owed everything to her.

They both became teachers giving lessons in everything from French, dancing, music, to reading, writing and elementary arithmetic. All this was arranged to give Audubon the maximum of free time and very long vacations. Lucy and he now knew what his life's work must be – he must paint the *Birds of America*.

Painting the birds that had so long captivated him was pure delight but then came the problem of finding an engraver with the necessary skill and experience to do justice to his paintings. He therefore hopefully travelled to Philadelphia where he had friends who were interested in the arts and sciences, and when they had seen the paintings he had brought with him, they had all urged him to go to England or France where he'd certainly find not only eminent engravers but where he would meet influential people who might well promise to subscribe to his *Birds of America*.

Lucy also insisted that he must go, and armed with letters of introduction and a portfolio of over two hundred of his paintings, he set sail for Liverpool.

He had met with great kindness but he'd had his moments of black despair. For instance he had once travelled north to Scotland to the city of Edinburgh. Here a well-known engraver, W. H. Lizars, had made some first-class copper plates of some of his paintings, but then he'd had trouble with the men who worked for him. They all walked out, and W. H. Lizars expressed his regrets, shook hands with him and walked out too.

At last he found excellent engravers in London, Robert Havells and his son. They agreed to engrave all his paintings, and they soon became the best of friends. But life was still far from easy, he was often lonely, homesick, he sorely missed Lucy and his children, and though he lived in one room in the poorest district of London, his money was fast running out.

Then who should come to his assistance but the English painter, Sir Thomas Lawrence. He'd visit Audubon in his squalid room and sometimes bring a rich friend with him and see that he paid a high price for one of Audubon's paintings.

'In that case,' cried Marie-Marthe, 'this English Milord well deserved to become a Chevalier of the Legion of Honour!'

Ah yes, agreed Audubon, he did indeed, for he also introduced him to the King of England and wrote to great English museums and libraries and presently Audubon had a list of English subscribers to his *Birds of America*.

But he still needed more. He also longed to revisit France. And here he was now, in Paris, and well, said engaging Jean-Jacques Audubon, he knew he could be frank with Pierre-Joseph. He was hoping he would introduce him to the Duke of Orleans and others who might subscribe to the *Birds of America*.

Now don't imagine for a moment that this had been one long monologue by Jean-Jacques Audubon. Certainly not. It is the story they pieced together as they talked and asked a hundred questions.

All, except Henri-Joseph. He was silent. And Marie-Marthe, seeing him so bent and looking so old, wished with all her heart he too could find a 'Lucy' to comfort and encourage him. Above all, if only his sight would improve!

Then came the moment when Audubon at last untied the tapes of his portfolio and they cleared a large table under a window of Pierre-Joseph's studio, and Audubon began to show them some of his paintings – in water-colours, Pierre-Joseph was delighted to see.

They were breathtaking, so lovely that at first they could only exclaim, and this was poignant, it was Henri-Joseph, stooping low and straining his eyes, who said: 'Now we understand, Monsieur, why you lost your heart to these wild birds of America.'

It wasn't only the beauty of Audubon's paintings that fascinated them; it was the eager way in which he spoke of every bird. He knew them, loved them every one. They could have listened to him all night.

The tiniest of all the birds he'd painted was the ruby-throated humming-bird, yet every year these gaily coloured tiny birds made incredibly long flights from Southern Canada to winter in far away Mexico. Imagine it, said Audubon, a minute jewel of a bird flying fast as the wind for endless mile after mile.

Then there was the Louisiana heron, a most dignified bird with its red-feathered neck, its slate-grey wings and tail, and its white body and underwings, so elegant and graceful a bird that Audubon called it the 'Lady of the Waters'.

But here now was an American song-bird, the whippoorwill. It was dearer and sweeter to Audubon than any nightingale. One could only see it if one stood silent and still at dusk in some forest for its brown and grey plumage made it seem part of the branch or log on which it perched. Its song was a plaintive refrain of three notes which it repeated over and over again in the deep shadows all about it, until the forest seemed to become a haunted secret place.

Ah, but this one, said Audubon bringing out another painting, was very different. It was a prim, trim, drab little bird, but what a clown, what a mimic! A great favourite with everyone for it was as tame as a robin. It could mimic a cat so well that it had been given the name 'Catbird', but it could also sing as sweet as a thrush, croak like a frog, cluck like a hen, and bark like a dog. And courageous! It would even tackle a snake if one was stupid enough to attack its nest, or the nests of its neighbours.

They would probably recognise this bird with its glowing red and yellow head, the Carolina parrot, though some called it the Parakeet. People in Europe kept them in cages, made pets of them, but in Carolina they lived wild and free, as many as a hundred of them, nesting together in the hollow trunks of trees. They were such beautiful wild birds – fatally beautiful – for they were shot to adorn the hats of fashionable women or to add to a hideous glass case of stuffed birds.

And they were so easy to shoot! If one poor parakeet was shot and fell to the ground, the others would continue to fly overhead, calling as if to comfort, to reassure it. But did this move the hearts of sportsmen? On the contrary, they would bang away and down would fall a dozen or more, recklessly, wantonly, shot to make a sportsman's holiday.

But this wasn't all that distressed and angered Audubon. When he saw the unthinking slaughter of so much wild life in America, he feared for the future.

'I tell you I have nightmares at times,' said Audubon. 'Nightmares of a future when there will be no more deer in our forests and millions of our wild birds will be driven away or slain by man, and fish will no longer abound in our rivers and lakes.

'But people laugh as if I were mad and say we have vast acres still unexplored, and all teeming with wild life. At moments like this I feel I am "the voice of one crying in the wilderness".'

'Then God add power to your voice,' said Pierre-Joseph.

'Amen to that,' said Audubon and began to replace his paintings in his portfolio.

It was then that Marie-Marthe began to bustle around, lighting the lamps, and insisting that Audubon had supper with them, ordering Pierre-Joseph to bestir himself and bring up a couple of bottles of wine, they must all drink to the success of the *Birds of America*, and over and over again she said that this had been one of the most interesting, fascinating days they had ever spent.

Late that night, Jean-Jacques Audubon wrote to his Lucy:

Found old Redouté at his painting. The size of my portfolio surprised him and when I opened the work, he examined it most carefully.

He gave me nine paintings of his *Choice of the Most Beautiful Flowers* and promised to send the *Roses*. Now, my Lucy, this will be a great treat for thee, fond of flowers as thou art. When you seest these, thy eyes will feast on the finest you can imagine.

Audubon put down his pen. He ruefully thought, not for the first time, that he'd never learned to write correctly in English, mixing up his 'thou' and 'you', and he wasn't much better when he wrote in French. But his Lucy would only smile and say all that mattered was that he excelled when he described his wild birds.

So he took up his pen again and scribbled a few more lines telling his Lucy that kind old Redouté had promised to introduce him to Louis-Philippe, Duke of Orleans, and Madame the Duchess, his wife, with whom he now had dinner every Friday.

He was also going to take him to meet the famous Gerard, 'Painter of Kings' who, it seemed, kept open house every Wednesday. Kind old Redouté would see to it that he met a host of the distinguished artists, writers and scientists who always came to these Wednesday receptions.

So his Lucy could be easy in her mind. Please God, he'd soon be sailing back home with a rewarding list of French subscribers to his *Birds of America* – thanks to kind old Redouté.

26

The Belvedere

A few days later when Pierre-Joseph paid 'Au Printemps Perpetuel' a visit, he was welcomed by Madame Prevost and ushered into the cool room behind the small shop just as on hundreds of other occasions.

But this time Madame greeted him with: 'Ah! so he spent a whole day with you, our romantic Monsieur Audubon from America!'

'Why yes,' said Pierre-Joseph, marvelling yet again at the way Madame Prevost was always so well informed. And he at once began to sing the praises of Audubon's paintings of the wild birds of America.

But Madame Prevost briskly brushed aside American birds, it was American Monsieur Audubon who interested her as it seemed he interested everyone in Paris. He was, said Madame, the 'topic of the day'. And she would permit herself to ask a blunt question. Did Pierre-Joseph think that Audubon was the answer at last to that unsolved mystery?

'Unsolved mystery?' echoed Pierre-Joseph.

'Yes, yes,' said Madame Prevost, now a little impatient. 'The mystery of the little Dauphin. Did he, or did he not die in that infamous prison? His body has never been found and there are many who prefer to believe that he was rescued and smuggled away to some secret hiding-place.

'There has been, of course, more than one accomplished liar who claimed to be that unhappy child, but every one of them proved to be an imposter. Now there are many rumours about Monsieur Audubon.'

And there stood Madame Prevost, obviously waiting for

Pierre-Joseph to impart some confidential information until he said he regretted it but he was mystified, he failed to see where all this was leading; and waited for Madame to lead on.

She obliged. There were many, she said, who firmly believed this French-American Audubon, yes, Audubon had been that child. He was the right age and appearance and there was something most mysterious about the way he'd been hidden away in a remote country house near Nantes.

As for his own memories of his childhood, a confused and terrified child comes to believe, in time, everything his kind protectors choose to tell him.

Now Pierre-Joseph had seen, with his own two eyes, the little Dauphin when he was called in to paint the cactus which his mother, Queen Marie-Antoinette, had been permitted to keep in their dark prison room. Surely he remembered the occasion!

'Yes,' said Pierre-Joseph, 'yes', and for a moment he saw again that dark airless room, that strange cactus coming slowly into bloom at the stroke of midnight and the tense pale face of a terrified little boy, intently watching, and then as if comforted, reassured, to see that flower gently unfolding its petals, he had fallen asleep.

'Come! Come!' said Madame Prevost. 'I'm no thought reader. I'd like to hear what you are thinking.'

'I'm thinking,' said Pierre-Joseph, very slowly and deliberately, 'that Monsieur Audubon is far happier painting the wild birds of America than he would ever be wearing the crown of France.'

And now it was he, not Madame Prevost, who abruptly changed the subject.

'Ah!' he exclaimed and turned to the table where Madame always kept her 'flower of the day'. It was a white tuberose, so delicate and scented that both he and Madame Prevost promptly forgot the 'topic of the day' as they stood lost in admiration before it.

'Surely one of the most beautiful flowers,' said Madame. 'No mystery about that!' and she expertly wrapped it, handed it to Pierre-Joseph, and cutting short his thanks, said, 'And now we both have work to do. So au revoir, my dear friend, come again soon.'

•   •   •

Pierre-Joseph lost no time in doing all he could to help Jean-Jacques Audubon. He spoke so warmly of him when he next had dinner with the Duke of Orleans and his family that the Duke said he was to invite this American artist to come and dine with them on the following Friday. And bring his portfolio of paintings with him of course.

Dinner that Friday was as merry as it was informal. The Duke was delighted to talk of his days in America when he gave those dollar-an-hour lessons in painting to American young ladies, and he roared with laughter when Audubon said he himself would often have been happy to accept half the price.

Pierre-Joseph, seeing them talking so easily to each other, thought how strange it would be if those fantastic rumours were true, that there sat the man who was legally King Louis XVII of France and who should be wearing the crown now worn so arrogantly by his father's brother, His Most Royal Majesty, King Charles X.

If so, God had preserved him from such a fate. Audubon would have made the most unwilling of kings, always truanting, always escaping from suffocating ceremony and tedious matters of state to go wandering in the forests. Now he was free, he could wander and paint to his heart's content to the end of his days. And surely the value of his work would be recognised. It would be of immense interest to botanists as well as all students of zoology. Pierre-Joseph had recognised the consummate skill with which Audubon had painted the American trees, bushes, and flowers among which his beloved birds sang, built their nests, hunted for food and fought their enemies.

Pierre-Joseph collected his wandering thoughts just in time; Audubon was now showing his paintings to the Duke and Duchess of Orleans. Both were clearly fascinated.

'This surpasses anything I have ever seen,' the Duke was saying. 'I'm not astonished Monsieur Redouté was so enthusiastic.'

Pierre-Joseph took Audubon home with him for the rest of that day and, as he told Marie-Marthe, Audubon had not walked, he had danced along.

The Duke and Duchess had done more than marvel. They had both promised to subscribe to the *Birds of America*.

Audubon had the same success when he went with Pierre-Joseph to meet the famous painter, Gerard, and the distinguished artists, writers and scientists who came to his Wednesday receptions. He was invited to show them some of his paintings and Gerard spoke for them all when he exclaimed, 'Monsieur Audubon, you are the king of painters of birds. Who would have expected such marvels from the forests of America!'

That visit brought Audubon still more promises of subscriptions and God knew he had great need of them if ever he was to publish his magnificent work. By this time Audubon had become a most welcome family friend and though he always joked, made light of the hardships, the disappointments, the counting of every penny he spent, they now knew how hard it had been for him to abandon his painting, leave his Lucy and children, and set out on this long quest for subscriptions. Even his buckskin jacket was no theatrical device to attract attention, it was a stern necessity, guaranteed to give a lifetime of hard wear – he was never conscious of the sensation it caused at times.

But now he had been away for three long years and he was longing to return to America. Everyone, everything, he loved was there in America. They noticed how time and again he would say 'back home in America.'

When the time came for him to go, he said he would never forget the happy hours he had spent in their home, and he would always be grateful for the help and encouragement Pierre-Joseph had given him. He was honoured to have found such a friend. His search for subscriptions in Scotland, England and France had not been in vain but they knew he would still have to find more 'back home in America'. Surely this would be easy, said Marie-Marthe. One said there were Americans as rich as Croesus and forever growing richer. They would be delighted to subscribe to the *Birds of America*. They'd regard it as a patriotic duty.

．　　　．　　　．

The cold truth was very different. Audubon found he had a far harder nut to crack in America.

This painter, said those rich Americans, was asking 1,000 dollars if one wished to own a complete copy of the *Birds of America*. There was that one word: 'complete'. And Audubon cheerfully admitted he needed time, maybe years, before he completed that work.

Sure, his paintings were admirable. But so was the sight of 1,000 good American dollars.

However, encouraged and sustained by the love and faith of his Lucy and his good English friend, the younger Robert Havell, he worked doggedly on, but it was often a 'nip-and-tuck' affair to keep the wolf from the door. There were more long separations from his Lucy as he travelled hundreds of miles to paint the astonishing variety of the wild birds of America.

At last, in 1838, the *Birds of America* was published. It was immediately recognised to be the world's finest book on birds, but how bitterly ironical it is now to think how hard it had been for Audubon to find subscribers to this masterpiece! Yet in our own day, a copy, one single copy, was eagerly bought for £90,000.

And how shameful to learn that some rich and high-born subscribers were sent their copies, kept them, and then ignored all requests for payment.

But better far to remember how Audubon once wrote: 'I never can remember the name of an enemy. It is only my friends I remember.' It is surely a tribute to human love, faith, and friendship that the magnificent work of one of the world's kindest and most courageous men was at last published.

And among the friends Audubon was always to remember was Pierre-Joseph Redouté.

All this while Pierre-Joseph was working as hard, as optimistically as ever. The first instalments of his *Choice of the Most Beautiful Flowers* were delighting the critics and he still confidently believed that once it was completed, in would come the money and there would be no more problems about settling bills, paying taxes, and repaying Monsieur Mercier. In fact he was so sure of the future that he now seized a golden opportunity to make a dream become a reality.

It was then, however, that Pierre-Joseph learned the bitter lesson that greed for land can make a man whom one thinks is a friend become, to one's horror, downright treacherous.

To put a complicated story into a nutshell, you must understand that the Marquis of Pastoret also had a country house in Fleury-Meudon; in short, the Marquis and Monsieur Panckoucke and Pierre-Joseph were neighbours. After long tedious negotiations, they had managed to buy, between them, a desirable stretch of woodland which they had agreed, very amicably, to share, each taking the land adjoining his own property.

So far, so good. Then to Pierre-Joseph's amazement he learned that Monsieur Panckoucke, his friend, neighbour and now his publisher, was scheming to acquire Pierre-Joseph's share as well as his own. This was unspeakable! But 'all's well that ends well'. Monsieur Panckoucke's conscience may have given him an outraged jab or maybe it was the icy contempt of his wife and the Marquis of Pastoret, for finally they all shook hands and agreed to forget the past and to share that desirable stretch of woodland.

Then came the momentous summer day when Pierre-Joseph proudly led Marie-Marthe and Josephine to a far corner of their garden in Fleury-Meudon. The wall was no longer there! And with a magnificent gesture Pierre-Joseph cried 'A dream come true, just as I promised you!'

Before them stretched a wooded hillside and Pierre-Joseph led them up it, and as they went he pointed out the lovely trees growing there, oak and chestnut, sycamore and birch, and tall slender poplars that seemed to quiver with every breeze, so it was no wonder they were known as 'tremblers'.

To add to all this, here and there were little streams and waterfalls, and in one clearing of their hillside woodland stood a graceful statue of Flora, goddess of flowers, and Pierre-Joseph had considerately ordered stone benches to be placed here so that they could sit and rest for a while.

When they came to the summit of the hillside, there stood a

belvedere! And this belvedere well deserved that poetical name for it was no commonplace summer-house. It was delightful to look at, it was simply but comfortably furnished, and what a view it commanded!

Far below they could see the Seine, with ships that seemed as small as toys sailing upon it, and on every side for kilometre after kilometre they could see the green countryside and the forests. On a cloudless day, said Pierre-Joseph, they would even be able to see the Bois de Boulogne. Julian, the Roman, would have been enchanted with the view from their belvedere.

Yes, there it was, the extensive, wonderful view Pierre-Joseph had promised Marie-Marthe, just as he had promised her so long ago – a house, a garden and an orangery in Fleury-Meudon.

Marie-Marthe flung her arms about him, Josephine hugged and kissed him and there they sat in their belvedere, enjoying the cool fresh air and exclaiming again and again at the magnificent view on every side. Nobody could claim a finer view, and as Pierre-Joseph proudly said, it would add enormously to the value of their home in Fleury-Meudon.

Presently Pierre-Joseph with the air of a conjurer producing a rabbit from his hat, pulled out a basket hidden under a chair, and there inside were two long loaves, and slices of ham and delicious sausage, a fine chunk of cheese and a couple of bottles of the local wine that centuries ago Julian, the Roman, had found so unexpectedly good.

There they sat that happy day until the sun began to set, and this too was wonderful to see, and as dusk fell they began to make their way down their enchanting hillside, back to home, and supper.

Late that evening Marie-Marthe said the moment had come to be serious, and as the old saying put it, 'to call a cat a cat'. They knew that Pierre-Joseph hated parting with any of his original paintings. Yet, no doubt to help make this dream come true, he had sold the originals of the most beautiful of them all, *Les Roses*.

And God bless him for making this sacrifice. But to continue. Madame the Duchess of Berry who so admired Pierre-Joseph's work had no doubt made it clear how much she would like her father-in-law, His Majesty Charles X, to buy and present her with these lovely paintings. And a fine royal haggler His Majesty had proved to be! In the end Pierre-Joseph had accepted 30,000 francs, exactly half the price he'd had to pay for their lovely hillside. By what miracle had Pierre-Joseph found the rest of the money?

How indeed! Pierre-Joseph, as carefree as you please, said it had been simplicity itself. He had raised a mortgage on their property in Fleury-Meudon, interest, five per cent per annum.

A mortgage, interest five per cent! For a moment Marie-Marthe was speechless, then she heard herself whispering: 'And Monsieur Mercier?'

'Ah yes,' said Pierre-Joseph, 'Monsieur Mercier.' Well, he had been distinctly chilly when Pierre-Joseph had written to him explaining that he'd had to pay money down for some land that would most profitably 'round off' his property in Fleury-Meudon, and would Monsieur Mercier now be obliging enough to defer for a while the repayment of the sum, together with the interest due to him.

Then airily dismissing chilly Monsieur Mercier, Pierre-Joseph began to sing of his *Choice of the Most Beautiful Flowers* which would solve all their problems, and how Monsieur Panckoucke had been most enthusiastic about Pierre-Joseph's decision to make his *Choice* even more appealing. He was going to paint and include some branches of 'The Most Beautiful Fruit' as well as flowers. It would be a joy to paint a purple plum, for instance, or an apricot, a peach, ripe to perfection, the velvet bloom still upon it.

Monsieur Panckoucke had been even more enthusiastic when Pierre-Joseph told him that he'd decided to pay an affectionate tribute to the two young daughters of the Duke of Orleans. He would dedicate this work to them. Monsier Panckoucke had immediately said this was an excellent idea. It should mean subscriptions from His Majesty Charles X, and the Duke of Orleans, the uncle and papa of the two young Royal Highnesses. The Duke was understandably tight-fisted. He had eight children, and he never seemed to forget the lean hungry years he had spent in exile and those American dollar-an-hour lessons. But Madame the Duchess could be counted upon to persuade him that he simply had to subscribe to a work dedicated to two of their daughters.

And how thankful he was, said Pierre-Joseph, that he could leave all the time-consuming advance publicity to Monsieur Panckoucke. The *Choice of the Most Beautiful Flowers and Fruit* would take up all his free time for some years but already he had ideas, such splendid ideas for the work he would then do.

He saw them already in his mind's eye – an album of paintings of little flowers, the ones that touch the heart to see their delicate minute beauty. Then another album of flowers that bloom in spring, those that blossom in summer, the ones that delight one in autumn and bravest of them all, those that defy the wind, rain, frost and snow of winter. He would call this album *The Seasons*, of course.

So many other ideas for work in the carefree years that lay ahead came crowding into Pierre-Joseph's mind, and as they listened to him Marie-Marthe and Josephine were carried away on the bright wings of his sunny optimism. They too forgot chilly Monsieur Mercier, the mortgage on their home in Fleury-Meudon; they too only saw the happy years to come, all brimming over with flowers.

And not a bill, a tax demand, left unpaid.

27

Painter of Flowers to Queen
Marie-Amélie

Pierre-Joseph stood in his garden at Fleury-Meudon one morning in June 1830, and thought there was only one word to describe this perfect day – glorious. Overhead the sun shone warm and kind in a cloudless blue sky, and never before had his flower-beds looked so gay, so joyous – the scarlet geraniums, the fragrant pinks, the many-coloured snapdragons and pansies. Never before had his roses, lavender and honeysuckle smelled more sweet.

His heart overflowed with gratitude and happiness. The garden, house, orangery and their woodland hillside, everything was again free of debt. He'd managed to pay off every franc of that mortgage. It had not been easy. He'd had to postpone the payment of bills and taxes and the interest on the money he'd borrowed from Monsieur Mercier.

But why think of this on so glorious a morning? He stooped and gently picked a few pansies, a white one, a golden-yellow, a purple and a blue and yellow one. He must paint them now, immediately, before a dew drop still shining on one green leaf lost its sparkle. And Pierre-Joseph hurried into his studio and as always time flew by as he sketched and then began to paint.

'Ah no,' said a voice behind him, 'the pansies are beautiful but I was about to touch that drop of water when I realised you had just painted it! It's unbelievably real! You intend, I hope, to include both the pansies and that dewdrop in your *Choice of the Most Beautiful*

Flowers. And to think that before I met you, I thought a most beautiful flower simply had to be some rare and expensive orchid!'

It was Jules Janin who had come to spend that glorious summer day with them in Fleury-Meudon.

All that June and until late in July, Pierre-Joseph spent every hour of daylight happily painting the most beautiful flowers in his own garden and greenhouse. He, and everyone else in peaceful Fleury-Meudon, were not in the least disturbed by the rumours of growing unrest in Paris. There was nothing new about this. As Jules Janin often said, His Majesty King Charles X had a gift for antagonising all manner of men, not only the embittered veterans of Napoleon's wars, but sober bankers, shop-keepers, scientists, lawyers – and journalists as well – no freedom of the press these days of course.

In fact, said Jules Janin, the only Frenchmen who approved of Charles X was the King himself and his band of 'Ultras', the ultra-royalists who, as someone had sourly put it, were more royal than royalty itself. They were now approving of His Majesty's decision to raise a billion francs – think of it, a billion francs! – to compensate them for the estates and fortunes they had lost in the Revolution. Yet what had those noble Frenchmen done for France? They had fled to save their own necks and abandoned the Royal Family of France to their cruel fate.

The widespread resentment in Paris suddenly exploded and July 27, 28 and 29 were to go down in French history as 'Les Trois Glorieuses'. But those 'Three Glorious Days' were decidedly in-glorious for Charles X. He had taken up summer residence in Saint Cloud but when August came he was on a ship with a band of 'Ultras' on his way back to England. No-one there seemed enchanted to see him again, but 'noblesse oblige', he was given an exceedingly draughty castle, so one said, in Scotland. And his cousin, the Duke of Orleans, who had once given those 'dollar-an-hour' lessons to American young ladies, was acclaimed Louis-Philippe I, King of the French.

'My dear friend,' said Madame Prevost when Pierre-Joseph next called to see her, 'one can in all modesty claim that France has already acquired quite a reputation for revolutions but this one was outstanding, a double-quick-time affair, all over and done with in "Three Glorious Days".

'Those narrow streets of Paris again proved so convenient for a revolution. I did not see them but I'm told the barricades were fantastic. One sacrificed tables, chairs, beds, and trees as well, alas, and any diligence or coach that happened to be on hand.

'As for the poor devils of soldiers sent to demolish those barricades, well, what can a soldier do when down from every window comes a devastating deluge of stones, pots and pans, chairs and tables, and heaven knows what beside.

'Demoralising, you must admit, resistance like this. And very effective for here we are now with Louis-Philipe, our Citizen-King, who must be hoarse as a raven, poor monarch, with crowds eternally yelling outside the Tuileries, "The King! the King!" until he appears at a window and joins them in singing the Marseillaise.

'And have you heard what one disapproving stickler for etiquette is reputed to have said, "Really, one will not be able to dine with the King. He keeps such low company".'

Pierre-Joseph roared with laughter, 'Yes,' he said, 'people like me.'

'I hear too,' said Madame Prevost 'that our incorrigible poet, Béranger, declared that the Palace of the Tuileries has become nothing more than an inn for itinerant monarchs. And one has to admit the truth of this. Just think, my dear friend, how many monarchs of France you and I have seen come and go: unhappy Louis XVI, the Emperor Napoleon, King Louis XVIII, Charles X, and enter now our Citizen-King, Louis-Philippe I.

'Tell me, my dear friend, when and where will one find the time, the acres of paper, and the gallons of ink to write the history of our day?'

It wasn't the first time Madame Prevost had asked this rhetorical question, and without waiting for an answer, which was fortunate as Pierre-Joseph still had none to offer, she turned and said, 'Well, what do you think of my "bouquet of the day"?'

On the little table stood a jug filled with the flowers known in

England as 'Sweet Williams', but to the French they are the 'Carnations of the Poet'. An appealing name, said Pierre-Joseph, for one at once imagined a poet, a poor one of course, who couldn't afford to buy his true love costly carnations and in any case much preferred these homely flowers which would fill with their rich colours the borders of the garden of the idyllic country cottage of his dreams.

Madame Prevost dryly said that the poets she'd met certainly wrote ecstatically of country cottages smothered in honeysuckle and roses but she'd noticed that they seemed to prefer to live in noisy, lively Paris. Pierre-Joseph wasn't listening, he was still admiring the 'bouquet of the day', and he began to say how Monsieur L'Héritier had once told him that a certain Greek philosopher – he couldn't recall his name – had been so enchanted with the rich variety of the family of pinks and carnations that he'd called them 'Dianthus', the 'Divine Flowers'.

'Well,' said Madame Prevost, wrapping her 'bouquet of the day' in soft paper, 'give these divinities to Madame, your wife, with my compliments, and tell her they have one splendidly down-to-earth virtue, they last a very long time.'

King Louis-Philippe I was undoubtedly delighted to be known as the 'Citizen King'. Not for him the elegant military uniforms, the glittering decorations, the regal hats adorned with white plumes, always worn by Charles X. He dressed so simply, so soberly that one would take him for some businessman as he strolled, unattended, along the streets and boulevards of Paris, sometimes stopping to chat to a group of workmen engaged in building a house. But Parisians soon learned to recognise their new king; he always carried a green umbrella and they began to call him the 'Green Umbrella King'.

'He must have lived too long in England,' said Marie-Marthe. 'It's always raining there, or about to rain.'

But Pierre-Joseph said that when he'd been in London the weather had been much the same as in Paris.

'Then it's probably a custom over there,' decided Marie-Marthe. 'It must be an English habit to carry an umbrella.'

Life in the Palace of the Tuileries was soon stripped of all stifling ceremony. Gentle, unassuming Queen Marie-Amélie would sit of an evening after dinner, crocheting or embroidering as she quietly talked to their 'low visitors' – among them Pierre-Joseph. She was quick, however, to show how much she appreciated the lessons he gave her two daughters for he came home one evening, flung open the door, and cried:

'Take a look at me! Here stands Pierre-Joseph Redouté, Painter of Flowers to Her Majesty Queen Marie-Amélie.'

Marie-Marthe caught her breath. For a moment she saw Pierre-Joseph young again, with the same joyous pride on his face as he cried:

'Take a look at me! Here stands Pierre-Joseph Redouté, Painter to Her Majesty Queen Marie-Antoinette.'

Then arms outstretched she and Josephine flew to hug and kiss him, and there too waiting to embrace and congratulate him was their faithful friend Jules Janin.

When the excitement had calmed a little, Marie-Marthe, mopping her eyes, ordered the Painter of Flowers to Her Majesty Queen Marie-Amélie, to bring out a special bottle to celebrate this royal occasion. And that evening, she and Josephine served up a supper fit for a king and they sat and talked far into the night.

Again and again Marie-Marthe would say who would have dreamed on that long-ago day when young Pierre-Joseph Redouté had arrived in Paris, perched among the luggage piled on top of a diligence, without a sou in his pocket, that he would become the royal painter to, and here Marie-Marthe ticked the list of royal ladies off on her fingers, Queen Marie-Antoinette, the Empress Josephine, the Empress Marie-Louise and now Queen Marie-Amélie.

And think too how he'd lost those valuable letters of introduction given to him by that gracious lady, Her Highness, the Princesse-Baronne de Tornaco. Heaven had certainly meant him to lose those letters; he would never have made a happy portrait-painter.

Jules Janin said ah, now this reminded him that he'd met a very happy portrait-painter, and he'd promised to introduce him to Pierre-Joseph. His name was Karl Christian Vogel; he came from Saxony, and never had a man been so aptly named since the German word for bird was 'vogel' and this Vogel was eternally on the wing. He had earned such excellent money with his fine portraits of high society, both in his native land and in Russia, that now he could afford to devote his time to a lifelong ambition – to amass a collection of the portraits of all the illustrious men of Europe. He'd already painted portraits in Berlin, Vienna, Florence, Copenhagen, Madrid, and now he'd arrived in Paris. And he was earnestly hoping to have the honour of adding the portrait of 'der Sehr erlauchte Monsieur Redouté' to his collection – in plain French, he hoped to paint the so-illustrious Monsieur Redouté.

'He'll regret that,' said the so-illustrious Pierre-Joseph, 'the moment he sets eyes on me. But if you think he can stand the shock, then by all means bring him to see me.'

On 30 October, Jules Janin arrived with Herr Vogel. Marie-Marthe decided he must be the best-liked portrait-painter in Europe. He was charming, he had excellent manners, and one could tell that he really was a happy man. There was something serene, modest and kind about him. And he certainly did not wish to waste the time of 'der Sehr erlauchte Monsieur Redouté'. He quickly brought out his pencils and paper and when Marie-Marthe decided Pierre-Joseph ought to brush his hair and straighten his cravat, Herr Vogel was so alarmed that he cried: 'Ich bitte Sie, Madame, ändern Sie nichts an den Haaren Ihres Gatten und lassen Sie auch das Halstuch so, wie es ist!'

Then he apologised for this torrent of German and said: 'Please, please, Madame, not to arrange hair and cravat of your illustrious husband! As I now see him, so I wish to sketch him.'

Herr Vogel was a lightning artist. In no time at all, his sketch of Pierre-Joseph seemed to be looking at them, an amused smile hovering on his face. And no flattering touches added by that honest painter. He at once set the sketch before Pierre-Joseph, held out a pencil, and said:

'Please, here, below, sign your name and the date.'

Pierre-Joseph obediently took the pencil and wrote: P. J. Redouté né à St. Hubert dans les ardènne le 10 juillet, 1759.

Paris ce 30 octobre 1830

Jules Janin and Josephine had no heart, no inclination to suggest that Pierre-Joseph ought to rub out 'ardènne', correct it, make it: Ardennes.

How right they were! This portrait of Pierre-Joseph Redouté, born in Saint Hubert in the Ardennes on 10 July 1759, is unique. This was just how he looked on 30 October 1830, his spelling as happy-go-lucky as ever.

When Josephine recalled the years that followed, she was always moved to think how hard her papa worked. He was now over seventy but he was, thank God, as hale and hearty as ever. He never had a day's illness; he would say he would not dare to be so ungrateful. Not every man could come home after a day's work humming, most untunefully, the song that Audubon had taught them, the one that was sweeping America and England and went: 'Home, sweet home, there's no place like home.'

But month after month, no matter how she and her mother made every possible economy, it was becoming more and more difficult to keep up appearances. And just when they needed the extra money there were fewer and fewer of those well-paid private lessons. Josephine would agree with her mother when she sometimes said – but never when Pierre-Joseph was there – that she wished a royal salary went with the title, 'Painter of Flowers to Queen Marie-Amélie'. The King had warmly approved of his wife's decision to make Pierre-Joseph Redouté her royal painter of flowers but he obviously thought this was reward enough.

In all justice Queen Marie-Amélie was very different from Queen Marie-Antoinette who not only never paid her royal artists, but treated them as so many superior lackeys. Queen Marie-Amélie was always kindness itself to Pierre-Joseph and later on she asked him to give her lessons in flower-painting – and never once forgot to pay him.

All this while the two young princesses were fast growing up of course, and in 1832, Princess Louise-Marie now aged twenty, married Léopold I, the first King of the Belgians. Before she went, she gave Pierre-Joseph a painting of a bouquet of flowers she herself had painted. To Pierre-Joseph this was the best of all gifts.

Jules Janin was there when Pierre-Joseph came home with that painting and as he looked at it he said he had to admit that Charles X had been right for once when he said his niece would do Pierre-Joseph honour.

Pierre-Joseph was so delighted with this painting and above all the marriage of the young princess, that Jules Janin declared one would imagine he had arranged the match himself. Whereupon Pierre-Joseph said Jules Janin seemed to forget that he was a Belgian to the backbone, and that he might not be an historian but he could well recall that in his young days his native land had been part and parcel of the vast Austrian Empire. Not that this had ever cowed his countrymen. Ah, no! The envoys of the Emperor had always shuddered at their lack of deference.

Then, as Pierre-Joseph saw it, after the fall of Napoleon, those victorious monarchs of Europe sitting in their velvet armchairs in Vienna had carved up the map of the world to suit their own convenience. For instance, the Cape of Good Hope had belonged to Holland but it was on the vital sea route to India, so it was given, lock, stock and barrel, to the English.

To placate the Dutch, it was decided that Belgium should be united with Holland, become one kingdom, under the Dutch King, William I. And, said Pierre-Joseph, it was one thing to be part and parcel of a vast empire, but quite another to be told that one's native land was now part and parcel of the small kingdom of the Low Countries, ruled over by a Dutch king. And no argument permitted.

Naturally Pierre-Joseph had not been astonished when his countrymen, inspired by the 'Three Glorious Days' in France, had decided to have a 'Glorious Day' of their own. They declared their independence, defied and defeated the Dutch, and presently invited Léopold of Saxe-Coburg to become their first king.

Pierre-Joseph had learned all this from Belgians visiting Paris. They had also told him that their first king was the most handsome and romantic of monarchs. He had been married to the English princess, Charlotte, who, if she had lived, would have become Queen of England, and Léopold would have been her Prince Consort. But a year after their marriage, the poor young princess died in child-birth, and the baby had died too.

Everyone said Léopold had truly grieved for his young wife, but there he was, a handsome and childless widower. And a man has to do something with his life, and he'd therefore accepted the invitation to become Léopold I, first King of Belgium.

A good king, however, said historian Pierre-Joseph Redouté, needs a good queen at his side, and who better than charming, kind little Princess Louise-Marie. And mark his words, his former pupil, the first Queen of the Belgians, would be loved by all his country-men.

Later on Jules Janin had to admit that Pierre-Joseph was right. The Belgians soon took their gentle pious little Queen to their hearts, respecting her as much as they loved her. But that evening he looked at Pierre-Joseph and said that he couldn't believe his ears. He had no idea that Pierre-Joseph had such a genius for what he'd call 'selective and oh-so-simplified history'. Pierre-Joseph said he regarded that as a compliment, so now they'd drink a toast to His Majesty King Léopold I, and Her Majesty Queen Louise-Marie. God bless them both.

Presently all the talk was of the sad death of Napoleon's son at the early age of twenty-one. Madame Prevost, when Pierre-Joseph called to see her, said that judging by all she heard it would need a genius like Shakespeare to write the tragic life of the son whom Napoleon had so ardently desired.

There could be no doubt whatever, said Madame Prevost, that he had cherished the memory of his father, and longed to see him again. But no, by order of his imperial grandfather, the Emperor of Austria, he had been kept virtually a prisoner, closely supervised all his short life long in the vast castle of Schönbrunn near Vienna.

He had also loved his mother, the ex-Empress Marie-Louise. She would write him the most touching letters with excuse upon excuse for not travelling to visit him. They said he'd died of consumption, but it was far more likely that he'd felt he had been abandoned, that he hated to be known as the Duke of Reichstadt and there had been no fight left in him when he began to lie awake, coughing all night long, remembering the days when he was a child and the father who had so loved and spoiled him. Death, for Napoleon's son had been the only escape from his vast palatial prison.

Now he lay, clad in the white uniform of an Austrian officer, in the gloomy burial vaults of the imperial Hapsburg family. And his father, who had once been Emperor of the French and the most powerful man in Europe, lay in a grave on the island of Saint Helena, lost in the grey waters of the Atlantic Ocean.

'But enough of this gloom,' said Madame, 'and tell me what you think of my two "flowers of the day".'

She brought out a glass vase in which were two perfect roses, one a golden yellow, the other a rich deep purple red. Again she and Pierre-Joseph stood side by side silently admiring them.

And Pierre-Joseph thought once more that Madame Prevost had an infallible instinct for reconciling one vivid colour with another, so that each enhanced the beauty of the other. Not that he had the words or the time to say this, for Madame Prevost was swiftly wrapping those two perfect roses in soft paper and handing them to him, saying, 'Au revoir, my dear friend, come again soon.'

Just as she always did.

Just as she would always do, please God, in the years to come.

28

The Order of Léopold

In 1833 the last instalment of the *Choice of the Most Beautiful Flowers and a Few Branches of the Most Beautiful Fruit* was finished, and Marie-Marthe told Josephine that one might not think so to look at her, but she felt years and years younger. This new work meant so much to Pierre-Joseph, he had devoted all his free time to it for six years. And it was truly beautiful.

But how beautiful too it was to think that it would bring in the money to pay the arrears of the rent of their apartment in Paris, the unpaid taxes and other overdue bills. They might even be able to pay back every franc Pierre-Joseph owed to rapidly chilling Monsieur Mercier. Think of it! No more peremptory demands for interest due. How easy it had been for Pierre-Joseph to borrow money from Monsieur Mercier and light-heartedly agree to pay interest on the loan, but how very hard it was to find the money to pay this interest, and yet never, never reduce the amount still owed to him. Yes, it would indeed be beautiful to say farewell for ever to Monsieur Mercier.

Jules Janin, sitting at his desk, preparing to write a review of Pierre-Joseph's latest achievement, decided it was another artistic masterpiece. The flowers, the branches of fruit, the butterfly or insect delicately poised or hovering over a flower, and here and there a stray dew drop, they were all most beautifully painted. More than once he had instinctively put out a finger to touch one of those dew drops, and then laughed, realising it was a painted one.

The title-page announced this new work was 'often animated by butterflies and insects' but made no mention of those deceptive dew drops. It was the first time Pierre-Joseph had 'animated' his work in this way, and Jules Janin warmly approved. The whole effect was delightful. This was how one saw a butterfly, an insect hovering over a flower, or a dew drop sparkling on some shaded green leaf, if one had eyes in one's head as one strolled in a garden.

Painting the thirty-six instalments of his new work had been pure joy to Pierre-Joseph but his Foreword – the 'Avertissement' he called it – now that had taken him long hours of hard labour to write. Jules Janin noticed that under his signature on the title-page Pierre-Joseph stated he was a Chevalier of the Legion of Honour, Professor of Painting of the Museum of Natural History, and followed this with an impressive list of learned societies to which he had the honour to belong, from the 'Children of Apollo' to the 'Geographical Society of France'. Then he had obviously decided enough was enough and added an all-embracing ETC. in capital letters. But not one. He had made it three: ETC. ETC. ETC.

Jules Janin had long been affectionately aware of Pierre-Joseph's naïve pride in the long string of distinctions he had every right to add to his signature. But now it was as if he wished to emphasise the validity of his 'Avertissement'. It was to be no polite everyday introduction to his new work. It was to be a solemn testament, a declaration of the creed which Pierre-Joseph Redouté, member of many a learned society, held most dear.

Poor Pierre-Joseph! He could capture beauty and truth so swiftly with brushes and paint, but with pen in hand and a blank sheet of paper before him, the writing down of words became tricky, treacherous, maliciously elusive. So he sought safety in using far too many words as he toiled to make himself clear. But shorn of the involved verbiage, the clutter of unessential information, there they shone, the major articles of the creed of Pierre-Joseph Redouté, Painter of Flowers.

He believed that the art of flower-painting should not be dismissed as a luxury, a pleasant pastime. It was far more than that. Only to look at flower-paintings, and even on the bleakest winter day, one ought to be able to recapture the fresh joy of spring or the lovely days of summer and autumn.

He therefore believed it was essential that strict accuracy of form and colour must never be dull and lifeless. At one time flower-paintings, if accurate, were considered to be of most value to professors and students of botany. But Pierre-Joseph believed that they should also delight the eyes of those who had no knowledge whatever of botany, inspire them to look more closely at flowers and so lead them to learn more and more of the infinite wonder and beauty of Nature.

Then Pierre-Joseph believed that the art of flower-painting should also be of value to those engaged in 'the choicest products of industry'. Jules Janin reading this enthusiastically cried, 'Très bien! Très bien,' as if applauding some telling point in a speech. He was doubtlessly seeing fine porcelain boxes, elegant vases and other 'objets d'art' decorated with flowers as painted by Pierre-Joseph Redouté.

Little did he imagine that today, over a hundred years later, we have only to walk around any great store to see not only expensive porcelain but a host of everyday 'products of industry' decorated above all by the roses, the many charming roses painted by P. J. Redouté.

But back now to 1833 and Jules Janin, sitting there at his desk, considering Pierre-Joseph's new work. He took up his pen. He would write the most glowing of reviews, proclaim that Pierre-Joseph had again proved he was unsurpassed, still the greatest of all flower-painters. Compared with him, other artists now so popular, painted with 'the brush of a butcher'.

Yet in his heart Jules Janin feared for Pierre-Joseph. He knew what influential authorities, wealthy patrons of the arts, were saying. Venerable Monsieur Redouté had had his day. He had enjoyed immense success, many years of well-deserved fame, but he was now seventy-four. His work was as beautiful as ever but there were already copies of his earlier work on the shelves of all the great libraries and museums of Europe. His flower-paintings already hung on the walls of many a palace and mansion.

There was now a new and gifted generation of flower-painters who needed financial help if they were ever to publish their work. Surely, with a limited amount of money at one's disposal, it was only just to recognise and encourage them. Then one had to be realistic, Monsieur Redouté asked so high a price for his work.

Jules Janin sighed. It was ironical but Pierre-Joseph's success, his vast output of work, were no longer an asset to him. His future was summed up in those ominous words: 'Venerable Monsieur Redouté had had his day.'

It was not only this that made Jules Janin fear for the success of Pierre-Joseph's superb new work. He had heard, on good authority, that certain botanists who could find no fault whatever with the meticulous accuracy of Pierre-Joseph's paintings, were showing a malicious delight as they sharpened their quill pens to point out that he had not given this or that flower its correct Latin name. Other botanists who warmly admired Pierre-Joseph's new work were also regretting that he had made 'slips' in naming his beautifully painted flowers.

Pierre-Joseph's publisher, Monsieur Panckoucke, had therefore, belatedly, engaged a professional and name-perfect botanist to write seventeen pages of text and an 'Alphabetical and Explanatory Catalogue of all the plants included in this work'. This had been rushed out in record time to accompany the final instalment with a lofty preface that said with the help of this text and alphabetical catalogue, it would be easy to rectify any error that had unfortunately crept into the naming of certain plants.

It was obvious that at first Pierre-Joseph had been badly shaken. Then Jules Janin smiled as he recalled the fury of Marie-Marthe. Who did they think they were, she demanded, these pernickety botanists? Jean-Jacques Rousseau had been right. They could chant you a litany of the Latin names of all the flowers in the Jardin des Plantes as glib and correct as you please, but set them down in a meadow or a cottage garden and they'd be lost. They wouldn't even be able to recognise, much less give the common or Latin names of the flowers blooming there.

And, in any case, demanded Marie-Marthe, who cared a rap about

Latin names? Pierre-Joseph's paintings spoke for themselves. Look, for instance, at these heavenly blue gentians with a delicate butterfly flying towards them, and these cheerful yellow snapdragons, this scarlet fuchsia, why, it was a tonic just to look at such beautiful flowers.

Then to Marie-Marthe's mind even the everyday names of some flowers were the inventions of someone weak in the head. These delightful flowers, for example, had been given the name: 'Oreilles d'Ours' – 'Ears of Bears'. Who in heaven's name had even seen a dancing bear with such flowerlike ears? For once Marie-Marthe approved of the Latin name of those flowers: Primula Auricula. It at least sounded poetical.

As for the beautiful fruit Pierre-Joseph had painted, wasn't everyone always enchanted to see just such a ripe peach, apricot, or pear on a branch of a tree. One felt one had only to put out one's hand and it would fall gently into it. Then what happened? One would stand and admire it, think it a crime to take a bite of so lovely a fruit.

Oh yes, Marie-Marthe had been most eloquent as she bristled at the very idea of anyone daring to criticise Pierre-Joseph in any way, till presently Pierre-Joseph began to laugh and say, come, come, why not admit the truth. His Latin wasn't in the least trustworthy, in fact it was riddled with holes. But had he had the good sense to say so when Monsieur Panckoucke suggested it would not be necessary to pay a more scholarly botanist to write the text, keep a vigilant eye on the Latin names of his *Most Beautiful Flowers*? No, no, he had at once agreed as foolhardy as you please. All that mattered, said Pierre-Joseph, was that not one of these Latin-name-perfect botanists could find fault with the accuracy of his paintings.

Jules Janin, sitting at his desk decided that staring in front of him, lost in thought, wasn't going to help Pierre-Joseph, and he dipped his pen into his ink-well to write a paean of praise of Pierre-Joseph's *Choice of the Most Beautiful Flowers and a Few Branches of the Most Beautiful Fruit* with a special mention that this magnificent work was delightfully 'animated by butterflies and insects'.

Madame Prevost, as well informed as ever, had heard of the text and the Alphabetical Catalogue that had been so hurriedly added to Pierre-Joseph's new work. In her own dignified way she was as angry as Marie-Marthe, above all with Monsieur Panckoucke. Why had he been so miserly and not engaged a professional botanist to write that text and index from the start?

However, she said nothing of Monsieur Panckoucke when Pierre-Joseph next came to visit her.

'Well, my dear friend,' she said, 'I hear some of our fanatical botanists have been enjoying themselves at your expense. I trust you have not lost any sleep over them. They are always so enchanted to quarrel with anyone. One would imagine they counted on a crown of eternal glory if they can prove how wrong someone else is. Their dissertations bore one to tears. Who will ever read them, indeed who will even remember these gentlemen's names in the years to come?

'Whereas your paintings, my dear friend, your name. . . . ' Madame Prevost left the rest unsaid and turned to the little table on which stood her 'flower of the day'.

This time it was a bunch of soft pink and snow-white sweet peas.

'Lathyrus odoratus,' said Madame Prevost, 'but don't let the Latin name spoil them for you.'

'No,' said Pierre-Joseph, stooping to smell them, 'I've already forgotten it.'

Then, as always, they stood for a while admiring those 'flowers of the day' till Madame Prevost swiftly wrapped them and gave them to Pierre-Joseph.

'For Madame your wife,' she said, 'I know she likes a flower with a scent.

'Au revoir, my dear friend! Come again soon.'

The sale of Pierre-Joseph's new work began slowly but became satisfactory enough to encourage Monsieur Panckoucke to bring out a second edition though he abbreviated the title to *Choice of the Most Beautiful Flowers and Fruit*. This too sold slowly but Monsieur Panckoucke regarded this as sufficiently satisfactory. It made an adequate profit.

Slow, satisfactory, adequate. Such bleak words when Pierre-Joseph had expected far, far more. But never had Jules Janin admired him so much than at this moment of harsh disappointment. He lost no time on useless lamentations but at once set to work in his free time painting his *Choice of the Most Charming Little Flowers*. And never once did he miss giving his lessons in the library of the Jardin des Plantes.

Jules Janin knew that these lessons were as popular and well attended as ever. It was so interesting to be taught flower-painting by venerable, famous Monsieur Redouté. The amazing skill of his enormous ugly hands, his warm homely Belgian accent, the way he hypnotised everyone into listening to him, all this was legendary, something one would be able to talk about in one's own old age. But pay him high prices for private lessons? That was another matter. Romance was in the air, there were so many exciting new novels, plays, operas, and the fascinating work of romantic artists like Monsieur Delacroix, one simply had to find time to be well informed, be able to discuss all this.

Jules Janin recalled that years ago a cynical dramatist, an English one by the curious name of Colley Cibber, had declared that 'one had as good be out of this world as out of fashion'. This was cruelly true now of Pierre-Joseph. He was 'out of fashion'. He was giving fewer and fewer of those well-paid private lessons. But his love and zest for his work, his courage and above all his optimism, never failed him. There was a childlike simplicity about Pierre-Joseph that touched and amazed Jules Janin. It was as if he saw a rainbow of flowers forever shining before him waiting to be painted, and there at the end would be a crock of gold as in the fairy tale.

But then, thought Jules Janin, the story of Pierre-Joseph's life had begun just as in the classic fairy tale, a poor boy setting out to earn his fortune, so why should he not believe that it would end in 'living happily ever after'? It was fortunate that Marie-Marthe and Josephine shared Pierre-Joseph's sunny faith in the future. Had he not more than once made a dream come true?

The truth was, of course, that Marie-Marthe and Josephine kept all their worries to themselves. They did not confide even in Jules

Janin, a friend they knew they could trust. At all costs, they had to be loyal, *believe* in Pierre-Joseph.

One morning in 1835, Jules Janin sat in his favourite café in Paris, a pot of coffee before him and a couple of newspapers he'd taken from the rack. He'd been away for a while on a visit to his 'good town of Saint Etienne'. He must now catch up with the latest Parisian 'one says'.

Jules poured himself some coffee, and opened one of the newspapers. His face lit up. Dear old Pierre-Joseph's name was in capitals in a headline.

The article below reminded its readers that it had already reported in a previous issue that His Majesty King Léopold I of Belgium, had created his own order of merit under the title: The Order of Léopold. The honour of belonging to this was to be the reward for distinguished services to the Kingdom of Belgium.

His Majesty King Léopold I had decided that the famous painter of flowers, Monsieur Pierre-Joseph Redouté, had added lustre and renown to his native land. He had therefore been awarded the decoration and the title of 'Chevalier of the Order of Léopold'.

Jules Janin sprang to his feet, called to the waiter, paid him, rushed to the bar, bought a bottle of champagne and went off at such a speed that the waiter wondered if he'd just read in that newspaper of the death of a rich elderly relative who had left him a fortune and was due to be buried in less than half an hour in 'Père Lachaise'. But even a journalist would hardly attend a funeral, a bottle of champagne under his arm. On the other hand there was no accounting for the erratic ways of journalists, ordering coffee, paying for it, not touching it, and then off like the wind, with a bottle of champagne, also paid for. And very pleasant it must be too, thought the waiter, to earn enough to be able to behave like this.

Jules Janin was, of course, on his way to congratulate the new member of the 'Order of Léopold'.

As he expected, Pierre-Joseph was as pleased and happy as a child but this time he was also profoundly moved. This honour from his native land clearly meant more to him than any he had received.

She had not forgotten him, the child he had once taught to paint, who had so loved the lessons he had given her, the quiet child who was now Queen Louise-Marie, the wife of Léopold I King of Belgium.

Pierre-Joseph was convinced that it was she who had spoken of him, suggested that he was worthy of this honour. And Pierre-Joseph pointed to the painting, framed and hanging in place of honour on one of his crowded studio walls. It was her gift to him before she left France to become Léopold's bride. It was a bouquet of flowers she herself had painted. Was it not lovely?

Yes, indeed, agreed Jules Janin. And said again that it was not astonishing that her uncle, Charles X, had made a special mention of his royal niece in the few words he had deigned to utter as he handed Pierre-Joseph his Cross of the Legion of Honour. It would be interesting, said Jules Janin, to know how his ex-Majesty, Charles X, was now enjoying life in his draughty castle in Scotland.

But Pierre-Joseph wasn't listening. He was bringing out his new decoration to show Jules Janin. Wasn't it beautiful in every way, cried Marie-Marthe, even the rich silk ribbon attached to it, a shade of . . . well, was it? A subtle purple-rose? No, no, that wasn't precise enough. Both decoration and ribbon were unique.

Then Pierre-Joseph had to relive every moment of that never-to-be-forgotten occasion, how he had been invited to the new Belgian Ministry in Paris, and how Monsieur le Hon, the Minister of Belgium, had made a speech that moved Pierre-Joseph almost to tears, even now to remember it. He had paid a glowing tribute to Pierre-Joseph's gift for flower-painting, he had spoken of every one of his major works from *The Story of the Succulent Plants* to his *Choice of the Most Beautiful Flowers and Fruit*. He had spoken of the work Pierre-Joseph had done for Monsieur L'Héritier and many other eminent botanists. He had spoken of the paintings Pierre-Joseph had added to the priceless collection once known as the 'Miniatures du Roi' and now as the 'Vellums'.

But better cut short that speech said Pierre-Joseph and simply say that Monsieur the Minister had gone to the trouble to be astonishingly well informed about all the work Pierre-Joseph had done.

Pierre-Joseph did not say that Monsieur the Minister had also spoken most warmly of the kindly way Pierre-Joseph had helped so many of his countrymen visiting Paris. His unfailing generosity, his hospitality, had become legendary.

Finally Monsieur the Minister, had uttered the words that would be forever engraved on Pierre-Joseph's heart:

Pierre-Joseph Redouté, in the name of Belgium I salute you. Your country, your native village of Saint Hubert, are proud of their son.

And Pierre-Joseph, standing there, aged seventy-four, thought again of his father. How proud he would have been to have heard those words.

Their country, their village of Saint Hubert were proud of him, proud of Charles-Joseph Redouté's son, born in Number 8, Street of the Oven, the Baker's Oven, in Saint Hubert in the Belgian Ardennes.

All the way home on that red-letter day Pierre-Joseph had seen in his mind a beautiful collection of paintings he would dedicate to Queen Louise-Marie, the first Queen of his native land. He would call it *Choice of Sixty Roses*. For this he would paint sixty of the loveliest French roses. He knew he could ask Jules Janin to help him with the Foreword which he would like to begin with:

Madame,
    Permit your old master to lay at the feet of Your Majesty a few beautiful flowers from your native France.
    Madame,
You are doubly my Queen for though I am an artist of France I was born in this Belgium which is so happy, so proud of their young Queen from France.

Jules Janin cried 'Bravo!' and said nobody could improve on that.

Then he caught Josephine's eye and knew that it was Pierre-Joseph's unorthodox spelling that might need a little professional editing. And he at once said he would be honoured to help to compose a Foreword in courtly language fit for a Queen, and fit to accompany sixty of the loveliest roses of France.

29

The Last Flower

Pierre-Joseph's illustrations for his next work, *The Most Charming Little Flowers*, followed by *The Seasons*, were beautifully painted. The critics, above all Jules Janin, enthusiastically agreed on this.

But enthusiastic acclaim was not enough. These two charming collections of flower-paintings only brought in enough money to settle the more urgent of bills and tax demands. Nothing more. And economise as they might, Marie-Marthe and Josephine were finding it more and more difficult to keep up appearances.

One evening Marie-Marthe took a deep breath to fortify her courage and then matter-of-fact as you please, said she was well aware why Pierre-Joseph was resigning from this and that learned society, with the excuse that he was now finding it difficult to attend the meetings he had so enjoyed in the past.

The time had again come, went on Marie-Marthe, 'to call a cat, a cat'. The real reason was that Pierre-Joseph was finding it difficult to pay the yearly subscriptions of the long string of learned societies to which he had the honour to belong.

Well now, said Marie-Marthe, it so happened that she had been taking a long, hard look at their expensively furnished apartment. And she was not given to being fanciful as they well knew, but it had seemed to her that their handsome furniture stared haughtily back at her as if reminding her that it demanded to be loved and cherished. And she had come to the conclusion that as time went on, possessions became balls and chains about a woman's feet. She had so loved and cherished that costly furniture. And what had happened? It had become a tyrant, eternally demanding to be dusted and polished.

Why not sell some? They had far too much both there in Paris and in Fleury-Meudon. Nobody would be in the least likely to notice the disappearance of some ornate bureau or massive mahogany desk.

Pierre-Joseph, God bless him, was working as hard as ever. His days were full to overflowing but he had the reward of knowing his work was acknowledged to be superb even if it did not bring in — for the time being — the money it merited.

And Marie-Marthe had made up her mind. She was not going to squander any more time loving and cherishing a load of ungrateful furniture. Ah, no!

Marie-Marthe had her way. From that day on, they began to sell an expensive piece of furniture to pay an overdue bill or the interest on the money Pierre-Joseph had borrowed from Monsieur Mercier. And never once did Marie-Marthe show any regret, or shed any tears, not even when Monsieur Mercier began to write the most menacing letters and they had to sell the handsome silver table-ware Pierre-Joseph had been so happy to give her. And of which she had always been so proud, so very proud.

One windy day in March 1840, Jules Janin paid a vist to Madame Prevost. He was looking so worried that Madame nodded to her son, Eugène — the signal that he was to attend to the two privileged clients who had been permitted to enter her scented and most exclusive shop. She then shook hands with Jules Janin and nodded to him — the signal to follow her into the small cool room behind the shop.

'You need not tell me,' she said quietly. 'You are concerned about our dear friend, Pierre-Joseph. It's no longer a secret that he is in such financial difficulties that he has been selling his furniture and even his silver table-ware. He has of course no gift for haggling and I fear he is learning, first-hand, that it is so easy to buy something costly when one's pockets are well lined; but try to *sell* it at a fair price! Now that's cruelly different, especially when the word has gone round that one is in need of money.

'Yet,' went on Madame Prevost, 'in some ways he is the most fortunate of men. Madame, his good little wife, and Mademoiselle Josephine are both admirable women.'

'I know, I know,' said Jules Janin. 'But one hesitates to offer to help them. They are so unrealistic, so optimistic.'

'Any why not?' icily demanded Madame Prevost. 'I've yet to learn that pessimism pays dividends or helps to pay one's taxes.'

'I've been wondering,' persisted Jules Janin, 'if I might suggest, tactfully of course, that they could find a far cheaper apartment or. . . .'

The look on Madame Prevost's face silenced him. 'You will do nothing of the kind,' she said sternly. 'It seems to have escaped you that one needs money to move. They have none. And far worse, it would be regarded as an admission of impending bankruptcy.'

To Jules Janin's relief she then seemed to relent.

'Don't stand there looking as if I were an avenging angel. I assure you that you can wipe that funereal expression from your face. I have my sources of information, and no, I am not prepared to tell you what I have heard. But I suggest you call on our dear friend some time soon.'

Jules Janin called on Pierre-Joseph that very evening and was greeted as warmly as ever. But it seemed to him there was something indefinable in the air, something joyously triumphant.

'Come and see,' said Pierre-Joseph, and Jules Janin obediently followed him into his spacious studio.

That canvas, eight feet high, which had been standing there for years and years, no longer had its face turned to the wall.

That night Jules Janin listened as Pierre-Joseph relived in detail the day when he and three friends had merrily decided to startle the artistic world with an imposing oil-painting, the combined work of all four of them.

Percier, the architect, was to paint a stately portico with marble pillars, as noble as any in ancient Greece.

Thibault was to paint a classic Greek landscape with a charming little stream meandering across it, and here and there a shady grove of trees. Overhead, of course, there would be the bluest of Grecian skies.

But Gerard, the 'King of Painters and Painter of Kings', had then assumed a fine show of artistic reluctance to paint his agreed share of the future masterpiece – two ravishing nymphs dallying on the banks of the little stream.

Yes, he said, he knew he had agreed to paint them but he had been thinking it over and he'd come to the conclusion that his two poor nymphs might well look as if they were about to swoon, overcome by the scent of the profusion of flowers with which Pierre-Joseph would certainly adorn that Grecian landscape. He'd have them everywhere, simply everywhere, climbing up the marble pillars of the portico, blossoming in every shady grove, growing thick and fast along the banks of the little stream and all about the lily-white feet of his two ravishing nymphs. Any nymph would droop and faint in the air charged with so much scent.

This had met with such shouts of derisive laughter that at last Gerard admitted that any ravishing Grecian nymph would be affronted not to have a carpet of lovely flowers about her lily-white feet.

Twenty years had flown since that merry evening. Twenty years! And Pierre-Joseph all unaware of their relentless flight.

His face clouded over. They were dead, those three merry friends, Percier, Thibault and Gerard. All three dead. But they had long since completed their share of that unusual oil-painting. And in all those twenty years Pierre-Joseph had not found the time to paint a single flower to adorn that Grecian landscape. Until now.

And this was strange. Pierre-Joseph was convinced that this masterpiece had been destined, yes, destined to wait – until now.

He was now going to spend every free hour painting his share of the unfinished oil-painting. He was going to make that Grecian landscape shine with the 'stars of this earth', the most beautiful of flowers, lilies, roses, violets and so many others he had loved to paint all his life long.

It would be his tribute to the memory of those three gifted friends. 'Yes,' said Marie-Marthe quietly. 'But it will also mean so much to us.'

Ah yes, agreed Pierre-Joseph and triumphantly announced that he had been most businesslike in his arrangements to sell the oil-painting, when completed – to the French Government! He'd had encouraging talks with sympathetic, high-placed politicians and finally with Monsieur the Minister of Home Affairs. It was he who ultimately decided how best to spend the funds at his disposal on the purchase of works of art. And to sum up, Monsieur the Minister of Home Affairs had agreed to buy the oil-painting, and at the price and terms suggested by Pierre-Joseph. Yes, at *his* price, and on *his* terms!

Monsieur the Minister had promised to purchase it for 12,000 francs payable in eight instalments, and Pierre-Joseph had undertaken to complete the painting down to the last blade of grass in three years.

And Pierre-Joseph leaned back in his chair, the picture of an astute man who had concluded a most businesslike transaction.

Jules Janin warmly congratulated him, and said he'd hate to brush the bloom from Pierre-Joseph's remarkable business acumen but had Monsieur the Minister signed a written agreement to buy that oil-painting on Pierre-Joseph's terms?

Pierre-Joseph, very taken aback, said well no, it had been an amicable verbal agreement, a very amicable one. In England, he believed, they'd call it a 'gentlemen's agreement'. Surely that was enough.

It would be enough said worldly-wise Jules Janin, if all Ministers of Home Affairs were at all times gentlemen. But if their present Minister lost his post, who could guarantee that the politican who stepped into his shoes would also be a gentleman?

No, his years in journalism had taught him one hard lesson: always have such an agreement in black and white, officially signed and sealed.

Pierre-Joseph still looked dubious but Marie-Marthe cried why, yes, it was an excellent idea. Josephine could compose a letter, a very polite letter, then all Monsieur the Minister would have to do was reply, confirming this 'gentlemen's agreement'.

And, proudly added Marie-Marthe, Josephine wrote such beautiful French with never a spelling or grammatical mistake. Josephine smiled at Jules Janin, and he smiled back. Kind sensible Josephine! She did not tartly remind her good little maman she was now fifty-four and not fifteen. Truly both she and Marie-Marthe were women in a million.

Later that night, as Josephine came to the door to see him go, Jules Janin quietly said, 'Mademoiselle Josephine, you *will* write that letter? I beg you to write that letter.'

'Don't worry,' said Josephine. 'I'll write it and send it tomorrow. I'm so very grateful you suggested it.'

The weeks that followed were happy indeed. Josephine's polite letter had been sent to Monsieur the Minister of Home Affairs. But they couldn't expect an immediate reply, said Marie-Marthe. Everyone knew that all Ministers of the Crown daily received sacks crammed with letters. So no need to fret and fume if there was no reply for days, maybe even weeks. One day Josephine's letter would surely be on top of the pile of Monsieur the Minister's desk, and he'd say, 'Ah, yes!' and send back a written and friendly confirmation of his 'gentlemen's agreement' with Pierre-Joseph.

Meanwhile a load of worry had fallen from Marie-Marthe at the thought of those 12,000 francs to be paid in eight instalments.

As for Pierre-Joseph, he faithfully gave his three lessons every week in the library of the Jardin des Plantes, and very occasionally, sold a painting or gave private lessons. Then he would spend his time in his studio, pencil in hand, deciding where he would paint his flowers in that sunlit Grecian landscape, and which flowers he would paint.

They must all be painted from life, of course, among them many of the ones which grew in their garden in Fleury-Meudon. Pierre-Joseph's heart overflowed with happiness thinking of the long summer days they would spend that year in their well-loved country home. At daybreak he would be up and out in the garden, listening to the most beautiful of all music – the dawn chorus of the birds. And as he stood there, he would be moved to see the cedar given to him by the Empress Josephine.

He would then stroll round his rose-beds and there it would be, a rose just about to open, the one he would paint that very day. Or he would suddenly stand still to see an iris, so perfect, so lovely, shining with dew below the cool morning sky.

Then Marie-Marthe would call to him and from the open windows of the kitchen would come the appetising smell of coffee, coffee as only Marie-Marthe knew how to make it.

After breakfast he would go to his orangery-studio and begin to sketch and paint his chosen 'flower of the day', make it bloom in that Grecian landscape as fresh and perfect as it had been at the moment he had seen it at dawn that day.

Sometimes he would leave his painting and Josephine would join him, and together they would work in the garden. And as so often happens when one grows old, the memories of childhood become clearer, more vivid than yesterday. He would talk to her of good Dom Hickman and how he too had loved all the flowers that grew, and valued them not only for their loveliness, but even more for their many God-given healing qualities.

When early evening came they would all three stroll around the garden and stop to admire their many coloured sweet williams, the 'carnations of the poet' and a great favourite of Marie-Marthe, or exclaim that their stocks, their lavender had never before smelled so sweet.

Then they would slowly climb their slope of woodland and come to the belvedere crowning its summit. There they would sit, and rest in comfort and watch the sun slowly go down over the peaceful landscape, the river far below, the meadows, the church-towers and the green shadowy forests.

Presently the first faint stars would appear and Marie-Marthe would exclaim, 'How fast time flies up here!' And they would begin to make their way down their hillside to the well-loved home waiting to welcome them back. And there would be the wondrous scent of tobacco plants, and their white roses would seem to glow in the mooonlight.

So happy, so tranquil it was to be, that summer of 1840. Only to think of it made Pierre-Joseph's heart overflow with joy and gratitude.

All this while Josephine's polite, well-written letter had been gathering dust on this and then that desk in the Department of Fine Arts of the Ministry of Home Affairs in Paris. In the cautious, time-honoured way of civil servants, one would refer such a letter to another. Monsieur the Minister could not be expected to read all the letters that came pouring in every day. He had to leave it to his competent and conscientious staff to sift and assess them.

In due time Josephine's letter arrived on the desk of a punctilious gentleman who had a long memory. Surely Monsieur Redouté painted the flowers for which he had become famous in water-colours? Hadn't some critic once written an article praising his painting of roses, and then said Monsieur Redouté showed great judgement in painting in water-colours as his oil-paintings lacked freshness and vigour. And this work of art he was now expecting to sell was an oil-painting.

One also had to remember that Monsieur Redouté was over eighty years of age. The amount of money at the disposal of the Department of Fine Arts was limited. Would it not be a grave risk to give a solemn written assurance to pay 12,000 francs for an oil-painting that might not come up to expectation, and remain unfinished?

Now one must be fair. On the evening of 13 June, Monsieur the Minister of Home Affairs was ready to go home after an exhausting day when a batch of letters was set before him and he was politely requested to sign them. Monsieur the Minister wearily took up his pen again, flicked over that pile of letters and scrawled his signature on every one.

He did not see, and no-one called his attention to the fact that one of those letters was addressed to Mademoiselle Redouté.

On Thursday, 19 June, Josephine returned from her early morning trip to the market with the usual supply of fresh vegetables. But she had also stopped at a flower-stall and bought something special for Pierre-Joseph.

It was a lily, freshly opened, the dew still on its pure white petals. She was well rewarded when she saw Pierre-Joseph's face, the delight with which he set it in a tall slender vase, the way he came back again and again to look at it.

Later that day, Pierre-Joseph was to give a lesson to a young student, Félix Rassat, so Marie-Marthe and Josephine decided to go out for a walk.

Félix arrived with a tight bunch of assorted flowers, and he had to admit it was a bunch though he had thought it a bouquet until he saw Monsieur Redouté wince; and watched him gently take those tightly packed flowers in his enormous and ugly hands, and lovingly, yes, that was the word, lovingly arrange them in a wide-necked vase.

And lo and behold, that bunch became a bouquet, an artistic bouquet, and as he arranged them, Monsieur Redouté explained in his homely Belgian accent how one could achieve such a miracle.

The young Félix listened, spellbound, as Monsieur Redouté taught him how to look at a flower, realise how lovely it was, and only then most delicately and accurately sketch it before he attempted to capture in paint the sheen of its leaves, the subtle colours of its petals, sepals and stamens and the grace of its stem.

It was Félix who realised with a start that it was high time he went. And he deferentially shook hands, and said, 'Au revoir. Et merci, Maître.'

As he walked home he thought that one would never imagine that Monsieur Redouté was over eighty. It was wonderful to listen to him. He seemed to have found the secret of eternal youth in his love of flowers. He was so very different from certain pedantic professors whom Félix had had to suffer. There was an endearing simplicity about Monsieur Redouté that made one respect him all the more.

When Félix had gone, Pierre-Joseph went back to his studio. He looked at the Grecian landscape and decided he had been right to paint those violets and daisies here and there on the banks of the little stream.

Then came a thunderous knock on the door. A messenger stood there with a letter for Mademoiselle Redouté, a letter from the Department of the Fine Arts of the Ministry of Home Affairs.

Ah, here it was at last! The reply to Josephine's letter, the confirmation signed and sealed of that 'gentlemen's agreement'.

Pierre-Joseph tore it open. So short a letter! But one didn't expect pages to confirm an agreement.

As he read it, the room began to spin around, and he had to sit down.

No, no, it could not be! There must be some mistake. He read the letter again but there was no reassuring word in any line of it.

Black phrases seem to leap from the paper and hammer blow upon blow on him.

'The funds at my disposal do not permit me. . . . '

'I regret to inform you that it will not be possible. . . . '

Blackest of all was the signature, the careless scrawl of a signature.

This curt, treacherous repudiation of that 'gentlemen's agreement' had been signed by Monsieur the Minister of Home Affairs himself.

It was providential that faithful Jules Janin came to see them that evening. As she opened the door to him, Josephine quietly told him how when she and Marie-Marthe came home from their walk, Marie-Marthe had looked at Pierre-Joseph and cried, 'But what is wrong? For God's sake, what is wrong?'

And it was terrible, said Josephine, terrible to see how cheerful Pierre-Joseph was trying to be.

It was true. It wrung Jules Janin's heart to see the stricken look in Pierre-Joseph's eyes and to listen to him, talking away, laughing so gay and carefree.

Far too gay. Far too carefree.

But what could any friend do but laugh too and say that all bureaucrats were notoriously unimaginative, thick-headed. Wasn't Pierre-Joseph known as the 'Raphael of Flowers', and the 'Rembrandt of Roses'? Pierre-Joseph would be able to sell that oil-painting for far more than 12,000 francs, if it was given the right advance publicity. And Jules Janin would be enchanted to see to that. He would enlist the help of every journalist in France, and in the rest of Europe, too.

Ah yes, there would be eager competition to acquire that unique oil-painting. Then what a fine blistering article criticising their Department of Fine Arts, would Jules Janin enjoy writing for his own influential journal!

When Jules Janin left them, it was already late but Pierre-Joseph insisted he must paint that lily, tonight, whilst it was still so fresh. And it must be on vellum for so perfect a flower.

So Josephine lit the lamps in the studio, persuaded Marie-Marthe to go to bed, and they left Pierre-Joseph to paint in peace.

As he painted, time as always stood still and he felt the swift surge of happiness he had known even as a child when he saw a lovely flower in bloom.

And once again Pierre-Joseph knew what it was 'for that time to be lifted above earth'.

But this time it was for ever.

It was Josephine who found him still in death in the silent lamp-lit studio. Before him was the lily she had that morning brought him. And on a sheet of vellum, it glowed as perfect as in life, Pierre-Joseph Redouté's last painting, his very last painting.

It was Josephine, sensible loving Josephine, who then had to find the courage to comfort Marie-Marthe, suddenly old, dazed with shock and sorrow, and quiet Henri-Joseph, helpless and desolate in grief.

But there were also many material responsibilities that now crowded thick and fast on Josephine. And if ever a man deserved the name of a friend, it was Jules Janin. He helped in every possible way and savagely thought that now Pierre-Joseph was dead, all Paris was eager to lay tribute upon tribute at his feet.

He was given the finest of funerals with all the traditional French 'pompe funèbre'. A host of mourners walked in his funeral procession, eminent men from every walk of life, representatives of the learned societies to which he had been so proud to belong, many of his students, past and present, and many a struggling artist to whom Pierre-Joseph had given a helpful hand.

There too, unrecognised among the mourners, walked a famous tight-rope dancer, remembering how he had once had a tragic accident and how he would have died of despair and starvation if Pierre-Joseph had not learned of his plight and come so swiftly, so unobtrusively to his aid. Now God reward him, prayed that tight-rope dancer. And he looked at the great crowd of mourners, and thought this funeral procession was surely the finest, the most telling of tributes to a great flower-painter and a great-hearted man.

Solemn Requiem Mass was sung in the church of Saint-Germain-des-Prés. Before the altar was Pierre-Joseph's velvet-draped coffin and on it lay his two most treasured decorations, the decoration of Léopold of Belgium and the one of the Legion of Honour of France. Encircling them was a lovely wreath of lilies and roses, Pierre-Joseph's last 'flowers of the day' from Madame Prevost.

The cortège then followed his velvet-draped coffin to the cemetery of Père Lachaise. But it was now Eugène Prevost who led the mourners. He was carrying a velvet cushion on which lay those two prized decorations encircled by another wreath of lilies and roses that he, Pierre-Joseph's pupil and friend, had fashioned at dawn that day.

Many eloquent speeches were made at Pierre-Joseph's open grave, praising 'the brilliance of his long career', and the kindness, the generosity that had endeared him to one generation after another. Most moving of all was the poem in which one of his students spoke for all his students, telling of their deep respect, their admiration, their warm affection for Pierre-Joseph. As he spoke the tears came to his eyes and many listening were also moved to tears.

Presently the last orations, the last prayers were said, all 'pompe funèbre' was over and done. And when dusk fell over the silent cemetery Pierre-Joseph lay peacefully in death by the side of quiet, gentle Adélaïde.

'Not dead,' wept Marie-Marthe. 'Not dead. But with God.'

For days after the funeral every French newspaper and journal had articles extolling Pierre-Joseph's lifetime of beautiful work, his illustrations for many a superb botanical publication, and the lovely 'Vellums', well over five hundred, he had added to the priceless collection of flower-paintings which Gaston, Duke of Orleans, had commenced two centuries ago.

But it was Jules Janin who wrote the most poignant of all articles. He told how Pierre-Joseph would stand silent, reverently, before the flowers he loved to paint, how he called them the 'stars of this earth', and how gently he handled them, always fearful of bruising them, marring their beauty in any way.

To him every flower was a miracle and in his paintings he had immortalised them. Yet to achieve these masterpieces, he had the most monstrous of hands with thick, ugly fingers. And he was highly amused when poets, who had never set eyes on him, proclaimed he had the 'delicate rose-tipped fingers of Dawn'.

One saw his flower-paintings in place of honour in palaces and mansions. No art gallery, no museum deemed it was complete without a work by Pierre-Joseph Redouté. He himself had lost count of all the flowers he had painted.

This gifted artist, wrote Jules Janin, was the kindest, the most generous of men. He was simplicity itself, a truly good man. Everyone who knew him recognised this.

And it was a bitter reflection on the times in which they lived when the funds for the encouragement of the Fine Arts were disgracefully squandered, a solemn verbal promise callously broken, and Pierre-Joseph Redouté had died poor to the point that he had been obliged to sell his furniture, the silver from his table.

Yet his warm generous spirit never failed him. One could assuredly say he had lived the happiest of men. And Jules Janin paid the warmest of tributes to the wife and daughter who had so loyally shared Pierre-Joseph's good fortune and his bad.

Marie-Marthe and Josephine were completely indifferent when Monsieur the Minister of Home Affairs blandly blamed his Department of the Fine Arts for that cruel curt letter. He admitted signing it but when one knew all the circumstances this would be seen to be an excusable error, and so on, and so on, hollow half-truths, half lies, expertly wrapped in diplomatic jargon. No, none of this meant anything to them. It was those words: 'he had lived the happiest of men' that Marie-Marthe and Josephine were to keep in their hearts in the difficult days that followed.

Even as the articles extolling Pierre-Joseph were appearing in the newspapers, in came a flood of reminders of bills to be settled, of taxes to be paid, and most peremptory of all, a demand from Monsieur Mercier for the full and immediate repayment of the money he had lent Pierre-Joseph together with the interest now due.

But better cut short those bewildering days and simply say that Marie-Marthe and Josephine were fiercely determined to pay every bill, debt and tax. Pierre-Joseph must lie in honour and dignity in his grave. And they had to find the money to do this as soon as possible.

They decided to sell Pierre-Joseph's fine collection of paintings, many by famous artists. Now this should have brought in a considerable sum of money but the sale had to be arranged so speedily that far too few people learned of it, and many valuable paintings were sold at ridiculously low prices.

Marie-Marthe and Josephine refused to part with Pierre-Joseph's last painting. To them it was beyond all price. As for the unfinished Grecian landscape, it went to Jules Janin. He outbid all other would-be buyers.

The disappointing result of the sale of the pictures was of course a real blow. Somehow, some way, they must find the money to pay every creditor. They also had to think of the future, they must have some capital left on which to live.

They faced harsh reality. They could never afford the upkeep of their property in Fleury-Meudon. They had to sell it, say good-bye to the garden they had loved, their wooded hillside crowned by a belvedere, and their unusual house with its two terraces, the home in which they had spent so many happy summers, and welcomed so many good friends.

They then put aside enough furniture to furnish a small apartment and sold the rest, keeping only one of the smaller display-cabinets. All the while Jules Janin still did everything in his power to help them and it was to him they turned when they had just a week in which to vacate their apartment in Paris. He had so often offered them hospitality and now he took them into his own home and made them feel most welcome.

Sensible Josephine had arranged to store the furniture left to them, and she at once began to search for a small apartment. By some miracle she found one at a very reasonable rent, and to make it even more attractive, nearby was a rank where little public coaches, the two-wheeled 'coucous', waited for passengers.

On a fine day they would be able to take the one that stopped outside the Jardin des Plantes.

They would stroll around, enjoy the fresh air, admire the flowers, trees and bushes growing there, and remember how this had once been a 'Paradise on Earth' to Pierre-Joseph. It was here that he had met upright Monsieur L'Héritier on the red-letter day that was to change his whole life.

To Josephine, finding that apartment was the answer to prayer. She also devoutly thanked heaven when they finally paid every creditor in full, and found that the capital left to them would bring in enough interest to enable them to live in frugal comfort.

So imagine them now in that small apartment, simply furnished but with the one display-cabinet they had decided to keep. In pride of place on one of its shelves shone Pierre-Joseph's two treasured decorations; on another were a few of the books their gentle Adélaïde had loved to 'devour', among them Professor de Candolle's *Flore Français* which recorded that it was Pierre-Joseph Redouté who had first discovered the delicate, star-like flower, Trientalis Europaea, growing in the forests about his native village of Saint Hubert in the Belgian Ardennes. This had always been of special pride to Adélaïde, an accolade to the thirteen-year-old boy who had become a famous flower-painter, her kind and gifted papa.

There too, you may be sure on another shelf, stood Marie-Marthe's beautiful teapot, undented, unscratched, forever too beautiful to consider making tea in it.

On one wall, framed and under glass, glowed the lily, Pierre-Joseph's last painting. There were also two more of his paintings, one of a bouquet of roses, the other of gay peonies. They had withdrawn them both from that disastrous sale, the price offered for them was nothing short of insulting. Now they were glad they had done so. Every time they returned from a walk, those roses and peonies seemed to welcome them back most joyously.

That small apartment soon became a real home not only for them but for desolate, half-blind Henri-Joseph who often came to visit them. Jules Janin also frequently came to spend a few hours with them, so did Eugène Prevost. And Eugène never came without some lovely flowers with the kindest of greetings from his mother.

Jules Janin confided in Marie-Marthe that Madame Prevost, now growing stiff with age, was nevertheless still reigning regally in her exclusive flower-shop. But it seemed to him that since the death of her 'dear friend', she was sterner, more autocratic, especially with the wealthy philanderers among her clients. They were mere *buyers* of her costly flowers. Only Pierre-Joseph had appreciated them as she did. The most innocent of passions, the love of flowers, had linked their lives and she sorely missed so old and valued a friend. No other, said Jules Janin, could hope to take his place. And no-one ever did.

Jules Janin would sometimes wonder at the way everyone always felt at ease, at home, in that small apartment. It certainly brimmed over with memories of Pierre-Joseph, yet this seemed to make it all the more hospitable.

The reason was simple. To Marie-Marthe and Josephine, Pierre-Joseph was never some 'sad-eyed ghost'. How could he be when all their memories of him were warm, kind and generous. So they were never doleful and it was a pleasure, not a duty, for their friends to visit them.

In this quiet homely way we come to the end of the story of Pierre-Joseph Redouté.

But the flowers, the many thousands of flowers he painted, live on, a golden treasury of beautiful flower-paintings, a galaxy of the 'stars of this earth'.

Take a look about you and when you see, as you surely will, a copy of one of the hundreds of roses he painted, think of the sturdy boy, aged thirteen, with enormous, ugly hands who two centuries ago, went trudging along the forest tracks, the lanes and roads of his native land, hoping to earn his supper and a bed for the night by painting a cut-price portrait or a pious picture of a saint.

Imagine him coming to a sudden halt at the sight of some lovely flower in bloom, and thinking how wonderful it would be to spend his life painting flowers, nothing but flowers. And then ordering himself to stop this dawdling and dreaming of painting flowers if he was to reach the next village or small town and earn his supper that night.

His dream, as you now know, came true, royally true, as in some fairy tale. But as the years go by it is the roses he painted that most delight us, the wild roses of the hedgerows and forests, the superb variety of roses that grew in the well-loved gardens of Josephine, Empress of France, the ones that bloomed in Pierre-Joseph's own garden at Fleury-Meudon and in the gardens of his friends.

He captured for all time the charm and fleeting beauty of those roses of two hundred years ago, the roses that still enchant so many of us the wide world over.

He became Painter of Flowers to two Queens and an Empress of France, but to us today he is above all Pierre-Joseph Redouté, the man who painted roses.